JIMI HENDRIX LIVE IN LVIV

Also by Andrey Kurkov in English translation

FICTION

Death and the Penguin
The Case of the General's Thumb
Penguin Lost
A Matter of Death and Life
The President's Last Love
The Good Angel of Death
The Milkman in the Night
The Gardener from Ochakov
The Bickford Fuse
Grey Bees

NON-FICTION

Ukraine Diaries: Dispatches from Kiev
Diary of an Invasion

Andrey Kurkov

JIMI HENDRIX
LIVE IN LVIV

Translated from the Russian by
Reuben Woolley

MACLEHOSE PRESS
QUERCUS · LONDON

First published in the Russian language as *L'vovskaia Gastrol' Dzhimi Khendriksa*,
by Folio, Kharkiv, in 2012.
First published in Great Britain in 2023 by

MacLehose Press
an imprint of Quercus
Carmelite House
50 Victoria Embankment
London w1u 8ew

An Hachette UK Company

A CIP catalogue record for this book is available
from the British Library.

ISBN (Hardback) 978 1 52942 782 0
ISBN (Trade paperback) 978 1 52943 033 2
ISBN (Ebook) 978 1 52942 785 1

10 9 8 7 6 5 4 3 2 1

Designed and typeset in Sabon by CC Book Production
Printed and bound in Great Britain by Clays Ltd, Elcograf S.p.A.

This translation is dedicated to the memory of
Olesya Sanotska (1970–2016),
founder of the Emmaus-Oselya shelter in Vynnyky,
as thanks for her tireless work for the people of Lviv.

I

A person's walk almost always gives away their age. A child, when young, has a laughing, curious gait. Sometimes they'll tippy-toe mid-stride, to see anything their own height keeps from view. Usually nobody minds until the little one reaches about a metre and a half tall. Once that height is reached, the short-lived gait turns a little wild and proud, or perhaps quite the opposite: taut, with a barely noticeable forward lean. This is, of course, already too much for some; for certain passers-by it may even carry an air of danger: just think of the damage a person could do with a gait like that! From then onwards: to each their own. Some walk straight for twenty years, some a little skewed – it depends by that point on one's way of life and how much anxiety they carry. But all of this applies only in daylight. At night, one can walk with no regard for one's day-gait, or one's age. Night is empowering. Especially the night between the seventeenth and eighteenth of September.

On that particular September night in 2011, the sound of footsteps drifted in from Hrushevskoho, from Zelena, from Fedorova, from Zamarstynivska and from the edge of Stry-iskyi Park, where at night the trees had long since housed heavy clouds of heavy crows, who ate away their days at the city landfill near the village of Hrybovychi.

These steps were the "solos" of those who walked alone, forever unable, even during the eternal Soviet era, to keep in formation. Were any little drummer boy to now try and bring their steps in order, he would quite quickly receive some "actual bodily harm". But these were people positively incapable of any "grievous bodily harm". Even if they were to find out that this "little drummer boy", now in some other, non-literal sense, turned out to be someone recently taken into their narrow social circle. The circle would only have truly narrowed very recently. Before then, twenty-five, perhaps thirty years ago, it would have exceeded fifty people, and every mid-September it would have swelled considerably, bolstered with arrivals by bus and train, and even some like-minded people who came here on foot.

The person who was passing the Monastery of St Alphonsus Most Holy Redemptorist had steps that sounded a little skittish. This person was in an audible rush. Zamarstynivska Street, down which he was rushing, could probably once have stretched its brick-built arm all the way back to Bryukhovychi, but for some reason it never had. Its length, even as it currently stood, would make any Parisian boulevard jealous, and if you cut it into equal sections, and arranged these sections into a proper intersecting grid, you would get a full-fledged German district centre, with a rich history. After all, over the course of its long and still very much ongoing life, was there anything Zamarstynivska had not been through? Streets live a long time, outlasting the humans that populate them, one generation after another. Zamarstynivska had always held many praying people, and many making –then drinking – vodka and liqueurs; there had been films in the local rental shop, and the same films had been played just next door at the Shevchenko Cinema; people had learned to tend gardens and grow vegetables, they'd learned to drive cars, and they'd treated sick and wounded policemen. They still treat them on this road to this day. And for those they can't get "back on track", they see them off in the hospital chapel. Everything must follow rules; any process must contain an indication of its future end, in much the same way as any sentence, no matter how many commas it contains, must eventually end in a full stop, an ellipsis, or a more emotive punctuational alternative.

This pedestrian, who had lived at the far end of this street for all his fairly eventful years, carried Zamarstynivska with him wherever he went. He had a feel for it, like a good driver's intuitive feel for the size of their car: an immediate sense for which gaps it can enter and which it can't.

The pedestrian's face was hidden from the sky by a brown leather hat with a wide brim. Long, grey-streaked hair fell from the hat to his shoulders. The other details need not be mentioned. Except perhaps the tall, seemingly military boots: ruthlessly laced, Ukrainian-made, a dependable model that for the last fifty years had been known as "shit kickers". The Chinese never learned to make boots like this. They thought it required too much plastic of a certain firmness and quality, and too much coarse leather. By now the last bastions of shit-kicker production were Belarus and Transnistria. But there were still lone craftsmen here in Lviv who were able not only to pierce the thick, thick slab of hog leather by hand with a gypsy needle, but also to bind the boot's upper section tight to its lower counterpart, tighter than the Soviet government had ever quite managed, over almost fifty years, to bind Western Ukraine to the East. Those same craftsmen can tell just from the sound of the wearer's steps if the cobbler has struck a wrong note, or if the shoe has been made by a true virtuoso. Both soles, after all, should ring out in unison. And in Lviv, a city with a subtle sonic culture, that takes on a particular importance. The left heel cannot hit the cobblestone sounding like a left heel, nor the right heel like a right heel! They should sound like a pair. Like a pavement-loving pair.

The pedestrian's phone rang in his pocket.

"Alik, you close?" asked the voice of an old friend.

"What's the rush? We're not Germans," replied the pedestrian. "Where are you?"

"Lychakivska."

"Alright," said Alik. "Be there soon."

Once Alik reached the closed gates of Lychakiv Cemetery, a group of about ten appeared from behind the row of trees lining the road. They appeared in no hurry, and gathered around him as he retrieved the key to the gates' lock from his pocket.

The key had already been slid into the keyhole's turning mechanism when someone's hurried footsteps approached the gathered group from behind. Alik turned to see a slouching giant, almost two metres tall. His long grey hair seemed to say: "I'm one of us."

"*Lābas vākaras!*"[1] he puffed quietly. "Apologies for being almost-late!"

"Audrius?!" Alik voiced his surprise, taking the measure of the giant with a quick glance from head to sharp-toed shoe. "Train?"

"Yep, via Kyiv."

They all rushed over to give Audrius a hug.

"You've not been in ages," Alik said. He looked back to the gates to finish turning his key, watching as the steel bolt jumped from its chamber.

They walked through the graveyard in silence. At the top of a hill, they surveyed their surroundings. Alik waved them all over and led them in single file between graves and railings.

They stopped at an iron crucifix, which seemed to be deliberately hidden from view by the trunk of an old tree and two overgrown bushes. There were no railings here. The long-haired and mature gathering crowded around the unassuming grave. Neither first name nor surname were legible on the rusty plate affixed to the centre of the cross. One of the group squatted before it, his knees pressing into the edge of the burial mound, and pulled a plastic bag from his jacket pocket. Unfolded it. Placed a small tub of white paint down on the grass. A paintbrush appeared in his hand.

His steady hand splayed oily white letters over the plate: **Jimy Hendrix 1942–1970.**

A twig snapped in the windless silence. Somewhere very nearby. Alik strained his ears. The cracking noise repeated itself. Fallen leaves were making sad little rustles under the feet of an approaching stranger.

Guard? thought Alik.

They were approached by a man of average height wearing a cap, following their exact path between the graves and railings. Just a regular stranger. Those gathered at the grave watched his approach indifferently. Curiosity is a young man's game, and they were all past fifty.

"Please excuse me," the unnamed guest announced in the curt voice of a newsreader. He kept a respectful distance. "I've always wanted . . . wanted to say something . . ."

"Go ahead," Alik said placidly.

"Don't you recognise me?" the man asked, removing his cap.

It was nighttime, but his face was lit well enough by the moonlight. Even well lit, however, it had no effect on Alik. It was a normal face, the world had produced billions just like it: ears, nose, eyes – all government standard; no faults, no memorable or eye-catching quirks or errors.

Alik shook his head.

"How could you?" The stranger's voice took on a faint note of offence. "We were close. Against your will, of course. I'm Captain Ryabtsev of the KGB."

"Woah," Alik let slip, squinting and looking more closely at the face of his unexpected interlocutor. "And what brings you here, Captain? Or by now, I suppose, former Captain?"

"Superannuated Captain," Ryabtsev corrected. "Although that's exactly why I'm . . . I wanted to apologise . . . and say something."

"So apologise!" Alik shrugged. "But be quick. We aren't here to listen to you." He nodded at the iron cross with its fresh white label.

The captain put his cap back on and coughed.

"Well in short, guys, forgive me! And forgive Mezentsev too. I buried him not long ago . . . bladder cancer . . ."

"Do we have to hear him out?" asked Penzel irritatedly. He was a large, long-haired, long-bearded guy in a leather jacket, more biker than hippie.

"Just for a minute." Alik sighed. "Come on Captain, cut to the chase! The guys are losing their patience!"

"Okay, just the short version." Ryabtsev now spoke more softly, less curtly. "Firstly, I'd like to thank you: thirty-five years ago, you introduced me to Jimi Hendrix! He turned my life around. Thanks to him I lost all interest in my career. That's why I'm a captain, not a colonel . . . But that's also why me and my guys, back in 1978, we managed to get a part of his body for you, his hand. So that Jimi could have his own grave right here in Lviv. So that you guys had somewhere to commemorate him on the anniversary of his death!"

"What?!" Alik's eyes widened. "But we got the hand from our guys in the Baltics, and they got it from the Lithuanian diaspora in the States! Tell him, Audrius! You'll remember!"

"Yep." Audrius nodded. "I remember those guys. Jonáš, Kestutis, Ramūnas . . ."

"Sure, they gave you the hand, but it was our people in the States who gave it to them." Captain Ryabtsev was back to firm and military curt, like he was conducting a drill or giving out orders. "Moscow didn't know about it. That was me and the late Mezentsev, here in Lviv. We cooked up a special operation in the States to partially exhume his body.

Moscow paid, but if they'd known the whole truth, I wouldn't be talking to you right now . . ."

Someone in the audience gave a heavy sigh. The captain paused and scanned the crowd for the culprit.

"I'm telling you this so you don't hold a grudge against us. We weren't just stupid bulldogs. Even now, I can tell you Jimi Hendrix's whole life story, year by year. I could recite his songs from memory, in the original. I can't sing, forgive me! My parents had no money for a piano or guitar. Whistling was the only musical instrument I had growing up. I'm still glad I never became an army man!"

"I remember you," Alik thought aloud. "If what you're saying is true, then we should find a table, at which we can all –" he gestured at the crowd – "sit together. And we should drink, and remember the past in a little more detail."

"Everything I told you is true," said Captain Ryabtsev. "There'd be no point deceiving you. I'm not in the service anymore. Fifteen years out already."

Alik looked at the floor and said nothing. He turned to the cross with its fresh white lettering.

"You hearing this, Jimi?" he addressed the cross. "The law are sticking their noses in our relationship again. But there's no need to discuss our relationship. We didn't give you up before the eighteenth of September 1970, and we won't do it after. There's not been a year gone by when we haven't gathered here to refresh your grave. Not even back when they really wanted to stop us!"

Somewhere nearby an ambulance squealed past. The siren gradually faded away.

"Alright, guys," said Alik. "I'm getting started!"

He pulled out a blister pack of Luminol, took one out, sat by the grave, dropped the white tablet on the earth and, after a moment's pause, pushed it into the soil with his index finger, just past the grass roots.

"Rest easy," he whispered, and got back to his feet.

The captain took a step back, like he was trying not to interfere. But he stayed there, watching everything unfold.

The bearded Penzel squatted by the grave, pre-prepared sleeping pill in hand. The ritual was repeated. Next came Audrius. He whispered something in Lithuanian. Then his index finger pushed another white tablet into the mound.

The sky over Lychakiv Cemetery darkened. The leaves that were yet to fall from their respective bushes and trees were catching patters of light rain. They rustled, whispered, lending a sense of encroaching danger.

Alik looked up.

"Just like last year," he said. "Time to go . . ."

They started back towards the exit, descending the hill, weaving between the graves and railings, the tombs and the statues.

In the dark Alik made out a large stone cross depicting the crucifixion. For just a moment, the face of the suspended Jesus Christ looked blissful.

Once the gates were locked, Captain Ryabtsev appeared in front of Alik, standing about a head shorter than him.

"Now then gents, shall we find ourselves a big table some-where?" Alik asked, and without waiting for an answer he turned right and started walking along the cemetery's brick lattice wall. The others followed him. The captain was left to bring up the rear.

They soon left the cemetery wall behind. The grey houses of Mechnikov Street now dozed on either side. Alik felt a weakness coming on in his legs. He walked in front, leading the way for these ancient friends of his, the people with whom he'd been taken off to the Regional Department of Internal Affairs as a young lad. As he walked, he realised that there were no specific big tables ahead of them that he was aware of. And they could really do with one right now. Before, in the old, unkind years of the Soviets, even a little square kitchen table with some stools around it seemed big. Those times and those tables were now in a "double" past: another age and another country. These days he required a worthy seat – evidently his backside now demanded more softness and comfort. But step after step, there was neither softness nor comfort to be found.

"Maybe the George?" The warm breath of an acquaintance filled his ear. "Genyk's on security there, he'll let us in . . ."

Alik slowed his pace and squinted at the person who'd said it.

The dark air trembled before his eyes, like someone had blown cigarette smoke in his face.

"Fog's coming down," said Captain Ryabtsev, who had suddenly appeared to Alik's right, between him and the wall. "It's a low one," he added in a knowing tone. "We'll be covered for a bit . . . Best to wait."

Alik waited. The others waited too. As they all stood under a street sign marked "Lychakivska 84A", weakly lit by a streetlamp, the darkness before their eyes filled with the fog's misty milk.

"Alik, I'm going," said the voice of Captain Ryabtsev. "Another time."

"What 'other time'?" asked Alik.

"You've not moved anywhere," said the captain affectionately. "I still remember your address from the seventies. I'll come over, tell you everything. Maybe tomorrow, even."

The guys bid their farewells and evaporated into the dark fog. Only Audrius was left beside him, his shoulder almost brushing Alik's.

"Let's go to mine," Alik suggested to his Lithuanian friend. "I've got herbal liqueur."

"Me too, two bottles of Triple Nine," Audrius replied.[2]

Alik pulled out his phone. He called a taxi company, but the dispatcher didn't respond. He called another – same result. Then suddenly he heard the sound of an engine, and remembered they were stood next to a road. He felt out the edge of the kerb with his foot and started peering in the direction of the oncoming car, still not visible, but audible. He stepped into the road, his right hand already raised.

Two headlights materialised out of the milky fog, right next to one another. Alik took another step forwards to make himself more visible. All of a sudden there was a screech of brakes, and the car skidded straight towards him across the wet cobblestone. The left headlamp hit him in the knee and he flew backwards, flailing an arm, trying to find a surface to keep himself vertical, but failing.

The car stopped. The inside light came on, and under that

light Alik saw two frightened faces. One belonged to a young man, perhaps thirty, the other to a man about ten years his senior. The older passenger's sharp nose and well-kept moustache gave him away as a foreigner, most likely a Pole. The young man opened the door and got out. His hands were shaking.

"Are you alright?" he asked Alik, who was already on his feet, rubbing his bruised knee. "I didn't see you!"

"It's fine, it's fine," Alik assured him. "Audrius, you there?" He looked around.

"I am," his acquaintance replied, stepping towards the car.

"Perhaps I could give you a lift somewhere?" asked the old Opel's driver, his voice still trembling.

"I was just trying to catch a ride off someone, as it happens," Alik said, a little aloof. "The far end of Zamarstynivska . . ."

"Take a seat!" The driver opened the rear door, and with a face that was still frightened, but also intrigued, he looked the middle-aged, long-haired pair of acquaintances up and down.

The car jolted and swam into the foggy milk, like a submarine traversing a deep, dark, opaque sea.

"You wouldn't be hippies, by any strange chance, would you?"

"Why 'strange'? There's nothing 'strange' about us being hippies!" Alik said firmly.

"I saw a film about you!"

"About us?" Alik and Audrius looked at each other in surprise.

"There's been no film about us," said Audrius with his faint Lithuanian accent.

18

"Well not about you personally, but about hippies!" the driver corrected himself. "About those American hippies who went to India and made themselves a city or something, for a better life! Maybe the city's already died out by now. This was way back when!"

"Way back when, exactly?" Audrius asked, almost annoyed. "It wasn't that long ago! What, you think we're in our eighties? We've got life in us yet! We're another ten or fifteen years from retiring, even!"

The driver's head shrank back into his shoulders. He went quiet and focused on the foggy road.

"So what do you think? Reckon Ryabtsev was telling the truth?" Alik asked Audrius.

Audrius shrugged. He didn't want to talk, and he didn't have an answer ready anyway.

They drove for half an hour, then suddenly the fog broke to reveal pine trunks, and the familiar fence of the police hospital.

"Alright." The driver gave a relieved sigh. "This where you wanted?"

"Yep," Alik nodded. "Near enough."

2

Having dropped off its long-haired passengers, the Opel turned around and headed back towards the centre.

"Where I'm from, hippies like that died out long ago," said the moustachioed passenger in lightly accented Russian. "Drugs, hashish . . . They didn't generally live all that long, but they had a fun time, with all the sex! Shall we give it a go?"

"Give what a go, pan Jarek?" The driver was taken aback; from everything the Pole had just said, all he'd picked up were the words "sex" and "fun time".

"What do you think I'm paying you for, kurwa-mać?!"

The driver looked closely at the road. The fog was lifting.

He nodded, pressing the accelerator. "We'll give it a go."

The cobblestones of Shpytalna Street had been scrubbed with the night's wet rag; Taras' Opel "raced" across them at twenty kilometres per hour, its body and headlamps disturbing the fog ahead. The car jostled, and the passenger's lack of a seatbelt made him bounce in his seat. Even this speed felt dangerous to Taras. But no fog had been thick enough to impede the last twenty years of Ukrainian capitalism. And capitalism is a violent thing. If you want to eat, best get to work!

Taras stopped the car. "Well, how are you doing?" he asked pan Jarek.

A month ago, this Pole had found Taras' advert online and been intrigued. So intrigued that he came over. How long did it take to get to here from Poland? It was funny just thinking about it. Poland might as well be a suburb of Lviv it was so close!

"I think that's enough for you today!" said Taras with a doctorly tone before his client had time to answer.

"No." The Pole shook his head and switched from broken Russian to Polish. "You know what . . . Maybe a little longer . . . fifteen minutes . . ." he said, his jaw clenched from pain in his teeth. His eyes were as dulled as his voice.

Taras waited a moment before trying to stand his ground, quieter and more cautiously: "Perhaps it would be better to try again tomorrow? With this fog . . ."

"Tomorrow?! That'll be too expensive . . . Have those hippies of yours tired you out? And on my money too . . ."

The grey Opel Vectra, which had a long and very international life story – Germany at the end of the eighties, Poland in the nineties, Belarus in the noughties and now Ukraine in 2011 – jostled once more and rolled along the bumpy, uneven cobblestone, passing every pothole and vibration through to driver and passenger alike.

Taras leaned towards the windshield. He was almost pressing his chest to the steering wheel. He stared into the road. The speedometer made it to 60. The passenger said nothing, bouncing along with the car and its driver.

Taras had worked out his "treatment" routes himself, and

he knew them by heart. Not just the street names, even the houses he passed and which cars sat outside them most often. If it weren't for the fog, there'd have been no problem at all.

Pan Jarek groaned loudly and threw his hands to his groin, squeezing them between his thighs; pressing them against his jeans like he was trying to warm them up.

Taras glanced over at the passenger, his mouth curled into a barely noticeable grin. He pressed more decisively on the gas pedal and the car shot forward, as if possessed.

His eyes filled with a simultaneous fervour and fear. The fear crept in at the very edge of his field of vision, getting caught up in the fog along with the headlamp beams. And although the lights could cut through about fifty metres of fog, were any kind of obstacle to appear on the road, alive or not, there would be no stopping in time. A wet cobblestone is a slippery thing.

The Opel gave such an unexpected jump that Taras, no seatbelt this time, smacked the top of his head against the car roof. The Pole got thrown even harder. He clenched his teeth as if he were trying to stop a scream pushing its way from his gut to the surface.

Taras looked nervously at his passenger.

"Stop! Stop!" pan Jarek groaned, and suddenly his whole body clenched, like a spasm. Clenched, then immediately released again. He went limp, his whole frame somehow contracted, his elbows dropping to his legs. His lips puckered on his pale face, as if he were about to whistle.

Taras slammed the brakes. The Opel screeched to the kerb. The Pole held his left hand out to Taras. His arm was trembling. In a swift and practised move, Taras pulled a litre-sized glass jar from under his seat and handed it to pan Jarek.

He turned off the engine and the lights. The car died. The fog drew in with an obstructive curiosity, enshrouding the "blinded" Opel and its inhabitants.

But the passenger opened his door, still groaning. He got out quickly and clumsily. Standing with his back to the car, he lowered his jeans and bent forward. The sleeve of his leather jacket caused a strangely harsh rustle as his hands moved.

Taras closed his eyes. Not due to any particular feeling of tiredness. His biological rhythm had long since accommodated these night trips across the city. It was just that the fog didn't usually factor into his plans. Fog always gets in the way. Though it was still a lot better than snow or black ice! Once the snow falls, then melts, and the slight frost comes in, that's that, goodbye income, see you in spring! It's surprising that some work, no matter how directly related it is to medicine, can still prove seasonal!

Through the complete silence came the sonorous clatter of pebble against glass, and then the immediate murmur of a stream – the Pole was urinating into the shaking glass jar.

Then the sound of a metal zip – the Pole doing up either his flies or his jacket.

Taras caught the passenger's heavy and uneven breathing. He was still stood there, now just completely still and silent. He was standing in front of a slumbering three-storey house, with slumbering city windows. He was about two metres from the front of the building, and still the fog crept into that small gap, pushing between the concrete and the man recently relieved of a small but vicious kidney stone.

Taras waited patiently. The stream sounded once more – pan Jarek was carefully pouring the urine in the jar out into the gutter drain.

After a couple of minutes, he returned cautiously to his seat beside the driver. He put the empty jar on the carpet next to his foot, and held out an open palm, on which sat a wet, grey globule, only small: a stone the size of a grain of buckwheat. Taras turned on the light in the car, carefully took the globule between two fingers, and lifted it up to inspect it.

"What do you want it for?" his passenger asked in Polish, his voice still rasping and strangulated from the memory of recent pain.

"A memento," the driver responded calmly, quietly. "So that I've got something to show the kids, when they ask what I did 'back then'."

Taras' tired smile gave his face a welcoming air.

"You got kids?" the Pole asked indifferently, his voice dropping to a murmur.

"No, no wife either."

"And you're how old?"

"Thirty-seven."

"Oh! So you're younger than your own motor!" He laughed.

"No, older. Just by a couple of years."

The Pole took his wallet from the inside pocket of his jacket.

"Here." He offered Taras a few twenty-złoty notes.

"Take you to the hotel?" Taras asked politely.

The Pole switched back to broken Russian: "I'll walk. It's nearby, in 'Old Krakow'."

Left on his own, Taras locked the car. He got out a small plastic tub for homeopathic cough balls and placed the pebble the Pole had given him inside it.

He had the sudden urge to take a nap. He reclined the driver's seat, lay down, and closed his eyes. The car was dark, warm, comfy. The warmth would last from half an hour to an hour, then the dry cold would naturally wake him up.

3

The dry air soaked through the slight opening in the Opel's window and brushed Taras' cheek. And he woke up. Half-awake, he immediately put his hand in his jacket pocket and pulled out the night's earned złoty then switched the light on. As he looked at the notes crumpled between his fingers, his eyes filled with acridity.

He looked at the clock. Half past four.

The headlamps lit up a thin fog, slicing eighty metres through it.

Taras snorted to himself, glad to see the fog ebbing. The houses of Shpytalna Street drifted lazily past the grey Opel.

He was so sick of this autumn. All the rain and fog. Almost like London, which he'd never been to. Still a long way to go until summer. It'd be a nice thing to just wake up in summer, in the warm. Go for a swim somewhere, the sea, a stream . . .

A pained grimace played over his face. Who came up with the idea of building this glorious city so far from the sea? Worse still – so far from any water at all?! Around here it was just endless drylands, the nearest beach was in Vynnyky, but Vynnyky was absolutely packed in the summer. Maybe he could move? Pack up and head to Odesa? Odesa was also a beautiful city, plus it was by the sea!

His favoured bureau de change appeared up ahead. The window was burning with a bright yellow light. Taras normally came to this window, on Ivan Franko Street, three to four times a week. If he'd found work, of course. Sometimes he could go a week without a visit. Those weeks he just sat at home, read books and newspapers, or roamed the internet.

But oh, think of the comfort he could live in in Odesa, and with no real pretensions either. He could live on the first floor there too. Just like here, in Lviv. He wouldn't mind that, even if people scraped their wooden chairs in this imagined Odesan house, and noises penetrated just as cleanly through the walls. He wouldn't care. He'd have the sea! And people around him! There'd be people there, he'd find clients for some dependable earnings. The main thing was locating Odesa's bad roads. But would that really be so hard? There probably wasn't a single city in the country where it would be difficult to find uneven cobblestones!

The car stopped outside the bureau. Taras got out without turning off the engine. He walked over to the gleaming window.

It was guarded by thick bars, with a small section cut out at the bottom for direct contact with customers. The clean glass gave a clear view of the kind-looking girl who always worked nights at this 24/7 bureau de change. Taras had no idea who worked there in the daytime. Somehow he'd managed never to use the services of the "daytime" bureau de change.

"Good evening!" Taras smiled, looking her in the eye and pushing his hard-earned złoty through the gap.

"Evening." She nodded.

The notes were whisked away by hands in white lace gloves, which disappeared under the sleeve of a red sweater.

Taras watched as her hands folded each note.

"Here you are." She offered the hryvnia through the gap.

"Is it not cold for you in there?" Taras asked playfully, his eyes on her slender fingertips hidden under the fabric of their gloves.

"Don't worry," she said. "I've got a heater in here."

"Well I thought I might invite you for a coffee . . . if you were cold."

"If I get cold, I'll invite myself!" Her voice carried something of a sneer.

On his way back to the car, Taras turned for a moment. The girl's face was no longer visible from where he was standing. The bright lamp behind the window cast out its light with a force that struck the eyes.

Taras dropped off the Opel near his house on Pekarska Street, then walked over to the nearest internet café.

The place was terribly lit. There were a few little desks with computers, a bare bar counter on the left, and to its right a glass-doored fridge filled with beer, Coke and water. But there was no-one around.

"Hey!" Taras shouted softly. "Anyone alive?"

"Huh? Who's there?" came a male voice from behind the bar.

Taras walked a little closer. He found a guy who looked sleepy and rough-faced, wearing a baggy sweater.

"Whaddaya want? Internet?" he asked drowsily, pushing his palms into the bar to hold himself upright.

"No, first a beer, then coffee."

"No coffee, but we've got beer. Get it from the fridge."

Taras took a bottle. Held it out to the guy. He opened it for him and took out a clean glass.

"Like me to switch you on some internet anyway?" he said.

Taras shrugged. "Why not?"

The guy sat at the computer. The monitor woke up, and its blue background filled row by row with program icons.

"Here then, sit!" He offered the chair up to Taras.

Taras thudded into it and moved the keyboard back. He poured the beer into the glass. Put it to his lips. Then he got out his homeopathic cough-ball pot from his jacket pocket. Opened it. And very carefully poured about twenty little pebbles onto the table. Some were darker, some lighter, but they were all grey.

"Don't have a magnifying glass, do you?" he shouted in the direction of the bar.

"Nope," the guy replied.

"What about paper?" asked Taras.

He was brought a blank sheet.

Taras immediately used his palm to sweep the stones onto the white sheet. Now they were more easily visible.

"What's that?" asked the "internet barman", still standing drowsily behind his customer.

"This lot?" asked Taras, turning to face him. "They're medicinal stones," he joked.

"What are they medicine for?"

"Don't know yet. I need to conduct a few experiments . . ."

The guy gave Taras a suspicious look, before returning to the bar.

Taras finished his beer, carefully poured the stones back into the plastic tub and stuffed it in his pocket before leaving.

The fog over Lviv had already begun lifting, like the very streets were pushing it up out of their way.

The front door squeaked. Taras looked at the wooden stairs, each of which gave its own particular sound, like the keys of a worn old grand piano. The fifth step was the loudest and most piercing. Its sound somehow always managed to wake up the neighbour on the first floor – the resentful Yezhi Astrovsky, former hairdresser, former bathhouse attendant, former book-binder and former supermarket security guard. These days you could just call him "the former Yezhi Astrovsky". He didn't work anywhere anymore, but he drank regularly, and once drunk he would search out interlocutors. Exclusively sober ones, too. He often picked fights with Taras over the noise, but from the thin, delicate, subtle facial features of his drunk neighbour, Taras could clearly see that he mostly just needed contact and pity – or he'd settle for attention – and his arguments stemmed primarily from a lack of other options.

Taras skipped the fifth step, and after making it up another ten, stopped in front of his door.

From the quiet little radio deceiver, which had sat on the kitchen table since God knows when, came the Ukrainian anthem.

"Six in the morning," Taras sighed. "Time for bed. God gives to those who fall asleep to the morning anthem!"

Ever since he was a schoolboy, Taras had always tried to be

a man of his word. So five minutes after saying that, he lay down trying to work out, through slow, unfocused thoughts, what exactly God had given him for the night's work. What was he paid in, and how much of it had he received?

4

The sound of a nearby tram flew in with the cool, dry air through the small open window of Taras' apartment. But Taras slept sweetly. He was dreaming of Zhirinovsky[3], rude and vigorous, and for some reason, in his sleep, he spoke to Zhirinovsky in Ukrainian, but he said the right words: "Ukraine should span from sea to sea! We will wash our Ukrainian boots in the Indian Ocean!"

Then suddenly, Taras dreamed that he was asleep, and dreaming of Zhirinovsky, while he himself, in his upper layer of sleep, in an almost controlled consciousness of cloudy dreaming, thought about how Ukraine needed its own Zhirinovskys, Ukrainian to the bone. And sure, let them be outright demagogues, even idiots, but they would serve the Ukrainian people faithfully and truthfully, instilling their people with an alertness to enemies, and carefully explaining the idea of an "enemy of the motherland". The doorbell rang, jolting him from his sleep.

Taras opened his eyes. The ringing had stopped already, but its echo hung in the air of the flat, in his ears.

He wasn't expecting anyone; that meant the person at the door could only be his downstairs neighbour. But what on earth for? Taras could remember very clearly avoiding the fifth step, after all.

He put on his white terry-cloth dressing gown, written off from the George hotel's supplies by a friend who worked there as a bathhouse attendant. He slid his feet into some flip flops and wandered over to the door.

Before Taras stood his old friend Oksana in a long grey-green coat. Her face carried an eternal smile, behind which could hide any mood, from catty and annoyed to joyous and celebratory. She had a bulky, zip-up laundry bag at her feet.

"What, not expecting me?" Oksana was surprised, looking over his terry-cloth gown with "George" embroidered in red on the breast pocket.

"Nope," Taras confessed, not moving an inch.

"What are you standing there for?" The smile vanished from Oksana's face. She looked down at the bag. "Go on, take it! But carefully!"

Oksana was generally listened to in the social circles the two of them shared. It wasn't that she was always giving instructions or deciding who did what. It was just that, though she was an actress, nature had given her the air of a director.

Taras lifted the bag, immediately noting its weight. He retreated down the hallway, carrying it straight into the main room. Oksana followed him in. Shut the door behind her. Took off her coat, hung it on a hanger and slipped off her boots.

"Let me give you a kiss, then! I'll be dragging you by the ear after that!"

She reached over to Taras, who had stopped by the table out of confusion.

"What, is it my birthday or something?" he asked. "What's the date today?"

Oksana smiled. "Might as well check your passport! September eighteenth!"

"Boy oh boy!" Taras sighed.

And then Oksana's strong hands got hold of him. Both palms gripped his temples like a warm vice, pulling his head towards her lips.

"Well, happy birthday little Tarasik!" she said, giving him a smacking kiss, first on the lips, then forehead, then cheek, just like a little kid.

After releasing the birthday boy, Oksana looked to either side.

"There's something I'm missing . . ." she said. "What about champagne? In the fridge?"

"I'll get some, gimme five . . ." he spluttered. "Let me get dressed. Got some hryvnia changed just in time, too!"

Taras threw his robe on the sofa-bed, then pulled on some trousers and a sweater.

"Back in a second!" he cried, already halfway out of the front door.

The door slammed shut. The stairs screeched, as if wailing underfoot.

Oksana settled into a chair. She was suddenly drawn to the barely audible buzzing coming from the lace-curtained window.

She approached, pulled back the curtain, and saw on the

wide windowsill a homemade plexiglass greenhouse, in which grew rotund spikeless cacti, with three long, skinny daylight-lamps glowing above them.

Oksana was so engrossed in watching the strange bald cacti growing in their plastic cubes that she didn't hear the door scrape open, nor Taras entering the flat with a shopping bag in his hand.

"Alright, got the champagne!" he declared proudly.

He quickly retrieved two flutes from the old sideboard. From the shopping bag he pulled out pre-sliced ham and kolbasa, and some cheese.

"Wait, what about your present?!" Oksana interrupted his bustling. "Come on, over here!"

She leaned over the bag, unzipped it and stretched it open.

First, she pulled out and presented the birthday boy with a new, quite small aquarium.

Taras squatted next to her, placing the aquarium on the parquet floor. He looked surprised, his eyes glued to the bag, as if Oksana were about to perform a magic trick, preparing to pull out a bunny by its ears.

"And here you go, lay these out nicely at the bottom!" Oksana presented him with a weighty bag of sea pebbles.

Taras quietly began to feel genuinely celebratory. How good of her, he said to himself. She can't come without a surprise!

After the sea pebbles she retrieved from the bag a six-litre plastic bottle of dull green water.

She explained the water's origin: "I went to the lake in Vynnyky especially. The distance my little car has driven today for you! Pour it in, but be careful!"

Taras had barely finished filling the aquarium when before him appeared a transparent plastic bag full of water (entirely clear this time) with rippling seaweed growing from little brown plastic pots.

"Can this go in too?" asked Taras cautiously.

"Sure!"

The aquarium filled with life before their eyes. The birthday boy arranged the three pots of seaweed; their long leaf-blades rippled as his hands disturbed the water.

Then came the next bag of clear water; in this one, small, blue, exotic-looking fish, no longer than Taras' little finger, swam about nervously.

"There you are. Now you won't be so lonely in here!" said Oksana, surveying her gift with pride. "You're excited, I hope?"

"Lost for words!" Taras shook his head emphatically. "But where should I put it?"

"What d'you mean, where?" his guest replied. "There's room on the windowsill! Next to the cacti."

"I was thinking of putting another greenhouse there ... Maybe it'd be better on the sill in the kitchen?"

"That's exactly where the second greenhouse would fit best!" Oksana cut in decisively. "A kitchen's no place for live fish! They might get the wrong impression!"

Taras smiled.

"What, can they understand humans?"

"Not all humans. But humans like you they can. If you behave normally around them. These are very useful fish, by the way. You can't even imagine. One day they'll save your life!"

"Wow!" Taras broke into a broad grin.

"This breed lives in Japanese lakes, and they can feel earthquakes coming. Get it? If they suddenly start drawing a figure of eight on the surface – get outside, quick!"

Taras went quiet. His face became deathly serious. He fixed his gaze on the red-blue fish as they slowly and peacefully grew accustomed to their new aquatic environs.

"So what, you think there's gonna be an earthquake sometime soon?"

"Doesn't matter if I believe it or not, it's best to be prepared! How many times have they written about it already, there's mountains just nearby! So get those fish on the windowsill, and let's have a drink!"

Taras promptly hoisted the aquarium up off the floor. He pushed the curtain back with his elbow and placed the fish on the sill, to the right of the greenhouse.

"So why do you shave your cacti?" asked Oksana behind his back.

"They just look like that! Bald by nature. They're called Lophophora Williamsii. Unique cacti! The Aztecs and Mayans used them to talk to the gods."

Just as Taras' champagne cork hit the high ceiling, someone's finger jammed into the doorbell.

"That mother—" Taras started. "That piece of shit! Just has to ruin the moment!"

"Who is it?"

"My neighbour! I must've accidentally stepped on the fifth step . . . When I went out for the champagne . . . And now he's going to pick a fight with me over it."

Taras started in the direction of the hallway.

"Wait right there!" Oksana stopped him in his tracks. "I'll do it."

Behind the door stood a man in a tracksuit with a pretty beat-up face and a disorderly, scraggly, slightly curly head of hair. His initially determined facial expression softened under the demandingly inquisitive stare of Oksana, then turned abashedly neutral.

"Have you come to congratulate Taras on his birthday?"

"Me?" he said, a little scared. "What, it's today? Yes, yes, of course!"

"But where's your bottle?" asked Oksana, lowering her inquisitive gaze to the neighbour's clasped hands.

"My bottle?" he asked back, still in no state to process this unexpected turn of events. "My bottle of . . . vodka?"

"Indeed, your bottle of vodka!" Oksana nodded. "Go and get it! We'll wait, right Taras?" She glanced back.

"Mhm . . ." came the host's uncertain response.

Taras' neighbour hotfooted it back downstairs.

"I'll leave the door open!" Oksana shouted after him. "But be quick!"

Five minutes later he was back, and he really did have a bottle of vodka in his hands. He was now dressed in an un-ironed brown suit. The short, broad green tie clashed with his pink shirt, which was somewhat poorly tucked into his trousers; he had slippers on his bare feet.

"Come in, come in!" Oksana shouted through from the living room. "Thanks for getting dressed for the occasion!"

The birthday boy and his guest were already sat at the

round table. The three full flutes of champagne invited quick action.

The neighbour sat on the free chair, set his vodka on the table next to the bottle of champagne, and gave the woman a quizzical look: not only did she have a commander's diction, but an air of authority as well.

"If I may," he said. "My name is Yezhi Astrovsky . . ."

"You may." Oksana nodded, reaching for her flute.

"I'm a former hairdresser. I could give you advice . . ."

"Later," Oksana interrupted and nodded at Taras. "First, a toast for the birthday boy!"

"Yes, yes." Yezhi grabbed his glass. "Congratulations! I wish you neighbourly peace . . . love –" on this word he squinted at Oksana – ". . . happiness and, most importantly, money . . . There."

The toast thawed Taras, who had been somewhat distracted by the sudden arrival of his own birthday.

The three flutes met over the table, which was covered in a yellow linen cloth with unwashed traces of past celebrations. The birthday boy's glass spilled a few drops of champagne that fell directly onto the sliced salami.

"Thank you!" Taras nodded. "I'm very touched."

The neighbour finished his champagne in one gulp. The birthday boy watched him, then followed suit. Only Oksana maintained her dignity – her flute was still half-full.

She opened the vodka with a practised twist.

"My father," she said, shifting her gaze from Taras to his neighbour, "when he was a soldier, would always make a

'Northern Lights' cocktail with his friends, and never – never!
– got a hangover."

"Well, what's in it?" Taras asked with a lively interest.

"Add half a glass of vodka to half a glass of champagne."

Yezhi Astrovsky flinched upon hearing the recipe.

"I must be going . . . apologies," he muttered, his eyes on
the bottle of vodka in Oksana's hand.

"No, you mustn't leave so soon! That's not neighbourly!"
Oksana's voice softened.

The neighbour nodded in despair.

The birthday boy poured himself and his neighbour a half-
glass of champagne each, and Oksana topped them up with
vodka. It was time for the "Northern Lights".

"You have to promise me something," Oksana said to Yezhi
as they finished their *zakuski*.[4]

"What?" asked the birthday boy's neighbour, gripping his
empty glass in fear.

"You have to remind Taras that he doesn't live on his own
anymore!" said Oksana.

The neighbour looked from side to side, quizzically and a
little perturbed, then looked back at Oksana.

"Okay . . ."

"Remind him that he needs to feed his fish daily." She
nodded at the windowsill. "And talk to the housekeeper, get
them to fix the step."

"I've told them a hundred times already, they're asking for
fifty hryvnia!" the neighbour exclaimed, back in his habitual
sulk.

Oksana took out her purse without a word and pulled out fifty hryvnia.

"Oksana! I'll do it, I've got the money!" Taras, whose face had already begun to express the cocktail's bewildering contents, raised his hand above the table. His fingers gripped some crumpled notes he'd got from his jeans pocket.

"Yeah, I'll . . ." Yezhi's eyes darted from the fifty in Oksana's hand to the crumpled twenties in Taras'. "I'll sort it out. I'll do it!"

He carefully slipped the three twenties from Taras' hand, stood up, nodded a farewell, and left.

"Shall I wash up?" Oksana asked.

"I'll manage, leave it!"

"If you insist!" His guest nodded. "I'm off too, I've got things to do! Don't forget about the fish!"

Left on his own again, Taras approached the window and observed his fish swimming peacefully between the seaweed.

"No earthquake today, by the looks," Taras whispered to himself. "Means I can sleep a little longer."

5

Alik and Audrius woke up just before the sun began setting, although it hadn't been visible that day anyway. The afternoon had a low-hanging gloom about it, but it was still putting on a brave face through the window of Alik's little apartment at the very end of Zamarstynivska Street. Their heads were both filled with a slight noise – the culprit was probably the glass each of "Nemirov", along with the several glasses each of Audrius' Lithuanian herbal liqueur that they'd knocked back in memory of Jimi Hendrix. They'd slept in their clothes, Alik on top of the duvet on his permanently unfolded sofa-bed, Audrius passed out in an armchair.

"What's Vilnius like?" Alik asked, rubbing his eyes.

"Don't know," Audrius shrugged. "Not been. I've got a *khutor*⁵ now, about forty kilometres outside of the city. No-one around."

"That's good." Alik nodded. "Sometimes I wish I had no-one around, too! But the opposite's also got its charm . . . Although nearby all I've got are my stepmother and a few peace-loving neighbours. My stomach's feeling a little lonely . . ."

This piqued Audrius' interest. "I could eat too . . . maybe even a drink . . . you got anything here to munch on?"

Alik shook his head.

"I fast every year in the lead-up to September eighteenth . . . Lose some weight . . ."

"Alright, shall we go somewhere then?" suggested the Lithuanian.

Alik thought for a moment.

"There's a twenty-four-seven cheburek place by the lake . . . But you can't have cheburek without a beer . . . What do you reckon, was our KGB guy telling the truth? You were there, after all . . ."

Audrius sighed. "My memory doesn't work on an empty head and a sober stomach."

"You sure you didn't mix those up?"

"Mix what up?"

"I mean . . . empty head . . . sober stomach . . ."

"Ah! What was it I said? I'm losing my Russian without realising, I don't have anyone to speak it with out on the *khutor.*"

"You already said, said there's no-one around, that you're out there alone."

"I'm telling you, no-one!" Audrius nodded to confirm his words. "Maybe you've got some Riga sprats?" he asked. "There used to always be loads of Riga sprats, in every house!"

"Where would I get Riga sprats from?! Come on, let's go!" Alik pulled himself briskly to his feet.

Outside it smelled of dry forest must. Through the gaps in a pine-trunk fence there were cars flashing past, heading in the direction of Bryukhovychi.

A car started up behind the backs of the two hippies, who

were fairly well-built for their age. Alik turned, and through the windscreen of a yellow Moskvich he made out the face of his neighbour. He waved.

"Give you a lift?" the neighbour offered politely through his open car door.

They got into the back seat, which was a little sharp and uncomfortable thanks to the springs pushing up through the leather.

The car pulled out into the road and turned left, towards the city.

"Where you headed?" The driver half-looked back.

"Well, we were thinking Bryukhovychi . . . to the cheburek place . . ."

"No, I'm headed to Povitryana," the neighbour said, hitting the brakes.

"Go for it, go for it!" Alik reassured him, not wanting to leave the Moskvich and end up back on the roadside having to pick and choose again, which had been getting irritating. "I'm sure there's a café there too!"

"Yes!" His neighbour livened up. "Café 'Café', 24 Povit-ryana! They've got crazy prices there. Zenyk went there with Tkatska the other day, spent fifteen hryvnia and got so drunk he didn't go to work for two days . . . They even left him there to sleep, that's service for you! Just try falling asleep in a McDon-alds! No chance! They'd throw you out like . . . like a . . ." The neighbour either lost his train of thought or couldn't think of a word, and he looked half-back at his passengers again.

". . . Like a dirty tissue?" suggested Audrius as a lightly Lithuanian-accented closer.

The driver nodded. "Exactly."

The old friends clambered out of the yellow Moskvich by 24 Povitryana Street.

"I'll be coming back this way too, I'll check in on you," the neighbour said as he bid them farewell. "I'll give you a ride home if you want!"

Inside it was loud and smoke-filled – so it was comfy. There was conversation humming at every table, beer was being drunk, dried fish was being crunched between unkempt but sharp teeth. Some light cursing added some spark to the chorus of slow, drunken male voices.

"Over there." Alik pointed at the far right-hand corner.

There were only two people sat at the table – they could fit at least another four in!

Their table neighbours, one in a freshly cleaned quilted jacket, the other in a suit and tie, lowered their conversation respectfully when Alik put down two glasses of beer and a shamelessly thrown-together plate of two cutlets, two salt-pickled cucumbers and two palm-sized dried fish.

"You still need to tell me what you think! Was our KGB guy telling the truth?" asked Alik once he'd sat opposite his Lithuanian friend.

Audrius shrugged his sharp shoulders. His jacket was next to him on the bench, and his threadbare sweater gave his bones too fatty and meaty a covering.

"Here, you take both!" Alik gave a casual but respectful nod to the cutlets. "You're in Europe now . . . Harder to survive out there . . ."

Audrius took a cutlet with his fingers, lifted it to his nose, sniffed it and smiled.

"Maybe it was the truth," he said, looking at the cutlet in his hand. "Think about it! Digging up a grave in the States, cutting the hand off a corpse, sticking it in plastic so it doesn't stink, transporting it over the Atlantic to Lithuania, and then by train to Lviv . . . Have hippies really ever known the meaning of the word 'logistics'?"

"What *does* it mean?" Alik asked, interrupting a gulp of beer.

"See?" said Audrius. "Our guys couldn't possibly have put that together . . ."

"That changes the matter fundamentally . . ." Alik mused slowly, resuming his interrupted gulp.

"Changes what?" Audrius looked his old friend in the eye.

"Well . . . Our map of the cosmos . . . Jimi Hendrix was an enemy of capitalism, and was in fact held in high esteem by the KGB!"

"Listen, young people get corrupted all over! I had a DJ friend of mine from Kaunas, a 'young bachelor', and one time he fell for a girl behind the bar so badly he nearly switched teams! Could happen to anyone! Not just the KGB. This captain of yours, by the way . . . He's a little soft . . . He's not a 'bachelor' too, is he?"

"They stuck the 'bachelors' in prison back then, not in the security forces. Maybe they put them in the KGB over there in Lithuania?"

Audrius shook his head, which almost made his hair converge in a curtain over his face, only his nose stuck through.

"That means . . ." The Lithuanian swept his hair apart again. "He's a romantic. He clearly ended up in the service by accident . . ."

"Yeah, but he said there were loads of them helping him trick Moscow, and use Moscow's money to bring us Jimi's genius fingers . . ."

"Cool it!" Audrius grabbed the second cutlet. "You're living in a fantasy land, a fantasy city, where even in the Soviet era, the KGB all loved Jimi Hendrix! They should get a statue in their honour, these agents of yours!"

"Well, you're a romantic too! What, should we stick that statue up next to Jimi's grave and be done with it?!"

"Old man." Audrius' face broke out in a slightly condescending smile. "Haven't you forgotten something? *'Make love, not war!'*" he said in English. "Love is the most important thing in our lives. And if the KGB agents loved us, and tried not to fuck us over as a result, all those years ago, is that not a beautiful thing?"

"It is." Alik chewed his lip, studying the two lonely cucumbers lying on his plate. "See, I got the pickles, but they don't go with the beer at all. One second!"

Alik got up and walked over to the counter. Audrius watched the barwoman thoughtfully, as she listened with an attentive smile to her tall, long-haired customer. Then she took two rippled glass bottles filled with a transparent watery liquid from the shelf behind her. She poured the vodka into two spirit glasses, which had fixed their uncut eye on the grey ceiling.

"Hey, you wouldn't happen to be from Vynnyky?" the man in the clean jacket asked Audrius unexpectedly.

"No, Lithuania."

"Oh!" The man in the jacket lifted his index finger in front of his friend. "I told you they weren't our people . . . They eat their cutlets with their fingers! It's a different culture!"

6

The entrance to the courtyard from Fedorov Street was blocked again – this time some oaf had left his asphalt-coloured "Zhiguli" in front of the gate.

Oksana searched for a while, then squeezed her Cheburashka[6] between two imports parked outside the Stauropegion Institute. She locked the car and made her way over to the courtyard. From the Fedorov Street side, this house had no number. Perhaps that's exactly why people left their cars in front of the entrance with such cruel regularity.

On her way up to her first-floor apartment, Oksana listened for any squeaking. The wooden steps in her hallway were distinguished by their quietness and flexibility.

After removing her tall autumn boots, she went through into the cosy apartment's sole room and settled on the sofa. She caught her breath. Listened to the soft sound of tiredness in her head. Yesterday evening had stretched out to one in the morning – she and the girls had been livening up an insurance company's office party. The women clearly ran the show, both there and in the firm more generally. A few quiet, scared men sitting between relaxed ladies, makeup complemented with a tipsy flush. The men probably weren't even employed by the company, just the husbands of those doing the celebrating.

Memories of the night brought a smile to Oksana's face, but it didn't last. She soon remembered this morning too, and the surprised look she'd got from Taras (who always forgot his own birthday). She remembered the fish she'd gifted him. And then she remembered the fish that she'd been given just yesterday!

Oksana looked up at the windowsill, where there now stood a small aquarium – the same one she'd bought Taras.

She walked over to it, pulled back the curtain, and leaned over her own little watery world.

She shook a little dry food into the water. The fish, swimming peacefully amongst the green seaweed, suddenly looked skyward.

"Eat up, my dear guests, eat up!" she laughed, and left the fish behind their curtain on the windowsill. She walked through the little kitchen to the bathroom and had a wash.

The cold water did nothing to liven her up. So Oksana decided to relax a little. She went back to the room and climbed the steep wooden stepladder up to her bed, which also served as the roof of a made-to-order wardrobe. Up there, almost three metres from the floor, she also kept a little table-top reading lamp and a few magazines.

She lay on her back, head resting on the pillow. Her eyes closed of their own accord. She drifted off, although she made sure it was only a very brief drift, a couple of hours perhaps, no more. It was the middle of the day, after all. Market Square was making noise next door, its fountains gurgling, trams rumbling by, and the heels of women's boots clopping against the wet cobblestones.

7

Taras' life gave him several breaks a day, as if his ancient computer had taught him how to "freeze". It was at just these moments, when a sudden emptiness filled his head, that he would automatically hit the ON button and fix his frozen gaze to the monitor. He watched passively as the screen woke up, listening to the secretive sounds that accompanied the start-up of the various computer programs. Once the desktop had decorated itself in "blossoming" icons, Taras got up and brought two or three cacti in their plastic cube-vases over from the windowsill. He placed them under the monitor, so that they caught all the harmful computer radiation, attracting it to themselves. What was it to them? They, like all plants, were created to filter air, to rework carbon dioxide into oxygen! Taras didn't know what cacti turned dangerous computer rays into. He wasn't even sure the rays were dangerous, and sometimes he even doubted they existed at all. But it was foolish to ignore folk wisdom. And if folk had at some point decided that it was best to place a cactus under a switched-on monitor, then Taras would take it further, and use not one cactus, but three!

"You have three new emails!" the monitor's "window" informed him with a little yellow drawing of an envelope.

Two of them offered to quickly and cheaply lengthen his penis by eight centimetres. The third was more constructive.

"I am in your city. I'm writing to enquire about your services. Call me on my mobile 096 – 7049657. Lenya."

The morning emptiness was driven from Taras' head. His "money-making" mindset kicked into gear. His hand retrieved his mobile from the pocket of his white terry robe.

"Hello, Lenya? You sent me an email! Are your kidneys giving you trouble?"

A suspicious male voice responded with another question: "Who's this? The urologist?"

"I'm the gallstones guy," Taras answered, not bold enough to call himself a representative of the medical profession.

"Uh-huh," said the voice. "So what, can we come to you now? Where's your office?"

"I work on the road, not in an office," Taras explained. "Vibrotherapy usually removes the stones in two to three hours . . . Although sometimes the procedure may take longer."

"What is it, a special vibrator?"

"No, a special car, in which I'll drive you down carefully selected roads . . . It's tried and tested."

"Alright, where do you want to meet?"

Taras looked to the clock on the wall.

"It's still early, we need to wait until the roads are empty. Somewhere around eleven, midnight would be best . . . But about two hours before the procedure you need to drink a glass of cognac and sit in a hot bath."

The potential client was unperturbed. "No bath here, but the cognac won't be a problem! No, I'll come over now. I've nothing better to do! Spent almost twenty-four hours on that train, which also vibrated, by the way . . . but it didn't help at all."

"No, a train wouldn't be suitable," Taras informed him knowledgeably.

"Well, let's get to know each other, so we can recognise each other better this evening!"

"Sure," sighed Taras. "Go to the Opera House, we'll meet by the entrance in half an hour. How do I recognise you?"

"I'll be wearing a grey cap!"

Interesting . . . I wonder where he's come from? Taras thought, trying to picture a person in a grey cap. Russia, maybe? People don't try to "shock" like that round here!

Half an hour later, at the Opera House, there was indeed a man in a grey cap standing outside. He was also wearing a light-grey mackintosh, black trousers and light-grey chamois shoes. He clasped a large cardboard envelope with FOTO printed on it in Latin letters. Slender, average height, he was shuffling from one foot to another and studying each passer-by a little nervously.

Taras walked up to him and introduced himself.

"Right, shall we go and find somewhere to sit down?" Lenya said very matter-of-factly.

"For a coffee?" Taras asked.

"What, you don't drink during the day?" Lenya's blue eyes grew momentarily sharper.

"I'll be driving, won't I?"

Taras could see Lenya losing his last shred of respect for him, but even if there was no need to get behind the wheel that evening, he didn't like the idea of drinking with a man in a grey cap. This was a very different kind of person, with a very different kind of life that was lived by a different set of rules. Taras could feel that. And then something new filled the space between them – the smell of petrol.

Taras looked to either side. They were standing a little distance from the road. Just in case, he lifted his sleeve to his nose to make sure the smell wasn't emanating from his own person.

"So what if you're driving?" said Lenya. "We need to talk to each other. Come on! Alright, you can get yourself a coffee."

Taras, liberated from the need to drink, walked his client briskly to a little café on Virmenska Street. They set themselves up there, although not without a taste of Lenya's well-expressed dissatisfaction when the barman revealed they had no vodka, only liqueur.

"Can't get a hold of a proper drink round here with you lot!" Lenya said, knocking back a glass of liqueur and eyeing up the other three full spirit glasses in front of him.

Taras almost laughed. His soon-to-be client's impression of Lviv spoke only to the great distance between Lviv and wherever he had come from.

"So, where have you come from?" he asked.

"Vorozhba . . ."

"Where's that?" Taras asked, surprised.

"What, never heard of it? It's the largest railway hub in the country!" Lenya explained. "Sumy Oblast!"

Taras thought he'd caught another whiff of petrol nearby. He looked to either side. There were two elderly ladies sat at the neighbouring table, drinking coffee and eating strudel in a very genteel manner. There was no way they smelled of petrol.

Taras nodded, returning his gaze to his companion. "I know Sumy."

"Here you go, have a look at my x-ray, so you know!" Lenya pulled an x-ray sheet from his photo envelope.

Taras took it from him, lifted it to his eyes and turned to face the window. The clear outline of the two bean-shaped kidneys calmed him. He immediately saw the three stones that were causing Lenya discomfort. Two in the left kidney, one in the right.

Taras thoughtfully considered the path that the stones would have to move down to make their way to freedom. It was unrealistic to call these little pebbles one night's work. They still had to get through the renal duct in the bladder, then along the urethra and out into the light of day.

Taras glanced at Lenya's face, imagining it in the grip of physical pain, imagining his voice crying out. He immediately lost interest in working with this client.

"Well, what's the verdict?" asked Lenya.

Taras sighed heavily.

"They won't come out in one session," he said.

"Not even if we drive all night?" Lenya leaned forward, and the smell of coffee was briefly overpowered by that of petrol.

"You wouldn't last all night," Taras said softly.

"I'm paying for it," Lenya said promptly, pursing his lips. "Or are you trying to say it'll be more?"

"Alright – we can try," Taras assured Lenya. "I'll pick you

up at midnight, back there, at the Opera! But right now, I've got places to be . . ."

Lenya nodded thoughtfully. He watched as Taras approached the barman and paid for the coffee. Then he went up himself and ordered three more glasses of liqueur.

At midnight, Taras found Lenya by the Opera House. He was leaning against the leftmost column, the peak of his cap folded over to the left. The light-grey coat was unbuttoned and his hands were in his pockets. His eyes were glued to the paving stones.

"Alright then. You ready?" Taras asked him politely.

"What?" Lenya lifted his head sharply and turned. "Ah! Yes, all ready!"

The city had gone quiet. A faint breeze blew. The windows of Lviv's houses were going dark.

"We'll be trying Lychakivska first, to disturb those stones of yours, then we'll head to Horodotska – it's a little more bumpy there," Taras started explaining once they were in the car. "And then, if they're still . . ."

"I don't care if we go all the way to Derybasivska[7] –" his drunk client waved a hand – "as long as you get these bastards out!"

Taras stopped talking and decided not to explain anything further to the client. Off set the Opel. The usual vibrations got the driver's head in gear. He looked over at his passenger, who was yawning.

Taras turned the radio on, and they came out on Lychakivska to a BoomBox song.[8]

The car found uneven paving beneath it, set with small

cobblestones. Grey houses flitted by on either side, along with closed grocery shops and hairdressers. Taras focused his entire body on the car's vibrations, trying to gauge which speed would best "disturb" and force out his client's stones. The client looked forward, gormless.

"Is it doing anything?" asked Taras.

"Ah? What?" The passenger turned to face the driver.

"Can you feel the stones moving?"

Lenya's expression changed. He was now clearly trying to pay attention to what was happening in his kidneys. He even started feeling his stomach with his hand.

Taras nodded. "You could massage it a little. That helps too!"

Emboldened by the specialist's advice, Lenya started kneading the bottom of his stomach with both hands. He continued this for about three minutes, jolting with the car over each uneven patch of road. Then he gave an "ohhh" and froze again.

"So, how goes it?" Taras asked.

"Something's going on down there," Lenya whispered, dumbfounded. He raised his frightened eyes, looking straight ahead at the road as it flew forward to meet him.

"Relax!" said Taras. "Now we'll go to Horodotska! Just to make sure . . ."

Taras turned off Lychakivska and the car weaved along cramped, dark alleyways. After making it through the old part of the city centre, the Opel came out on a wide street and began to pick up its pace again.

"Wait!" cried Lenya, holding his stomach. "It hurts!"

"The process has already begun." Taras smiled. "Can't stop now! Best grin and bear it!"

Lenya's eyes rolled upwards from the pain. He gave the driver a crazed look and leaned forward against the dashboard without removing his hand from his stomach.

"And will it be like this for long?" he asked, defeated.

"About fifteen minutes," answered Taras. "Then, if it hasn't come out, we'll have a break and try again."

Taras thought that night would never end. After four full lengths of Horodotska Street, which is comfortably thirty kilometres long, Lenya was beginning to look really awful. And suddenly, there was a glint in the road from the illuminated striped baton of a traffic warden. Taras stopped. The warden asked politely for his licence and cast a suspicious eye over Lenya, specifically over his face, which was a mask of pain.

"I'm taking him to the hospital," Taras improvised. "Poor guy's not feeling good."

"Hope you make it okay!" The traffic warden returned his licence.

Three hours later, having already exhausted the "long vibrations" of both Horodotska Street and Lychakivska Street, Taras moved towards the "short vibrations" of Lisna Street. Lisna was quite a small and jagged backstreet, with such big potholes that the car would jump almost half a metre into the air. This street managed to shake out Lenya's first pebble. Lenya stood wincing, his back to the car, facing the stairs that led up the hill to Znesinnya Park. Once the pebble clinked into the glass jar, he froze and stood completely still for a couple of minutes, his legs apart, lit by the scattered yellow light of a sole streetlamp.

Taras looked at the clock – almost half past four. It would be getting light soon. He yawned. His body was habitually preparing for its morning sleep.

"Here, take it!" Lenya said, deflated, holding out the jar.

Taras took it silently, opened the door on his own side and carefully poured the urine into the road.

"Are we going to try and get the next stone?" he asked.

Lenya's head wrenched towards him. His scared expression betrayed a desire to never discuss the matter again.

"Where shall I take you?" Taras asked a little more quietly.

"The Opera House, where you picked me up," his client managed. "I'll call you tomorrow . . . I don't know yet."

He reached into the pocket of his unbuttoned light-grey coat. Pulled out three crumpled ten-dollar bills. The car set off, trundling quietly down the street with the engine turned off. Taras had simply released the handbrake. The engine kicked in at the foot of the hill.

After dropping his client at the Opera, he drove a little further to his beloved bureau de change. Its little window, full of light, made Taras feel very happy. Even if he had nothing to exchange, he would still be drawn back here, just for the sake of catching a glimpse of the pretty, brightly dressed girl, always working away in those long gloves that seemed so ancient and old-fashioned.

"Good morning!" He slipped thirty dollars into the hatch.

A hand in an emerald-coloured glove elegantly picked up the crumpled bills.

"You're a little late today," said the girl.

"He proved a tricky client."

"You work in a nightclub, I'm assuming?"

"No ... I'm in medicine." Taras didn't want to explain much further, so he leaned a little closer to the glass. "You promised to come for coffee with me!"

"Me? I couldn't have! I don't go for coffee with strange men!" she joked, counting out the hryvnia.

"So let's get to know each other! My name's Taras. And you?"

"Darka," the girl replied. "But I still won't be going to a café. But say, if you brought me a cup, I'd drink it! I'm already falling asleep, it's been dead tonight."

"I'll bring you one!" Taras promised. "I'll be back in literally ten minutes!"

The girl laughed. "You boys always make promises!"

She was in a good mood this morning. She'd never chatted so eagerly with Taras. The exchange had perked him up. His body forgot about the forthcoming radio performance of the Ukrainian anthem, about the moment he'd close his eyes and be sent off to sleep.

Taras returned to the car, stuffing his hryvnia into his pocket. He checked he hadn't forgotten his travel Thermos – Thermos in place! Now he had to find some coffee.

Just down the road, he noticed a kiosk that was lit up from within. He applied the brakes.

"Could you do me a little coffee?" he asked the woman who opened the sales hatch when he knocked.

"Jacobs? Nescafé?" she asked sleepily.

"What about real coffee?"

"You don't drink real coffee at this time," she declared knowingly.

"Alright." Taras handed over his Thermos. "Pour it in there for me! Two cups! No sugar!"

Back behind the wheel, his Thermos placed carefully, if not downright tenderly, in the passenger seat, Taras released the Opel's handbrake. The car didn't take off in a hurry – it was more like a boat leaving its mooring.

"Here you are," he said sweetly, leaning towards the window at the bureau de change, pressing the silver Thermos to his left cheek and feeling its cold exterior. "Coffee's ready!"

"I thought you were kidding!" Darka laughed behind the barred window.

"Do you have your own mug? Or shall I stick it in the lid of the Thermos?"

Darka turned away briefly and a ceramic cup appeared in her hands, but her face suddenly revealed a child-like, naive sense of confusion.

"You can't pour it," she muttered, showing Taras the mug.

"What, can't you just open the window?"

She shook her head. Her right hand in its emerald-coloured glove slipped into the gap meant for notes. She pressed the back of her palm against the gap's upper border and strained vexatiously to prise it open further.

"What about the door?" asked Taras. He took a step back, trying to find her eyes.

To the left he spotted another, larger window to this strange "bruised" brick hut, painted a mousey colour, under a sign saying: WATCH REPAIR. Taras saw no doors. He stepped back to the bureau de change window.

"The door's locked," Darka said sorrowfully. "Until morning. For security . . ."

"But what if there's a fire?!"

"I've got a red button and a telephone," the girl explained in a more serious tone of voice. "The police can be here in just five minutes!"

"You ever had to call them?"

"Yes, twice . . . All sorts of things happen at night."

Considering his options, Taras opened the Thermos, poured out a lid's worth of coffee and drank it. It tasted vile. Perhaps for that precise reason, at that moment he was hit by an unexpected thought. He asked Darka to wait, left his Thermos on the sill of the bureau de change and ran back to his car. He tipped everything out of the glovebox, but he couldn't find the item he was looking for. He went back to the window deflated.

"I'll think of something," the girl promised.

8

"You sure you have to go?" Alik asked, looking at his old comrade warmly but somewhat questioningly. "You've not found it too cramped here, have you?"

He looked around his little room, whose every wall reminded him of his wonderfully free hippie past. There was a lot more past on the walls than present, of course – it's always like that. It's simple: the past accrues, and the present, though clutching on to its moment, will inevitably be assimilated too. A human being is, generally speaking, the most ordinary and elementary apparatus for turning the future into the past. But Alik was no ordinary piece of apparatus. He kept his future notably inquisitive and bright. This meant his past always stood out correspondingly – none of your usual Soviet Pioneer ties or Little Octobrist star-badges, no locks of hair from girls at school.[9]

Audrius also looked around, squinting at dozens of old black and white photographs glued to the wall above the eternally unfolded sofa-bed. He looked at the handbasin with an Amnesty International sticker on it, at the placards, at the fan portrait of John Lennon, at the prehistoric stove with its inch-wide gas pipe, no longer stoked by logs or coal, but scandalous Russian gas, which burned, like all scandalous things, with a blue flame.

"I need the toilet!" Audrius got up, walked out into the little hallway and straight through the front door into the courtyard.

Alik's accommodation – this room, which amounted to no more than seven square metres – was distinctive not only for its size, but also its complete lack of so-called "comforts". But that didn't make Alik at all uncomfortable. He'd spent his whole life in here, despite there being a much larger one-roomed area just through the wall – that territory belonged to his stepmother, who had replaced his mother by his father's arrangement before he was eight years old. Alik's room felt like an extension to the house, a strange extension, extending the corner of the building furthest from the road by a good two metres. If you exited through its separate door, you'd find all your comforts – on the left, twenty metres along a pathway by the fence, was the toilet; on the right, five metres over concrete, was a well with a uniquely shallow depth – no more than half a metre. It wasn't really a well, but a water source, which had erupted from the earth when the old lady next door had decided to expand her veranda past the stand-pipe. No sooner had their picks hit the paving stones than the water sprang through – and, to their surprise, it tasted alright. They diverted the flow a metre from the veranda, dug it out a little and built a well ring above it. And so they had a well. But the standpipe had gone permanently dry, as though it had calmed down once it was satisfied that the courtyard had found another water source.

Alik smiled at the thought that his little courtyard, practically the last on the street, had survived a regime as grand as the USSR. Not that he, Alik, had ever really resisted the Soviet regime. He'd never fought against it. He'd just ignored it. And, just for that, the regime took offence and refused to ignore Alik and his friends. But they – Alik and his friends – rather than hiding away, chose to live their lives in close proximity to the regime, to the extent that even the location of their traditional gatherings, known to Lvivians as the "Holy Garden", was practically visible from the regional party committee offices. And not one of the officials behind the windows of those grey offices ever thought to wrap this whole unfettered territory in barbed wire, this oasis in the shadow of a block of flats, partially walled-in by an ancient monastery – a territory from which occasionally, and really quite loudly, thanks to the extension lead sneaking from the window of one flat, blared strange music that the regional party committee didn't recognise, with strange but, thank God, incomprehensible foreign lyrics. This territory could have had a distribution hub built over it, or even worse, a recycling centre! Yet nobody seemed in any hurry to yank this plot of grass from under the feet and backsides of those long-haired youths with guitars in their hands! In retrospect, it could have been decency or short-sightedness. Although maybe it was all due to the cloth ears of the workers in the office. A district officer made regular inquiries, but conversations with him never ended in any unpleasantness and it was clear that he wasn't disturbing the youths with his presence voluntarily.

Alik was still sat in the armchair. Audrius' voice appeared above his head. "What are you so lost in thought about?"

"You won't believe me!" Alik laughed, jerking out of his reverie. "I was remembering our younger years!"

"What's there to remember?" Audrius was nonplussed. "Anyway, I'm off! Algis is waiting for me – old friend of mine. He's got his own lorry. He's transporting Lviv chocolate to Lithuania. I offered him my services ages ago. Looks like it's finally paid off!"

Alik got up from the armchair briskly, as if to demonstrate that he was still in good athletic form.

They went out into the courtyard.

It was dark outside. Cars hummed past occasionally, zipping down Zamarstynivska.

The gate creaked, they went out to the street and turned left, in the direction of the city centre.

A sharp horn of yellow moon bared itself in the sky, and immediately took cover again behind some clouds. A harsh bird's cry-laugh fell from above straight into the ears of the pedestrians.

Alik shivered as he walked.

"Just like we have in Palanga," sighed a surprised Audrius.

"What do you have in Palanga?" Alik said.

"Well, our seagulls cry like that too . . ."

"We have no seagulls. Where's that coming from?" Alik shrugged.

Audrius looked into the dark sky, from which came another bird's cry-laugh, only it was quieter, like the birds had already outrun their earthbound counterparts.

"We don't have any sea here either," Alik said pitifully, also throwing a glance at the sky. "It's what this place needs . . . the only water we get is rain or out of the pipes . . ."

"There's sea everywhere," Audrius protested. "Sometimes it's visible, other times it's not . . . Sometimes it's above, sometimes below . . ."

"Well, yeah," nodded Alik. "They say the Carpathians used to be a seabed, and now you can find fossilised molluscs there . . . By the way, we still haven't made it to San Francisco!"

Audrius sighed heavily. After a few steps he stopped. Alik stopped too.

"You know," the Lithuanian started assuredly. "Some cities only exist so people can dream about going there. And sometimes the dreaming is more important than the going . . ."

Behind their backs they heard an approaching police siren. Alik and Audrius moved over to the edge of the road, which they had previously been walking along freely and peacefully. They waited for the car to whizz past, then moved back into the middle.

Half an hour of unhurried walking later they stopped on Tkatska Street, not far from the gates of the chocolate factory. The air was heavy and sweet.

Audrius got out his mobile, dialled a number and talked to someone in Lithuanian. Then he turned back to his old friend and nodded.

"It'll be on the road in about five minutes. They're already loading."

From the tall open gates came a long, covered Volvo lorry, moving slowly. It stopped. Audrius and Alik embraced.

"Well, Alik," said the Lithuanian, throwing back his long, straight hair. "If all goes according to plan, then same time next year, same place, after dark . . ."

Audrius climbed the steep steps to the cab so lightly that it seemed the earth's laws of gravity had stopped working for a moment. The door slapped shut behind him, and forty tonnes of Lviv chocolate, with an old friend in tow, left Alik standing at the already-closed gates.

Alik walked back home again, waiting at the deserted crossings for the red traffic lights, and continuing on his way again once green appeared. In the sky up above him he heard that harsh cry-laugh a few more times, from some type of bird he'd never heard in Lviv before. And the air around him tasted briny, too.

Maybe Audrius was right? Alik mused as he walked. Maybe it's seagulls heading south for winter. From the Baltic to the Black Sea . . . and the air seems salty because all the sweetness in it has gone into the nearby chocolatier – the Svitoch factory. Everything in this life has a logical explanation . . .

And Alik's thoughts led themselves back to Lychakivska Cemetery, to the grave with its renewed label, daubed in white oil paint on an iron cross: **Jimy Hendrix 1942–1970.**

9

The lilac-blue Tavria Slavuta nicknamed "Cheburashka" slowed obediently outside a little grocery shop on Gogol Street. Out of the car stepped Oksana. She shut the door neatly behind her and, after whispering "don't worry, I'll be back in five minutes!" to the car, set off in search of her forthcoming dinner with a lively gait. She still didn't know what she was going to buy, as she wasn't in the habit of putting together a personal menu in advance. Food made her happy not just by tasting good, but by arriving unexpectedly too. Her usual policy was to go into the shop and look over the counters and stalls disinterestedly, assessing all edible items, everything laid-out, hung-out, dried-out, cured-out. Right up until her inspection stopped being so disinterested. This happened spontaneously, it wasn't pre-determined, it seemed to happen outside of conscious thought. Three days ago, her eyes had brightened at the sight of entirely regular mushrooms, which then became her first purchase. The mushrooms then "accrued" some onions, potatoes, brisket, carrots and spices, and back home they were transformed, almost naturally, into a tasty ragu, which Oksana then ate for two and a half days, right up to this morning. But today her eyes crept past the mushrooms and stopped on the glass-roofed freezer, full of both full-bodied and filleted fish of various sorts. Oksana inspected the frozen fish and, despite the attention she'd already devoted to them, took a step back and turned around. She remembered feeding her own aquarium fish today. She fell into thought. Then she came back to life and turned her eyes to the glass shelves of sliced and salted fish. Fish really seemed to have a monopoly on her attention on this particular evening! She focused in on the herring, at twenty-five hryvnia a kilo. It was plump, fatty, probably quite tasty if you made sure to slice it right, pick out the bones, smear it in unrefined sunflower oil, decorate it with rings of onion and, of course, put it on a bed of fried potato, which she wouldn't even have to buy, as she had enough at home.

"This one, please!" Oksana pointed out the chosen fish for the assistant.

"Seven hundred grams, you want it all?!" asked the assistant, whose white coat looked like she'd wiped her working hands on it a few times today already.

"Yes, I think so." Oksana nodded. "And these too – three pieces!" She indicated the small, palm-length salted capelins.

Having paid and got herself together to leave, she suddenly came face to face with a slim man who wore a brown jacket over a blue turtleneck sweater and blue trousers – and had the blueish face of a professional drinker.

He's going to ask me for money! Oksana thought, already displeased in advance, preparing to deploy her protective rudeness.

"Oh, I'm sorry! Don't you recognise me?" The man pulled a welcoming smile onto his gaunt face.

"Me? You?" Oksana studied him, thinking that you could find a man with those features in any dive bar you wanted.

"Well, you're obviously . . .Your name's Oksana!" he added.

Oksana looked nervously over the shoulder of her irritant, where Cheburashka would be stood waiting for its owner. All the more so as its owner had promised to be back in five minutes!

"You've probably made a mistake!" she said gently but firmly, and her entire body prepared to take a decisive step forward.

"We drank together! You sent me down for vodka! What, you don't remember?! At Taras' place! He had a birthday . . . really not that long ago! I'm Yezhi Astrovsky!" The man looked fearfully from side to side, clearly feeling some discomfort at the looks he was getting from shoppers. "Let's go outside! I've already got what I came in for . . ."

They went outside. Oksana felt uncomfortable. She now remembered this neighbour of Taras', who had come to start a row, but found himself at a birthday. She wanted to apologise and get away as fast as possible – drive away, specifically. Cheburashka was waiting!

"Could I ask you to go for coffee?" the man asked unexpectedly, like he'd picked up courage from the discomfort he could read on Oksana's face.

"There!" He waved a buoyant hand at the awning of a café over the road. "Let's go! It's so great to see you again!"

Oksana looked sorrowfully at her Slavuta, then turned her

attention to the café. It was only fifteen metres away, and from its window she would be able to see Cheburashka.

"Alright," she sighed. "But I don't have much time, just ten minutes . . ."

"Oy, how long d'you need for a cup of coffee?!" he joked in an exaggeratedly Jewish accent, his confidence clearly growing.

Yezhi ordered a small piece of chocolate with his coffee. As they ate and drank, he told Oksana about how the finest ladies of Pekarska Street and its neighbouring alleys had got him to do their hair, and how he used to do home visits once the hairdressers was sold and an "Everything for a Hryvnia!" shop opened in its place.

Oksana, her coffee finished, looked at the clock and shook her head in surprise.

"Please forgive me Yezhi, but I'm a busy woman . . ."

"I understand, I understand." He nodded and turned straight to the bar. "Check please!"

The waiter appeared in a flash and placed a small piece of paper on the table before Yezhi.

"Thirty-five?!" he blurted in surprise.

He reached into his right-hand jacket pocket, pulled out a few five-hryvnia notes, then reached into the left – where he found two tens – and re-counted with trembling hands, visibly relieved. Before him sat thirty-five hryvnia exactly. He pushed them proudly into the centre of the table and stood up.

"Everything's got so expensive!" he said once they were back outside. "It didn't used to be like that!"

"When?" Oksana queried.

"Eh, before. When I visited establishments like this more

regularly . . . Even now I know places where the beer's cheaper than the coffee is here . . . But next time I think it's better we have coffee at mine . . ."

Oksana gave Yezhi a stern, shocked stare.

"I think at Taras' would be better. By the way, have you been reminding him about the fish?"

"Ah! Well yes, of course I have!" he rattled off quickly, then paused for a moment, before asking: "About which fish exactly?"

"In the aquarium! The one on his windowsill! I asked you to remind him to feed them . . ."

"Yes," Yezhi said confidently. "I reminded him a few times, then I forgot. Forgive me! I'll remind him! I promise! Now, are you driving?"

"Yes, but I'm going in the other direction," Oksana declared courteously to the now entirely full-of-himself Yezhi. "See you!"

She sat in the car, switched on the engine and, without looking back at the man staring after her, drove off, his saccharine-sweet voice still cloying in her ears.

He's certainly an odd one, Oksana thought. As a means of distracting herself, she rubbed her hand on the Slavuta's dashboard. "Forgive me, little Cheburashka! I made you wait! It's impossible to slip away from these suitors!"

10

During his long sleep beginning straight after the Ukrainian anthem's morning radio reprisal, Taras dreamed many things: sounds, pictures, the night. Several times an entirely real, recognisable noise tore into the dream, and to his sleeping surprise, Taras recognised it immediately as the squeaking, screeching fifth wooden step of his own stairway. Soon after the sound's fourth or fifth ingression into his dream, there was a knock at the door.

It was bright and noisy outside. The street noise lightly dislodged the dream soundtrack from Taras' ears. He opened the front door and froze when he saw Yezhi Astrovsky standing before him.

"Good evening! I promised our mutual friend to remind you about the fish!" Yezhi said with exaggerated forthrightness. "Are you feeding them?"

Taras grunted in surprise. "Of course I am! What, you think I've got amnesia?"

"Could I take a look, perhaps?" asked Yezhi.

Taras shrugged and gestured at the living room with his right hand. "Come in, go ahead!"

His guest took off his shoes and stomped through in his odd socks – one black, one blue. Taras followed.

"They look a little thin," Yezhi whispered accusatorially, squinting at Taras stood beside him.

Taras shook the box of food over the aquarium, and an array of little brown flakes scattered over the water. The fish darted up to the surface and started gulping greedily.

Yezhi watched the unfolding scene and curled his lip in dissatisfaction.

"They're always hungry," Taras grumbled in annoyance. "You need anything else?"

Yezhi looked away from the aquarium and turned to Taras, his face now affable again. The neighbour's eyes drifted higher than the host's, and stopped on his unkempt, sleep-mussed hairdo.

"You know, I tidied my place up today." Yezhi lowered his gaze and now looked Taras straight in the eyes. "I found forty-seven hryvnia! In an old jacket – not this one." He looked down at his brown jacket. "It's nice, you know, when your home's in order . . . Maybe you'd like to come over?"

"Now?" Taras was nonplussed.

"Well yeah, you've never come round before . . ."

"I have work later," Taras lied. "I'm not going to drink . . ."

"And I've got nothing to drink," Yezhi replied coolly. "Let's just go down."

They went down to the ground floor, careful to avoid the fifth step. Yezhi opened the door, and a strange, unpleasant smell hit Taras' nose immediately. There was a coat hook nailed into the wall on the left-hand side. A mirror hung opposite the door. The wooden floor beneath the coat hook was home to three pairs of ragged slippers.

"Go on through, go on through!" Yezhi hurried him in from behind. "The main room's straight ahead of you!"

Taras was already aware that the main room was ahead of him. Three steps left him standing in the centre of the living space. On the wall opposite the window a rug was hung above a large iron single bed, draped in a plaid blanket. There was a writing desk, strewn with old papers and journals, and between the table and the corner of the room closest to the window sat an old barber's chair, turned to face an old black-and-white photo of an elderly lady in a hat in a carved wooden frame.

Taras' eyes were fixed on the chair. Yezhi scooted past his guest, spun it around and gestured for Taras to take a seat.

"So, this is where I live," he said. "For the last few years it's been very uncomfortable in here, I didn't invite anyone over . . . but today I tidied up, and I wanted you to see straight away! Have a seat!" He repeated his encouraging hand gesture, looking at his disconcerted, uncertain guest.

Taras sat in the barber's chair.

"You work a lot," Yezhi said, looking up at his guest's hair again. "You don't even have time for a trim! Go on, I'll neaten you up! Don't worry about it." He lifted his palms level with the face of his seated neighbour. "I'm decent – my hands don't even shake. I want to talk to you, but I know what a busy man you are . . . Plus, it's usually easier for me to chat when I've got my hands busy . . ."

He walked over to the dresser between the barber's chair

and the window, opened the top drawer and took out a pair of scissors, a comb and a strangely coloured piece of folded fabric.

"As long as you've no objection?"

Taras put his hand through his hair, which he still hadn't brushed since waking up.

"Alright," he said, not entirely convinced.

Yezhi unfolded the fabric, which turned out to be a British flag, and tied it around Taras' neck. He spun his neighbour to face the wall with the portrait of the elderly lady once more.

"You remember how in the eighties they had 'Britain days' in the USSR? They hung this flag up in our building and forgot to take it down afterwards – our caretaker was a drunk. So I took it for myself! It's the perfect size!"

A buzzer's sharp row of teeth sank into Taras' hair. Taras shivered and froze. But the buzzer's further movements were very graceful, causing no unpleasant sensations.

"So you don't have a mirror?" Taras asked.

Yezhi lifted up a round tabletop mirror to Taras' face.

"Just you wait and see," he said. "In fifteen minutes' time you won't recognise yourself. In a good way!"

The mirror disappeared. One of Yezhi's hands picked up the buzzer, the other the scissors, and they danced around the head of his guest. The guest's shoulders, covered with the flag of the British Empire, were slowly powdered with small snips of hair.

"You see?" Yezhi boasted from on high. "My hands don't forget a thing! So have you known Oksana long?"

Taras sighed. "Oksana? Yes." He tried to turn his head.

"Don't wriggle!" his neighbour instructed. "It'll end up uneven! She's a good woman! Got real character to her, you know ... She and I went for a coffee today ... And wow, you wouldn't believe the prices these days! In my day it all cost kopecks!"

"In your day? And how is the present day not your day?"

"I just like to think out loud ... Personally, I just make my coffee at home, but when I'm out and about I drink beer, because I know the price of beer ... And it makes sense for beer – it's got alcohol in it. What's coffee doing getting so expensive?"

"Same as everything else in life." Taras shrugged, realising immediately that there was no need to argue with his neighbour, he was just sharing his thoughts, "thinking out loud".

"I'll make you some real coffee in a minute, the kind you used to get for seventeen kopecks!" Yezhi went on. "Do you usually have a side parting?"

Taras considered this. He realised suddenly that he didn't know how he wore his hair. He just got it cut, end of story.

"I don't have a parting. Keep it simple."

"Yes, that works." Yezhi walked around the chair, surveying the result of his hard work. Then he stopped.

"Freshen up?" A glass vial of eau de cologne appeared in his hand.

Taras nodded.

The fragrance of mixed sweetness and spirits reminded Taras of the unpleasant smell in the corridor. In here, in the room, it had smelled fine up to now.

"What's that smell in your corridor?" he asked.

"A mouse died, I just found it under the floorboards. I've taken it out already. It'll air out soon! Here's the mirror for you!"

Taras inspected the reflection of his new hairdo. He was perfectly satisfied.

"You see, no experiments!" Yezhi said proudly. "I based it on what you already had! You don't happen to know where Oksana gets her hair cut, do you?"

Taras stood up from the chair and turned.

"No, I don't."

"And does she have anyone else in her life?" the neighbour asked more quietly and cautiously.

Taras shrugged.

"She helps the homeless in her spare time. She's told me nothing else about her . . ."

"The homeless?" Yezhi repeated, deep in thought.

"So is this your mother?" Taras looked to the portrait of the lady in the hat.

Yezhi smiled.

"Absolutely. You think I look like her?"

Taras nodded.

"You show Oksana how I cut your hair!" A wily flame gleamed in Yezhi's eyes. "And, if she asks, tell her that I've got everything neat and tidy round here." He looked around his room. "You won't find that too hard to slip into conversation? I'll make sure I tell her that you feed the fish regularly, and change the water in the aquarium . . ."

"Oh, does it need to be changed?" asked Taras.

Yezhi nodded.

Upon returning to his flat on the first floor, carefully avoiding the fifth step and carefully shutting the door behind him, Taras went straight over to the windowsill to look at the fish. The surface of the water was clean and smooth – there wasn't a trace of fish food left.

11

After watching his fill of the fish, Taras walked over to the mirror in the hallway. He studied his appearance and was again surprised: on the one hand at his own stupid acquiescence, thanks to which he had ended up in his neighbour's old barber's chair; on the other hand at the pleasant haircut that now sat atop his head as a result. But time can't be rewound like an old VHS tape. And nor should it be. Order atop his head. And order within. September was coming to a close outside the window. The sun was now an infrequent visitor. The rain would sometimes drip, sometimes pour. Against the background of a Lviv September, simple human contact gained additional value, and became more desirable than it was on hot summer days. And Taras caught himself, for the first time in his life, having positive feelings for his neighbour. He even felt a certain fleeting pity for this strange man, always too fussy and unsettled in life, who probably missed regular human warmth in the warm months too. Taras might have kept developing this line of thought, but then his mobile rang.

"It's me, Lenya!" a familiar voice said. "I've made up my mind. I'm ready to go all the way, so to speak!"

"It might end up being more painful than last night!" Taras warned seriously.

"But I'll bring a bottle with me. I didn't think of it yesterday, somehow . . ."

"Alright, midnight, same place, at the Opera House! Just don't forget to drink your glass of cognac two hours before!"

Taras put his phone on the table. Was he happy that he had work tonight, or not? On one level he was. But then the work suddenly felt trivial, unimportant. Twenty to thirty euros for a sleepless night – it's money he could live on quite easily, with no pretensions. But he'd be living alone. And living alone, even if it's cheap, is somewhat uncomfortable. And dangerous too – he might end up like his neighbour, Yezhi Astrovsky, and suddenly notice one day that his life had passed him by, and nobody loved or needed him. And then you end up cutting your neighbour's hair or cooking their eggs, just so someone will listen to you!

His thoughts were clearly trying to conform to the melancholic melody of autumn. Taras realised he needed to put a stop to it, perk himself up! He went to the kitchen and brewed a strong coffee. He drank it, experiencing the unmistakeable scald against his tongue. He thought of Darka in her nighttime bureau de change. He thought of his unsuccessful attempt to treat her to a nighttime coffee. A smile played across his lips. Tonight it'll all go perfectly! he decided. Ground coffee – here, in the kitchen. Thermos – in his car, outside. But how was he to pass her the cup?! Taras lifted his right hand and stared at his thumb and index finger, trying to recreate the height of the gap in the window through which the money was passed back and forth.

I'll have to be more inventive, he told himself, and after changing into jeans and a sweater, throwing on a windbreaker and doing up his trainers, he went outside. Right next to his house was one of the city's many little shops with the optimistic name "Everything for a Hryvnia!".

Five minutes later he was browsing in the kingdom of bargains, where hundreds of unnecessary items lined the shelves, waiting to play their part. Some of them really did cost one hryvnia, others pushed the price boundary, but not by much. There were ceramic mugs for seven hryvnia, and plastic plates too. Taras looked attentively over shelf after shelf in the hope of seeing any short, squat-as-squat-can-be teacups. But the shop had no teacups of the required height. The saleswoman stood at the door reading a book. Taras got her attention and described as best he could what he was looking for. The brunette girl lazily walked along the shelves, as if refreshing her memory. Her eyes stopped at a black Dutchware ashtray with VENEZIA printed on the base. The ashtray's lip was straight and tall, with little square notches to rest your cigarette.

"I don't smoke," he said.

"I'm sure you don't, but you need a flat vessel." The girl gave her customer a wise, exasperated look. "This is the flattest we've got."

Taras looked down at the book in her hand. It had *Pharmacologist's Handbook* on the cover.

"And what would you think if someone offered you a coffee in that ashtray?!" he asked acerbically.

Placing the book on a shelf, the saleswoman took the ashtray in her slender fingers and looked it over, rotating it in her hands. Finally, she placed it in her palm like an imaginary teacup and saucer, to try lifting it to her lips.

Taras was almost scared, the girl was a talented actress. Her lips were barely parted, and yet they became so sensitive, as if the ashtray she was just preparing to brush them against were alive, not an ashtray at all, but lips, the lips of a man.

"Interesting." The saleswoman sighed languidly. "I'd never thought of that . . ."

"What's interesting?" Taras asked her.

"Just something I was thinking about." She looked at the customer. "But I'd say overall, it would depend on the environment, the atmosphere." Her voice grew stronger. She put the ashtray back in its place. "If the atmosphere's right, then yes, you can drink coffee from an ashtray. Not just coffee, either."

Taras was struck by the certainty in her voice. He immediately paid for two ashtrays and left the shop.

12

Lenya's out-of-place grey mackintosh and cap would have caught the eye of any passer-by who happened to be walking through the Opera House entrance just before midnight. But at this time of night, Lviv is not exactly packed with unhurried, observant passers-by, so Taras was the only one paying him any attention as he approached the theatre from the direction of Virmenska Street.

"Right, you ready?" Taras asked promptly, not even bothering to greet him.

Lenya's manners and general behaviour yesterday had suggested to Taras that his client, who was regularly accompanied by the smell of petrol, lived outside the regular rules of etiquette. He was like a word in an endless agglomeration of words, which didn't follow the laws of punctuation and was thus unable to form a sentence. He didn't greet Taras either. Probably because he hadn't bid him farewell last night, so technically they had never parted.

"Ready," said the client.

As they walked to the car, Taras remembered the x-ray of Lenya's kidneys. It was clear that last night a pebble near the urethra had made it to the outside world. Thinking more in geometric than medicinal terms, Taras imagined the simultaneous movement of all three stones – the first stone's path to freedom was the most straightforward, the other two would still need to escape from the kidneys into the bladder. Yesterday's procedure would almost certainly have shifted them. These brief rationalisations led Taras to the conclusion that today had to start with sharper "short" vibrations. After that, taking account of his client's state, he could temporarily switch to less intensive, "long" vibrations, only to return to the sharper, stronger ones at the end to get the job done.

Lenya thudded into the front seat so habitually and idiosyncratically that it seemed like Taras was his permanent chauffeur. The old Opel got going on the small, even cobblestones, drifting fluidly from the kerb.

Taras already had a plan in his head for today's stone-extraction route – Lisna Street (5–6 circuits), Lychakivska Street (4–6 circuits), Horodotska Street (4–6 circuits) and then back to Lisna again at the end (4–6 circuits). He drove the car confidently to his selected start point.

He caught a whiff of petrol and instinctively looked down at the plastic mat under his feet. Then he turned for a moment and looked at his passenger. He wanted to say something encouraging to him, but the frozen expression on Lenya's face forestalled his good intentions.

The plan he'd put together in his head was proving effective. It was nearing four in the morning on Lisna Street, not far from the uneven steps up to the park, to the left of the "smiley face" statue – a curious sculpted construction consisting of a concrete foundation and a small concrete ball, on which some kind soul had drawn a smiley-face emoji giving a "cry of liberation". To Taras' joy, not one window in the four-floored orange-yellow house opposite the hill was illuminated. Lenya's hand was shaking as he passed Taras the glass jar.

"Alright – do we try again tomorrow, or are you done?" Taras asked once they reached the Opera House.

Lenya contemplated this. His face was no longer pained – just spitefully exhausted.

"I'll have a think," he said after a pause. "I'll call if I come up with anything," he added, before leaving the car without a goodbye.

Taras watched him go, then shook the grey pebble, no larger than a grain of rice, into an unfolded tissue. He patted it dry and deposited it carefully into the plastic tub for homeopathic balls. He wanted to sleep. But then a sudden unpleasant thought jolted him awake – Lenya hadn't paid for his procedure! Taras shook his head bitterly; his eyes dropped to Lenya's seat. The bitterness suddenly turned to surprise – on the seat lay three crumpled ten-dollar notes. His mood improved. Taras remembered the Thermos in the boot, wrapped in a towel and stuffed into a bag, so that the strong, lovingly brewed coffee wouldn't suffer after all the "long" and "short" vibrations. In the same bag sat the two new ashtrays.

It was getting ever closer to four a.m. Only one thing could now give any purpose to the hours before sunrise – a date with Darka, the enigmatic girl in the satin gloves, custodian of night money, locked up with said night money in her little brick tower on Ivan Franko street.

The ageing Opel led its owner to his date quietly, as if it were happy at the chance to enjoy some more or less even road, with no need to shake stones and curses from its passengers.

Taras stopped the car at the corner of Kostomarova. He decided to surprise her with Thermos in hand.

He freed the Thermos from its towel and got the ashtrays out, giving them a quick wipe down then storing them in his jacket pockets – one on each side.

He was surprised, turning onto Franko, at the lack of the usual electric light coming from the window of the bureau de change. He picked up his pace.

There was a lit candle placed behind the window. Taras was frightened. He nervously swallowed some saliva and squinted past the trembling flame. To the right of it, in semi-darkness, sat Darka. She was sitting completely still.

"Good evening!" Taras whispered. "What are you doing in the dark?"

Darka leaned forward, trying to make him out.

"Oh!" She sighed in relief. "It's you! Thank God!"

"Something happened?"

"Electricity's out," she whispered. "I called the boss. He said to light a candle and keep working."

"And what, he can't come here himself?" Taras was annoyed.

"He's not in the city – but my replacement comes at six to let me out. He's got the key."

"This is slavery, not work!" Taras said indignantly. "You need to find yourself something better than this!"

"Working with money is always slavery," Darka replied calmly. "But I need night work . . ."

"In that case, I suggest we drink coffee!" Taras said firmly, placing the Thermos on the outside ledge.

"I'd love to." Darka didn't sound scared anymore, but her voice did have a note of sadness. "But how?"

Taras smirked, but the girl didn't notice.

He placed the two black ashtrays next to the Thermos, filled them with coffee and carefully slipped one of them through the slot for exchanging notes.

"I've never had coffee from a dish before!" Darka exclaimed happily.

Taras could barely suppress his laughter as he lifted the ashtray to his mouth.

"Ah! That's the stuff!" Darka suddenly smiled, and her laughter sounded surprisingly joyous, earnest, sonorous. "What lovely . . . Tobacco coffee!!"

Taras had "achieved" a moment of happiness. He was the "perpetrator" of her laughter, her joy. He was filled with a thunderous pride. It gripped him, carried him over the city and let him go again. He became light and bodiless, like a magician or a fairy-tale hero. And Darka's face in the window suddenly lit up, and the fire in her eyes grew fun and wild. The empty ashtray stood in front of her next to the burning candle, the word VENEZIA now easily legible.

"More?" asked Taras.

Darka nodded and slid the ashtray back out.

A gust of wind suddenly hit Taras in the back and nearly blew the candle out. Darka clasped her hands around it quickly to shield the flame.

"Oh, when the light went out – there was such a wind then

too. One gust and that was it! And the birds started crying this strange, loud cry, like a hoarse laugh! They're normally silent at night, aren't they?!" Darka said, leaning forward to see Taras more clearly.

Her face in the soft light of the candle looked at once like a child and a painted icon. Even her fear made her somehow more desirable.

"You've already told me a little about yourself . . . You're a medic, right?" asked Darka. "So at night, I guess you must be out on call?"

"On drives!" Taras corrected her. "I have something of a private practice, using my own methods. I draw out kidney stones. This isn't coffee-break talk, though . . . So you . . . You dress so interestingly! I've only seen your gloves before . . . You always have them on . . ."

"Oh, just don't think I'm fashionable!" Darka's voice became pure, alive, freed from all fear. "I'm allergic to money . . . Specifically banknotes and change . . . When I was little, if I so much as touched them, my skin would start burning straight away, the fingers first, then my hands would be red and itchy for two or three weeks. It was awfully painful! I've worn gloves ever since. They really saved me! Here, look!" In her hands appeared a banknote – fifty Russian rubles. The money rustled as the fingertips of a dark-blue glove played around with it.

"I'm not quite getting this," Taras pondered aloud. "You're allergic to money, and yet you work with it?!"

Darka shrugged.

"The pay's good, and the doctors recommend night work,

so I can sleep in the mornings. I have very sensitive skin, it's not just with money. When I used to sleep at night it took me ages to drift off. I twitched, rolled around from side to side, and then I'd get red blotches and itching again . . . If you weren't a doctor, I wouldn't be telling you this . . ."

"Shame I only do stones," Taras sighed. "But who knows?! Maybe there's some way I can help . . ."

A bird of some sort cry-laughed loudly above the bureau de change. Then it dropped down straight onto the roof, gave another wailing chuckle, and after beating its wings in farewell, shot up into the black sky.

"Did you hear that?" Taras could hear fright and fear again in Darka's voice.

"I didn't just hear it, I saw it too!" he said entirely calmly in response. "A crow! But a white one, by the looks of it!"

"A crow?!" said Darka. "Crows don't make sounds like that . . . Crows caw! And they sleep at night anyway. In Stryiskyi Park. Then they fly over to the landfill in Hrybovychi in the morning."

"How do you know all that?" Taras was surprised. "Do you track crows or something?"

"They fly over our house. They've flown like that ever since I was a kid, all through the city centre. The park in the evenings, then by morning over to the landfill. There's thousands of them there!"

Taras didn't even get the opportunity to make an excuse for his lie. He hadn't actually seen the bird, only its shadow, but it was, it had seemed, larger than the average crow. The coffee was forgotten. Its taste, much like the energy boost from the caffeine, had taken flight from his tongue. The tiredness was beginning to take over, and Taras was finding it harder and harder to resist.

At about half past five, a white Lada stopped opposite the bureau de change, and out of the car stepped a man of around fifty in glasses and a leather jacket.

"Step away from the window!" he sternly instructed Taras.

"On what charge?" Taras replied resentfully.

"Taras, step back," Darka's voice called from inside the bureau. "This is Orest Vasilievich, he's about to let me out!"

Taras took a few steps to the side. He watched the man in glasses. The man walked around the left window of the building, the side which housed the WATCH REPAIR sign, keys jangling in his hand. Suddenly, the window of the bureau de change filled with light – the lamp had come on again. And straight away a few lights came on in the house opposite.

"There you are then, all sorted," said Darka, appearing suddenly beside Taras along with Orest Vasilievich. She stopped for a moment: she proved to be on the short side, petite and dainty.

"In which case, could I give you a lift home?" Taras offered.

Darka looked over at the man who'd arrived in the Lada, paused before responding, then shook her head.

"Orest Vasilievich knows the way better."

She nodded farewell, and the car whisked her away along the empty street.

Walking upstairs to his first-floor apartment, exhausted and lost in thought, Taras almost put his foot on the fifth step. At the last moment, he managed to use his last reserves of strength to thrust his entire body forward, and land his right foot on the one above.

Even while sleeping, he heard the sound of the anthem on the radio. A smile appeared on his face. It was followed by a fleeting thought about how similar he and Darka were – after all, they both went to sleep very tired early in the morning.

Outside the window, life was already in full swing; lorries rumbled past, cars too. The soles of cheap boots clattered against the pavement. The awakened city made thousands of noises, none of them able to penetrate Taras' deep sleep.

13

Long past midnight, Alik was walking back home along Zamarstynivska, back to his comfortable, private little corner of the city, where the courtyard he shared with five families – some broken, some not – wasn't home to a single dog. The lack of a dog allowed you to come home at any time of night, without any fear of disturbing the silence or the sleep of your neighbours.

His mood was easy and romantic, a mood he'd picked up from performing his duties as the "left" light technician at the Opera House, up in his box, lighting specifically the left-hand side of the hall with a powerful spotlight, for a rather pleasant production of Lehár's *The Merry Widow*. In the intermission he'd been joking with the ladies working the cloakroom, who'd treated him to tea. Scenes from the operetta, which he'd seen plenty of times by now, still brought the occasional smile to his face. The show had something of a dual meaning to him. He saw more in it than the average viewer, because he knew the actors and actresses and their relationships with one another, and he smiled at moments when the actors, at the whim of circumstance and Offenbach, suddenly began playing themselves. Actual former lovers played operatic lovers with great flair – the sparks that lit up their eyes during those scenes were by no means theatrical. Up in his side-lighting box, Alik was the only one who could read their eyes like this. The audience were far more taken by the bright costumes, gestures, phrases.

The dark sky was turning sullen. Alik felt it closing in, as if it wanted to land rain or showers on him in particular. He increased his pace. The sound of his steps, the only rhythm being laid down over the late-night Lviv silence, grew slightly louder.

After work at the theatre he had headed to Hrushevskoho to visit an old friend, and had sat with her at the kitchen table chattering away until almost two in the morning. Time always "chatters away" more quickly and stealthily at night. It doesn't follow the clock. It sits down next to you at the table, an invisible third party protecting your conversation, letting you relax and sink into reminiscing. It's in no rush.

But once the chatter is long behind you, and you come out of your cosy little private world into the less cosy one you share with everyone else, where it also happens to be night and it's just about to rain, then time starts hurrying again, and there's nowhere to run from it, because instead of ticking hands it counts with clopping soles on cobblestones or tarmac.

From somewhere high above Alik's head came a strange sound; he adjusted his wide-brimmed leather hat and pulled it down a little tighter, so that the sudden gust of wind didn't tear it off.

Up ahead, about ten metres away, something weighty and dark fell into the road. Alik walked over to it cautiously and squatted over a large dead crow splattered on the tarmac. Its black head was bloody. After glancing worriedly up at the dark sky, Alik got up, stepped around the corpse and carried on. Only now, his light thoughts and feelings had left him. The silence of the night city brought a corresponding silence to his head.

Alik was happy at the sight of his front gate, and then his little single-storey roadside house. Another couple of minutes and he'd be in his extension room with its two windows: one looking out at his stepmother's fence and the wooden toilet stall, the other at the narrow alleyway between the house and a few connected brick sheds.

"A good evening to you!" It came from behind Alik, once his hand had already grasped the top of the gate.

Alik froze, tense. He didn't want to look around. He remembered the turbulent seventies and eighties, and the representatives from various internal state organs that had tailed him – police, KGB – appearing completely out of the blue, often delivering their words of greeting with an incongruous playfulness and verve.

"Who's that?" asked Alik, without turning or moving an inch.

"Ryabtsev . . . Captain Ryabtsev," came the answer from behind his back, the voice now normal, no longer subdued, the tone notably more welcoming.

Alik turned around.

"What are you doing here?" he asked in surprised annoyance. The former KGB agent's pleading expression led him to believe that Ryabtsev had come to borrow money. The thought made him smile – there could be no funnier address at which to borrow money than 270 Zamarstynivska, Lviv.

"I haven't come empty-handed." Ryabtsev looked down at an old-fashioned black diplomat's briefcase.

"Well, what's in there?" Alik asked suspiciously.

His uninvited night guest breezily unlatched the briefcase and something clinked inside.

"A bottle of something," Ryabtsev said sweetly. "To have while we talk . . ."

"Alright." Alik opened the gate and let Ryabtsev go first.

Ryabtsev, as though he were a regular guest at Alik's, walked straight past the house, turned left and stopped by a narrow door plastered with placards, stickers and various memorable flyers from the previous century.

The light came on in the little room. The old photos on the wall came to life.

"Nothing's changed! Just incredible!" Ryabtsev marvelled.

"Have you really been here before?" Alik asked, placing his hat on the upper shelf of the coat rack in the hallway.

"Of course – just in your absence . . . Forgive me, that's just the way it was back then. You wouldn't have invited me . . . But I really liked your place!" Ryabtsev walked over to the sofa and sat on it without waiting for an invitation. He settled in, seeming to feel it out with his skinny backside, checking it for springiness.

"Eh, youth!" he said romantically. "When I first came to visit you, I was meant to plant narcotics. To remove you from society. But it was so cosy here . . . I couldn't bring myself to destroy your world!"

"Tea? Coffee?" Alik asked politely, deciding not to react to his guest's romantic reminiscences.

"What are you doing? Don't worry about it! I've brought everything with me!" Ryabtsev got up, opened his briefcase and laid out on the table a bottle of vodka, a pickled sea-cabbage salad, bread and sausage.

There was nothing left for Alik to provide.

Ryabtsev was no longer annoying Alik. He'd blended into the micro-landscape of the little room too easily somehow, like he'd shrunk in size so as not to stand out amongst the general paraphernalia. He'd also made very easy and familiar use of the washbasin fitted in the left corner over the cabinet, inside which was a regular water bucket, and he'd wiped his hands with a towel he'd taken from the nail in the wall.

"Please don't think I was trying to scare you!" Ryabtsev picked up a full spirit glass. "Sometimes the old instincts kick in. It's why I whispered 'good evening' behind your back like that . . . You see! That's not really who I am at all, of course . . . I've come to you with a serious matter . . . I don't know many people around here, after all . . . Just you and a couple of old colleagues, who I very rarely see . . . But my head still works, I was taught to work over information properly, and I've no longer got anyone to approach with my findings . . ."

"What about the Security Service?" Alik joked, lifting his glass to his lips.

Ryabtsev waved him away.

"Serious matters, after all . . . Let us drink!"

They drank. Alik put some sea cabbage onto a plate for himself. He hadn't eaten it in years. Since Soviet times, it would have to be. Back then, just before the end of Soviet rule, sea cabbage was sold everywhere, it was almost the only non-deficit produce.[10] And back then he, Alik, had eaten thirty years' worth. But now, on this night, it seemed that perhaps he hadn't eaten thirty years' worth, only twenty! And the taste of it refreshed his tongue after the glass of vodka that had passed over it.

"Alik, I've had insomnia for many years now. I wander around the city at night, thinking, remembering. And just recently, something's not been quite right with Lviv . . . There's something going on . . ."

Alik shrugged.

"There's always something going on here – and there's usually something not going right too," he sighed.

"No, I don't mean the city itself, I mean something else . . . a particular sensation, like some sort of catastrophe is just about to occur. A natural disaster. An earthquake, or a flood . . ."

"A flood? In a city where there's never enough water, and the only river has been hidden underground?!"

"Let me explain." Ryabtsev held a pause. "A few times recently I've found myself in places where I detected a distinct oceanic smell in the air, the smell of iodine and seaweed. And I could clearly hear the cries of seagulls. At these moments the air seemed to tremble, you see. Something started to seem off . . ."

Ryabtsev filled his glass again.

"I dug into my books and, of course, I immediately discovered that the city was constructed on the site of a prehistoric Carpathian sea. That is, we're living on the seabed! This, of course, resonates with the current situation in the country, but I'm not talking about politics! Then I thought – what if the sea is returning, rising up from under the earth, leaking out?! But it could only come through sewers or pipes. The city, of course, is built over it, concreted. The water might push against the basements and foundations, but in the places where it finds an exit it will burst out and throw up an iodine, salty smell. You see . . . the Carpathian sea wants us to become its bed once more!"

Alik smiled.

"We had a water source appear in the courtyard eight years back," he said. "I'll pour you some now!"

He took a water pail from the stove, filled a glass and offered it to Ryabtsev. The captain lifted it to his lips.

"Not salty?" asked Alik.

Ryabtsev shook his head.

"But something's definitely going on!" he said determinedly. "I can feel it . . . Don't think I'm joking . . ."

Having run into some resistance to his theory from the long-haired owner of the annex, Ryabtsev grew less talkative. This quite quickly brought their catchup to a close.

"Perhaps I can call you a taxi?" asked Alik.

"No need, I have my Piaggio in the bushes," answered Ryabtsev.

"In the bushes?"

"By the pond. I'm off to Sykhiv you know, it's not exactly down the road! My pension doesn't cover taxis!"

Alik walked his guest to the pond. Once they reached it, Ryabtsev got on his scooter and turned to Alik. The through-and-through hippie was struck by the the vehicle's bright yellow.

"Next time you're coming to mine!" said the captain. "You've never been to mine, after all!"

Alik nodded.

"I'll call! I'll call soon!" Ryabtsev promised as he drove away.

The air at the pond was moist and fresh, and heavy too. Suddenly Alik felt like he really could smell the sea – iodine. He looked to either side, wrinkled his nose, pushed his tongue around his mouth. It still tasted of sea cabbage.

That'll be where the illusion comes from! thought Alik. He probably eats that seaweed every day! It's cheap, after all!

14

Taras slept until lunch. He had a bright but imaginary taste of women's lipstick on his lips, with a raspberry aroma – he had dreamed of Darka kissing him a few times.

Outside it was loud and bright. The sun peeked out, and its rays beat through the gap in the curtains, falling on the room's trampled old parquet floor.

After washing himself, Taras remembered the fish and poured them some food, then thought he wouldn't be against some lunch himself. But before stepping away from the windowsill, he scooped some tank water out and splashed it on the cacti by the aquarium.

As he was consulting the internally lit and barren depths of the fridge, his phone rang.

Lenya's lively tones informed him that he was ready for the procedure to remove the third and final stone.

"Perhaps in a day or two?" Taras offered after a pause. "You've already put stress on yourself two nights in a row . . . it still won't be that easy."

"God loves a trinity," Lenya said bluntly. "Go on! I'll pay extra . . ."

"He had a different trinity in mind," Taras said pensively.

"Call me back at about six, please. I'm not feeling up to it right now. If I cough myself better, we'll do it!"

"I will!" the lover of grey caps promised fervently.

Taras shut the kitchen window and it was immediately quieter and cosier. He sat at the table, remembering his wish to eat something, but then someone rang the doorbell.

Judging by the silence of the fifth step before the ring, it was someone he knew. Most likely Yezhi. This calculation brought Taras no joy.

"Hi Tarasik!" Oksana waltzed in through the open door. "I was passing by. If you don't mind, I think I'll take a look in your fridge!"

His friend walked through to the kitchen with a blue shopping bag in her hand. The fridge door clicked open.

"Just as I thought!" Oksana's stern voice rang through the apartment. "Do you want to give yourself an ulcer?!"

By the time Taras got to the kitchen Oksana was already decanting produce from her bag.

"Here, take these." She handed him a packet of veal ribs. "For soup! Do you remember how to make soup?"

Taras nodded. He actually did remember, as Oksana had shown him four times, forcing him to recite each step aloud, in order.

"Right, I'll take eighty-five hryvnia from you! Here's your receipt!" she said, standing upright.

Taras reached into his pocket for the money. As he was getting it out, Oksana slipped into his living room and came back with a satisfied smile on her face.

"Well done for not forgetting the fish! I wanted to tell you something, by the way!"

"Maybe you'd like to sit down?" Taras suggested.

"No, I'm in a rush! We have rehearsal in an hour, we have to learn new numbers . . . So, last night there was a magnetic storm, so powerful that the lights went out in the city centre! And on the radio they said that LvivEnergo had announced that there didn't seem to have been any outages, and there had been an uninterrupted supply of electricity! Do you understand?"

Taras shook his head.

"Well, all the readers showed that the electricity was running, but in actual fact, for a few hours there wasn't any! It means that the magnetic storm pulled all the energy towards itself . . . Hey, you had a haircut!" Oksana was suddenly distracted by Taras' hair. "Well done! Nice cut! You've probably fallen in love!" She smiled slyly.

Taras gave a barely perceptible nod.

"Alright, I'm off!" She made a start towards the door, but stopped and turned back to face him. "Your neighbour invited me for coffee! But I didn't recognise him at first! Is everything alright between you two?"

"Yes."

"And did he sort out the step?"

"No."

"Say hello from me and remind him about the step! He promised to call a carpenter!"

Taras sighed in relief as Oksana's Cheburashka pulled away from the pavement. The hurricane had passed, without hanging around too long or destroying anything!

Cooking the simple veal rib soup returned Taras to a state of comfortable peace. And once consumed, it lifted his mood so much that he wasn't even daunted by the prospect of driving his petrol-scented client from the Sumy Oblast around tonight.

God loves a trinity! he thought with a smirk.

15

Alik was sitting on a bench in the little square by Gunpowder Tower.[11] Sitting and thinking. After the restless and short sleep that Captain Ryabtsev's stories had imposed, he'd wanted to get out of the city centre. He'd shaved and put on a denim uniform that he didn't have to iron, then gone outside.

The sun was gleaming in the sky, interrupted here and there by clouds. At first, Alik had taken the gleam to mean warmth, but then a cool breeze flew in to disabuse him. He remembered he'd left his trusty wide-brimmed hat at home, but decided against going back.

He'd felt the sun's warmth on the crown of his head a few more times on his walk, but thoughts of his hat were far behind by then. He was thinking about the little café on Virmenska Street – the only place he knew that had preserved the atmosphere of accessibility and "do-it-yourself-ness" from times long gone: places where you go up to the staff yourself, order yourself, pay for yourself, and then carry everything over to your table yourself. Alik didn't like cafés with table service. At some point he'd realised that there were too many trained waiters in the country, and there weren't enough restaurants to employ them. It was around then that they'd flooded into the cafés, raising the price of coffee and expecting tips. After that, cafés all became "Cukiernia",[12] "Chocolateries" and other glamorous establishments for customers who respected the Polish words "Szlachta" and "Szlachetna" and applied them to themselves. Alik had abandoned these establishments one after the other, until Virmenska was his only remaining regular haunt.

Take today: he started with two coffees "Eastern-style", followed by a glass of Vana Tallin liqueur, and then set off for Gunpowder Tower. His rest in the little square by the tower calmed his thoughts, his nerves and his eyes. Nobody here was in a hurry. Two mothers were pushing their buggies along an alleyway, chatting calmly about something. A bald plump man in a blue tracksuit was walking his ashy, prim poodle. The dog kept looking back at its owner, as if it wanted to say something nice to him.

Alik decided to spend the day slowly. He needed to be at the theatre by six this evening. In a couple of hours he'd find somewhere to have a bite to eat. But for now he could relax and listen to the birds.

Alik looked up at the tall treetops crowned in mistletoe. He listened in. His ears caught the rustle of reddening autumn leaves.

He thought of the Holy Garden, where he'd spent so many wonderful hours, he remembered his hippie youth, from which he'd transitioned fluidly into hippie maturity, he remembered songs, guitars, long homemade extension cables, stretching from the student dorm all the way to their little space in the garden. He remembered the police officer on shift at the door to the local Party office, located some fifty metres from their den, from their grass, from their universal love. Police didn't live by love, they lived by statute. That's why conflict arose, that's why they cut the extension cables used by the group "Super-Vuiki" to share music and songs with a world that had not yet developed its own universal love. What had changed since then? The hippies had left, the police had stayed. As had the former KGB agents, who it turned out didn't find universal love so strange a concept; they were wilier and smarter than the police, they hid behind their statutes, like they hid their service behind civilian clothes, but some of their souls weren't necessarily against the idea of joining this party they couldn't condone, this government of universal love. And, if you were to believe Ryabtsev's stories, they had joined it – at some risk to their careers, maybe even to their lives!

A faint sound roused Alik from his reflections. He looked around and saw that a small crowd of homeless people carrying assorted bags were approaching the third bench from the stairs that led up from the tram lines to Gunpowder Tower. Some of them were still walking over, but others were already standing around, talking animatedly. The homeless assembly diverted Alik's thoughts down a new path. He remembered the constitution and its right to assembly. Alik smiled. All of God's creations love to assemble, he thought. And once again in his mind's eye he saw a fleeting image of their hippie congregations not far from here, in the garden. He saw sun-warmed clusters of red soldier ants, assembled on tree stumps in the woods behind his house, and scenes from long ago party congresses on a black-and-white television, with thousands of humanoid soldier ants in identical dark suits. And after that he extruded an image from another television broadcast he'd once watched, of marching soldiers in his childhood, regular soldiers this time, not ants.

The homeless people had now all gathered, and Alik saw that among them were people that weren't necessarily homeless, just old men and women slightly worn down by life, with slightly different gaits and body movements, movements that seemed to suggest that these old men and women had stoves or hobs, that they had a table to sit at.

A pirozhki van suddenly appeared in the alleyway: white, with a sign that said OSELYA. It stopped by Alik's bench, just verging onto the grass. The assembled public, united by their poor circumstances, formed a queue. Some nicely dressed girls and women, who had arrived with the van, started walking up and down the queue, which already had about twenty-five people in it, stopping to explain something to those in line. The double doors at the back of the vehicle burst open, and a wave of excitement passed through the assembly.

Alik studied the queue, examining the people's faces, not noticing that a pretty, round-faced lady, who was wearing jeans and a short blue puffer jacket, was paying close attention to him. She had a camera with a large lens hanging from a strap over her chest. Turning away from Alik, she stepped to the side and took a couple of photos of the queue and the girls who were stood by the doors of the van, pouring hot soup into identical plastic bowls from a large Thermos. The third girl was handing out disposable plastic spoons and black bread to those who'd been given soup.

Alik, who had already snapped out of unconsciously surveying the van and the people assembled around it, now started thinking about human values, about simple and important things. About love and warmth, about trees flowering, about soft grass, about butterflies and children.

"Don't be too shy to come over!" a strong woman's voice said above his head. "It could happen to anyone, after all!"

He lifted his head. In front of him stood the pretty, round-faced girl. Her camera bounced against her chest, and she was offering him a plastic bowl of hot soup.

Alik didn't even notice the bowl finding its way into his lap, while his hands were suddenly holding bread and a spoon.

"Eat up!" The woman took a seat, her kind, green eyes trained on him. "I'm guessing it's your first time here . . ."

Her unexpected arrival had robbed Alik of the gift of speech.

"Eat up, eat up! It's pea soup, not from concentrate! With smoked ribs. It's tasty," she said, and her voice became softer and more thoughtful, like she was just about to go quiet and sink into reflections and memories herself. "For main course we have puree and frankfurters. And a fruit kompot!"

The woman's countenance suddenly grew stern, like a nursery teacher, and Alik started wolfing down the hot soup, realising what was wanted of him.

The face of the caring woman with curly short hair regained its smile.

As soon as the bowl was empty, the woman took it from Alik's lap, along with the spoon, said "Back in a second! We take all the rubbish with us!" and walked away.

A couple of minutes later a disposable plate with puree and frankfurters appeared on his lap.

"What's your name?" asked a surprised Alik.

"Oksana."

"I'm Alik."

"Eat up while it's hot!"

Alik nodded and got started on his main course.

But Oksana kept looking at him, and her face showed real sorrow, a sympathy for the hardship of others.

"In Vynnyky we have a hot shower and a washing machine!" she said after a pause. "Come over! Wash your clothes, have a shower. You're probably quite a recent rough sleeper . . ."

"Well, I came here this morning—" Alik began, but Oksana's face became teacher-stern again and he shut up, returning to his hot puree and frankfurter.

"I could book you in with a free hairdresser, not far from here," Oksana suggested after looking at his long hair.

"No thanks," Alik forced out of himself while chewing a mouthful of frankfurter.

"You don't need to be shy about your situation," Oksana said softly, with the intonation of a frontline nurse. "Remember us! We're here on Thursdays from one o'clock!"

She left once Alik had finished his main course, taking the disposable plate and fork with her and leaving him a little leaflet with the address and phone number for a hot shower in Vynnyky as a reminder.

Alik folded the leaflet in four and put it in the pocket of his denim jacket. He looked at his jeans, which he'd always valued, as it happened, because dirt was practically invisible on them. But maybe they could do with a wash? he thought, before getting up from the bench.

The white pirozhki van with the OSELYA sign on it drove off down the alley. The assembly of people that had gathered for the occasion also dissolved, petered out, dispersed. Getting up, Alik searched for Oksana, but there was no sign of her in the square.

16

Large drops of evening rain were crawling slowly down the outer surface of the kitchen window. Taras poured freshly brewed coffee into his Thermos. Whenever he poured or brewed coffee now, he couldn't help thinking about Darka, about her fun eyes, her charming quirks.

His thoughts had never turned to a woman so easily or pleasantly. It couldn't be said that his life was lacking in romantic adventures, but the women he ended up with, no matter how strange, fell into two categories: the silent, languishing type, who always expected something from him and loved to hold his hand while they walked; and the dragons, who were always making loud demands, which always curtailed their relationships, and every time one ended it would bring his soul incomparable relief, reminding him of the inestimable value of loneliness as a way of life. He had to choose between silence and shouting, although is it really a choice? After each dragon Taras would feel charmed by the languishing and pregnant silence of any thoughtfully phlegmatic beauty he came across, and he would take her by the hand and lead her to a café, and she would go, easily and wordlessly submitting to the path he'd chosen. But no, right now, he had no wish to think about them, those former romantic companions of his. Just about her, Darka, like it was for her that he forced himself and his shabby car over the bumpy streets of Lviv, shaking kidney stones out of passengers, so he could then drive over to her, to her glowing late-night window, behind which hid less the banknotes of various nations than her, Darka herself, a sorceress in colourful elbow-length gloves. And he came to her in the earliest hours, just before dawn, slipping his hard-earned notes through the low slit in the window, like he was reporting back to her at the end of each and every working night of his life.

It was nearing midnight, and by the time Taras was approaching the Opera House, the rain had already stopped. At the entrance to the theatre stood a lonely figure in a grey mackintosh and cap. Taras briefly watched Lenya through the windscreen. Then he opened the door and called out to him, and his client walked over to the old Opel with a bustling, non-Lvivian gait that forced a condescending smile out of Taras.

The next few hours passed surprisingly slowly, despite the speed the ageing Opel reached on the cobblestones of Horodotska, Lychakivska and Zelena. Once or twice Lenya cried out, clutched his groin and asked Taras to stop the car. But the third stone was holding on like the last soldier in Brest Fortress. After just a few short rides over the potholes of Lisna Street, Lenya's eyes began burning with a strange electric light, and Taras thought he noticed the inside of the car grow suddenly brighter. Lenya was past the point of speech, but his hand suddenly gripped Taras' right shoulder, and his sharp fingers dug so far into Taras' clavicle that he understood what was needed. He slammed his right foot on the brakes and turned the engine off immediately. The car juddered and froze on the spot. The sudden silence assaulted the ears. Lenya was sat still as a statue. His face had frozen into a nauseatingly haughty expression. His thin nose seemed to grow even sharper.

Taras offered him the glass jar. Lenya didn't budge, only the movement of his eyeballs confirmed that he had noticed it. A few moments later he waved it away with a shaking hand, opened the car door and swivelled outwards, his knit-together legs resting against the doorframe.

Taras waited patiently.

A few minutes later Lenya swayed forwards and slid out of the seat. He was now standing in front of the car with his back to the driver. His movements were restricted. Taras watched as the client unbuttoned his mackintosh, his head bent forward, fiddling with his trouser fly.

Time stopped, and the extended pause began to act on Taras' nerves. Finally, Lenya turned around. He stood, his left hand gripping the bottom of his unbuttoned grey mackintosh to his chest. His right hand was held out, and in its wet palm Taras saw a larger grey pebble than usual. He took it and tipped it into the jar in his lap. The pebble clinked against the glass and all was quiet again.

"I pished myself," Lenya said in a strained, tragic whisper. "Like a youngster . . ."

"It happens," Taras said softly. "It's because of the stone . . ."

Lenya nodded almost imperceptibly.

"Can I sit down?" He looked down at his seat.

And without waiting for an answer, he slowly sat down. Then he took out of his mackintosh pocket a thousand-Russian-ruble note and offered it to Taras.

"Where am I taking you?" asked Taras.

"Where do they take the piss-pants?!" Lenya asked back in a bitterly dejected tone. "To the train station!"

In the square in front of the station, before bidding Taras farewell, Lenya thanked him and said that if he were ever passing through Vorozhba, he would gift him a full vat of real "ninety-five".

"We have a sea of petrol in our city," he bragged. "We get tankers from Belarus and Lithuania coming through, and we siphon off a few gallons from each! That's what the city lives on!"

Taras watched Lenya climb the stairs to the station entrance.

Ten minutes later he was already standing by his favourite late-night window, behind which the light was burning bright and Darka was smiling, her hands in dark-blue gloves tonight, retrieving a clean black ashtray with VENEZIA written on it in gold from the slot for notes. As they drank their coffee, each on their own side of the bureau window, they talked, chattered, listened to each other's voices. The conversation turned, by itself, to the possibility of a date in a different place and at a different time, and Darka, to Taras' sheer joy, agreed. They arranged to meet on Prospect Svobody, by the Virgin Mary, the following evening at six.

"But why didn't you agree before?!" queried Taras, still jubilant at the news.

"My Papa wouldn't let me before, but yesterday he said he wasn't opposed to the idea."

"But surely he needs to get to know me?"

"He already does." Darka reached up to the upper left corner of the window, removed something from it, and showed it to Taras.

It was a small webcam.

"He looked into you and said that you were a harmless simpleton without any criminal or political connections." Darka smiled, securing the webcam back in its former spot.

"What is he then, a policeman?" The smile had disappeared from Taras' face.

"No, he just worries about me! So where are you taking me?" Darka asked playfully, looking Taras straight in the eyes.

"Let's just have a walk outside and go into the third café we see," he said, a little calmer now, resting his palm on the window.

Darka placed her own palm on the other side of the glass. Taras thought he could feel its warmth.

17

There were no more than twenty minutes to go to the performance of the national anthem. Taras' body felt exhausted, but the light in his head was radiant. And this internal light made the space for his thoughts feel so boundless that it seemed there'd be room for a thousand more pleasant reflections. Reflections, of course, that started and ended with Darka, and then started and ended with her again. She occupied every corner; every cell in his brain responsible for his emotions and imagination worked entirely on her, on her image, on doing her "PR". His brain was now an ingenious machine for making images of Darka. Her hands, in dark-blue velvet gloves, tenderly caressing Taras from within, like she had moved entirely inside his body and brain, and he had no need to search for a means of touching her, it was enough to feel her presence inside himself, inside his own personal membrane.

He lay on the sofa under a blanket, gathering his own warmth for an easy entry into sleep, sleep that was so vital and necessary if he was to be lively and happy on their first date. He didn't need much, four hours, maybe five.

"The glory and freedom of our Ukraine has not yet perished . . ." sang the well-accustomed radio set.

Taras shut his eyes and froze. All thoughts stopped, his body waited to be transported to another state.

While he slept, he could hear a very distinct patter of slanted rain against the window. But when he woke there was neither wind nor rain. Instead, Taras' attention was caught by the silvery blue of the pure, darkening sky. The kind of blue with which women of a certain age sometimes colour their grey hair.

From his home on Pekarska to the Virgin Mary on Prospect Svobody is a fifteen-minute walk at a push. They met at the designated spot and stood by the statue for a while, watching as others stopped before the Mother of God to pray before setting off again.

They headed in the direction of the Market Square and stopped at precisely the third café they found on the way.

Her emerald gloves were in surprising harmony with the interior of this establishment, while her green slim-fitted jacket highlighted her love for thirties fashion. Her tapered tweed skirt in the same colour, and her darker but still green leather ankle boots completed the look. In such an outfit, she could hardly resemble a bureau de change employee. Her style was closer to that of a bank branch manager. However, for a manager, there was something missing. And Taras soon realised what. Her face was a cosmetics-free zone. But this didn't strike you at first. Her cheeks had enough of their own rouge and freshness, her lips had a natural raspberry sheen.

"It looks like it's our lucky day! It's perfectly cosy in here!" Darka smiled as they sat at their table. She adjusted the collar of her jacket, looked around and cast an eye towards the bar, where a tall waiter with greased-back black hair was stood waiting.

"You know, this is actually the fifth one I counted, you just didn't notice!" Taras confessed. "I like this place more! The coffee machine never breaks! And they always have bitter chocolate!"

"Ah, do you like your chocolate bitter then?"

"No." Taras giggled. "But they always have it here, look at the ad in the window!"

When her emerald fingers lifted the coffee cup to her lips, Taras froze. He had the feeling that, as soon as she took a small sip, his world would change. As if it wasn't coffee in her cup, but a certain elixir, an elixir that changes the world's sights and feelings, changes its sizes, shapes and sounds. Taras felt hot. He took off his jacket but kept on his long, knitted sweater, which he'd bought especially to wear with his jeans.

"So what do you normally do during the day?" Darka asked suddenly.

"Sleep," replied Taras vaguely, but then roused himself straight away and added, "but I water my cacti and feed my fish too."

"Cacti and fish?" She sounded surprised.

"They don't disturb one another, even though they're sat together on the same windowsill. How about you, what do you do in the daytime?"

"I sleep too. I only fall asleep easily when my body's really tired, that's why I work nights . . . And then after I've slept I read and help my father."

"You live with your father?"

"Yes. My mother was a strange woman. She left when father got ill. And then moved to another city, to Chernivtsi. She calls sometimes."

"Yes, that is strange!" Taras shrugged. "She left because your father got ill?"

"Judge not and you shall not be judged!" Darka sighed. "She was just tired of my sores. After all, all I've brought them is trouble, ever since I was a child. They had to get anti-allergenic air filters installed in the apartment for my sake. And then my father too . . ."

"You said you were allergic to money, not dust."

"There's more than just dust flying about in the air. Money's in the air too, tiny little particles of it. And when you handle it, little microparticles stay on your fingers, little acids. Little reactions take place, which you don't notice because you're thick-skinned."

"I'm thick-skinned?" said Taras.

"In the medical sense, I mean," Darka emphasised softly. "Thick-skinned people aren't susceptible to allergens, but thin-skinned people – people like me – are. People always have moisture on their fingers, after all, even when they think they're dry and they've rubbed them with a towel. And when the fingers touch money, the body moisture reacts with the acid – it's on both notes and coins. For thick-skinned people the reaction happens on the surface, but for thin-skinned people the money acid gets into the blood . . ."

"And what's the air got to do with this?"

"Our body temperature is thirty-six point six," Darka continued explaining calmly. "The temperature of the reaction between body moisture and money acid is a little higher, and as a result, if the acid doesn't end up in the blood, it evaporates and remains in the air. And it reaches the blood of us thin-skinned people through our lungs."

"You mean to tell me that the world is made up of the thin-skinned and the thick-skinned, and the thick-skinned are to blame for the thin-skinned people's problems?"

Darka shook her head and smiled.

"No, it's the money that's to blame, not thick-skinned people."

"But all the same, I'm a thick-skinned person?" Taras asked again, a little calmer.

"Yes." She nodded. "A very likeable thick-skinned person, red-faced, inventive and very funny!"

At around eight in the evening Darka had to go home. To Taras' delight, she allowed him to accompany her, and they walked under the weakening rays of the setting sun to her home on Dudaev Street and climbed to the third floor.

"Will you come and say hi tomorrow morning?" asked Darka, her key already in the lock.

"I don't have any work for this evening yet," Taras admitted. "But if you want, I can arrange a coffee delivery!"

"I do want."

"What time?" Taras took up the pose of a waiter taking an order.

"Let's say ... around four! That's when I start yawning horribly!"

"Say no more!" Taras promised. He willed his entire body forwards, trying to hold his lips as close as possible to hers.

Darka took half a step backwards, the smile still on her face. Then she did the opposite, leaned forward a touch and brushed her lips against his. But just for a moment.

It was long enough for an electric shock to pass through Taras' entire body, from top to bottom. He froze.

"That's a trial kiss," Darka joked before disappearing behind the door to her apartment. "In the morning I'll tell you if you have money acid on your lips or not!"

Taras left feeling weightless. He didn't see anything around him. His legs took themselves to Pekarska. Sluggish thoughts stumbled into his head one after the other, but he paid them no attention. The entirety of his self-perception was currently focused on his lips, which still held the taste of morning fresh-ness, raspberry and coffee.

18

Captain Ryabtsev's yellow Piaggio stopped by Alik's gate just after five. The air was already full of evening heaviness, gradually losing its lightness and transparency. The sky over Zamarstynivska Street darkened too, and so too, therefore, did its reflection on the lake over the road from Alik's house.

Alik hadn't been particularly surprised when the former state security captain had rung him that morning on his mobile and reiterated his promise to have Alik over. The memory of Ryabtsev's strange confession at Lychakiv Cemetery, back on the night of the eighteenth of September, was still floating around Alik's head, reminding him that he had not accepted that information as the decisive, thrice-checked truth. It hung there in his consciousness, as if a book were hanging in the air above its shelf, rather than sitting on it. Alik felt a simultaneous pity and curiosity towards Ryabtsev. The captain's modest height was certainly playing a role there, as well as his obvious Russian-speaking discomfort in Ukrainian-speaking Lviv, although he had learned to speak Ukrainian perfectly adequately. The ageing fragment of the state machine of the Soviet empire inspired no antipathy in Alik, though no great sympathy either.

When Alik sat behind the captain on the soft seat of the scooter, it seemed almost as if he would be the one driving. It wouldn't have been hard to grab the handlebars – the crown of Ryabtsev's head barely reached Alik's chin. On the other hand, Captain Ryabtsev sat assuredly and compactly in the driver's seat, and his legs fitted comfortably in the bottom of the scooter. If you'd sat Alik in his place, his height, which could be described as "considerably above average", would have made it uncomfortable.

Zamarstynivska at rush hour was not a pleasant street for driving, particularly in an open form of transport. They were forced now and then to weave between lorries and vans. The spluttering fumes broke Alik's concentration. He turned away, trying to breathe some "side" air, adjusting his long hair under his wide-brimmed leather hat, which was only held on his head thanks to the buckle strapped under his chin.

Sykhiv finally appeared on the horizon, its white multi-storeys rising above the nearby residential area. The road here was an even tarmac, and the lorries had all disappeared some-where along the way.

"Alik, I won't invite you to mine. It would need tidying first," Ryabtsev said, lowering his speed. "But I can guarantee you that you won't have been anywhere like where we're going today!"

Ryabtsev turned right and drove down a road that ran between a few nine-storey buildings and a green pine forest. They took an unexpected turn onto a narrow track leading into the forest. Alik looked over his shoulder in surprise at the houses behind him, then looked forward again, and saw that the path ended at a green wooden dovecote tower, beyond which there was nothing but trees.

The Piaggio stopped at the dovecote.

"Well, here we are." Captain Ryabtsev smiled. "Welcome!"

Alik slid off the scooter and stretched, loosening his shoulder joints after the somewhat uncomfortable journey. Ryabtsev, meanwhile, removed the padlock from the door of the dovecote, pushed the scooter inside, then poked his head out. He caught Alik's eye and beckoned him in.

In a darkness filled with the smell of potassium fertiliser, a dim lamp came to life, lighting a crudely knocked together wooden staircase that led to the next floor. The dovecote's owner bolted the door and began to clamber upstairs. Alik followed.

For some reason, Alik found the second floor more spacious than the first. This was probably because it had a small table, two stools and an old-fashioned nightstand. Every item of furniture was covered in unfolded newspapers. Dry dove droppings crunched under their feet. Over their heads cooed the doves, inhabiting two large cells that were partially visible from below. A sole silent, unmoving white dove sat on a wooden crossbeam between the two cages.

"I only invite the closest of acquaintances here," said Ryabtsev, sweeping some newspaper to the floor and taking a stool by the table. "You, Alik, are the second person I've ever brought here . . ."

Alik took the paper from the second stool and sat down. His eyes were fixed to the table. Under the copies of *Izvestiya* covering it he could make out an array of dishes and bottles. The newspaper itself was marked by fresh traces of dove inhabitation. A dull lamp was lighting the room here too, hanging on a black wire from the upper wooden crossbeam, the one on which the lonely snow-white dove was perched.

"Alright, the table!" Ryabtsev announced ceremonially, grabbing the *Izvestiya* copies at their edges before throwing them to the floor.

A pleasant and familiar picture revealed itself to Alik: an open jar of sprats, a bowl of sea cabbage, a plate with sliced kolbasa and cheese, bread, a jar of salted pickles, a bottle of vodka, two vodka glasses, and two other, larger glasses.

"This is my little temple," Ryabtsev said lovingly, and the warmth you could hear in his voice once more made Alik look to either side.

A strange feeling came over him: it was as if he had spotted an icon hanging on the wall in an unassuming little corner of the dovecote. Or maybe even a portrait of Stalin or Beria. But the dovecote had neither icons nor portraits. Alik's eyes returned to the light above the table.

"So how does the electricity make its way over here?" he asked.

Ryabtsev smiled and shook his head.

"I installed an accumulator. Take it home once a week to recharge it. I usually spend more time here than at home, so ... All my friends are here." He looked up. "And my biggest friend of all is Nikishka!" Ryabtsev pointed at the large snow-white dove with unusually curled wings sat on the crossbeam. "He's not just a regular dove, he's sickle-winged! Beauty and brains!"

Ryabtsev filled a glass of vodka and placed an aluminium fork on Alik's plate.

"If I were a married man –" Ryabtsev looked a little critically at the snacks – "there'd be other smells in here! And the forks would be cupronickel. But my late motherland taught me that the state comes first and family second! So I never found anyone . . ."

"Ah, what's there to find?" Alik tried to console the captain. "I've always had everything simple too! And you've got everything a man needs in here!"

"Yes, you're right about that!" Ryabtsev lifted his glass. "I thought you were right thirty years ago too. But now it's simply a fact for me! Here's to good memories!"

After they'd had their drinks, Ryabtsev poured them each a glass of water.

"They used to teach us it was wrong to wash it down with water. You had to eat something! But I think we should be free to choose which we prefer, eating or washing it down. I like both, on occasion."

Alik nodded, chewing a sprat and spreading a hunk of black bread with the fish's oil.

"The old world was held together by conventions, and that's why it fell apart," he said thoughtfully. "This world is held together by conventions too, just different ones! It'll fall apart too, with time. The most important thing is to protect your own personal, internal world from all these conventions!"

"You're talking just like a priest!" Ryabtsev was surprised.

"It's this place." Alik suddenly felt embarrassed. "I usually talk normally. This place has clearly had an effect on me," he sighed.

"This place has an effect on me too, it returns me to myself . . . I look after them, let them out to fly around, sometimes let them have little playdates, you see, they sit in separate cages. The boys in one, the girls in the other . . . Only little Nikishka there is always free, I trust him. And he doesn't seem attracted to the girls . . ."

Alik pursed his lips and Ryabtsev suddenly went quiet.

"Something taste bad?" he asked cautiously, and his hand reached out for the vodka bottle.

"No, it's nice," Alik sighed. "It's just that there's something KGB-ish to your words . . . girls in one cage, boys in the other . . ."

Ryabtsev smiled and raised the neck of the vodka bottle to avoid spilling any.

"Wherever there are human beings, something 'KGB-ish' arises . . . But you can't do anything else with doves. It'd be pandemonium, they'd crush their own eggs, they'd fight . . ."

Ryabtsev began lovingly describing the doves, his dovecote and the psycho that was currently running the Lviv dove-breeders club – but Ryabtsev couldn't care less! He took no part in competitions and, unlike the other dove-lovers, he didn't throw his dead birds in the bin, he buried them just here, a little way into the forest.

The former captain's expression while singing the praises of his relationship with his doves put Alik in a good mood again, and as he listened to Ryabtsev, he was at once both taking in his monologue and half forgetting himself, taking in his own thoughts, which had burrowed all of a sudden into the distant Soviet past. In the old days he had encountered his fair share of KGB agents and cops, but he hadn't yet managed to run into doves or dove enthusiasts. The fact that the dove fan also happened to be a former KGB agent, as well as a secret hippie sympathiser, made the evening all the more bizarrely entertaining. Alik, however, was already of the age where not all fun things made him laugh, or even smile.

The half-litre of vodka had emptied quietly, and Ryabtsev almost as quietly took the empty vessel from the table without a break in conversation, holding direct eye contact the entire time.

The captain suddenly fell abruptly silent, turned to the nightstand and pulled a stereo cassette player from a drawer. He checked which cassette was loaded and turned it on.

The voice of Jimi Hendrix, familiar to Alik from an age gone by:

And the wind whispers: Mary.

Alik froze. His thoughts hid themselves, ceding all territory to his ears.

Something dripped onto his head, but Alik paid it no attention. He listened to the song, a song he'd heard a thousand times and not once tired of.

"You'll be rich!" said Ryabtsev, pointing at the crown of Alik's head.

Alik stroked his hair with his palm and hit a moist spot. He held the palm out to inspect it. He sniffed, then looked up at the snow-white sickle-winged dove sat on the crossbeam above him.

"Well, I don't think I needed riches," he said. "I was alright as I was!"

Half an hour later the lamp above the table began to dim. Ryabtsev got nimbly to his feet and covered the table once more with the newspapers from the floor.

"You can't go home like that," he mused, looking at Alik.

"Why not? I'm not drunk!"

"No, you need to clean up!" the dove-keeper explained, pointing at the white splodges on the sleeves of Alik's jean jacket, barely visible in the dying light.

They went downstairs. Ryabtsev locked the dovecote door and turned to face his guest.

"You'll have to come over to mine – the washing machine works! I'm just over there." He gestured at a multi-storey building overlooking the forest around a hundred metres from where they were standing. "Forgive the mess!"

It was only in the glare of a streetlamp that Alik could evaluate the level of "avian presence" on his clothing, including the hat, which he was now holding in his hands.

"It's nothing," Ryabtsev reassured him on the way. "It'll come out in a jiffy! There's no fats whatsoever in dove droppings!"

The captain's one-bedroom apartment proved very cosy, and Alik found no real evidence of the great mess that Ryabtsev had described. Except perhaps that some of his belongings were in cardboard boxes lined up by the wall next to the balcony door.

After showing him the apartment's main room, its owner diverted his guest to the kitchen. He sat him at the table and began arranging snacks on the countertop. Another bottle of vodka appeared, and two clean glasses.

"You get undressed in the meantime! Don't be shy!" said the host as he worked.

Alik pulled his boots from his feet, then slipped off his jeans, feeling distinctly uncomfortable.

"I'm worried it'll be cold if I'm just in my underwear!" he said.

Ryabtsev thought for a moment.

"I'm a size smaller than you, but you could wear my old uniform . . . However! One minute!" Ryabtsev left the kitchen.

Alik could hear him opening cardboard boxes, moving them around, muttering something to himself. Finally he came back in, holding a blue overcoat.

"Here, it'll be warmer in this! Plus the vodka'll warm you!"

The overcoat's sleeves ended up being a touch short, and the coat itself barely covered Alik's knees. Ryabtsev had already taken his jacket and jeans to the bathroom, and now Alik could hear the water gurgling. The captain returned and sat at the table. He began pouring again. Alik thought he seemed troubled.

"When I'm sat in the dovecote, I only feel positive," he began. "But then back here at home . . . at home very different thoughts come to me! Maybe not even my own thoughts, but my neighbours'. The walls here are thin! There's more than a hundred apartments in this building! What a concentration of asynchronously working minds and hearts! But do you remember our last conversation, at your place?"

Alik nodded.

"I wasn't joking! It's all very serious! Soon anyone, even the most ordinary person, will start noticing the anomalies, they'll feel them for themselves! Have you been noticing anything strange?"

Alik thought. He remembered that a few minor details had in fact seemed strange to him in the last week.

"Yes." Alik nodded. "I have. And I heard the birds that shout like seagulls!"

"I went into the office, to see my old colleagues. They just laughed at me! There's already almost no-one from the old guard left! Just newbies who don't understand anything!"

Alik suddenly lost the urge to drink. He just touched the glass to his lips and lowered it again to be polite. Ryabtsev got the hint and continued to drink alone while chatting. Drink, but not get drunk.

At some point the washing machine and the host both went quiet. And a heavy, dismal silence set in, which let the chill penetrate Alik. He tried to push his wrists into the sleeves of the slightly short overcoat, but got nowhere. Ryabtsev sat opposite him just as before, behind him the gas stove was gleaming white. Outside the window the night was ink black. The feeling of normal kitchen cosiness disappeared, it drained out of Ryabtsev's kitchen like sand drains from the top of an hourglass, leaving it empty to signify that a period of time has elapsed. The period of comfort had also evidently elapsed. The time on his mobile phone read half past four in the morning. The phone, which Alik was gripping tightly, also felt too cold.

Ryabtsev left and returned with an ironing board, which he put up. He turned the iron on at the plug, brought Alik's washed jeans in from the bathroom and, after arranging them on the board, began to iron them. Steam was forced out of the iron with a hiss and hit the surface of the jeans. The air smelled of warm damp. Alik began to feel warmer too. He realised that the captain was using the iron to speed up the drying, and watching the process distracted him from his strange internal discomfort.

At half past five Alik took off the KGB overcoat and put his jeans and denim jacket back on. The clothes passed on warmth from the iron. Alik started to say goodbye, but Ryabtsev insisted on walking his guest out to the main road.

On the stairs just outside the door was a bottle of port and a nibbled-at spring onion, surrounded by bread crusts.

"The bums have scattered!" Ryabtsev sighed bitterly.

He walked Alik to Chervona Kalina Prospect, bid him farewell and, after promising to show his face again soon, set off back to his apartment with a firm gait.

After half an hour Alik came out on a people-less and car-less Zamarstynivska and headed towards home. At the corner of Tatarska it was as if he were struck by a bolt of electricity. He stopped. His arms and legs felt cold again and a shiver ran down his spine. He touched his forehead and his fingers felt wet. The air smelled of iodine, of the sea, of rotting seaweed on the beach. A sharp bird cry, like that of a seagull, dropped from the dark sky above. And Alik felt scared again, scared to walk forwards. He took a step back, tripped, and his backside thudded onto the wet tarmac. His right palm, stuck out to cushion the landing, hit something wet and coarse. He lifted the object up to his face. It was a five-limbed starfish. One of the limbs twitched, as if the starfish were trying to reach out for Alik's nose. He threw his strange finding aside. He stood up, surveying the tarmac around him, and took another couple of steps backwards. The inner cold quietly began weakening. So too did the smell of iodine as it left the air. Silence replaced the bird cries. Alik looked to either side once more, then stared at the road that he needed to walk down if he wanted to get home. He started walking forwards again, and straight away a new wave of cold and unease stopped him. And the smell of the sea hit his nose even stronger, the harsh cackle of the seagulls spilled from the sky like thunder, hurting his ears. He ran back again, looking carefully under his feet, and stopped. He squatted, giving in to the weakness that had deadened his legs. He listened in to the returning silence, thinking feverishly of what Captain Ryabtsev had said.

"Looks like he's right," Alik whispered, sick of trying to continue down his own street, suddenly impassable for reasons as yet unknown, refusing to let him through to his own home.

19

Verging on five in the morning, Taras put to one side the fifth volume of the Concise Medical Encyclopaedia that he had bought at a book stall near the Ivan Fyodorov statue. Of course, he would be better off with the first volume, for the letter A, as he sought to understand the nature of allergies and the types of treatment available, but the fifth volume started at the letter L; more specifically it started with a description of the effects of the anti-tuberculosis medication Larusan. So Taras leafed freely through the alphabetised reference book of medical wisdom, stopping to look at individual articles which, despite how strange it all sounded, refreshed fragments of knowledge that he'd picked up during his two-year attempt to become a licensed paramedic. If it weren't for the bright-green cover, the title in which the word "Encyclopaedia" took pride of place, and the ten-hryvnia price tag, then he wouldn't have bought this book. But now, flicking through it at leisure, Taras felt the need to bolster his unfinished secondary medical education by buying the remaining eleven volumes. No matter how you twist it, he earned his money through medicine! Health is the most dependable commodity possible, better than bread!

But all the same, he had to start from the letter A. From the very beginning. That wasn't just natural, it was perfectly necessary! Once he'd made sense of Darka's allergy, he could personally take her long gloves off her hands, he could kiss her fingertips, he could touch her skin!

He poured coffee into his Thermos. When he went out into the courtyard with a sports bag over his shoulder, he stood for a minute in front of his Opel before walking over to the archway leading out to the street. Driving the car in the courtyard that early in the morning, with thirty apartment windows above him, seemed a little impolite.

The sleeping Lviv was peacefully breathing a cool, moist breeze. Not a single window was lit on Pekarska. The traffic lights were left to decorate the night alone, with their aimlessly switching signals. The peaceful surroundings compelled Taras to walk as quietly as possible, but he didn't quite manage for one reason alone – he had a date to get to.

As he came out on Franko Street, Taras completely forgot about his careful relationship to the nighttime quiet, and the echo of his steps hit the walls of the old homes, ricocheted off and flew up higher, higher than the city's roofs.

Before him appeared the small bureau window, full of yellow light. A person's silhouette stood before it. On the road opposite was a taxi with its headlamps lit.

Taras stopped. He waited until Darka was alone.

"You ordered a coffee?" Taras nestled up close to the window.

A hand in a green glove gave a welcome wave from behind the glass.

"Where are our Venetian cups?" he asked jauntily.

"You know, my co-worker and his friends used them as intended." Darka smiled guiltily. "But I washed them out. And I've warned him not to do it again!"

She slipped the ashtrays through the gap.

They chatted a little, until her eyes fell on the wristwatch she had on over the glove.

"But now you have to go!" she said. "They'll be coming for me in fifteen minutes!"

Taras slid his hand through the gap and drummed his fingers against the counter. Darka brushed a tender, gloved finger over the back of his hand.

"Come tomorrow!" she whispered.

Her words electrified Taras' thoughts so much that even as he walked away from the bureau, he felt he wasn't walking, but instead floating above the earth grandiosely, like a ball of lightning, ready to explode from internal excitement at the slightest contact with any reality beyond his feelings.

He was also surprised at his complete lack of physical tiredness. The hour of the anthem was approaching, after which the Lviv courtyard-sweepers would start rustling their brooms. The lights in the homes he was passing should be coming on at any moment. But it was like someone had pressed the snooze button on the city's central clock. And the night stretched out longer than usual, the morning was late, dreams didn't leave the sleepers, the crows of Stryiskyi Park were held up by a changeover somewhere near the city landfill by the village of Hrybovychi. And nothing could distract Taras from enjoying the excitement of falling in love, his new lease on life.

He made it to the corner of his street and suddenly the pre-sunrise but still transparent air lost its usual amenability. The change in the air brought Taras' easy gait to a stop as if it were a strong facing wind, piercing his body with cold, unpleasant vibrations, which suddenly made him feel unexpectedly, helplessly lost. He stopped. His gaze sidled uneasily over the familiar environs, the familiar houses and shop windows. A shiver ran down his arms, the cold air brushed his bare neck with wet fingers. A bird's aggressive and unpleasant cry-laugh poured forth from the sky. The sharp smell of the sea struck Taras' nose and he sneezed. He didn't understand what was happening to him; he moved back and the cold left him. The birds went quiet and the smell of the sea disappeared too. But all of it was replaced with rain. His mood changed for the worse all of a sudden, his heart felt heavy, and fear of the encroaching winter took hold of his mind without either grounds or explanation. His thoughts grew confused, like a startled flock of sparrows. He stood there for ten to fifteen minutes, troubled. The windows of the apartments on the first floor of the building to his right lit up with a kind yellow light. From the corner of his eye he noticed windows lighting up on the other side of the street too. An old woman walked past with a lapdog on a lead. The dog sniffed Taras' trouser leg, then suddenly jumped at the wall of the building and caught something between its jaws. It came back over to Taras and left a dark object in front of him on the tarmac. The old woman tugged on the lead and the lapdog set off to catch up with its owner. But the object, which Taras had not stopped watching, suddenly slipped back over to the wall of the building. Taras squatted down. He couldn't believe his eyes: scuttling across the tarmac, dragging its finger-shafts, was a starfish about the size of a human hand. It reached the wall and disappeared into a dark crevice.

20

Taras' hunger was very nearly ready to wake him, but alas, it was five minutes too late. The screech of the fifth step, violently dreary, penetrating, sharp like a whetted sickle, forced the sleeping body to start. The screech penetrated into his being through both ears and made its way down. Taras grasped his legs and stared at the ceiling. Poor Yezhi!

The doorbell rang a moment later. Taras got up, pulled on some jeans and, naked from the waist up, with a head not entirely capable of comprehending the world, went out into the hallway.

He opened the door to find his downstairs neighbour. The pained look on his face put Taras on guard.

"You forgot to skip the fifth step this morning!" Yezhi's voice sounded gloomy and threatening.

Taras could feel the oncoming argument, which, evidently, had been refining itself in the brain of a man so unsuited to this life since six this morning, and had finally taken shape. A home delivery argument, so to speak.

"You just stepped on it yourself," he said.

"So you heard it? That means you know what I'm talking about!"

Taras began to feel agitated. His mood had been ruined. But he collected his thoughts and planned the most expedient way to put out this spark, which was about to be fanned into a flame nobody particularly needed.

"My bad." Taras lowered his head decisively, and saw the fluffy slippers on Yezhi's feet. "Something strange happened to me this morning, just out there, near the building . . ."

Taras took a few steps back and gestured for his neighbour to come in.

"Sit down! Oksana was a fan of the haircut you gave me!"

"But what happened?" asked Yezhi, sitting at the table.

"I wasn't drunk, right." Taras sat opposite him. "At the corner of Pekarska and Franko I was stopped by a cold wind. It felt scary. The smell of the sea hit my nose, and above me it was like a seagull was crying . . . And then I saw a starfish crawling off the street into a little hole in the wall . . ."

Yezhi considered this.

"You got something to drink?" he asked after a short pause.

Delighted to see that the fifth step had lost its urgency, Taras shot straight up from the table.

"Vodka?" he asked.

"No, get me a tea!" said Yezhi unexpectedly. "I had something similar happen a little while back, five days ago, at night . . ."

Stood in the kitchen by the simmering kettle, Taras couldn't help but start reflecting on the oddities he'd been noticing recently in Yezhi's behaviour. Clean-shaven cheeks, tea instead of vodka. It was all rather suspicious.

The room was a little dark. After putting the teacup on the table, Taras pulled open the curtains.

Yezhi turned to the window.

"You fed the fish?" he asked.

"Yesterday morning I did."

"And today?"

Taras took the fish food box and tipped it over the aquarium. And froze. The fish were "stood" unmoving in the water, collected into a compact flock, in the corner of the aquarium nearest the edge of the windowsill.

"Something's not right with them," whispered Taras. "Oksana said that they can predict earthquakes."

"No, they're scared! Look! Someone's thrown a rock at your window!"

Taras followed Yezhi's gaze and saw on the window's outer glass a rose of cracks, travelling outward from a small hole at precisely the level of the aquarium.

"I've never seen scared fish before," confessed Taras.

"Don't worry about it! They'll calm down once they've eaten."

Taras poured another generous helping over the water's surface.

The fish flurried towards the food. The men returned to the table.

"I'll need to get the glass changed," Taras said sadly, but without any great feeling.

"Yep. Winter soon after all! And that's a hole in it there." Yezhi nodded. "But as for what's going on at night around us, we'll need to give a statement to the police."

"But perhaps it's magnetic storms?" suggested Taras. "They say that storms like that can drive a person mad, if he's weak or ill . . ."

"Well, are you weak or ill?" his neighbour asked irritably.

"I— no, I'm healthy . . ."

"If I go and make a statement, the police will laugh and send me packing! But if it was you, let's say, then what, perhaps, would they do about it?"

"What indeed?" Taras shrugged. "Send a patrol? And what if it's an apparition? The police aren't going to trouble themselves with an apparition! Apparitions don't give out bribes, and you can't take anything from their pockets as a souvenir!"

"Call Oksana." Yezhi suddenly came to life. "She's so clever! She'll tell us straight away what needs doing!"

Taras gave his neighbour a suspicious look. He wasn't thrilled about Yezhi's enthusiasm for Oksana. But she was, in fact, someone who could not only put everything in its place, but also find answers for the most complex of questions.

Taras called her and asked her to come over, saying only that the fish she'd gifted him were acting somewhat strangely.

Half an hour later the familiar sounds of Cheburashka's engine came through the window. In the entrance hall the fifth step screeched and immediately afterwards the trill of the doorbell chased Taras out into the hallway.

"What on earth's going on with you then?" Oksana gave her acquaintance a quizzical look.

"Come through, I'll show you!"

Oksana's face turned stony at the sight of Yezhi Astrovsky.

"You were supposed to be getting that step changed!" she said strictly, like a teacher.

"I remember . . . Yes," the downstairs neighbour babbled. "It's just that I had a bit of a mishap, and had to spend some money . . . I'll do it . . . There's something more serious going on here!" The neighbour nodded towards the windowsill.

"Someone threw a rock." Taras showed Oksana the dent in the window glass, from which thousands of little cracks and splinters splayed out. "When I came over here, all the fish were stood in the corner, completely still, they looked dead . . . It was like something had shocked them."

"Okay." Oksana turned from the fish to Taras. "But they're swimming around normally now?"

"They are now, yeah. But also, this morning I . . . I was frightened too . . ."

"By the stone?" Oksana asked mockingly.

Taras shook his head and started explaining in detail what he had experienced on the way home.

The smile disappeared from his guest's face. She listened to Taras intently, forgetting entirely about Yezhi.

"And something similar happened to me," added the neighbour once Taras went quiet. "But not here on Pekarska, by the Krakow Market, at nighttime. I had to take a detour, because the air was shaking and it made my body shake too. I thought I was drunk, but now I realise it wasn't that."

Oksana sat at the table, rested her elbows on it. Palms cradling her cheeks, she froze, sinking into contemplation.

"Tea, perhaps?" Taras offered. He immediately noticed his neighbour waving agitatedly to get his attention.

"It'd be better if we went down to mine for coffee instead," he whispered, as though he were trying not to interrupt Oksana's thoughts.

Oksana turned around.

Yezhi Astrovsky stretched out into a string as he felt her eyes on him.

"You keep thinking – in the meantime I'll make coffee! Come down in five!" he said quickly and disappeared immediately into the corridor, as if he were scared to hear any kind of reaction.

"Was it him who put you up to calling me?"

"No, we both decided together. If you don't want to go down to his, we can tell him to bring it up."

"Well, are you gonna come with me to drink his coffee?"

"Of course, I wouldn't leave you alone with him!"

"See, you know your own neighbour!" Oksana laughed.

"No, he's just regular crazy, he's no maniac!"

It turned out to be tidy and bright in Yezhi's apartment. Even Taras, who had been there recently, was surprised by the change. A new oval mirror in a carved, bronze-painted frame hung on the wall. In front of it sat the old Soviet barber's chair, covered in a snow-white sheet.

"What's that over there?" Oksana took Taras by the elbow and nodded at the chair.

"His workplace," Taras replied, looking around.

Yezhi wasn't in the room.

"He's a hairdresser," he added.

"And I thought he was just an alcoholic!"

"One doesn't rule out the other. But he smelled of shampoo

this morning." Taras switched to a whisper as he heard the door open.

Yezhi walked into the living room. He was carrying a tray with three porcelain coffee cups and an old-looking porcelain coffee pot. Both the cups and the pot were decorated with a tableau of a hunt with Borzois.

"Take a seat!" Yezhi indicated the round table in the far corner of the room.

"This table wasn't here last time, was it?!" asked a troubled Taras.

Yezhi nodded. "I didn't have these cups last time either. I wasn't quite up to scratch, although I did my best." Yezhi looked at Taras' haircut, his own handiwork. "I bought everything with hard-earned cash!"

"You found work?" Oksana let slip admiringly.

Upon hearing this, Yezhi blossomed. "Yes, yes, of course! Work enriches a person, remember? First I had to enrich myself – then I got everything else . . ."

"What else?" Taras enquired.

"What do you think?! My equipment! Look!" He nodded at the chair, covered in a sheet. "I bring women here, make them beautiful . . ."

"What, they come with you?" asked Oksana.

"Well the ones like you don't, of course." There was a sad note in his voice. "But those a little plainer do. I give them a new hairdo. I've already bought a blow dryer with my earn-ings, and a broom, and a stool." He looked to either side, as if making sure he hadn't purchased anything else. "By the way, I can do men's cuts too, but I don't want to invite men over . . .

They'll get the wrong idea. But women, even if they do get the wrong idea, sometimes they'll come over anyway . . ."

Oksana smiled a little cruelly. "I'll believe it when I see it."

Yezhi pursed his lips. He poured the coffee in silence. Walked over to the phone on the side table. Dialled a number.

"Alla Ivanovna, this is Yezhi Astrovsky. Remember me? You wouldn't be able to recommend me, as a hairdresser, would you? I've got a lady acting all suspicious on me. Yes, thank you! One second!"

Yezhi looked over at Oksana and gestured for her to come to the phone.

Oksana unwillingly picked up the receiver and put it to her ear.

"Hello! Hello?" cried a crackly woman's voice on the other end.

"Yes, I can hear you," Oksana said, deliberately stern. "What did he do, trim you?"

"You know, Yezhi has wonderful hands. I'll only be getting cuts from him now. So don't be scared! You won't regret it!"

"What won't I regret?!" Oksana grumbled. She turned around and held out the phone to Yezhi. "Talk to your fans yourself!"

Yezhi took the phone gingerly from his guest's hands. His face expressed patience and peace, which was most likely why Oksana's irritation didn't last long. She returned to the table. And looked guiltily at Taras.

"Forgive me," came Yezhi's voice next to them, as he continued his phone conversation. "As you well know yourself, sometimes women just get in a bad mood! I'll call you back tomorrow. Yes, and don't forget – I still don't have hairspray yet!"

Over the table hung a silence as heavy as an axe. None of them were quite themselves.

Yezhi took the empty coffee pot and silently left the room.

"I'm miles away." Oksana shrugged, watching the host go.

"Sometimes women just get in a bad mood," Taras repeated with a smile. "Don't worry! Someone should be a little more sceptical with him. It's too dangerous for me. Sometimes I step on that damn step . . ."

Yezhi came back to the table ten minutes later. He looked at both guests, sighed, and immediately turned his gaze to Oksana's hair, which made her a little uncomfortable.

"Have you had many customers yet?" she asked, trying to distract his scheming attention away from her head.

"Eight." Yezhi looked her in the eyes. "There'd have been more if I weren't so shy. It's not easy to walk outside and choose a woman who doesn't look after herself and isn't in a hurry either."

"So you just find them on the street?" Oksana livened up. "You literally just walk up to them and start introducing yourself?!"

"It's not straightforward, by any means." Yezhi was now very serious. "After the first customer, I couldn't fall asleep for half the night. My heart ached. But I need something to live on, especially as I've decided to start from zero . . . with a clean slate, that is."

"That's not easy." Oksana nodded. "You made that choice at the right time too! I know a lot of people who'd envy you!"

"What's there to envy?!" Yezhi waved his hand timidly. "And it wasn't really all that complicated. I stopped drinking, started brushing my teeth five times a day, even though tooth-paste costs a lot these days. But it's tastier than it used to be! I started shaving." He stroked his cheek, confirming the smoothness of his skin. "Bought one of *our* colognes, Ukrainian. Bought an iron too. Taras was my example. I've been watching him for a long time, after all! He was the shyest of the shy, used to come home with beer. And now he feeds fish! That's your influence, of course!"

Yezhi's gaze crept back upwards and fixed itself to Oksana's curls.

"In what way was I 'the shyest of the shy'?" Taras protested belatedly. "I still love beer now! Less of it, sure. But it's an evening drink, and I usually have to drive at night! For work!"

"Is something up there not alright?" Oksana asked tersely.

"No, what do you mean? You have wonderful hair! Although you don't make the most of it."

"What do you mean I don't make the most of it?" Tired of her own irritation, Oksana stared right at the host.

"Well, you could attract the eyes of many men, if you wanted . . ."

"What do I want their eyes for?!" Her voice became barbed. "Just yours are driving me nuts, if it were three or four pairs of them I'd explode like an atom bomb!"

Yezhi spoke calmly again. "You really are a strange one, Oksana!" He looked at Taras. "I'm offering you a free haircut, and you're getting angry! Believe me, a new haircut is a new chance in life!"

"Taras, let's go back to yours!" Oksana stood up from the table. "I don't think this conversation is going to end well!"

Taras stood up too. He looked furtively at the host, who had frozen in a pose of utter confusion.

"But do you go to a hairdresser at all?" asked Yezhi pitifully.

"I do not!" Oksana cut him off. "A friend sometimes trims it for me, that's all I need!"

Yezhi started shaking his head bitterly.

"This friend of yours probably has a dacha too, where she practises on the bushes!" he muttered.

"Right, thank you for having us!" Oksana said firmly. She shot Taras a significant look, assuming that he would move towards the door and she would follow him.

But Taras stayed where he was.

"It's a shame you're leaving," said Yezhi. "Let me at least show you my chair! It's a Soviet antique, but all the mechanisms work!"

He walked over to the barber's chair, took the sheet from it, and swivelled it to face his guests.

"You know, I'd even pay you if you'd let me give you a trim!"

"Listen here, Yezhi! There are so many unhappy, hairy, unkempt homeless people walking around Lviv, but it's my hair you're hung up on! You get them sorted out for starters, then worry about me!"

"And how many of them should I get through before you let me?"

"Well at least ten or twenty for starters!" Oksana smiled again, feeling once more that she'd been overly harsh on the former alcoholic's hairdressing ambitions.

"I'd be ready to give at least fifty homeless haircuts for your sake," Yezhi muttered.

"So get to it! Meanwhile, Taras, let's go to yours!"

"So when should I start?" Yezhi asked.

"Start what?" she asked back.

"Well, cutting homeless people's hair?"

"Any Thursday! On Thursdays they give lunch out at Gunpowder Tower. All Lviv's rough sleepers go there for food," Oksana said angrily and walked out of the apartment.

"You should forgive him," Taras said to Oksana after catching up with her on the stairs. "At least so he doesn't start drinking again! He's trying so hard, he came and visited me a couple of times on your orders, to check if I've been feeding the fish or not!"

"Alright, enough about your Yezhikins. I'm sick of him! And I'm sick of you today! I'm going home to my fish. At least they don't shred my nerves and offer me haircuts!"

Oksana kissed Taras on the cheek and, waving a quick goodbye, left for her Cheburashka, parked in the courtyard.

21

Oksana was overcome by a creeping unease as soon as she parked Cheburashka outside Café Dominik on Fedorova. Her steps sped up by themselves. The gate to the entrance to her building was unlocked. Oksana went up to the first floor and surveyed the doors. Intact! And behind them a secondary set of doors, which also had a lock. Her apartment had been burgled a few years ago, literally a month after she'd bought it. They didn't take much, but she'd never had much to start with. Her computer, some ornaments and her new Teflon frying pan.

She sighed with relief, opened the first door, then the second. She stepped inside and froze in fright. On the floor in front of her, in a pool of water, lay her fish. Two were still moving, flipping languidly from side to side.

"God, what's happened?" cried Oksana, before running into the kitchen, grabbing the first saucepan she saw, filling it with water and diving to her knees to collect the fish. She felt a pain in her right knee, examined it – blood. Her hand brushed over the wet floor and was met with shards of broken glass.

She turned to look at the window, where the aquarium had sat behind a curtain. And suddenly, a noise from behind the curtain plunged her into a stupor. She was paralysed with fear. But the noise continued, a strangled wheezing, as though someone were desperately struggling to inhale.

She crawled backwards, forgetting about her cut knee. Grabbed her mobile phone. Dialled Taras' number.

"Come over, quick! I'm at home! There's someone here!"

"Got it, on my way!" Taras shouted in response.

Oksana ran into the kitchen, where she crouched on the floor, her eyes trained on the curtain from which, just a few moments ago, had come the soul-chilling wheeze of someone choking.

For what must have been the first time, as he ran downstairs, Taras deliberately trod on the fifth step. Its heart-rending cry blended seamlessly into the trilling of the doorbell outside Yezhi's apartment, as Taras pushed down with all his strength. He was still holding it even once the door had opened and Yezhi Astrovsky's scared face had appeared in the gap.

"Quickly, we've got to go! There's robbers at Oksana's place!" Taras screamed, and only then did he release the doorbell and run into the courtyard to his car.

Yezhi, still wearing his slippers, came flying after him.

The old Opel tore out of the courtyard entrance onto Pekarska with the speed of a Ferrari. Taras paid no attention to the brakes' sudden screeching. He took a sharp right and accelerated away.

"Slow down, will you? My heart'll jump out of my ribcage!" Yezhi shouted.

"We'll be there any second, it's just over there!" the driver said without taking his eyes off the road, and the car, darting through a red light, shot out onto Fedorova.

Having stopped right in the middle of the entrance to Oksana's courtyard – there were no parking spaces – they jumped out of the car. Taras ran into the courtyard and almost dived into the entrance hall, his soles smacking against the wooden stairs as he raced to the first floor. He tried the door to Oksana's apartment. Both the first and the second set were open.

"Oksana, where are you?" he asked, stopping just inside the apartment.

"I'm here," she whispered from the kitchen.

Her face was unusually pale, her eyes wet.

"And where's the . . .?" Taras also switched to a whisper.

Oksana, trembling, pointed at the curtain over the window.

Yezhi arrived, breathing heavily. He was about to open his mouth to say something, but Taras raised a finger to his lips, and then with that same finger pointed at the curtain.

From behind it came another wheeze. Yezhi jumped.

"A knife, give us a knife!" he whispered after looking round and noticing Oksana on the floor. "And a stick!"

Striding into the kitchen, Yezhi Astrovsky stepped neatly over Oksana, grabbed a bread knife from the table in his right hand and the mop in his left and rushed towards the window. Taras wouldn't have thought his neighbour would have the strength to swing a mop around with such force, hitting the curtain hard enough that the breeze from the blow swept a few paper napkins from the kitchen table. The hearty thwack drew another wheeze from behind the curtain.

"Have you not called the police yet?" Taras asked Oksana. She shook her head.

Taras was suddenly uncomfortable at the zeal with which Yezhi was doing battle with an unknown danger. He armed himself with a broom and smaller kitchen knife.

"Yezhi," he whispered. "Use your mop to pull the curtain out of the way! Then we'll take him down together."

Yezhi nodded. He swung the mop and knocked it against the rings holding the curtain up. The curtain travelled to the far end of the wooden rod.

Oksana screamed and clapped her hand over her mouth. A shiver went down Taras' spine. Yezhi froze, his mouth wide open.

Writhing in the middle of a cracked hole in the window was an enormous seagull. Blood was dripping from its feathers onto the white windowsill. From the sill the blood dripped further down onto the floor, onto the broken aquarium, onto the pebbles and seaweed.

Oksana got up from the floor. She came a little closer, staring at the wounded bird.

"I'll cut the feathered cretin's throat right now!" Yezhi announced emotionally, the handle of the bread knife still tightly gripped in his right hand.

"Why?" Oksana asked, confused.

"Well . . . So it doesn't suffer." Yezhi looked at her. "It'll die either way, right?"

Oksana shook her head and leaned over the seagull.

"Careful!" Taras warned her. "It could peck you!"

The seagull, as if Taras had reminded it of its own arsenal, lifted its beak and fixed its beady eyes on Oksana, wheezing once more.

Taras noticed a roll of sellotape on the kitchen shelf; he tore off a piece and wrapped it quickly and confidently around the wounded bird's beak.

"Now it's less dangerous," he said.

"We have to call an emergency vet," said Oksana. "Call the help desk, find out the number!" Oksana showed Taras the phone, lying on a pouffe.

"You sure those fish are alright?" Yezhi pointed at the saucepan on the floor.

Oksana nodded without taking her eyes off the bird.

"They have a paid service!" Taras shouted from the other room, the phone still held to his ear. "Hundred hryvnia for a call-out, more for any medical care. Shall I do it?"

"Do it!" said Oksana.

Twenty minutes later a vet in branded green overalls entered with a hurried gait, plastic briefcase in hand. Her face was full of concern. Her cropped red hair was dishevelled – either a random effect of the wind, or the concerted work of a hairdresser.

"Shoes off?" she asked Oksana.

"Don't bother." Oksana waved her into the room. "Here, look!"

"Hey, how could you leave it like that?!" the vet exclaimed upon seeing the seagull. "You need to free it!"

"But couldn't it hurt itself more like that?" Oksana suggested.

"You're not a vegetarian?" The vet eyed her nervously.

"No."

"Then get me the hammer you use for tenderising!"

"Oksana dear," Taras interrupted. "Yezhi and I will go get a new aquarium, and some water for it!"

Oksana nodded. She brought the hammer from the kitchen. The woman in the green overalls assessed the glass under the seagull carefully, paying no attention to the bird's weak wheezes. Then she hammered the glass just above the lower edge of the frame.

A piece of glass flew out from under the seagull, but it still wasn't freed, suspended in the little hole with glass digging into both of its sides.

"Get yourself a cloth and stand next to me!" the vet commanded, measuring the hammer up to the right-hand side of the window. "I'm going to hit right on the glass now, and you're going to catch it immediately!"

That's what happened. The right side of the glass shattered. The seagull awkwardly flapped its injured wing and fell straight into the hands of Oksana, or more precisely into the old green blouse that Oksana had grabbed at short notice.

She put both bird and blouse on the floor, which was already clear of blood and broken glass. The vet brought over her briefcase and opened it up. The seagull began wriggling, which scared Oksana.

"Ah! What do I do? What do I do?"

The vet, thick rubber gloves already pulled on, pinned the seagull down with her right hand, then turned the bird onto its back and showed Oksana how to keep it in place. Oksana stayed exactly like that, both hands pressed down on the open wings. The vet leaned over the seagull and began surveying its wounds.

Taras came into the hallway with two big bottles of water.

"Yezhi not back yet?" he asked.

"Not yet. Come here!" Oksana called. "Take my place, I'm tired!"

Taras squatted down next to them.

While Taras watched the vet pour a hydrogen peroxide solution on the bird's wounds, Oksana put the kettle on.

"I'm gonna lose my mind today," she said angrily. "First there's something up with you, then Yezhi tries to force me into a haircut, then lord knows what this is! Can all that really happen? All in the same day?!"

"There are a lot of magnetic storms at the moment," the vet butted in. "We've had three calls from dove breeders today – seagulls have been mauling the doves! These storms affect animals too, not just us!"

Yezhi entered the hallway, breathing heavily. In his hands was an aquarium.

"Here, they didn't have any smaller ones," he said, showing Oksana his purchase as she peered out of the kitchen.

"Hm, it's twice the size of the one that broke," she mused.

"You could always buy more fish," suggested Yezhi Astrovsky. "For those guys, the bigger, the better! Oh!" He turned his attention to the now-calm injured seagull. "Will it live?"

"It will." The vet nodded and got to her feet. "Well, that's everything. Let it rest in its bandages for three days. You'll need to feed it, of course. You can buy it some frozen gobies.

Just make sure you thaw the fish with warm water before you feed them to the bird!"

"But will it need a cage?" Oksana asked as she weighed up her new responsibilities.

The vet shrugged. "Why spend the money? Just get an old cardboard box and keep it in that. If it wears out just throw it away and get another. It won't be flying anywhere any time soon, regardless!"

"And its beak?"

"You know, before feeding it I would probably tie up its feet. Just in case. They're crafty little things! If its feet are tied, you can release the beak . . ."

Oksana looked over at Taras and Yezhi.

"You'll have to remind me of all of this, or else I'll forget," she said, her voice tired.

After paying and seeing out the vet, Oksana decided to feed her guest-rescuers. She sat them down in the living room at a small wheel-out table and warmed some potatoes and mushrooms in the microwave.

"You can pour yourself something from over there if you want it," she shouted from the kitchen. "Everything's under the table!"

Yezhi looked under the table. He found some vodka and cognac. He grabbed the vodka and looked questioningly at Taras.

"Just a glass," Taras nodded. "For the stress!"

After finishing their drinks, both Taras and Yezhi looked around. Taras was drawn to the new aquarium on the floor by the window, a metre from the bandaged seagull still wrapped in Oksana's blouse.

Taras got up, brought the two bottles in from the hallway and poured the water into the aquarium.

"Oksana, where did the fish go?"

"Just here, in the pan, on the stove!" she replied from the kitchen.

Taras walked over and looked nervously underneath the saucepan that the fish were swimming in – there was no flame. He sighed in relief.

He carried the pan to the aquarium, pulled out the fish by hand and set them free to swim in their new "apartment". He found a packet of dry fish food on the windowsill, poured some in, and watched as the fish raced towards it. He noticed the seagull directing its sharp, crafty gaze at the fish. Taras thought its beady eyes looked evil.

"Don't even think about it!" he scolded the bandaged bird.

After eating, all three of them drank another couple of vodkas. Oksana relaxed a little after that.

"So what are you going to do with it?" Yezhi asked her, nodding at the seagull.

Oksana shrugged. "Take care of it then let it go, what else is there to do?"

"It's probably in pain," Yezhi thought aloud. Then he poured a glass of vodka, and downed almost all of it. He got up and walked over to the seagull. Then he squatted next to it and poured the remaining vodka into the bird's beak.

"Maybe it'll land on its tongue! It'll be like an anaesthetic!" he explained, returning to his chair. He looked around again.

"Interesting place you've got!" he said, as his eyes stopped on Oksana's hair.

"Don't start!" the hostess warned him curtly.

Yezhi lowered a sorrowful look to his plate.

22

"Address?" The woman behind the post office window studied Ryabtsev interrogatively.

"Osvytska thirteen, apartment sixteen."

There was a shuffling of pension-roll papers.

"Ryabtsev?" she asked.

Ryabtsev nodded and offered her his passport.

After being signed onto the roll, he counted out his pension – one thousand two hundred hryvnia – and stood to the side. This monthly ritual always ruined his mood: standing in a queue for between half an hour and an hour, identifying himself to a post office worker, signing onto the roll and receiving his sum, equivalent to one hundred euros. And that was it, for thirty-five years of faithful service in the ranks of first the Soviet, then even the independent Ukrainian Chekists!

A drizzling rain was falling outside the post office's glass door. A regular Lviv autumn day that would have a negligible effect on the former KGB captain's plans. Now he needed somewhere to have a coffee – he'd grown accustomed to observing this tradition back in the Soviet era, only back then, having received his wages, he would bravely walk into any Lviv café and order a cup of coffee – always in Russian. For some reason he had enjoyed people looking at him with a mixture of fear and distaste. Now, every time he received his pension he would order himself a cup of coffee in Ukrainian. Now he wanted to be loved, but nobody paid him any attention, the same way they ignored any other customer, regardless of which language they ordered their coffee in.

Parking his yellow Piaggio under a tree, he took himself to a nearby bar at the corner of the street. He ordered a coffee and paid. Then he took a seat by the window.

Just as the pleasant bitterness reached his tongue, a sadness and conscious self-pity surfaced in Ryabtsev's thoughts. He wasn't old yet, after all, but even now he meant nothing to anyone but his doves. He had strong arms, a clear mind, his height was – well, no less than Putin's, and nor was his education. But even with all that, and despite his other good qualities, he felt the soul-crushing uselessness of his own existence. A uselessness underlined by a laughable pension. No, he wasn't one to complain about life. On the contrary, he used to tell himself that life had a right to complain about him, about Captain Ryabtsev, because back then, life couldn't dictate its terms to him! Life trailed behind him, it stared at his back with envy as he peered out from behind the corner of the Party building. He wasn't gloating over the matter by any means, he didn't look down on others, he didn't make a big deal of himself, making out that he could strike down enemy spy rockets from outer space. He always maintained an even and modest character, and the inner workings of his brain, anything that reflected his heart, rather than his reason, remained invisible and undetectable to the outside world. It all stayed within.

Especially the weaknesses that he had confessed to himself after his motherland – the Soviet Union – had met its end. Weaknesses that had, at the right time, proved to Ryabtsev himself that he wasn't as simple a person as he seemed to the higher-ups. They – the weaknesses – had added spice to his thoughts, but in doing so they hadn't created any doubts, they hadn't deprived Ryabtsev of his strong, dependable contact with the soil, the earth, the structure of the gone-away Soviet world. One question had always worried Ryabtsev, it's true: why had they not given him the rank of major? Why had his colleagues of a similar vintage left as lieutenant-colonels, and one even a general, while he'd remained a captain all his life?

His second sip of coffee shifted the sadness a little. He remembered two co-worker friends with whom he'd sometimes spend nights in the office listening to records that had been confiscated from the international postal service. The stereo player, made somewhere in a secret Siberian military radio factory, could knock spots off any Sony, Philips or Grundig when it came to sound quality. The fifty-watt columns sped up the blood in your veins and arteries. The body itself became a musical instrument. Ivan Sukhikh, whose body corresponded entirely to his surname[13], and who retired a colonel, would change his facial expression at the very first sound of Western rock music, and only now, looking back, did Ryabtsev recall his utter disinhibition and independence, his face transfiguring into that of a free Western man – although it was true that as soon as the record was taken from the platter he would return to his "default position". Ryabtsev's other associate in secret rock appreciation, Nikita Ryumachov, did not change facial expressions during their "harm-carrying music" listening parties. It was only his eyes that were affected, burning in a peculiar manner until the final chords. Nikita Ryumachov retired a lieutenant-colonel, then became Mykyta Ryumachov, while his son Vasily ran for election with the nationalists in independent Ukraine under the surname Ryumach.[14] The Lord works in mysterious ways. If he himself, Ryabtsev, had had children, who would they have been by now? On one side of the ethnic front, or the other? Or at the back? Or in the Czech Republic for work?

Ryabtsev sighed and turned to the window. A sudden sun had begun to shine, and the drops of recent rain on the outside of the glass now sparkled, refracting the sunlight.

In his mind he began playing one of Jimi Hendrix's first songs: "Purple Haze", from his first album *Are You Experienced?*. Ryabtsev hadn't heard it in a long time, a very long time. He tried to strengthen his memory and raise the volume a little. It seemed to be working. A soft, kind smile came to his face. And to go with the Hendrix soundtrack, his memory suddenly filled with the image of a young Alik Olisevych, and a few of the other hippies that Ryabtsev had dedicated the largest – and yes, you could even say the best – portion of his professional life to surveilling. What a colourful gang those hippies were! And what colourful guests they had visiting them too. Just Audrius from Lithuania alone! And the bearded Penzel too! And what about Yuzik, who let nothing grow on his head except sideburns?! They had their share of invisible types as well, but where *doesn't* have them? The state organs were *mostly* invisible types! Just as invisible as

Ryabtsev himself! But back then he'd been on assignments! Daily. Or at least, that's what his bosses thought. For his part, Ryabtsev had always understood that he was studying global tendencies through the example of a bunch of guys that had been infected by them. Sure, he himself had pretty quickly caught the bug of one of those tendencies – a love for rock and for the physical sensation of freedom that this music incited, this music that was so dangerous from the point of view of communist ideology. This very song, "Purple Haze", was dangerous, detrimental to the psychic health of those who understood its lyrics. After all, it was a song regarding the act of smoking weed! And it is, after all, true that Soviet music, in accordance with ideology, was much more "constructive" and in no way prejudicial to either psyche or health. They now say it helped order people into files to march; helped them build the future, or just new cowsheds. In every Soviet song you could hear the concrete task the authors had set themselves. Rock songs had no concrete, they engaged the animal instinct of joy, the sense of freedom, of sudden urges. It was impossible to manage a person who loved such music. Which might explain why, after the three colleagues had listened to Jimi Hendrix in secret, either for the sake of sonic camouflage, or just to return themselves spirituo-physically to the Soviet citizen's regular state of being, they listened to a couple of Magomaev numbers, or the heroic songs of Iosif Kobzon. And only then would they go their separate ways, either back home or to their duties. In theory neither Vanya Sukhikh nor Nikita Ryumachov had any official responsibility for monitoring the hippies, it was just a hobby for them.

The three of them were first brought together by the confiscated records; it was only later that they became interested in the packages' addressees.

Ryabtsev sighed. He remembered how much had never made it by mail to Alik Olisevych and his friends. And he felt bitter and ashamed.

"It wasn't me, it was the system," he said to reassure himself.

He remembered how many years it had taken before he could go to them and confess. The people who met him that night at Lychakiv Cemetery hadn't stopped being hippies, but they'd grown, aged. Yes, that was difficult information to come to terms with. Difficult, but necessary. For the sake of justice. Justice is integral to history, and history is the highest judge. Ryabtsev knew that. The Lviv hippies had one history, and the Lviv KGB had another. But that's not to say that these two histories only met one another on the ideological front. There are always collaborationists and sympathisers, as well as simple traitors and those weak of will. Ryabtsev didn't want to think about the latter – he considered himself and his two co-workers true sympathisers, upholders and arbiters, in their own way, of the highest justice; arbiters of the fact that, ultimately, in the eyes of history, even his old employers – the KGB – weren't to be painted solely black, as they so often were. That's what he reckoned, at least.

Yes, I'm still indebted, he thought. I haven't rehabilitated myself yet. But we'll get there. I've still got to return something to them, and then . . . Then I can die peacefully.

Ryabtsev imagined his own funeral: a yellow bus with a

black stripe entering the gates of Lychakiv Cemetery, an open casket raised on the shoulders of the tall, long-haired, elderly hippies. All of them in denim. At the front on the left-hand side, Alik Olisevych. Behind him Penzel and Igor Zlyi. At the back, a few old co-workers in their uniforms . . .

Having chased away these thoughts, Ryabtsev began to think about his feathery responsibilities. He called a dove-breeder acquaintance with a question about vitamin availability. The answer was affirmative.

And Ryabtsev drove his yellow Piaggio over the wet Sykhiv tarmac. Past the multi-storeys and churches (both Orthodox and Catholic) built on former wasteground, past the Arsen shopping centre, the Santa Barbara market.

Ilko Narizhny, for whom doves were not just a hobby but a small business, welcomed Ryabtsev into his home, a two-room apartment on the fourth floor.

"All nice and fresh, haven't even unpacked it," he said, folding a sheet of paper in four. "Here, have a look!"

Ryabtsev ran his eyes over the list of names. He looked back at his host – a sullen, sturdy man with a moustache, around ten years younger than himself.

"What would you recommend?" he asked.

"Well, last time you took those Belgian vitamins . . . I didn't get any of them this time. But I've got Omniform. It's the same thing – also Belgian. Are all your birds healthy? No mites?"

"Healthy? Why would they be sick?!"

"Omniform then, but there's also Fortalite and Dextro-tonic, so they don't lose their sporting shape in winter!" Ilko Narizhny suggested more forcefully.

"Why would they need sporting shape? I'm not taking them to competitions . . ."

"But maybe that's a bad decision? It's not just people who live longer if they keep active! Anything to drink?"

Ryabtsev shook his head.

"I'll take the vitamins, but not any of this other nonsense," he said firmly.

Having received a shopping bag with the vitamin food supplements in exchange for twenty hryvnia, he said farewell.

The day was heading towards sunset. Moisture weighed down the air, making it evening-like, painting it grey.

Ten minutes later, the captain had already unlocked the door to his dovecote, rolled his scooter inside, and turned on the light.

The lamp was dim – the accumulator needed a recharge. But the distinct dove chatter upstairs was in full swing. Ryabtsev smiled. Now he had something to do: he'd mix the vitamins in with the food, then treat his feathered fellows to a hearty dinner.

23

Right at the end of Zamarstynivska, at the crack of dawn, Thursday was approaching. Alik didn't realise this at first; he woke up as usual. He sat on the sofa, turned to the "short-view" window that looked out straight onto the brick wall of a neighbouring shed, then shifted his gaze to the old stove, long ago fuelled by wood, now running on gas. He lit a match, opened the stove door and, holding the flame to the flattened end of the pipe, turned on the gas. A blue flash agitated the still stove air, and the flames began to lick against the bottom of the old metal rings of the two wide burners. Alik tipped ground coffee into the Turkish coffee pot, filled it with water and looked out of the "long-view" window. This one revealed sunshine outside. Its unexpected appearance made Alik think about the date, which made him remember at first that it was October outside, while in his apartment, where everything is more concrete than the outer world and even the bathroom has a quietly ticking clock high on the wall, Thursday was approaching.

"Thursday?!" Alik whispered, and for some reason he began to feel anxious.

He remembered how worried Ryabtsev was by the strange

events that had been happening at night in the city. But that was clearly nothing to do with Thursday, he and Ryabtsev hadn't sat in the dovecote on a Thursday. It had been another day of the week.

Alik stopped thinking about that Lviv night and began to remember last Thursday in more detail: Gunpowder Tower, the homeless queuing for free food, and Oksana, the round-faced lady with a harsh beauty to her, watching to make sure he was satiated and insisting on offering him a free hot shower somewhere in Vynnyky. Yes! She'd also said that he could wash his clothes there . . . But Captain Ryabtsev had already washed them!

Alik smiled and glanced towards the back of the armchair, where his denim jeans and jacket were draped, clean, washed and hand-pressed personally by a former full-time employee of the KGB.

He got dressed and brushed his long hair, which evened it out and gave his face a near-monastic air.

"Thursday," he whispered. "I need to make the most of the sun. It'll be gone soon!"

An hour later he was sat on the bench in the little square by Gunpowder Tower. From Market Square came the midday clock tower chime. The clouds parted to let a few tired autumnal rays of sunlight pass through. One of them fell directly on Alik, and he immediately took off his wide-brimmed hat – what good was the sun's warmth to a hat?! A woman of about thirty in a blue dress walked by with a baby in a buggy, and Alik, having caught her glance, nodded at her. She nodded back. He reckoned she must have walked past last Thursday too, in that same blue dress, pushing that same claret buggy in front of her. The city, with all of its noises and problems, lay all around this little square. But here, even if it wasn't bright, there was always at least a little sun, and instead of the usual city roar there were rustles, squeaking wheels from children's buggies, the footsteps of people passing by, human utterances that couldn't be made out as words, because distance and wind turned them to music and echoes. This had Alik thinking about how every little corner, be it a square or a courtyard, lived its own constant, and constantly repeating, life, starting at sunrise, with the opening or closing of windows, the flicking on and off of lights, the screeches of wooden steps in the hallways of old Polish houses, and the slamming and shutting of entrance doors.

If Alik were to come here every day, he would learn not just the names of the mums, but the names of the kids in the buggies too; he'd know the nicknames of the dogs that were walked here, and the names of their owners, who were always shouting "Buddy! Tiger! Jolly!". Dogs don't know their owners by their names. They know them by their smells.

Caught on these thoughts of dogs and smells, Alik tried to remember the smell of his own apartment, his own home. He tried, and he failed. "That's probably normal," he sighed. "I don't know my own smell, after all, do I?! I wouldn't be able to say at once: 'oh, this person smells just like me!' Because I'm not a dog . . ."

Alik laughed. It was then that he noticed the pirozhki van with the OSELYA sign driving into the little square. People of unfortunate appearance rushed over from different corners of the square towards it. Their movements were jerky, scurrying. They started to form themselves awkwardly into a queue, but then three nicely dressed girls came to their aid. They skirted around the knotted queue, which gradually untangled itself.

Alik caught himself wondering if he'd be able to make out the round-faced brunette in jeans and a short, dark jacket in the crowd, either holding her large camera or letting it dangle around her neck.

By now the first citizens were already walking away from the vehicle, cheered up by their free soup. They cautiously carried their disposable plastic bowls to the nearest benches. Three minutes later, five of them were already sat shoulder to shoulder on the closest bench to the vehicle, almost synchronised in lifting their single-use spoons to their mouths.

Alik watched them thoughtfully, not noticing that a tall, thin man was watching him from the neighbouring bench; at his feet sat an old, yellow leather carpet bag. He was dressed modestly, but well: a brown suit from the late eighties with sharp lapels and a blue diamond patch from some Soviet university above the breast pocket, grey chamois shoes and a beige thin-brimmed hat. For a moment he was distracted by the queue for the truck. He swallowed some saliva, making the Adam's apple on his slender neck jerk sharply up and down. The sight of the queue clearly worried him for some reason, and he quickly shifted his gaze back to Alik.

Alik's stomach had awoken. He began subconsciously searching for the pretty, kind, round-faced woman that had fed him here last Thursday. But he couldn't see her. The shabby folk who had finished their soup went back to the queue, this time for their second course. Alik's memory brought the taste of the kompot he'd had a week before back to his tongue. His stomach grew louder. He started trying to jolt his memory: where around here did cheap and tasty food?

At around this point, the man in the brown suit lifted his yellow carpet bag from the tarmac, and walked over to Alik's bench. He sat down next to him, so quietly that Alik didn't hear a thing. And nor did he see him, he was so caught up in his own thoughts.

"And why aren't you over there?" asked the man, nodding towards the van.

Alik jumped in shock and stared in surprise at the new neighbour he'd suddenly acquired.

"Find it awkward?" the man proffered aloud.

Alik nodded.

"Me too," the man said. "But I'll bring you some. You just look after my things!" He indicated the carpet bag.

The man came back with three plates. He gave one to Alik and sat beside him. Alik looked at the buckwheat porridge, generously covered in gravy, and at the cutlet.

"Thank you!" he said, turning to the kind stranger.

"Don't mention it!" the man responded. "Forgive me, I haven't introduced myself. Yezhi Astrovsky, former Pole."

"Why 'former'?" Alik asked. "Can you really be a 'former' Pole or Russian?"

"You can't be former KGB or communist – the body and soul can't be washed of those marks. But the Soviet years beat all the Polish out of me, there's nothing left now but my name and surname. And even those they suggested I change! Hence, 'former'."

The buckwheat porridge melted just as lightly in the mouth as the kind man's words melted in Alik's ears, leaving a mental aftertaste.

"My name's Alik," he said. He wanted to add something about himself to match his bench neighbour's earnestness and openness. "I'm more or less from a hippie background . . ."

"A former hippie?" asked Yezhi Astrovsky.

"No." Alik shook his head. "Not 'former'."

"What, are there still hippies?" His interlocutor seemed surprised.

"There's still me!"

Yezhi nodded. Spearing his cutlet on his fork, he lifted it to his mouth and bit a third of it off with relish. He chewed slowly and concertedly. Then he turned to Alik.

"You know, I recently started my life afresh!" he informed him almost ceremonially.

"How are you finding it?"

"I like it. I like it a lot. Now I understand that I wasted twenty years of my life, but that there's still something left ahead of me!"

"That's good! I'm an optimist too," Alik said, but his voice sounded a little wistful for some reason.

"If you're an optimist, then God himself ordered you to start your life anew too!"

"But where do I start?" the hippie asked with a barely noticeable touch of irony.

"The small things," Yezhi responded firmly. "Showering

with soap, cleaning your clothes, rejecting dangerous habits, cleaning your home and, of course, going to the barber's, getting your hair in order." He was now staring at Alik's head.

Alik suddenly felt that in the blink of an eye his new friend's nose had become beak-like and wily. Yezhi was a touch shorter than him and now, as he studied Alik's hair, he was craning his neck a little to get a better look. Alik didn't quite feel himself. A strange smell tickled his nose. It was not the smell of the food or the city.

Alik sneezed. Yezhi was finally torn away from the hair of his bench neighbour. He polished off his second course.

"I'm going up for kompot," he said as he stood up.

As soon as the "former Pole" had left, the smell that had been disturbing Alik disappeared too. Alik looked around. The queue for the van had dispersed, although there were still clumps of homeless people dotted around the mobile kitchen.

"So what do you think?" The "former Pole" sat back down next to Alik and handed him a plastic cup full of kompot.

"About what?"

"About starting life afresh?"

"I still haven't really thought about it," Alik confessed. "It's too serious a topic."

"Yes," Yezhi agreed. "But, like I said, you have to start with the little things!"

He leaned over his carpet bag and opened it without lifting it from the ground. He pulled out a square mirror around the size of a book, hairdresser's scissors, a square of green fabric and a large plastic comb.

"I found all of this at home, when I cleaned up after twenty years of aimless living," Yezhi explained, handing Alik the mirror.

Alik peered into it. His reflection looked bewildered. He looked over at the green fabric that Yezhi was waving in the air, as one waves a tablecloth to free it of crumbs.

Alik's nose twitched again from the unpleasant smell.

"I could give you a haircut right now, entirely for free," the "former Pole" said confidently.

"But why?" asked Alik.

"It's important for me. I'll gain respect!"

"Respect from where, up there?" Alik pointed at the sky.

"No." Yezhi shook his head. "Here!" He pointed down, at the earth.

"I don't think I will, all things considered," said Alik. "I have a close friend, a lady, she evens out the ends of my hair every three months. But I don't want it cut!"

"Oh, come on, a new life always starts with a new haircut!"

"I don't want a new life," Alik confessed. "I'm very happy with my current life. I'm quite conservative in that respect. I like my room, my courtyard. I don't like new things or new smells . . . By the way, I think you've got something on you that smells sort of strange!"

"Yes!" Yezhi nodded. "Forgive me! I went overboard! I sprayed myself with insect repellent . . ."

"Why?" Alik opened his eyes wide in surprise.

"Well, so the bugs don't jump ship onto me . . . From the people I'm giving haircuts to!"

"I don't have any bugs," Alik said, offended.

"Come on now, I didn't mean you! That's why I offered you

the first free haircut! I saw you had no fleas or lice on you! I meant *them*!" He looked over at the bums that were still standing nearby. "They're more in need of my help. A new life means more to them than it does to you. I can see that. I just find it hard to make myself walk up to them. But I've got to, haven't I?"

"Are you a believer?" Alik asked.

"I wouldn't say so." Yezhi dropped his scissors and comb back into the carpet bag. He carefully folded the green fabric.

Alik suddenly held a hand out and felt the fabric between his fingers.

"I cut it from an old Bologna cloak," Yezhi explained, and paused briefly. "I'm not a believer, although faith is also a good stimulus for starting one's life over again. I have a stimulus too . . . a woman . . ."

Yezhi picked his yellow carpet bag up and, nodding goodbye to Alik, set off towards the nearest group of rough sleepers.

Alik watched as he walked over to them and started talking. He talked for a long time, about fifteen minutes. Then one of the women sat on the nearest bench and took the cloth from her head. Yezhi pulled a comb from the carpet bag, which he'd set down beside her, and began combing her hair. And it was clear from both their faces that this activity was bringing neither of them any pleasure.

24

After three lazy days, Poland sent Taras a client. Sławomir – for that was his name – immediately informed him that he was ready to pay one hundred euros, so long as the procedure lasted only one night. Excited by this generosity, Taras forgot to convey his indispensable condition: that the stone, once retrieved, would be his to keep as a souvenir. He was to pick the customer up from the Leopolis hotel on Teatralna, which made the man seem even more respectable. Not all Poles had the means for such luxury.

It was still fifteen minutes before midnight when Taras, skipping the fifth step, walked out into the courtyard, sat behind the wheel of his Opel and drove out onto Pekarska. Sławomir was standing by the hotel entrance. Stopping a short distance away, Taras got out of the car, waved at him, and immediately felt the night air's saturating moisture settle on the skin of his palm.

"Old motor," he said with a thick Polish accent.

The Pole looked to be around forty. Tweed coat down to his knees, umbrella-walking-stick in his hand.

"It's special," Taras explained. "For procedures, not pleasure!"

"I bought myself a Porsche Cayenne a week ago," Sławomir bragged.

"A useless car," Taras sighed. "Only good for driving girls around!"

"That's why I bought it." The Pole smiled. "Well, here you are, you asked for an x-ray!" He pulled the photo, rolled into a tube, from the inside pocket of his coat.

Taras turned on the light in the car, raised the photo to eye level and squinted.

"No problem," he said in a professional tone. "We'll get it sorted tonight!"

Five minutes later the car set off down Lychakivska. The road was empty. His client was unusually peaceful, as though he were in no pain at all!

"Right then, you ready?" Taras asked Sławomir.

He nodded. Taras pressed down on the accelerator. The car shot forwards, and the Pole was jolted so heavily he knocked the crown of his head against the roof. He yelped, and a pained grimace flashed across his face like lightning. Taras smiled. Another couple of kilometres and there wouldn't be a trace left of the Pole's self-assured calm.

After their nighttime jolt down Lychakivska, Taras drove his client back and forth along Horodotska, and after that, having judged from the colour of Sławomir's face that they were near their goal, he headed for Lisna. Right there the Pole screamed, gripping his hands to his private area as if a heavy football boot had just thudded into his groin. Taras stopped, noticing that once again he was by the entrance to a familiar four-storey building, where many of his clients had relieved themselves of their burden of small but painful stones.

The Pole gripped the litre jar held out to him, and folding himself in two he dragged himself out of the car.

"Hey!" Taras said behind his back. "Just don't throw away the stone! I collect them!"

The seconds went by painfully slowly. The Pole froze, hunched over, leaning forwards. A cool, dry breeze blew in through the open door of the Opel.

Taras felt uneasy. At first he thought he was concerned for his client, but a few moments later a small, unpleasant tremor set into his fingers. He put his hands to the steering wheel, gripping it with what strength he had, and felt with his whole body how everything around him was trembling – him, the steering wheel held tight in his hands, and the rest of the car too. The gluey silence surrounding the Opel bothered Taras even more, until suddenly it was broken by the sound of a shattered jar. The Pole hadn't been holding it properly. He'd dropped it. Then came the sound of a gurgling stream. Sławomir groaned and straightened out his back.

Taras still felt the steering wheel shaking in his hands, but now, with no more silence around him, his unease gave way to fear, pushing all other thoughts from his mind.

The Pole turned around slowly, buttoned up his tweed coat and gingerly sat in his seat.

Taras was just about to ask him to slam his door shut when the sound of shuffling footsteps reached his ears. He leaned forward and saw that lower down the street a man was staggering along; gloomy, hairy, average height, either in a *vatnik* or a torn jacket that looked like one.[15] The air filled with the smell of a dumpster.

Once the man passed out of sight, the trembling in Taras' fingers disappeared. The worried sensation let him go. His soul was filled with peace, and Taras felt this sudden change of condition in the smallest details, as if in different places on his body no fewer than a hundred little needles had been piercing his skin, and someone had somehow managed to take them all out at once.

He took off the car's handbrake. It rolled forward unhurriedly. The engine kicked into gear as it rolled, and the headlamps switched on.

Taras stared at the space lit up ahead, trying to make out the homeless man from a couple of minutes before, but he was nowhere to be seen.

"To the hotel?" he asked the Pole.

"No, let's go to a nightclub! Need to feel myself again."

Taras shrugged and took his client to Club Pozitiff on Zelena.

The club was humming with music. They sat at a table, and a tired waiter floated towards them through heavy air.

"You got Lagavulin?"

The waiter nodded.

"Two!" said the Pole.

"I'm driving!" Taras said firmly.

The waiter froze. His eyeballs strayed of their own accord to take in the person who was "driving", then returned to Sławomir.

"Two anyway," he repeated. "Neat, one glass."

Taras studied the back of the retreating waiter, trying to work out if he was high.

"Tell me, do you treat other illnesses?"

"No, I only do stones."

"Well, perhaps you have friends? Who could be turned to regarding other conditions?" The Pole was insistent.

Taras had an inkling of what his client was aiming for.

"Are you interested in heavy venereology?" he asked.

"Heavy?!" repeated Sławomir, his laughter showing off a row of bright white teeth. "Good term! You came up with that yourself?"

Taras nodded. And felt a momentary pride. While studying, he had jokingly split venereology into "heavy" and "light", making a comparison to artillery.

A ten-euro note appeared unexpectedly in front of Taras on the table.

"That's for the copyright!" said the Pole. "I'm gonna use that one!"

A hundred and ten! The calculator in Taras' head totted up the night's income.

On the table in front of the Pole, the waiter placed a thick-cut glass full of amber-coloured liquid. The sharp smell tore into the nostrils; Taras instinctively leaned back in his chair.

"I need people with rare diseases," the Pole said more plainly and distinctly, his eyes fixed on the whisky.

"My friend has an allergy to money," said Taras, not because he had any interest in the conversation, but because at that moment he was thinking about Darka, and about how it was probably time for him to be drinking coffee from a Thermos with her.

"Interesting." Sławomir took a gulp of whisky. "She had it long? What symptoms?"

"Lesions all across her body, reddening . . ."

Taras suddenly went quiet out of embarrassment, as if he had realised he was doing something bad. Yes! He had been talking about her body with a third party he didn't even know. He'd talked about her illness, about her. Why?

"I have to go," he said in an apologetic tone.

"Just think about it! Rare diseases – they're good business! I could offer you a partnership!" Sławomir started talking more quickly, recognising that Taras really was leaving now, without hearing him out. "I work with pharmacological labs in Belgium. They need patients to try out new treatments."

"But what's the point in making new treatments for rare diseases?"

"You don't get it! Some rare diseases have a great potential! They might just become regular illnesses. Allergies have already completely taken over America! Your acquaintance – she's, as we say, the first swallow! She'd receive free treatment, you'd receive three hundred euros a month for your administrative services and patient monitoring . . . Three hundred euros for each patient!"

Taras felt tired. Something had finished him off; either the humming vibrations of the club, or the sleepless night, or that sudden inexplicable worry that had taken hold of him on Lisna Street. He could no longer think clearly, and nor did he want to.

"It's a solid deal!" the Pole continued, offering him a business card. "You really could administrate ten to fifteen sick people, and that would be five thousand euros a month! What could it cost you to drive around the hospitals? Any good doctor will give you a list of his recent diagnoses for twenty euros! All you'd have to do is take your pick!"

"I really have to go." Taras got up decisively from the table, stashing the Pole's business card in his jacket pocket.

The Pole caught up to him at the exit, held out a hundred euros and clapped him on the shoulder.

Once he was outside, Taras looked down at the banknote in his right hand. He looked at it and realised that he had nearly left without his earnings! He sent a mental note of gratitude back into the club to the Pole, for his honesty, then he sat in his car.

By around five in the morning he had made it to the window of his favourite bureau de change employee. He slipped a hundred euros through the slit.

"Out of hryvnia today," said a familiar voice. "Oh, it's you!" Darka smiled. "You know, half an hour ago a black man ran over here, I think he was a doorman for the Split casino, and he took all the hryvnia!"

"Ah well." Taras laughed. "Then we'll just drink coffee! Are the ashtrays clean?"

Darka slipped both of the "Venetian" ashtrays out of the window. Taras opened the Thermos. The pleasant smell tickled their nostrils.

"Are you free this afternoon?" asked Darka.

"Yes!" nodded Taras.

25

After waking up the following afternoon, Taras checked his emails. There was only one in his virtual postbox, and that was from last night's client, Sławomir.

"I thank you kindly," wrote the Pole. "Don't forget about the business opportunity! With your inventiveness and energy, you could be earning even more than 5,000 euros a month!"

Taras smirked, switched to a weather forecast site, and saw that this evening in Lviv would be a rainy one, but the news didn't make him bitter. Let it rain! Who was scared of it here, in Lviv? Besides, in just two hours he'd be meeting his own little ray of sunshine, and taking her to where they'd both be warm and cosy!

They met at Café Kabinet. By the time Darka entered, furling her wet umbrella as she walked, Taras was already sat at the table leafing through a book he'd picked from the shelf. She gave him a fun, mischievous look. Walked over. Brushed a fingertip wrapped in a claret right-hand glove gently across his lip. Sat opposite him. Waved over a waitress.

"Latte!"

"And for you?" The waitress looked at Taras.

"Espresso, and a glass of Zakarpatsky." He turned to Darka. "How's things at home?"

"All fine! How about yours?"

"What would happen at mine?" Taras shrugged. "I live alone, don't I? Well, not entirely. There's cacti and an aquarium with fish. I fed them."

Darka laughed.

"What do you feed them?"

"What? Fish food. From a box. Have you had lunch, by the way?"

"Of course," Darka replied. "I also had food from a box. A dry breakfast!"

"Dry breakfast for lunch?"

"You know . . ." Darka smiled gleefully. "A person usually has three breakfasts a day, they just call the second one lunch and the third dinner. For some variety. Do you understand?"

"Well sure." Taras nodded. "Understood!"

He listened to Darka, who was more talkative than usual, and from time to time he glanced out of the café's rain-washed windows. He was waiting for them to give him a signal, he didn't want to miss a pause in the rain. And once the windows lit the café up by just a touch, he sprang into action, helping Darka put on her coat, and picking her umbrella up from the floor himself.

Outside they managed to catch a fleeting ray of sunlight.

The break in the rain brought them back to the bar Dominik, where they were forced to wait for an hour until a renewed downpour quietened down or even stopped, giving the lovers a chance to step out again and head for the city's oldest quarters.

"How's your allergy?" Taras asked tentatively.

"Not causing me any trouble for now. I'm clever about it! I don't provoke it!"

"You know, a client of mine who came over here from Poland said that in Belgium they're thinking up new treatments for allergies." Taras' voice was quiet, uncertain.

Darka shook her head.

"Caution is the best medicine!" she said.

At around six, she asked Taras to put her in a taxi and went home to rest before work.

The rain had turned to drizzle. Taras walked home in good spirits. Passing a small shop, he couldn't help going in to buy a small bottle of cognac. As he entered his courtyard, he noticed that the light was on in Yezhi Astrovsky's apartment. He fancied a chat with his neighbour.

Yezhi was thrilled to see him. He ushered Taras in, but asked him to immediately take off his boots.

"I've cleaned up in here today," he said proudly.

The room really was spotless. It seemed like the cleaning had only just finished. On the windowsills, revealed by the tied-back curtains, stood flowerpots holding century plants. The hairdresser's seat was covered once more with a sheet. The table at which they'd very recently drunk coffee was now decorated with a green glass vase. The red head of an artificial rose peered shyly out of the neck.

Taras placed the bottle of cognac next to the vase and looked at his host.

Yezhi shook his head.

"I don't drink anymore," he declared softly, not wanting

to offend his guest. "Only in cultured social environs. I've got great tea, by the way. And I bought a new kettle. With a whistle!"

"Well, I'd kind of set my heart on the cognac." Taras looked towards the windows, through which clouds could be seen descending over the courtyard.

"One doesn't prevent the other," said the host, leaving for the kitchen.

He brought a spirit glass and two teacups. Taras filled the glass with cognac. He tasted it.

"I wanted to get some advice," he confessed to his host.

"From me?" Yezhi looked surprised.

"Sure, as a neighbour."

"Of course, anything I can do to help." Yezhi nodded. "I'd be happy to, you know that . . ."

"By the way, you don't happen to have any rare diseases, do you?" Taras asked, lowering his voice suddenly.

"No, why?"

"It's just that . . . my girlfriend has a strong allergy to money . . ."

"To money?" Yezhi sounded surprised.

And then the kettle began to whistle from the kitchen. The conversation was interrupted briefly, but a minute later Yezhi was back at the table.

"So, what, she can't stand money?"

"Not her, her body. She gets lesions, rashes, itches . . . But yesterday this Pole offered me some treatment for her . . . Belgian treatment . . ."

"Means it's expensive, probably . . ."

"No, you could say it was free even, she pays by being the first to try it . . ."

Yezhi considered this. His face became so serious that Taras froze.

"You know," Yezhi said eventually, "I'm not sure I'd let her be treated, if I were in your place . . ."

"Why's that?"

"What, you rolling in it or something? If she's allergic to money, it means she'd be fine without it too! My ex-wife . . ." Tears twinkled in Yezhi's eyes. "She was the opposite, she loved money so much we had to break up. If only she'd had an allergy! I'd already be a granddad by now . . ."

They didn't talk any more of Darka at the table. Taras' neighbour was riding the waves of his own memories. He could sense that Taras was a gracious listener, and he started telling him about his marriage and his ex-wife, Teresa Vladimirovna. He talked about her tenderly, like a lost treasure. Outside the window it was darkening and lulling, which made the light of the three-pronged chandelier on the ceiling seem brighter and brighter.

At one point Yezhi went quiet, thinking. Then he got up and went over to the cupboard. The veneer door creaked. Taras looked around and saw shirts and jackets lined up on hangers.

"Here!" The host's voice sounded joyous. "Come and look!"

In Yezhi's hands was a long dress. He held it out in front of him so that the hem just brushed the floor. Dark blue, with small bright red and yellow flowers; it was genuinely beautiful.

"Come here! Hold it like this," he requested.

Taras took the dress by the hanger. It felt surprisingly light, almost weightless.

Yezhi, meanwhile, took a couple of steps off to the side and froze, fixing his gaze once more on the dress.

"You see?" he asked after a minute. "No, you can't see it! She was so shapely! And when she collected her things, she caused a right scandal over this dress! Tore up the whole apartment! But I'd hidden it with Arkadievna, the old lady who lived opposite. Had to keep something for old time's sake . . . That and I didn't want her to be twirling around in this dress for anybody else. Sniff it, by the way, go on, give it a sniff!"

Taras lifted the dress to his face and buried his nose into the fabric. He could pick up a barely noticeable sweet scent.

"Red October perfume," Yezhi explained. "Her favourite. I spray the dress with it once a year . . . And you see, the moths don't take to it!"

Taras returned to the table, laden with the thought that he had never seen Darka in a dress. And she was never without her gloves, ten different colours probably, right up to her elbows. But she couldn't exist without the gloves, she wasn't allowed not to wear them!

Yezhi, after carefully folding the dress and hiding it back in the cupboard, brewed some fresh tea. His face showed a quiet happiness and calm. It shone so brightly from the peculiar purity of his thoughts and feelings that Taras paused, looking his neighbour in the eyes. He paused and listened to the encroaching silence. He didn't want to talk anymore.

And suddenly, the silence was blown to smithereens.

Something outside rang out, thumped, a woman's scream hit the closed windows of the apartment and faded away before Taras and Yezhi were able to make it out. Yezhi ran to the nearest window, opened the ventilation pane, pushed the century-plant flowerpot to one side and clambered up onto the sill. Taras jumped up too.

"Quickly! Outside!" Yezhi commanded him, jumping from windowsill to floor. "They're beating a woman out there!"

Yezhi managed to run to the kitchen and grab a frying pan. They made it to the courtyard at the same time. The light falling from the windows lit up a squatting woman covering her head with her hands. By her feet lay a torn paper bag; next to it were a white baguette, canned fish, a disc of half-boiled kolbasa that had spilled out of its packet, and a whole herring.

Taras looked to either side, listening carefully. The sudden quiet scared him. It seemed like the bandits that had attacked this woman had quickly taken cover somewhere just nearby.

A strange briny smell tickled Taras' nostrils. He bent down to the woman and touched her on the shoulder.

"Everything's okay!" He tried to calm her down. "They ran away! Stand up!"

The woman slowly lowered her arms and looked at Taras fearfully. He grew scared, seeing blood on her face.

"Come up to my apartment," Yezhi said to her. "Let's go!"

While Yezhi helped the woman to her feet, Taras gathered her purchases back into the bag, and held it up from underneath – the handles had been ripped off.

After settling the woman in the kitchen, Yezhi fetched a wet towel. Taras called the police and an ambulance.

"Bastards!" Yezhi whispered, using the towel to wipe away the blood that was pouring from the wounds on her face. "What did they hit you with?"

The woman twitched but didn't respond. She would just lift a scared face to Yezhi from time to time, then at Taras next to him.

After a few minutes a police jeep entered the courtyard. The officers greeted Taras and stamped their dirty boots into the kitchen.

"Who did this to her?" asked a youngish sergeant.

"We didn't see," answered Taras. "By the time we ran out they'd already gone."

"They attacked from above," came her weak, trembling voice. "From above, like birds! And they were laughing while they did it!"

The ambulance arrived five minutes later. The female paramedic looked over the victim.

"Again . . ." She sighed heavily.

"What again?" the older of the police officers asked guardedly.

"Face and arms lacerated with a thin, sharp object," the paramedic explained. "Third time this week! Some maniac has got his hands on a weapon!"

She helped the victim get up, and with the assistance of the sergeant, who held her by the other arm, she led the woman from the apartment.

The older police officer held back a moment and took down Taras and Yezhi's phone numbers.

Both vehicles left, and it was quiet again.

Yezhi quietly picked up the mop and started mopping the kitchen floor. His eyes caught the paper bag filled with produce. He laid its contents out on the table. The disc of kolbasa went into the fridge.

"Perhaps some cognac after all? To counteract the stress?" Taras suggested.

"It's already late," said Yezhi. "And sober heads are met with pleasant dreams, free of horrible things like that." He nodded at the window, through which the autumn evening was just ready to turn to night.

Taras couldn't sleep at all. He twisted and turned, lying on his back with his eyes open. A few times he got up and went over to the window. It was quiet and still outside. He lay down again, but found no way of getting to sleep. The whole time he was thinking of the woman, the one whose attackers had come "from above, like birds". Her cries from the courtyard. The blood on her face. The terror in her eyes. These memories caused some kind of strange stupor in his body. This is probably how a hare feels just as a boa constrictor eyes it up, ready to swallow.

Taras reached for the dresser and grabbed his mobile. He called Darka.

"How are you?" he asked.

"Fine," answered a familiar voice. "It's quiet, nobody here. They came from the casino, got ten thousand dollars changed. I'm out of hryvnia again. Everyone needs hryvnia at night, for some reason. But dollars in the day . . ."

"Well, I can't sleep," Taras complained.

"Have a drink!" Darka advised.

"Already did. Didn't help."

"Then come here! We'll have a chat!"

"I've had a drink, haven't I?" Taras began to explain. "I can't get behind the wheel. I can only walk."

"Then walk!"

"You know," Taras started speaking more slowly. "I'm scared. A woman was attacked today in our courtyard . . ."

"Well, women get attacked all the time. And men are only attacked when there are no women around." Darka's voice grew sly and playful. "And all of a sudden I want coffee!"

"Right now?"

"Right now!"

"Okay, I'm up!" Taras put a foot on the floor.

"Get up, get up!" Darka egged him on. "No point in lying around!"

In the courtyard Taras listened carefully to the night-world surrounding him. What first seemed like silence gradually differentiated into a plethora of micro-sounds, some coming from Taras' own bodily core. He could hear distinctly his own heartbeat, not even in his ears, but in his skin. He heard the distant hum of a plane somewhere high up in the dark heavens. He heard something not entirely intelligible, but rhythmic, with the qualities of a certain industrial melody, almost like an eternally running lathe or conveyor belt. Once this melody went quiet, Taras realised that somewhere in the distance a train had passed.

Taras calmed down once it was beyond the boundaries of earshot. He went out onto Pekarska. Now he himself became the main source of sound. He listened to his own steps as he walked, trying all the while to tread as softly as he could, to make his steps as quiet as possible.

Near Halytsky Market Taras was gripped by a now-familiar discomfort, and started walking more briskly, like he was trying to escape the danger zone. And in actual fact, after walking thirty to forty metres, he stopped at the corner of Franko Street and froze, realising that the sensation had released him as quickly as it had seized him just a few moments before. He looked to either side and listened carefully. Nothing out of the ordinary, just a slight saltiness on the tongue. After adjusting the bag carrying the Thermos over his shoulder, Taras took a few steps backwards, towards Halytsky Market. And immediately he felt strange, unpleasant vibrations. But when he paid close attention to his own body this time, the sensations that arose didn't cause any further discomfort, just fear and curiosity.

The cognac he'd had that evening could absolutely have been the reason for the curiosity. Taras took another few steps back, and there he felt a jolt. A shiver went through his entire body from top to bottom. He froze. The curiosity disappeared. All that was left was fear and the salty air, which was hard to breathe. A sudden cry came from above, reminding him of an ancient laugh, some kind of bird. It flapped its wings. Taras jerked his head and saw something white falling at him. He hit the white with his hand as if it were a ball, and the white, which turned out to be heavy and soft, flew off to one side and, with a flap of its wings, started to rise into the invisible night sky. Taras ran back to the start of Franko Street, but he stumbled on the road and barely kept his footing. He looked over his shoulder and saw something strange, that reminded him of a crab, quickly running off to the wall of the nearest house and falling through the opening of a ventilation pipe, down into the sewers. A cold sweat appeared on his forehead. He wiped it with his palm and felt a prickling pain. He stepped a little closer to the dully lit window of a café and lifted his palm to his face. He saw blood. He looked back and listened closely. And suddenly he tore off, running headlong to Darka's bureau de change, which was just around the "boomerang" of the street up ahead.

26

Alik Olisevych was woken before dawn by the sound of his phone ringing from over near the door somewhere. It may have woken him, but he wasn't getting up from the sofa. It was still dark outside. A light drizzle rustled almost inaudibly, and the melody of the phone against the background of the rain sounded pleasant and not at all irritating. Alik turned onto his stomach and drifted off again.

At somewhere around nine he woke up and remembered his ringing mobile. He fished it out of his jacket pocket. Five calls from Ryabtsev. The first at six in the morning!

What's gotten him so worked up? he thought. He called back.

"You heard the news on the radio?" Ryabtsev asked worriedly, not even greeting him.

"I only just got up!"

"Then listen! There was a robbery overnight, of a fishmongers on Lypynskoho, a whole live fish was taken through a smashed shop window. A few bird feathers were left behind at the scene of the crime. In the last two days there have been five identical attacks on women. Nothing stolen, but their faces and arms were lacerated with thin, sharp objects. The attacks all took place in one region. One of the victims swears that she was attacked by two huge, white birds."

"Okay, so what?" Alik tried to understand the former captain's agitation. "So a shop was robbed? What's new? It's sad about the women, of course! But thank God they're still alive!"

"All five victims confirm that before their attacks they felt ill, they were nauseous, and they could taste salt on their tongues! It's what I told you about! Remember?"

"About the Carpathian sea?" Alik asked.

"Exactly! Are you home right now?"

"Yes."

"Don't go out, I'm on my way!"

Alik lay back down on the sofa. And suddenly it was like he'd been thrown back up. He remembered walking back that night from Ryabtsev's not too long ago, from Sykhiv. Ryabtsev said that the women had also tasted salt on their tongues. Did that mean something similar had happened to them? But no, they were then attacked!

Alik made himself tea. He took his mug into the courtyard, under the light, drizzling rain.

Thanks to the wet road, the cars were passing down Zamarstynivska more loudly than usual. The low sky promised continuing rain, perhaps even an escalation from drizzle to downpour.

In such weather it's nice to stay at home, even if the home is as small as Alik's. Such weather only emphasises the cosiness of any space covered by a roof and protected from the rest of the world by one's own walls.

After half an hour Ryabtsev knocked on the unlocked door, walked in without a word, and sat in the armchair by the stove.

"Well, hello!" He stared at Alik, who was sat on his permanently unfolded sofa-bed. "What are we going to do then?"

Alik shrugged. "What is there to do?"

"We need to save the city! Is it not our city, after all?! All bells must be rung! Tell the tabloids – they'll probably make some noise! Just look at all the noise they made over that rascal 'Doctor Pi'![16] And this is a much more serious matter! Perhaps by now even the police and the secret service have twigged what's going on?"

Alik nodded. There was little doubt that this was a matter of more interest to the tabloids than it was to him, a serious person working as a stage light operator in the Opera House. But then why had the captain come here, to his place on Zamarstynivska, and not gone straight to the office of the *Express*?!

"So, what then?" Ryabtsev's voice broke the silence. "Let's put our heads together!"

"I'm happy to." Alik looked at the former captain entirely seriously. "Only I don't know what I'm meant to be thinking about – or how!"

"Don't you worry!" Having received a positive signal from Alik, Ryabtsev relaxed. "I'll talk, and you listen and react! That way we'll come up with a quick plan of action! That's how we did it in the service: one talks, the other two or three listen and question. So, what do we have? Anomalous natural occurrences . . . ?" Ryabtsev stared into Alik's eyes.

Alik understood what his old acquaintance wanted from him and nodded. Ryabtsev gave a no-nonsense smile.

"Anomalous natural occurrences which we have already identified: the release of salty sea air with a clear presence of iodine in different regions of the city."

Alik nodded.

"In the places that this air is released, there is also a disturbance in the atmosphere and, you would imagine, in the magnetic fields, which throws any person situated in that location into disarray and panic."

Alik nodded again in response to the former captain's fixed stare. He was suddenly enjoying the clarity and precision with which Ryabtsev was laying out his thoughts. It wasn't at all like when he had tried to explain his worries over the telephone that morning, to a much sleepier Alik. He now understood why Ryabtsev had explained himself so cryptically on the phone – he'd had nobody in front of him, nobody to absorb his stare!

"These very local anomalous changes in the atmosphere don't just send people into a panic, but also any birds that are programmed by nature for a life by the sea – that is, the seagulls!" Ryabtsev lifted his right hand, pointing at the ceiling while clearly intending the sky. "This must mean the sea air awakens some kind of instinct in the gulls . . . Most likely their hunting instinct! Seagulls live in flocks. One such flock most likely broke into the fishmongers on Lypynskoho, and once inside they stole all the live fish they had in stock . . ."

Ryabtsev froze, as if he were struck by his own thoughts

being said out loud. His mouth opened. He looked at the stove, then lifted his eyes to the window.

"Listen, where would seagulls have come from to reach Lviv?" he asked suddenly, returning his gaze to his host.

Alik shrugged.

"The landfill, probably, by Hrybovychi . . ."

"But before the landfill they lived somewhere near the sea, surely?"

"No idea," Alik sighed.

"Alright, we'll get back to our analysis. So, you and I have agreed that the salty air seeps up from underground? Yes?"

Alik considered this. This proposition still gave him doubts, but everything else Ryabtsev had laid out was so logical and coherent! Maybe it really had come from underground!

He nodded indecisively.

"We need as many people as possible to pay attention to this issue! Which means we should kick up some kind of sensation in the papers! What do you think?" said Ryabtsev.

"I agree," Alik said firmly.

"If you were the one to go to their offices and tell them about it all, they'd think you were high!" Ryabtsev's voice lost some of its assured intonation. "If I go, they'll think I'm a psycho. We need someone else to do it . . ."

"Who?" asked Alik.

"We need a person who you can trust, relatively well known in the city . . ."

"A writer?" Alik blurted out.

"Why a writer?" There was a live spark in Ryabtsev's eyes.

"Well, who else are they going to believe? A politician?"

"You're right," agreed the former captain. "Nobody believes politicians. But they'd believe, I don't know, some university professor or other!"

"I know a guy." Alik sensed an inexplicable passion taking control of him. "He's a writer *and* he teaches in a university!"

"Who is it?" Ryabtsev leaned forward with his entire body.

"Yurko Vynnychuk! He's about my age . . ."

"Is he just as hairy? A hippie too?"

"No, the opposite, he's balding. He was never a hippie, he just drank . . ."

"I reckoned as much, I never heard the name back then . . ."

"I've got his number. He lives in Vynnyky!" said Alik, and mentioning the Lviv suburb turned his thoughts suddenly to the free shower and free clothes-washing that he'd been offered there.

Alik thought of round-faced Oksana. And he thought about a hot shower. He suddenly really wanted a hot shower. No, not just to soap up and pass a loofah over himself. He could do that any day he wanted, after the end of a performance, in the shower next to the dressing rooms. No, he wanted to just stand there and "listen", with his whole body, to hot water pouring across his skin. And he wanted a sheer, cold, unbreaking rain outside.

"What is it?" Ryabtsev asked impatiently. "Have you got any better ideas?"

"No." Alik broke out of his daydream. "But I'll call him now . . ."

Ten minutes later, in gushing rain, they were already driving the yellow Piaggio to meet Yurko Vynnychuk. Alik sat on the back again, uncomfortably holding onto the former captain with his arms, clasping them round his stomach. Alik's wide-brimmed leather hat was partially protecting him from the rain, but his hair was still messy from the wind, and rainwater was channelling through it in streams. Ryabtsev's bald spot, which Alik's chin would be sure to crash into if he were to suddenly brake, was gleaming with water, despite being barely noticeable in dry weather.

Yurko Vynnychuk was waiting for them at the Magic Lantern, a bar on Fedorova. He was sat at the bar with a glass of white wine. His ironed grey trousers, shiny black pointy shoes and beige chunky-knit sweater gave him an unusual gravitas. People don't drink vodka in an outfit like that! Alik thought.

"Yurko." Alik introduced his ancient acquaintance to the former captain.

"Ryabtsev." The captain presented himself and held out a hand.

"And your name and patronymic?" Yurko Vynnychuk asked, taken aback at his abruptness.

Alik wanted to quickly supply Ryabtsev's name and patronymic himself to move to the matter at hand more quickly, but he realised with some surprise that he didn't know either. Dumbfounded, he "jumped" back into his memory, but there all he came up with was "Captain Ryabtsev".

"Pan Yuri," Ryabtsev addressed Vynnychuk with exaggerated politeness. "To be honest with you, I haven't used my first name for forty years now, if not longer. While my mother was still alive I used it, then I stopped . . . The thing was, I served in the KGB."

"In Lviv?" Vynnychuk asked.

"Yes, but we're here about something else . . . Can we sit?" Ryabtsev suggested, looking over at a free table by the stained-glass window.

"So what's this 'sensation' you've got then?" Vynnychuk asked impatiently.

Ryabtsev, making attentive eye contact with the writer, told him in great detail all about his theory about the anomalous occurrences taking place in Lviv. Yurko Vynnychuk listened to the former captain with a frown; a couple of times an ironic smile played on his lips. Ryabtsev couldn't help but notice it, and his voice as he finished sounded quieter and less assured. Alik reckoned that he was pining for his old service "handler". He wanted Vynnychuk to take Ryabtsev's words seriously, but at the same time he remembered the benders they used to go on together, back when Yurko loved to make cruel jokes, always opted for irony, and never took anything seriously.

"Yes-ss," Vynnychuk sighed after hearing Ryabtsev out and holding a two-minute pause. "We'd be able to kick up a twenty-four hour sensation over this . . ."

"Pan Yuri," Ryabtsev interrupted him. "Ask Alik, he wouldn't lie . . . This is really all happening!"

"Perhaps it's happening for you in Lviv, but here in Vynnyky it's just peace and quiet!" Vynnychuk continued patiently. "The nighttime releasing of salty air or gas, that might be interesting . . ." Vynnychuk's eyes gradually lit up with an idea. "If, for example, there was a narco lab in operation, there would have to be some sort of gas build-up . . . They could be storing it until nightfall, then releasing it . . ." Vynnychuk surveyed Ryabtsev with an entirely serious and inquisitive look. "Do you not remember that in the Soviet era they stored chemical weapons in this city's territory?"

"Sure, they stored them everywhere," Ryabtsev shrugged. "Then they took them away ... Chemical weapons don't smell, if something's up with them, they just kill ... And poisonous gases smell different, not like iodine ..."

"You know your way around gases then?" asked Vynnychuk.

"Hardly," Ryabtsev confessed. "I didn't do gases, I specialised in hippies."

Vynnychuk's expression became briefly more upbeat, and he looked to Alik.

"So what, you've been together since back then? Bound by one chain?" he said in a sing-song voice.

"No, Pan Yuri." Ryabtsev sighed. "Until this September, Alik and I hadn't seen each other since 1986! I always respected him and I always will! There was just something important that I had to tell him. That's why I went and found him in September."

"And what was that something?" Vynnychuk enquired.

Alik was just about to open his mouth to tell him, when from the corner of his eye he noticed the former captain's palm rise above the table.

"No need," Ryabtsev said in a voice that had some unexpected steel in it. "If pan Writer doesn't believe what we're telling him now, he won't believe the rest either!"

"Pan Ryabtsev, don't think I'm making a joke of you." Vynnychuk's face became more welcoming. "I've remembered everything and I'll think it over. I very much enjoy thinking, but usually in solitude . . . It's just a habit of mine. Me, a glass of wine and some thoughts. I have Alik's number. If I think of something, or more questions come up, I'll find you . . . Do you read my column, by the way?" Vynnychuk looked at the former captain with a disarming smile on his face.

"Column?" Ryabtsev asked, lost. "I don't normally buy the papers . . ."

"Do you use the internet?"

"No, I have other forms of entertainment," Ryabtsev admitted. "Doves . . ."

27

The rainy morning brought Taras a surprise email from Russia. An unknown man named Arnold offered himself as an exclusive agent for Taras across the Ryazan Oblast.

Where'd he find out about me?! Taras wondered, reading through the long and detailed email, which read more like a business plan.

Arnold promised to get him twenty to thirty clients a month for a thirty percent commission and a share in the business. "Share in the business" made Taras exert his tired brain even more. The previous night's work hadn't been particularly arduous – the latest Polish client's stones proved small and amenable. There were three of them, but they had all come out relatively easily. Taras was already free by three in the morning and spent an hour and a half at the bureau chatting with Darka, and slowly sipping strong coffee from the "Venetian" ashtrays. There was a bitter taste on his tongue from the coffee even now, and Darka's alarmed voice was still ringing in his ears. It had happened once he'd already got home, just a couple of hours ago. Darka had suddenly called him and told him about a strange customer who had come up to the window at half past five and asked for a glass of fresh water.

"Maybe he was drunk. I explained to him that I didn't have any water. He left, but then he came back and spent half an hour rocking me, until Orest Vasilievich came for me," she told him in a still shaky voice.

Why had she called him a customer, Taras wondered, remembering their conversation almost word for word.

He looked back at the email from Ryazan on his laptop screen.

What the hell does a "share in the business" mean? An implacable irritation took hold of Taras. So what, I'm meant to buy an old bus just to shake some stones out of the citizens of Ryazan in bulk?!

He shook his head wearily. He looked at the clock – just past eight.

Taras got undressed and lay under the duvet.

Sleep came immediately, but it brought with it a nightmare, from which Taras didn't manage to escape for the following several hours. In his dream, he and Oksana were walking along Kopernyk, and as they went past the shop "Semena", Taras wanted to show her the courtyard where an old acquaintance of his had once lived. In the little courtyard, woven with grapevines and ivy, they were suddenly attacked from above by birds – enormous white seagulls. The seagulls crashed into them feet first and started to peck. Taras lay on his back, kicking the birds away with his legs; he couldn't see them, but he heard them. He used his hands to cover his cheeks and eyes. But the birds pressed down onto him, beating their wings, and swiped their sharp claws across the back of his hands and his arms. Oksana was crying next to him. He threw his hands from his face, which scared the birds off momentarily, and turned to look at her. She was sat on the ground, waving her arms. Her face and hands were bloodied. A few seagulls were circling her, bobbing their heads and preparing to attack. One of them dropped down from above.

"Look out!" Taras shouted.

But Oksana couldn't hear him. The attacking seagull gripped her hair in its claws and gave her a strong jab with its beak. Oksana cried out, lifted her hands and tried to grab at the bird's side, but the gull wasn't scared, and simply twisted its neck to bite Oksana's hand. Then suddenly, a sharp pain in his neck forced Taras to forget about Oksana. He grabbed at his neck and blood poured over his fingers, warm and sticky. He looked up and saw several seagulls circling above him. They were dropping lower and lower. A sharp pain in his leg made him look down. The seagull that had just bitten him shot off a metre to the side and tensed its neck once more in preparation for an attack. Taras, full of pain and malice, jumped at the seagull and kicked it like a football. It flew off to the side, but the pain in Taras' leg grew stronger, making him clench his teeth. He leaned forward to look at the wound and realised that the right leg of his trousers, blood seeping through it, was sticking to his shin just below the knee. He looked over at Oksana – she was lying unmoving, face-down on the ground. Two seagulls stood on her back, swivelling their bloodied beaks from side to side.

Taras only woke up once he'd died in the dream, torn apart and mangled by the vicious birds. He was drenched. He took a long time to come to his senses.

It was only by three in the afternoon that Taras could entirely distinguish between nightmare and reality. And even once he'd distinguished, he couldn't get away from it at all. He could still hear the evil birds cackling, and their great white wings beating. He could still hear Oksana's screaming. And now a new, real worry took over, a worry for Oksana. Perhaps it wasn't a coincidence that she, specifically, had been in his dream? Not Darka, to whom nothing unpleasant, unless you counted her strange "customer" asking for a glass of fresh water, had occurred last night – specifically Oksana!

Taras remembered the smashed aquarium in Oksana's apartment, the smashed window, the blood dripping from the windowsill, the terror caught in her eyes.

He remembered the Hitchcock film, the one about birds attacking people. But in that film, the birds were small and black, they looked like thrushes. But this morning's nightmare had been much scarier and more realistic than any horror film. The raspy gull laugh-cry was still tearing into his ears, scratching at his eardrums.

Taras called Oksana.

"Everything alright with you?" he asked.

"Yes, what is it?"

"I had a nightmare about you, about me and you."

"A nightmare? About me?" Oksana's voice was trembling. "You busy?"

"No."

"I'm at home today. Come over, tell me about it! It might be serious ... I'll feed you potatoes and mushrooms. I'm assuming you haven't had lunch yet?"

"Nor breakfast. Alright. With you shortly."

"You look so pale," was Oksana's reaction as she let her friend into the apartment. "Come through, I've already warmed it all up!"

Taras sat at the movable serving table.

"I've already eaten," Oksana told him, putting a plate of mushroom ragu down in front of him and a dish with thinly sliced lard. "But you eat up and tell me about this dream!"

Taras told her, and as he did so he listened to his own story, surprised at what he was saying, how it now seemed bigger and more detailed than how he'd actually experienced it in the nightmare itself.

And suddenly a loud sharp seagull cry burst into the room, making Taras jump; his fork fell from his hand, hit the edge of his plate and dropped to the floor.

"Oh, it's mine!" Oksana jumped down from her stool. "I forgot to sellotape its beak up after feeding it! Come and help me!"

They went over to the window. Oksana pulled back the curtain and Taras saw the familiar seagull in its cardboard box, wings tied up, beak fearsome. Oksana cut off a strip of sellotape with scissors. She looked over at her guest.

"Grab it by the neck, and use your other hand to close the beak, but be gentle, softly!"

Taras reached for the bird with shaking hands. Oksana used practised motions to wrap the beak in sellotape, then sighed in relief. She went back to the table. Taras took his place on the sofa. A little rat plush toy fell on his shoulder, one of Oksana's "Sofa Zoo" collection.

"She loves you," Oksana smiled. "You're not in a rush then?"

Taras shook his head.

"It's just that this isn't the kind of dream that people usually have." The smile disappeared from Oksana's face.

"That's why I called," said Taras. "It's probably best you get rid of it!" Taras looked over at the window, where the sellotape-muted seagull was now covered by the curtain again.

"I'll let it out once the wounds heal."

"And where are the fish?" Taras wondered aloud.

"On another windowsill, in the hallway."

The room was quiet for a couple of minutes. Taras silently finished his potatoes and mushrooms, looking at Oksana's face, which was reflecting the full emotional palette of her thoughts: worry, doubt, self-confidence and uncertainty. Her face suddenly came alive, her eyes lit up by something that had occurred to her.

"Will you come with me?" she asked.

"Where?"

"Just next door, to a friend of mine." Oksana faltered, picking the right words. "I sometimes confer with her on the matter of dreams . . . it's her job."

"You're taking me to a fortune teller?" Taras clarified.

"Not exactly," Oksana replied evasively.

28

The Laboratory for Paranormal Occurrences was two blocks' walk from Oksana's apartment. Taras was aware of this strange little building, the ground-floor exterior of which was painted a rich blue. On several occasions he'd stopped while passing by chance to stare at the elephants that decorated the facade and read the unintelligible, almost deliberately confusing quotes stencilled onto the window glass. No matter how many times he stopped, his curiosity could never compel him to go inside. But now the force leading him – or more precisely, shepherding him – into the building was Oksana. She stopped just outside and sent a text from her phone. The door opened a minute later, and a large lady in a long black dress let them in.

"This one's with you?" The lady indicated Taras with a heavy, brown-eyed gaze.

"Yes." Oksana nodded and went on ahead, forcing the lady in black to follow her.

Oksana approached a broad writing table covered in a burgundy cloth and sat herself in a semi-antique high-armed chair. The lady skirted around the table and lowered herself, grandiosely, into her own armchair. She pulled an open laptop towards herself, clacked her manicured nails on the keyboard and raised her head.

Taras hovered behind Oksana's back.

"Grab the little chair over there." The lady indicated the neighbouring table, which was simpler and had no tablecloth. "And sit down!"

From that point onwards the woman's face took on a completely different expression, less strict, less formal. Her face became invitingly inquisitive, and she now looked Oksana straight in the eyes.

"Tell me everything!"

"He . . . had a dream about me," Oksana started nervously, glancing at Taras.

The lady looked over at the young man.

Taras started describing his frightful dream blow by blow, looking somewhat indifferently at the employee of the Laboratory for Paranormal Occurrences. On the one hand, this complete waste of time was dampening his mood; on the other, the meeting was clearly important and meaningful to Oksana, so Taras tried to sound convincing and engaged, and didn't skip a single detail.

As the dream's recounting approached its finale, the recounter's dry mouth forced him to look either side in search of, if not a bottle of mineral water, then at least a pitcher. The lady in black got up as he cast about. She walked out of the room, leaving the visitors on their own.

The dim lighting almost seemed to make the opposite corner of the room disappear. Taras tried with some difficulty to make out, over there in the veiled, windowless depths, yet another table, where some books were stacked to the left of a computer monitor. One of the books was open. A table-top lamp was hanging over the pile like an old overhead projector. Taras imagined turning it on and "saw" a pretty, gentle, almost homely cone of light falling onto the books. This table had no pompous tablecloth, but on the wall next to it was a schematic map of the city.

Taras was just about to get up and walk over there when the door suddenly opened without a sound, and the lady in black walked back into the room.

She sat back in her seat and trained her eyes on the laptop screen for a moment, clacking one more nail against a key.

"Young man." She fixed a stern eye on Taras.

Taras gripped the back of the chair, sensing some kind of non-physical pressure emanating from the custodian of this poorly lit space.

"Young man, you wouldn't happen to be a cinephile?"

Taras was caught off guard by the question.

"No, I almost never go to the cinema," he said.

"And do you enjoy horror films?"

Taras shrugged.

"Okay, we'll be more specific," she continued. "Do you know of the Hitchcock film, *The Birds*?"

Taras nodded.

"Perhaps you've watched it in the last few days?"

"I can't even recall the last time I watched it. I remembered it all of a sudden thanks to that dream, that's for sure. And also ... I forgot to say! An actual seagull attacked me! It tried to nosedive right on my head, I punched it away and it flew off."

"Really?!" The lady was truly surprised. "This happened in the daytime? Who else saw it?"

"No, at night. In the dark. Walking down the street. There was nobody around."

The lady's eyes flashed with doubt. She blinked a few times, squinted at Oksana and looked back at Taras.

"There was nobody around," she repeated thoughtfully. "Tell me, do you have a woman?"

"There's a woman I like," Taras replied noncommittally.

"Do you dream of her?"

"Sometimes, yes."

"Would you call the dreams that she's in nightmares?"

"No," Taras sighed hurriedly, glancing at Oksana. "But why were you asking about horror films?"

"People who enjoy horror films often see continuations of those films in their dreams, and sometimes even in real life."

"Ahh." Taras thought for a moment. "I see ... but I think ..." He looked at Oksana again.

"You think what?"

"I think I might know where I got the seagulls from ... Oksana! Have you told her about your window?"

"No." Oksana jolted in her seat as if waking up; her voice had a child-like surprise to it. "What, should I?"

"Your window?" asked the lady in black.

And Oksana told her the story of the smashed window and the seagull that got caught in it.

"And this seagull is still with you?!" The lady in black was amazed. "Why didn't you come to us sooner?"

"I didn't think . . ."

Taras sighed heavily.

"You know," he began. "Nightmares are nightmares, but something very strange is going on! And these seagulls are everywhere! A couple of days ago a woman ran into our courtyard covered in blood and said that she'd been 'attacked from above, as if by birds' . . ."

The lady in black grew irritated.

"I'm primarily a dream specialist." Her voice trembled unexpectedly, as if from fright. "What you're describing now . . . that's something else entirely, I'm not the person to come to with that!"

"But he had the nightmare about me, didn't he?" Oksana began talking quickly. "And last time you really helped me, when I told you about my dream with the underground tram and the falling town hall . . ."

"That was a pure dream. But this . . . these are evidently vibrations . . . You absolutely must go to Simon Fyodor-ovich . . . only he won't take you, Oksanochka. He only does men!"

"What? Is he gay?" Oksana was taken aback.

"No, don't say that! It's just that interpreting dreams is a matter that primarily concerns women. But only men can properly explain vibrations and put them into words . . . Men can also sense them better than women . . . Because men aren't so emotional. I think –" the lady looked at Taras – "that you absolutely must schedule an appointment with Simon

Fyodorovich. You won't find a better expert on vibrations in all Ukraine! I'll write to him myself on your behalf, right now! For the day after tomorrow, at one in the morning! You'll be the first of the day!"

"So then what am I supposed to do?" Oksana asked, a little disconcerted, suddenly cast adrift in the conversation.

"Sweetheart, don't worry!" The lady in black's hand reached over to her visitor, as if she wanted to stroke her shoulder. "It'll all be okay!"

29

The midnight Chornovol Prospect was slowly leading Alik in the direction of home. The sky, which fifteen minutes ago had been driven back by heavy, gloomy clouds hovering over the Opera House and the old town, suddenly relaxed, cleared, and even surprised those living under it with the appearance of a round yolk of moon.

Winter lay ahead. It was perhaps two weeks away, a month maybe. Alik was reminded of the previous winter, a little protracted, but entirely pleasant for one sole reason: snow is better than rain! Living under constant rainfall isn't so bad either – people live in London, where it rains far more often than in Lviv! But snow is like a pure, fresh desert. Snow gives you a renewed sense of life. It rejuvenates. A person can use the snow to focus their eyes afresh. It's good that your eyes aren't worn out by looking at so many things. It was good that Alik could still take in the world without glasses. And even at night, he always felt he could see as clear as day.

Alik was surprised at how light his step was. He thought about how, over so many years of his life, he must've walked this road from the Opera House to his home on Zamarstynivska thousands of times! Here, before his eyes, the old had disappeared, and new buildings had taken their place: the St Paraskeva Medical Centre; the mast with the big yellow letter "M" of McDonalds, which he hadn't entered once in his etire life. If it were possible to even approximately count up all the kilometres he'd walked, and then put them in a straight line, tracing them on a map, setting off from Lviv, would it reach Berlin or Paris, perhaps? It probably would!

Alik smiled, thinking of how close Paris felt all of a sudden.

But something made a noise up above. Jerking his head upwards, Alik saw a flock of crows in the sky, between himself and the yellow moon, flying in the direction of the city centre. He stopped, keeping his eyes on the hundreds of black spots breaking up his private, nighttime sky. The crows flew silently, not cawing amongst themselves; it was like they'd long since agreed on all the details. All that was left was the collective rustle of their wings falling to earth, like invisible autumn leaves.

By now even the short Warsaw Street was left behind, and he was walking along his own, not particularly short Lviv street – Zamarstynivska.

Thursday was dawning again, but it would still be seven or eight hours until it matured into a fully-fledged day.

I wonder if that round-faced woman with the strict face and big camera will be there today, in the square? Alik thought. Thought, then laughed.

He wondered how it could be that he, a free man, could be taken for homeless?! That thin fellow too, the one who had sat next to him on the bench last time, he'd also talked to him like he was homeless . . . Although the homeless are also entirely free people, he supposed. At their core they're hippies all the same, only not by choice, but by dint of circumstance. They were drawn there by drunkenness or a certain instinct towards the street, so they did everything necessary to make it their native home.

"Our roof is the light blue sky, our joy is to live this life." Alik hummed the song from the old Soviet cartoon *The Bremen Musicians* to himself as he walked.

And suddenly a somewhat indistinct fear took hold of him, tearing away the cartoon song. Alik stopped, reached into the pockets of his denim jacket, grabbed his mobile from the right-hand side and moved it to the left. He checked his jeans pockets. And then he realised what the problem was. He searched for his house key. That key was always in his right-hand jacket pocket or, if he'd left his jacket at home, in the right-hand pocket of his jeans. But now it wasn't there. It wasn't anywhere.

Alik, at first more lost than annoyed, checked his pockets over and over, fingering through debris, scraps of paper that fell out of a box of cough tablets long ago, and other little things and particulars normally referred to as "pocket fodder". There was no key. The last doubts over its disappearance were banished, and now he needed to decide what to do next. The door was plywood, of course. It wouldn't be costly to break down, but that would disturb not only Alik's inner world, but the outer aura of his living space too. Breaking down doors is an act of violence. It's just the same as breaking a living thing's arm. No, he couldn't break it down! But that was his last key! A few years ago he'd had two, but then he lost the spare one, and now he'd lost the only other one as well . . .

Alik got out his mobile and twirled it in his hand, pondering. Who should he call, who to ask for help? Sure, there were firms which could open any lock for a hundred dollars. But he didn't have a hundred dollars. Better to stay somewhere overnight, and then in the morning, with a fresh head, he could peacefully resolve the conundrum.

Alik's recent musings on rough sleepers and freedom now seemed sneeringly fitting. He'd also become a rough sleeper. Even if just for one night.

His phone beeped in his hand – his finger had accidentally pressed a button. Alik looked down. Who would he be able to trouble now, at this time of night? He didn't want to disturb his friends over something so stupid. They had families, and besides, they would already be long asleep by now. The only people awake at such hours are romantics and fundamentally unhappy people, people who haven't found themselves a dependable place in life.

While he was having these thoughts, Captain Ryabtsev appeared before his eyes; lost, frightened, full of doubts and fears.

Alik dialled his number.

"Good evening," he said after hearing a lively "Hello!". "I lost my key . . . I don't know what to do . . ."

"Your key? Your house key, you mean?" Ryabtsev asked worriedly. "Well, where are you?"

"Zamarstynivska, just at the start of it . . ."

"Well then take a taxi or hitch a ride and come over to mine! Spend the night!"

"No." Alik sighed heavily. "There are no cars here . . . And I've not got the money for a taxi to Sykhiv . . ."

"Alright, then walk towards me, I'll come and pick you up . . . Somewhere in the region of thirty to forty minutes. Where can you get to in half an hour?"

Alik worked out an estimate.

"Somewhere by Verbova, I guess."

"Okay, that's where I'll look for you! See you there!"

Stowing his phone in his jacket pocket, Alik turned and walked back towards the city centre.

Former KGB captain Ryabtsev picked him up earlier than promised, which was a pleasant surprise.

The road to Sykhiv seemed much longer to Alik on this occasion. A couple of times he drifted off into daydreams, but then jolted his head up immediately and forced himself, through sheer willpower, to the "surface". He tightened his grip on the scrawny, grey-jacketed Ryabtsev.

Alik was only fully revived once the yellow Piaggio had stopped outside Ryabtsev's home on Osvytska. The captain asked Alik to wait there while he walked his vehicle down the thin path to the dovecote.

Alik stood swaying by the entrance. He looked at the block's dark windows and sensed his body become almost plastic, stretched out, but ready to suddenly clench, snap back and re-form, small and unnoticeable.

When they got up to the apartment, Ryabtsev poured Alik a glass of "cognac sedative".

The real Thursday morning only started for Alik at eleven o'clock. He lay on the sofa with his eyes open, listening to Ryabtsev's raspy breathing next to him.

Alik went into the kitchen and made himself tea. It was drizzling outside. The forest next to the building looked dark, the dovecote just about visible among the trees. In one of the neighbouring flats a radio was playing loudly. Alik looked out at the dovecote, and the forest, and started thinking about his return home. He reckoned that his flimsy door, pasted with all sorts of hippie nonsense, could probably just be jimmied up with a chisel or something, and then the latch of the lock might jump out of the bore itself. How deep could the latch go, one centimetre, maybe one and a half? No more than that. And he could ask the neighbours for a chisel, they'd probably have one. There might even be some metalworking tools of some sort in his shed, left over from his father. There might be something suitable in there.

"What, you didn't wake me?" The host peered into the kitchen in long boxers that went almost down to his knees.

"I've not woken up myself yet," Alik admitted.

"Had breakfast?" Ryabtsev nodded at the fridge.

Alik shook his head.

"Sit down then, I'll do some now!" Ryabtsev turned and left.

A couple of minutes later he peered in again, but he was now dressed and booted.

"Have you checked your pockets?" he asked. "Definitely no key?"

"No," sighed the guest.

The door slammed. It grew quiet. And Alik noticed that the neighbour's radio had also gone quiet. A solution to his key problem had been found. Now he just had to get back to his place on Zamarstynivska. But first he had to wait for the owner of the flat to return so he could drink a cup of coffee with him, nibble on a sandwich and thank him kindly for shooting across the city in the middle of the night to help out a person to whom he was in no way obligated.

Ryabtsev returned with a plastic bag, from which he carefully retrieved a few eggs and placed them on the kitchen table.

"Right then, shall I make eggs, or are we going to drink a couple raw?" he asked.

Alik thought. The question demanded a considered answer. In the past it wasn't uncommon for him to drink an egg or two in the morning, especially after a heavy night. He'd make a hole in the top of the egg, break through the opposite end and suck the contents out in a few seconds, which would then land on the pinch of salt he'd thrown on his tongue as a precaution. He didn't drink like he used to these days. There was nobody to drink with. His old Lviv friends had given it up. Penzel, Lyonya . . . Only his Lithuanian friends were still game, but they didn't come over that often.

Alik's reminiscences about the morning taste of raw egg made his decision for him. Ryabtsev was overjoyed to hear it. He put two dishes on the table, held out a teaspoon to his guest, and retrieved the salt from the windowsill.

The two eggs went down so quickly that Alik cast a sly look at the three that remained, sat there on their own plate.

"Go for it!" Ryabtsev nodded. "It's almost lunchtime, and you don't know when you'll next be able to eat!"

I do know, Alik thought, grabbing another egg from the plate. If only you were planning to drive back to the city centre!

"Forgive me for not giving you a lift home," Ryabtsev said to Alik fifteen minutes later as Alik tied the laces of his heavy boots.

"Don't worry about it." Alik, squatting on the floor, looked up at his host. "You've done way too much for me already!"

"Well, not quite too much yet . . . I've got a little something else for you," he said mysteriously.

Alik got up and did up all the buttons of his denim jacket without taking his eyes off Ryabtsev.

He took a folded piece of cloth from his trouser pocket and held it out to Alik.

Alik shook out into his palm . . . a key . . . a little sticky, smeared in something.

"You haven't changed the locks?" asked Ryabtsev with a hint of worry in his eyes.

"Not for the last thirty years."

"There you have it, how excellent! The past occasionally has its unexpected uses."

"So that's for what, my front door?" Alik was taken aback.

Ryabtsev nodded. His face took on a momentary guilty expression, which was almost immediately displaced by one of light, almost romantic sadness.

"Some time I'll tell you all the details of your life that you've forgotten yourself . . . If you want to, and if I'm in the mood . . . But really, I've taken very little from the past into the present . . . almost nothing. Besides, what I've taken doesn't rightfully belong to me, like this key here . . ."

The captain earnestly, fearlessly looked his guest in the eyes; his own showed neither embarrassment nor doubt. "But I never took anything from you, never switched places. I had to look into your home every two to three months and write a report. I came, sometimes I drank your coffee and sat on your sofa or armchair. Only when you weren't in the city. Usually at night, just before morning, when your neighbours and stepmother were fast asleep. Those really were magical moments . . . You aren't offended, are you?"

Alik shook his head.

"Thanks for the key!" he said, walking towards the door.

As he took his seat on the bus, his mobile rang in his jacket pocket.

"I completely forgot to mention the anomalies!" The agitated voice of the former captain exploded into his ear. "We mustn't forget about them! Have you seen your writer friend again?"

"No, not yet."

"My advice to you: take detours to avoid the start of Chornovol, as well as Hrushevsky, Franko and Pekarska. There've been more than twenty attacks on nighttime walkers in that area in the last month!"

30

The key he'd received from Ryabtsev slid so smoothly and easily into the keyhole that Alik nearly exclaimed in surprise. The one he'd lost the previous evening sometimes got caught in the lock, probably because many long years of service had scuffed and deformed its metal teeth. But the new key instantly found a "common tongue" with the lock, and Alik entered his home in awe, almost ceremoniously. He took his boots off at the door, sat in the armchair by the stove, and felt an unusual influx of emotion. As if a miracle had taken place, preserving the comforting aura of his home.

"Alichek, are you home?" He heard his stepmother's trembling voice from the courtyard.

She looked in through the open door and searched him out.

"Alichek, could you come and help me?" she asked. "I want to move the wardrobe."

The home's large main room, which his stepmother owned, had been cleaned.

"Where do you want to take it?" asked Alik, waiting by the tall, old-fashioned wardrobe.

"Just here," his stepmother gestured. "Do you remember where it was five years ago?"

"So what, back in its old spot?" Alik clarified.

"Yes! Today's exactly five years since we moved it. We also moved my bed away from the window back then, remember?"

"I do."

"Let's move that too."

"Back to its old place as well?"

"No, by the wall, where the table is. And the table closer to the window."

"So you've decided to change round all of the furniture!" Alik couldn't hide his surprise.

"It's helpful at my age. Gives you a fresh feeling. And lets you clean the floor under the wardrobe. There's so much dust under there!"

After spending fifteen minutes on the task, Alik drank a cup of tea with his stepmother and returned to his apartment.

He was tempted to move the furniture around in his own room too, but once he'd run an eye over the contents of his home, the urge disappeared. The old brick stove couldn't go anywhere, for a start. The sofa was in the only spot it could fit. The sink was in the corner left of the window, there was a coffee table under the window itself, and an armchair jammed in between the dining table and the stove. What fantasies could he be having here? None! There was nothing unnecessary and everything was in its rightful place. Perfect feng shui, as his friend, the theatre's costume designer, liked to say about situations which couldn't be changed.

Thus resolved, Alik called Yurko Vynnychuk and they agreed to meet.

31

They met in a café on Virmenska, where they'd been meeting for ten, twenty, even thirty years by now.

". . . And why are you messing around with this KGB guy?" Yurko Vynnychuk wondered aloud, sipping his coffee. "He's raving on about something insane, and you're listening to him!"

"You think it's insane?" Alik asked entirely seriously.

"Well, if he's not crazy, then it isn't insane, just complete nonsense! I asked our university's geologists. Only ground-water can be drawn upwards. If the earth is contaminated with construction waste or fertiliser then that rising water could be salty or full of chemicals, but it's got nothing to do with a prehistoric Carpathian sea. Are you sure he's normal, this acquaintance of yours?"

"I'm not sure." Alik sighed. "But I'm not sure I'm normal myself, and I'm not sure you are either. What's 'normal', anyway? Ninety-sixty-ninety? Vodka-beer-dried fish?"

"Normal –" Yurko gave his old friend a teacherly look –"is when an individual avoids the breaking of accepted written and unwritten laws in any given society. You, by the way, have never been normal. That's why people fought with you so much in the Soviet times!"

"Ahh!" Alik smiled. "Exactly – they called us 'abnormal' back then! But in that case captain Ryabtsev is entirely normal! It was him who tried to bring us, the hippies, back to 'normal'! Although, as it turns out, he wasn't personally interested in doing that! And he listened to Jimi Hendrix himself! And helped us out . . ."

"Which therefore means he's not 'normal'." Yurko quickly reached his conclusion. "And how did he 'help you out'?"

"Ryabtsev recently confessed that it was him and his friends who organised the transport of Hendrix's dead hand from the States, through the Baltics, all the way to us in Lychakiv."

"What?!" Vynnychuk's eyes, wide at the best of times, were now nearing circular. "You're telling me you actually believe that it's Hendrix's real hand in there?"

"Of course I believe it, I saw it. And me, Audrius and Vitas dug it out together. Penzel was there too. He can vouch for it."

"And what did you see?"

"What? The hand, dried out and vacuum-packed. And there were burn marks on it!"

"Alright, if you want to believe in miracles, be my guest!" Yurko waved him away. "You can go on helping your KGB friend to track down a prehistoric sea too! I've got no problem with it! In fact, I'm all in favour! I like it, an ironic performance by a former hippie and his former KGB officer."

"I'm not a 'former' hippie." Alik was offended.

"Well sure, and he's not former KGB! You're right, there's no such thing as 'former KGB' or 'former hippie'!" Vynnychuk smiled, proud of his pithy line.

"Something's not right with you today," Alik mused aloud,

staring purposefully into the eyes of the writer. "Maybe you're feeling insignificant?"

The smile slid off Vynnychuk's face.

"Damn you!" he snorted. "Who, out of the two of us, is the engineer of human souls? You? ... Yes, you figured it out! My liver hurts ... I drank some questionable wine with a neighbour yesterday."

"So you should've stayed home. Why'd you come?"

"But you asked me to!" Yurko Vynnychuk lifted his hands in exasperation. "How can I say no to you? Really, I feel dreadful today for some reason ... So pay no attention to me castigating you! I've also noticed strange smells in different parts of the city. Perhaps there really are old chemical weapons being stored somewhere under the houses? Lord only knows ... Anyway, better for your KGB friend to rummage around in the military archives. That'd be a damn sight more useful than searching for where the Carpathian sea is going to rise up out of the earth!"

It was no more than ten minutes on foot from Virmenska to Gunpowder Tower. The dry weather allowed Alik to walk at a leisurely pace down the ancient alleyways of the city centre, and when he reached the little square by the tower he noticed immediately that his usual bench was free.

Alik sat down and looked around. He noticed a few homeless people in the distance, by the tower. The pirozhki van with OSELYA across the top was in the exact same place, but he could only see two women wearing hi-vis jackets over their neat coats, instead of the usual three. They seemed to have already wrapped up their charitable work for the day.

Alik got up and wandered towards the vehicle. He stopped about ten metres away. The young women were busying themselves around the open rear door, shutting large Thermos vats of food.

One of them, a brunette of about thirty, noticed him.

"Why would you come so late?" she said sympathetically. "We've already run out . . ."

"Thank you, I'm not hungry," Alik responded amicably. "A colleague of yours told me that you have a hot shower . . ."

"Yes, in Vynnyky." The brunette nodded. "You could visit today if you'd like. Showers run until six in the evening."

Alik thought for a moment.

"No, I won't make it today," he said pitifully.

"Well, we could give you a ride," the brunette offered, looking at him attentively from his feet to his head. "It's just that we can't bring you back again . . ."

A hot shower against the backdrop of a cold autumn was an unbelievably tempting prospect. Alik's Spartan way of life, his body, grown accustomed to cold water, bearing it with humility even in winter, his entire past and current life, being deprived by fate of a hot water supply, it all suddenly started pressing down on him, with such force that for the first time in many years he felt lame, aggrieved, stuffed into a silent corner.

Meanwhile, the women closed the rear doors of the van. The brunette looked over at him. Alik nodded firmly.

He got in next to her on the back seat. And the van drove cautiously out of the square, hopped over the kerb onto the road and began rolling along, picking up its pace.

An hour later, he was stood under a hot shower. The water

poured generously over his head and shoulders, flowed down his back, his stomach, his legs. It poured over him, warming his body to an unbelievably enjoyable temperature.

"We have three shampoos!" came an uncertain woman's voice from outside the shower cabin. "Pear, anti-dandruff and lice, and nettle! Which would you like?"

"Nettle!" Alik said, and immediately a plastic bottle with thick green liquid in it appeared above him, hanging from the top edge of the shower cabin.

"I'll leave the towel here on the table!" the woman with short red hair who'd met him here in the shower room added before heading out. Wearing a white gown and towelling slippers, she'd greeted him warmly and, without another word, ushered him through. Bookshelves lined the walls, and in the middle of the room he saw a table and a box full of games as well as a chess board – the shower cabin itself only took up a fraction of the available space. On another table by the window was an electric kettle, a few teacups and a sugar bowl.

The woman knocked first, and only afterwards entered the room again.

"You've got a whole hotel in here!" said Alik, already dried and dressed.

"No," she laughed, "our hotel's next door, not here! It really is a hotel – just free. I spent a year there. Now I rent a room . . ."

Alik nodded understandingly. It was like this woman's turbulent, alcohol-soaked biography was written across her face. But her eyes were alive. Not only because of the mascara. The eyeballs themselves were talkative, and even if she was silent, they kept talking for her.

"I used to be homeless too," she said after a minute. "I was scared I was going to die, then they brought me back to life." She nodded towards the window. "They picked out good clothes for you," she said, indicating Alik's jeans and denim jacket. "I need to go and see Sonya too, see what new stuff they've got in! They're bringing us a lot of clothes at the moment, even more than usual, because it'll be winter soon . . ."

The mention of winter derailed Alik's train of thought. He had been planning to explain that he wasn't homeless, and that he'd come in his own clothes, but perhaps there was no point. Let her think what she wanted! Maybe it was nice for her to imagine that she'd become a benefactor to a homeless person, like she once was herself? Let her! Besides, she was a benefactor, a bringer of hot water.

Alik sat there, thinking how he didn't want to leave. The woman also sat at the table, but now she was thoughtful and silent.

Alik turned to the window, staring at the brick wall of the single-storey building six or seven metres away that housed either the dining hall or the washhouse. The air outside was greying; evening was drawing in.

After asking the woman directions to the nearest stop for a *marshrutka*[17] back to Lviv, Alik thanked her and left.

His body seemed surprisingly light to him now, as though the shower had taken ten kilos off him. He found the *marshrutka* stop quickly, and about fifteen minutes later the road was jolting him with its bumps and potholes, as the ageing minibus bravely pulled itself up to the main road. Vynnyky was left below and behind; it had taken on the weight and responsibility of washing and feeding Lviv's homeless and adjacent citizens, one of whom, on this day, had turned out to be Alik Olisevych.

32

For a while, the nighttime appointment with Simon Fyodorovich in the Laboratory for Paranormal Occurrences was slow
in approaching. Taras remembered about it "in passing", like
he'd remember something of no particular importance. But as
the evening of the fifteenth drew near, he was gripped with
anxiety. If only he'd had a client, that would have provided
a distraction, but the next Poles would only be coming on
Sunday to fill the early hours of Monday morning with his
habitual occupation. And today was Friday. Quiet and dark
outside, though that in no way meant "peaceful". The occasional sound of a car passing down Pekarska would find its
way into the courtyard and in through the window's ventilation hatch.

Taras sat in the kitchen, flattening out a white sheet of
paper. His right hand held the handle of a magnifying glass
he'd bought in the "Everything for a Hryvnia!" shop. On the
white expanse of the paper lay little greyish pebbles, which to
the uninitiated observer might have seemed entirely identical.
Taras rolled one of the pebbles a little closer to him with
his index finger and started to inspect it through the magnifying glass. This stone, like the others, as it happened, was

round-*ish*, but not round. This wasn't that surprising, after all. These stones were comparatively soft, and in the process of passing along their troublesome path to "freedom", they lost their sharp corners and protrusions, sometimes causing their unwilling hosts absolutely unbearable pain.

Their ultra-enlarged surfaces reminded Taras of the moon. This thought made him smile, edging the appointment at the laboratory in a few hours back to his "passing" memory.

Yes, exactly! Taras thought distractedly. Maybe the moon is the same, maybe it comes from a kidney?! Maybe it formed and grew in the kidneys of some giant, and as it came out it killed him, tore him apart . . . And that's how the Universe came about! And maybe Earth came from the same place, from the kidney of a giant? Only Earth got luckier – it got shaken out into a virile spot, where life and decay could transform the planet into something green and flowering!

Taras pushed three more stones to the centre of the white sheet with his finger. They were like brothers! Even the warped grooves that could be seen through the magnifying glass were somewhat similar from one to the next. Like bullets fired from the same gun.

Looking over his stone collection always calmed Taras, bringing his soul into equilibrium and harmony. On top of which he always got a feeling of deep satisfaction from the realisation that he had done, all in all, a good deed in helping these men through their pain and suffering. And they, his clients, had given him the means to live. Not to live richly, but not poorly either. His tastes were not extravagant; it was as though they'd tailored themselves to his income.

By around midnight Taras began to feel uneasy. It was time to plan his journey: should he walk to the laboratory, or take the car? He normally didn't touch the Opel unless it was absolutely necessary. But walking alone felt a little scary after the recent nighttime occurrences.

Taras thought about his neighbour as he stepped over the fifth step. He checked out his windows from the courtyard, and to his delight he saw light coming from inside. Yezhi was awake!

"Something's up," Taras whispered conspiratorially as Yezhi opened his door a crack, dressed in tracksuit bottoms and a vest.

"What is it?"

"I've got an appointment at the Laboratory for Paranormal Occurrences, at one a.m. . . ."

Yezhi's eyes widened, and condescension formed on his lips.

"Is that one of those places where they do the predictions with the cards?" he asked after a pregnant pause.

"They do the cards there in the daytime, but they only do serious consultations at night! There's this fella there, Simon Fyodorovich, a specialist in paranormal vibrations, he's got a PhD . . . He doesn't work with women, by the way. Only men . . . Want to come?"

Yezhi thought, chewing his thin lips.

"I'd have to dress a little nicer for that," he said eventually, looking Taras up and down.

"Well, if possible." Taras nodded. "It's a serious matter . . . the thing with the seagulls . . ."

"Alright, hold on." Yezhi shut the door, leaving his neighbour in the stairwell.

A few minutes later the door opened again, and Yezhi Astrovsky stepped out into the dark courtyard in ironed trousers and a shirt, jacket and tie. In his hands were an umbrella and an old-fashioned leather briefcase, which looked empty, judging by the way he was carrying it.

It was a little brighter on Pekarska than in the courtyard. Cars drove past, pushing aside the opaque night air with their headlamps.

"You feed the fish?" Yezhi asked as they walked.

"Yes," Taras lied, resolving to see to it as soon as he got home.

"I've already cut the hair of seventeen homeless or worse-off volunteers." Yezhi switched topics of conversation breezily. "Tell Oksana! I have a list too, I could give it to her . . ."

"With the names and addresses of homeless people?" Taras joked.

"They're normal people, as it happens." There was a clang of dissatisfied metal in Yezhi's voice. "And some of them have addresses . . . You insulated your windows, by the way?"

"Not yet." Taras was taken aback by the question. "There's still another month and a half before snow!"

"Well, they've already insulated their basements!" Yezhi said patronisingly.

The windows of the Laboratory for Paranormal Occurrences were not lit. The entire junction, and the little square opposite, were cloaked in darkness.

"Shut!" whispered Yezhi.

Taras pressed the button on the intercom system.

"Who to see?" a male voice screeched immediately through the device.

"One a.m. with Simon Fyodorovich," Taras recited.

The click of the lock mechanism indicated that they were free to enter.

Taras and Yezhi found themselves in the corridor, where it was just as dark as it had been on the street.

"Through here!" the man's voice called to them from somewhere on the right.

"Where's 'here'?" Taras asked irritably.

"Straight up the stairs, through another door!"

The darkness was left behind as they climbed to the first floor. In a setting that Taras now found familiar, the tabletop reading lamp was glowing on the doctor's desk. Taras could now see the doctor himself – a man of about fifty, balding, in a white suit. His tight, light-blue turtleneck went right up to his chin and was turned over in a neat "cuff", completely covering his neck.

Taras smiled, delighted that the desk lamp projected precisely the cone of light he'd pictured on his first visit.

Simon Fyodorovich waited for his guests to be seated on the other side of the table.

"I won't offer you tea or coffee," he began in a cautious, not overly loud tone. "Because hot drinks make conversation pleasant, but too light-minded. So then, what can I do for you?"

Taras and Yezhi looked at one another, then Taras, slightly more patchily than a couple of days prior, told the doctor about the sudden nighttime terror he had experienced while out walking, about the woman who had come running into their courtyard at night, and about the dream in which he and Oksana had been attacked by seagulls. And when he described how an enormous seagull had dropped on him from a great height, like an eagle on a hare, he was overcome with trembling, like his body wanted him to remember the fear he'd experienced that night.

Simon Fyodorovich listened attentively, glancing from time to time at the nodding head of Yezhi Astrovsky.

When Taras finished his account, the room was filled with a silence that lasted several minutes.

"Yes," Simon Fyodorovich sighed eventually. "A familiar story."

He pulled out the top drawer of his writing desk and retrieved a thin stick around the length of two pencils, which he handed to Taras before turning to his left to stare at the large plan of Lviv hanging on the wall.

"There's a button there, press it!" he urged Taras after realising that he had no idea what to do with the laser pointer he'd been given.

Once Taras had figured it out, Simon Fyodorovich turned again to the plan of the city.

"Show me where you live!" he instructed.

The red dot of the pointer travelled along Pekarska and stopped.

"And where else have you experienced these events?"

Taras tried to remember. At first he indicated a section of Pekarska at the junction of Dontsov and Filatov. Then he remembered how scared Darka had been, and pointed out the spot on the map where her bureau de change was located.

"Mhm." Simon Fyodorovich nodded. "I see."

He opened the desk drawer again and took out a wide folder, from which he removed a dozen sheets of A3 paper. He laid them over the open book under the cone of light.

The top sheet turned out to be a contour map, cross-hatched in pencil.

"Look here." Simon Fyodorovich turned the map to face Taras and Yezhi. "These are the recorded anomalies for the thirteenth of September at two-twenty a.m."

Taras leaned in closer and saw that the map showed a fragment of the city centre, Prospect Svobody, by Kopernik Street. The corner of the prospect and Kopernik was cross-hatched.

The doctor laid another contour map over the first, showing a different section of the city centre. On this one a whole section of Franko Street was cross-hatched, from Hrushevskoho to Zelena. "15th September 3.45 a.m." was written in pen at the top.

"And what does all this mean?" asked Yezhi Astrovsky.

"It means that we are dealing with an anomaly that is not linked to a concrete location, or with multiple anomalies linked to several concrete locations," Simon Fyodorovich responded calmly. "You aren't the first to notice these, shall we say, unpleasant phenomena. I am in the middle of conducting a study into negative vibrations . . . If you'd like to help me . . ."

"Of course," Taras blurted out.

"In which case, I will provide you with a device of my own invention and a map of the city, and instruct you on what to do and how. What do you say?"

Taras considered the offer.

"Okay," he said after a minute's pause. "And how will your device help?"

"It measures the quantity and intensity of negative vibrations. Your role will be to record the boundaries of these vibrations on the map. Then we can discern patterns in the times and places of their appearance, and by combining our efforts – perhaps even involving the police or other organs of the state – we could encircle those responsible and drag them out into the light of day."

"Those responsible?"

"Well, yes. This is most likely the result of a group of lighthearted and talented students entertaining themselves, not understanding the full consequences of their experiments."

Taras sagged in his chair. Simon Fyodorovich's last words provoked a sudden wave of suspicion. Blaming these occurrences on a group of students?!

"You noted, after all, that at the onset of fear, the air suddenly became salty?" Simon Fyodorovich went on.

Taras strained to remember.

"Yes, it seemed to," he said.

"There you have it! It could all be your body's reaction to some sort of gas collecting in a particular region of the street . . . The kind of thing that student chemists could absolutely be dabbling in . . ."

"Some dabbling!" Yezhi Astrovsky jutted his head upwards, visibly annoyed.

"Dabbling for them," the vibration specialist clarified. "A serious problem for the city."

"But what about the birds?" asked Taras.

"You know, if you breathe in enough of certain gases, you'll see and hear dinosaurs, not just birds! Please forgive me." Simon Fyodorovich looked at his watch. "I have my next visitor in ten minutes. Let's wrap this up! Are you going to take the device?"

"Yes," Taras responded decisively.

"It's very simple to use. I'll give you a demonstration and talk you through it!"

The apparatus was at once reminiscent of a Geiger counter and an old portable transistor radio. A green, rectangular device with two indicators and a comfortable, gleaming handle. The arrows on the first indicator seemed to suggest that the left zone was determined "normal", while the red background of the right-hand side screamed "danger" louder than any words or symbols could. The indicator's semicircle was covered in vertical dashes, above which were numbers. The background of the second indicator was entirely red. At no point during his explanation did Simon Fyodorovich name the units in which the vibrations were measured, but Taras only realised this once back outside, as he and Yezhi were already walking silently in the direction of the Halytsky Market. Yezhi was looking business-like, carrying a file containing a dozen identical contour schemes of the city, folded in two.

A cat suddenly ran across the empty pavement in front of them.

Yezhi stopped sharply. "Black?" he asked, his voice trembling slightly.

Taras tried to pick the animal out, but it had already disappeared round a corner.

"I didn't see," he confessed. "It wasn't white, that much I can tell you . . ."

"Go on, turn that thing on, so that we don't accidentally stumble into some vibration that we can't escape alive!" Yezhi was consumed by fear.

Taras pressed the button on the contraption. Both indicators lit up. The arrow for the left indicator shivered and moved upwards but froze in the green zone. The second arrow didn't even flinch.

"All good." Taras looked at his neighbour.

Yezhi sighed in relief.

"Shall we get going?" he asked cautiously, looking from side to side as he walked. They came out by the statue of Danylo Halytskyi.

"Let's walk a little, along Pekarska, not far . . . We need to see how it works!"

"So what's the second arrow for?" Yezhi tapped his finger against the second indicator as they walked.

"If it doesn't have enough of a negative zone on the first indicator, the second one – which doesn't respond to positive vibrations at all – turns on automatically." Taras repeated the words of Simon Fyodorovich, surprised at his own ability to recall them so precisely.

They turned onto Pekarska.

Taras felt an inexplicable wave of energy. The street was calm, the occasional lit windows of old Polish houses broke up the darkness. Every now and then a car would go by, and the arrow of the indicator would respond with a light shudder.

"You're not thinking of going to Lychakivska, are you?" asked Yezhi. "Let's go back now, and we can carry on tomorrow morning. It's less scary by day, somehow . . ."

"We can't do it in the day."

"Can't?" the neighbour asked, surprised.

"In the daytime the city is taken over by natural negative vibrations, from cars, gas contamination, human aggression. That makes it difficult to distinguish the anomalous ones . . . Were you really not listening to Simon Fyodorovich?"

"The fella in the blue turtleneck? I listened! But he was looking at you the whole time!" Yezhi seemed offended. "No, I listened . . . he was saying which signals on the apparatus meant you weren't allowed to bring it near a source of vibrations! I remember some of it!"

Taras nodded. If the arrow entered the second zone of the second indicator, that was a sign of imminent fatal danger. But for now it slept peacefully.

Taras stopped, and Yezhi understood the interruption as the start of their journey home; he turned around and began walking back. Taras decided to continue his nighttime walk on his own.

After bidding his neighbour farewell, he called Darka.

"Hi, how're things with you?" he asked.

"Fine. I'm bored," replied the familiar voice.

"Got it! On my way!"

When he reached the bureau de change, Taras placed the device on the outer ledge of the bureau's window and immediately noticed that the left arrow floated up and stopped almost at the boundary of the green and red zones.

"What's that?" asked Darka.

Taras looked through the window at her hands in their dark-green gloves. The gloves were tucked into the sleeves of a blouse in the same dark green, above which Darka was further insulated by a knitted, sleeveless black jersey. On her left wrist, over her gloves, she wore a watch with a red plastic strap.

"I'm borrowing it from the Laboratory for Paranormal Occurrences." He smiled. "You can use it to find ghosts!"

"Hey, cool!" Darka clapped her hands excitedly. "Like in *Scooby-Doo*? Will you take me with you?"

"Aren't you at work?!" Taras asked mockingly.

Darka nodded, crestfallen.

"It's fine, it's fine, we can start finding ghosts right here in your cell!" Taras said cheerily, moving the apparatus right up to the window.

He watched as the arrow jolted then started rising smoothly. It stopped in the red zone, although only by a couple of milli-metres.

"You've got something up with you in there." Taras was serious now.

"Of course something's up." Darka's eyes twinkled with a light irony. "Look!" she said confidently, reaching down and placing on her side of the glass several wads of dollars, euros and hryvnia.

Taras was awestruck when he saw the arrow rise even higher into the indicator's red zone.

"Well, that's a bit of a cliché." Taras sighed bitterly. "Money is dirty, that much is obvious. But what do negative vibrations have to do with it?"

"Well maybe it's not the money, maybe it's me that's causing it!" Darka hid the money under the counter and the arrow retreated again.

"You need to get out of there," Taras said entirely seriously. "Find some other work!"

"I will. But not right now." Darka's eyes were full of dreams. "You'd better tell me something fun, so I don't fall asleep in here!"

They chatted for no less than an hour.

"You know," Darka said just before he left. "I was promised an anti-allergic lip balm! Perhaps I could try it out on you?"

"Which of us would be using the balm?" he asked jovially.

"Which of us?! You, of course!"

Despite the early-morning darkness, Taras set off home with a lively, carefree gait. Only on Pekarska, at the very start of the street, did an unpleasant anxiety take hold of him. Seeing the device light up, Taras stopped suddenly. The first indicator's arrow was at its limit!

Taras' ears were ringing. He took a couple of steps back, his eyes still fixed on the indicator. The arrow dropped from the limit and slowly crept towards the green zone. A shiver ran over his body. Taras looked from side to side. His eyes stopped on the door to a block of flats, which he couldn't have been more than two or three metres from.

The door somehow drew Taras over to it. Ancient, carved, painted in a deep blue.

Taras gathered his courage and, lifting the apparatus so that it was at chest height, he stepped forward once more. The arrow of the first indicator crept upwards. A cold breeze hit him in the face. His legs grew weak. The arrow approached the upper limit. His hands, even the device itself, trembled before Taras' eyes, which stayed fixed on the indicator. He stood still.

His lungs were beginning to run out of air, forcing him to take a deep breath. He immediately felt salt on his tongue, sea salt. The familiar avian laugh-cry broke out above him. It seemed like one more step would allow him to reach out to the door's massive bronze handle. Reach out, open the door and look into the entrance hall. Taras, clenching his teeth, forced his body forwards, compelling his right foot to take a step, to maintain equilibrium. But the leg wouldn't lift, and the body itself didn't fall from leaning forward, it recoiled.

Taras straightened up against his own will. An invisible force pushed him away from the door, as though a fast-flowing river was stopping him from moving towards it. Even just standing in place now seemed a difficult matter. But Taras held his ground, not taking his eyes from the unreachable door. It seemed that a great animalian fear had been born somewhere in his liver or kidneys. And it became harder by the second to stand in one place. He could barely contain the urge to run.

His eyes dropped down to the indicator: the arrow had fallen back from the limit a little. Taras took a few steps backwards, stopping once the arrow retreated to the green zone. Silence suddenly returned, the laugh-cries faded away. Taras sighed in relief. His fear evaporated. He looked into the dark sky, now free of bird cries. And then the salt on his tongue reminded him of his own self, and he remembered the terror he'd just experienced.

He remembered the doors, remembered the building, remembered the silent dark windows that he couldn't quite reach. First thing in the morning I need Yezhi to give me the maps from the laboratory, and I need to shade this place in, Taras decided.

33

After getting up and listening attentively to the radio news in the kitchen, Ryabtsev shaved and washed. His autumn somnolence hadn't yet left him. He used to feel wide awake as soon as he opened his eyes in the morning. Now – and this was no doubt a consequence of his approaching age, his autumn years, as it were – Ryabtsev began every day slowly, uncollected.

While the kettle came to the boil, he pulled on his trousers, a vest and an old green sweater. Two cheese sandwiches brought the captain to working condition. And immediately something clicked inside him, clicked and turned, like a cog in a watch. This influx of energy, even if a little meaningless, revived him somewhat and made him quietly happy, a feeling he wished to share with his feathered companions at once.

Pulling his umbrella-walking-stick from the rack, Ryabtsev slammed the door and hurried downstairs.

Once outside, he opened his umbrella and ploughed ahead under the monotonous drubbing of raindrops.

Another twenty steps and he would dive into his own personal world, where it was easier to collect his thoughts and feelings, where he was always in harmony with nature and nature was always kind and curious towards him, a person of pensionable age who meant nothing to his surrounding environment.

Stopping at the wooden door, gripping the key in his hand, Ryabtsev noticed a suspicious white spot on the wet grass, about two metres from the dovecote. He walked over to it, squatted down, and was struck with horror. In front of him lay one of his white sickle-winged doves, mangled, blood clumped on its feathers, its little head thrown backwards and its wings splayed.

Ryabtsev lowered his umbrella to the ground, carefully took the dead bird in his free hand, and lifted it up. And he noticed another three doves lying unmoving in the grass a little further away.

"How?" Ryabtsev whispered, looking up at his dovecote.

The wet gable roof, fitted with rib-like protrusions for the doves to sit on, was glinting in the morning light. Ryabtsev walked over to the side and peered up at the landing platform. The door was open and one of his doves was looking fearfully out from the loft.

"How?" repeated a shell-shocked Ryabtsev. He began going over last night and the day before it in his mind.

He remembered bringing his freshly charged accumulator from his apartment and turning on the light. He remembered sitting under the doves on a stool and listening to their cooing. He remembered a slanting rain suddenly driving against the dovecote's left wall. It started just as he'd lifted a glass of vodka to his lips. And then? Then he'd drunk it, clambered up the ladder to the loft and opened the door. Why?! Ryabtsev groped for an answer. And here his memory gave him a hint: it had been very stuffy in the dovecote. The rain was filling the air with ozone, and he'd wanted some ozone, both for himself and for the doves ...

Sighing heavily, the former captain walked back over to the mangled doves and stood over them. His eyes fell on an alien, incongruous feather, large and white with a grey fringe.

"Forgive me. Forgive me," he whispered.

He strode into the dovecote and threw his open umbrella into the corner. Stopped by his yellow Piaggio. Wiped slow tears from his unshaven cheeks.

To the left of the scooter, under trampled straw, was the square hatch to the cellar.

He thought of Alik Olisevych, to whom he had recently handed the key that he'd collected from down there, from his secret coffers, from his past. The key to Alik's hippie cell on Zamarstynivska. Ryabtsev climbed up to the first floor, placing the dead dove on the newspaper-covered dresser. And he climbed higher again, up into the roof space. He closed the door to the landing platform. The doves recoiled from him as if he were a stranger. He counted them. Instead of twelve pairs around him there were now nine.

His left hand felt out his mobile in his pocket. Felt it out and gripped it, like it was alive and able to help him in this difficult moment. And the moment really was difficult. Difficult and bitter. He was finding it as hard as six months ago, at Mezentsev's funeral.

But Ryabtsev didn't call anyone. Telling his dove-breeder friends about his stupidity and guilt?! No! They would never take him seriously again! His old friends in the service? They had their own problems. Alik? Alik would, of course, get it, and sympathise, but what good was sympathy to Ryabtsev?!

As the tears dried on his cheeks, his thoughts regained their former rigidity.

"Yes, I made an error, and that error will be exploited by my enemies," Ryabtsev concluded. "Now it is a matter of honour to settle my accounts with them!"

Lowering himself into the cellar, Ryabtsev neatened the large cardboard boxes piled on top of one another, then crept into the gap between them and the brickwork of the interior wall, into the very back, where he kept his tools. He found his shovel.

Drenched to the bone under the continuous rain, he dug out four small graves under a nearby pine tree. He lowered the doves into them and replaced the earth.

He thought of his fellow dove-breeders again. None of them had become a friend, or even a good acquaintance. When their birds died, which didn't happen too rarely, they simply threw them in a rubbish bag, as if a dead dove is just rubbish. Ryabtsev could neither accept that nor understand it. Yes, doves live short lives. Yes, it could happen that some stranger brings in an infection, that the disease 'kills off' the doves, and then you have to start all over again, disinfect the dovecote, go to the bird market. But to have no respect for death like that?

The rain slackened. The sky seemed to become a touch lighter. Ryabtsev surveyed his surroundings.

After wiping the earth from the shovel with a newspaper,

he threw it inside onto the straw. He secured the weighty lock on the door of the dovecote, picked the large white feather with its grey fringe up off the ground, and set off back to the flat.

34

The city couldn't sleep that night. It was overpowered by dryness, cold and fear.

Ryabtsev was whipping along on his Piaggio, wearing his buttoned-up grey coat with the collar raised and leaning over the handlebars, which pulled the strap of his sheathed shotgun so tight that the weapon stuck up and forwards, like the mast of a yacht being buffeted by the wind.

The captain killed the engine after stopping at the corner of Hrushevskoho and Drahomanov. He listened closely to the night and looked tensely at the dark windows of the buildings. He took a few steps into the centre of the junction and peered down the dark road as if it were a pit.

Something cracked up in the sky. Ryabtsev whipped the shotgun from his shoulder, unsheathed it, slid a pellet-filled shell into the chamber and, holding the gun at the ready, tried to burn his gaze through the dull grey city ceiling. But no further sound came from above. Ryabtsev lowered the gun, screwed up his eyes, which were tired from the unnecessary strain, and nodded, as if acknowledging his weakness. A couple of minutes later he returned to the yellow Piaggio and, with the sheathed shotgun still over his shoulder, turned on the engine.

He drove a little slower further along Hrushevskoho. The emptiness of the street gave him a sharp sense of personal responsibility for all those sleeping behind the windows of these houses. Ryabtsev felt like a guard, a city guard keeping the nighttime order, the urban nighttime peace. The fact that there was evidently nobody besides him watching out for this order both scared Ryabtsev and gave his nocturnal mission a sense of urgency. Where were the police? Where were their patrol cars?

And right there, as if mocking him, he saw a wet front door open and shut again, throwing out the reflection of a green flashing traffic light onto the wet cobblestone pavement. The traffic light switched to yellow, but Ryabtsev had already stopped the scooter and turned off its engine.

He pushed out the steel kickstand and, leaving it by the kerb, crept along the wall of the building he'd parked by, where he crouched in hiding.

The night itself seemed to be laughing condescendingly at his suspicion. He stopped, leaning against the brick wall, and felt doubts regarding his own sense of reason begin to wash over his already exhausted thoughts.

But he didn't let them get the upper hand. That same door, which he was now thirty metres from, opened again, and a man in a long coat and a hat peered out from the hallway before stepping outside. It was the same person who had entered in such a hurry just a couple of minutes earlier.

Ryabtsev's thin lips expressed, almost imperceptibly, the tense smile of a hunter spotting his prey. It were as though the man's suspicious behaviour at once explained and justified Ryabtsev's own presence.

The man looked to either side, crossed the road and carefully, stealthily disappeared through the front door of the house on the corner opposite.

"Interesting," whispered Ryabtsev, not moving an inch.

His eyes now concentrated on the dark windows of this house, as if he could sense that one of them was about to ignite with yellow light, giving Ryabtsev a hint as to where this strange and suspicious night-dweller wanted to go, and what, or who, he was searching for.

Ryabtsev came alive through an ancient professional instinct. He even clenched his hand muscles for a moment, assessing their combat readiness. The shotgun, however, stayed behind his back. He didn't reach for it yet. Probably because the old KGB agent's intuition suggested to him that if the man in the long coat was an opponent, then he was weak and presented no real threat. Strong opponents don't look fearfully from side to side.

The door of the house on the other side of the road opened again, and that same man stepped out of the foyer and onto the street. He stopped, looked around, and slowly got down into a squat. He froze in this strange pose, his elbows leaning on his knees, his chin lowered into the open cup of his palms.

Ryabtsev smirked, struck by his behaviour. There was no longer a drop of potential enmity or opposition in this night stranger. All suspicious behaviour had been outweighed by this one pose. Perhaps he's drunk, looking for a woman he barely knows to spend the night with, Ryabtsev thought, getting ready to "unstick" himself from the wall and return to the Piaggio.

But at night the temporal gap between decision and action lengthens. At that very moment, before Ryabtsev had managed to take a step towards the scooter, the man got to his feet, a lamp suddenly lit up in his hands, and he set off decisively towards the nearest courtyard entrance, disappearing into it.

Ryabtsev walked about seven metres to the left, so that he was positioned immediately across the street from the archway. At night, any courtyard entrance looked like the neck of a bottle filled with pure darkness.

And suddenly this darkness was cut into by the lamp's light. It crawled across the walls, whipped momentarily into the inner archway of the entrance, and its yellow beam even lit up the house on the other side of the road. Then it returned to the courtyard.

Ryabtsev ran across the road and ducked into the archway, arriving in complete darkness and silence. Not a murmur.

The troubled former captain of the KGB froze on the spot with bated breath. The darkness before his eyes slowly dissipated, revealing the walls and windows of the house and the vast well of the courtyard. Ryabtsev took three silent steps with his back to the wall. His jacket sleeve rustled unpleasantly as he took the shotgun from his shoulder.

A door screeched open. The fourth or fifth on the left. From it, hurriedly but silently enough, came the now-familiar figure. He crept along under the low first-floor windows towards the next door. Then he disappeared behind that door too, pulling it in carefully, to avoid slamming it.

Ryabtsev evaluated the situation. If he, this man, was checking every hallway, then he'd soon complete a circle of the square courtyard, ending up outside the last door, just five metres from Ryabtsev and the archway.

There was nowhere to hide and there was no sense in going back out to the street. If he wanted to understand the reason for this person's suspicious behaviour he would have to remain right there, in the courtyard.

But in the meantime, the person in the coat and hat hurriedly came back out into the courtyard and, holding open a door, shone his lamp inside. Then he shut it and set off to the next one.

Tiredness was beginning to get the better of Ryabtsev. He yawned. The shotgun nearly fell from his hands, so he put it down, leaning it against the wall of the building behind him. He walked to the nearest entrance on the left and went inside. Alas, he had no lamp. But there was a dim light burning inside, by which the former captain could see some worn wooden steps that had not been decorated in a while, a recently installed iron door to apartment number one on the right, and to the left, in the deep dark, a low, one-and-a-half-metre door, concealing the way down to the basement. A moist smell hit his nostrils. He pulled the low door open and saw steps littered with rubbish. He began to go down, lighting the way with his mobile.

In the basement, two metres from the bottom step, Ryabtsev walked into a "bed" made out of an old sofa. He squatted down and lit his immediate surroundings with his mobile. Before him were the living quarters of an evidently well-educated homeless person. On the other side of the "bed" was a small table. Under it were a few plates and a plastic bucket of water. On top of it was the third volume of the complete works of Ivan Franko.

"Wow," Ryabtsev sighed, getting up. "Life is everywhere . . ."[18]

The phone screen went black. The unknown homeless person's living space was once more plunged into darkness. From the direction of the open door to the basement a dull light shone in. He had to get out. But the rubbish on the steps would crunch under his feet. If he's reading Franko, the bum could at least sweep up his stairs! Ryabtsev couldn't help feeling sad.

A door slammed in the hallway above and someone came in loudly, in a manner Ryabtsev thought he recognised.

A new wave of light rolled from the door to the cellar to fall on the stairs. A moment later, a dirty black boot landed on the top step.

Ryabtsev took a couple of steps into the darkness and knocked his head on something hard. He felt out the obstacle with his hand and realised it was a water pipe.

"Who's there? Anya, is that you?" asked a nervous male voice.

The owner of the dirty boots came cautiously down the stairs, holding a burning candle in his hand. He stopped by the "bed" and lifted his candle up higher, looking into the corners. After a few seconds he froze, and Ryabtsev realised that he'd been spotted.

"Hands up!" barked the former KGB captain. "And stay where you are, or I'll shoot!"

"Don't!" the man said, terrified, lifting his left hand closer to his right, which was holding the candle. "Who are you?"

"Who are you?" asked Ryabtsev, his nervousness quelled by the stranger's fear.

"I'm living here . . . temporarily . . . Trying to start my life over . . . Gave up drinking, started reading . . ."

"Name and surname?"

"Petro. Why would you need my surname?"

"Alright, I don't need your surname . . . Lower your hands. You didn't see anyone outside just now?"

"No."

"And you've been living here a while?"

"Almost a year."

"Notice anything strange in the basement? A salty smell and the appearance of water, perhaps?"

"The pipe burst once . . . But smells . . . No, nothing salty. Sometimes it just stinks. They're old pipes, you know . . ."

"Okay. Thank you. Stay where you are!" Ryabtsev commanded. He strode over to Petro and looked him attentively in the face, trying to remember it, just in case. After that he got himself out of the basement and shut the little door behind him.

It was quiet in the courtyard. Ryabtsev walked out to the street. There, seeing the red traffic light, he remembered his shotgun and rushed back. It was just where he'd left it. He threw it over his shoulder and, still agitated by his dangerous forgetfulness, he crossed the street, got on his scooter, and switched on the engine.

After passing the next junction, he noticed the person in the coat and hat walking unhurriedly along the pavement. He braked.

"You couldn't tell me how to get to Halytsky Market?" Ryabtsev called out to the stranger.

The man stopped, turned around, and stared silently at his interlocutor.

Ryabtsev found his face familiar, even half-hidden in the nighttime darkness.

"You're lost?" the man in the hat asked, his voice full of trickery.

"A little," answered Ryabtsev, still trying to remember where he'd seen this person before.

"I suppose you're looking for the sea?!" His voice was dripping with irony. "Or off on a hunt?" His eyes reached for the shotgun protruding over Ryabtsev's shoulder. "And why alone? Why's Alik not with you?"

"Pan Vynnychuk?!" asked the former captain of state security. "Is that you?"

"Yes, it's me, pan Captain!"

"But what are you doing here?"

"Walking. Finding inspiration."

"In basements and hallways?"

"What? Have you been you following me?" It seemed to Ryabtsev that Vynnychuk had suddenly turned bitter.

"No, I was following a suspicious type, who I noticed walking around an area in which there have recently been a good number of crimes and strange occurrences . . . How bizarre that this 'suspicious type' turned out to be you!"

Vynnychuk smiled condescendingly. "A writer, much like an actor, pan Captain, could turn out to be any person at all, any character from the books they write."

"Forgive me, pan Vynnychuk, I don't know the characters in your books. I haven't read them. If you gave me them, I could have a read and we could discuss your craft."

"What kind of behaviour is that, asking an author to gift you their own books?!" Vynnychuk was incensed. "What, would they be so hard for you to buy?"

"Don't be offended, but if I have to choose between a book and vitamins for my doves, I'm choosing the latter. It is my firm belief that modern books don't give you wings and don't make you think about the meaning of life! So, did you find anything interesting in those basements and hallways?"

"Two homeless guys," Vynnychuk replied after a moment's pause, taking from his pocket a portable Dictaphone and lamp. "I'm collecting people's stories for a future novel." He shone the lamp on the Dictaphone and stared into Ryabtsev's eyes deliberately, with a questioning look.

"Sorry," Ryabtsev sighed. "I see that you're just a man looking for adventure . . . it means I wasted my time on you! Goodbye!"

The captain, glum and suddenly experiencing a new wave of exhaustion, turned on the engine and left. Vynnychuk saw him off with a wry smile.

35

Taras had wanted to dedicate the coming night to searching for anomalous zones, with the help of the apparatus that Simon Fyodorovich had given him. These plans, however, were destined not to come to fruition.

"There's three of us," some guy called Wacław with a Polish accent was saying down the phone. "So we're asking you to give us a discount!"

Taras agreed. He asked them to drink a glass of cognac two hours before the meeting time and to sit for no less than an hour in a hot bath. They arranged to meet at midnight by the Leopolis hotel.

As he left for the courtyard, Taras still grabbed Simon Fyodorovich's contraption, as well as the contour maps of Lviv. He also remembered his Thermos of coffee.

An unpleasant drizzle hung in the air, wetting his face and hands. Taras placed the bag in the boot, took out a cloth, wiped his mirrors and windscreen. Before leaving the courtyard, he noticed Yezhi Astrovsky at his window. His red terry robe made him a character from a *Peredvizhniki* painting, while the yellow, homely chandelier light added some antiquated romanticism to the tableau.

The new clients proved to be both polite and likeable, tongues clearly loosened by the cognac they'd drunk. Each of them proudly presented their x-rays. Then one of them, the youngest, called Taras aside and asked him to be a little more respectful towards Wacław. "Wacław is from a princely family," he whispered. "He has royal blood in him!" Taras smiled inwardly, but nodded politely and respectfully. He returned to the car. Wacław, sitting up front with Taras, immediately started making jokes about his three stones. After just five or six kilometres down a relatively "soft" road, however, the smiles had left the faces of all passengers. Wacław had gone noticeably pale. Taras went down Horodotska three times, twice down Lychakivska, and decided that it was time to try some "shorter vibrations". With Krymska Street behind them, he stopped the car, turned on the inside light and looked over at his clients.

"How are you feeling?" he asked.

His clients' suffering faces answered Taras' question for themselves.

He realised that it was not going to be a quick process and made peace with that fact. He turned the car around and took the route back to Horodotska once more.

At nearing five in the morning, one of the passengers in the rear howled and punched the back of the driver's seat. Taras automatically slammed the brake pedal, and the car squealed and stopped on a dark kerb by the fence of a concrete factory.

The passenger hunched over, turned to the side, opened the door and seemed to pour out onto the road. Taras jumped out of the car holding the glass jar. The Pole took the jar with his left hand, simultaneously trying to undo his flies with his right.

This Lviv night was full of sounds, but the moisture in the air made them distant and deformed. Taras froze a metre from the awkwardly hunched-over Pole, his ears pricked attentively. A few minutes later a little stone hit the bottom of the jar, not too loudly, and a stream gurgled into life.

The Pole straightened out his back, turned around and set his eyes on Taras. Taras took the jar from him, squatted down, and carefully poured out the urine while holding back the kidney stone with his finger. Then, pulling a tissue from his jacket pocket, he wrapped the stone up and stowed it safely away.

The second Pole's stone was "expelled" half an hour after the first's. But the suffering of the third, Wacław, continued, as yet without results. Princely stones take longer, Taras thought with mild irritation. Sunrise was approaching, cars had appeared on the roads, and Taras was no longer able to really rev his old Opel over the uneven cobblestones. At around six he drove onto Lisna and bolted upwards along its pitted surface, without trying to avoid the potholes or mounds. Here, finally, Wacław's face noticeably paled, and he threw a pleading look at the driver.

Taras braked. While Wacław stood there, hunched, facing the hill, Taras looked at the yellow-orange house he was now very familiar with, in which, as he watched, first two windows, then another three lit up. A new day had begun for the inhabitants, but Taras was yet to finish his night's work. But it would conclude any moment now. The only thing that annoyed him was the fact that he wouldn't see Darka this morning: her shift was already coming to an end. Remembering his Thermos, Taras pulled it out of the boot and offered a cup of coffee to his clients in the back seats.

The air grew lighter, drier. Here, on Lisna, it was still quiet, much quieter than an hour ago on Lychakivska. Here, evidently, active morning life started later, and the hill with the park atop it protected the street from some of the city noise.

Taras finally heard the clink of stone against glass.

Wacław, groaning, sat slowly in the car. Taras squatted down. He poured the urine from the jar, holding back the stone with a finger. He immediately noticed that this specimen was a lot larger than usual. That was why it took so long to come out. So Taras was right when he had jokingly told himself that princes had larger, more princely stones. After putting it in a tissue, he brought it up to his eyes, paying close attention to its strange colour. In the murky pre-sunrise air, the stone seemed to glisten. Taras laughed at the tricks his eyes were playing on him. I really must be tired!

He turned the car on, and looked over at the still-pale Wacław.

"I have another two in there," the Pole informed him sorrowfully. "I was hoping they'd all come out . . ."

"Yours are too large," Taras said quietly. "Rest up and come back in a few weeks!"

The Poles paid at the hotel. They bid him farewell warmly, personally.

Back home, Taras first threw his fish some feed. He was again reminded of his downstairs neighbour, who wanted to ingratiate himself with Oksana, and so constantly reminded Taras about the need to care for his aquatic dependents. He got undressed down to his underwear and decided before bed to look over his night's earnings. He sat at the cold kitchen table, laid out the three "Polish" stones, and grabbed his magnifying glass. Two of the stones were entirely normal, like little moons, but Wacław's made Taras' eyes bulge. It was genuinely multi-coloured; it seemed iridescent, like mother-of-pearl after passing through the hands of a good jeweller. Taras looked it over as attentively as he could.

"It couldn't be!" he mouthed. "But that's a pearl! An actual pearl!"

As he stared at the pearl, he became aware of the sound of the sea in his head, the sea he had never seen, on the shores of which he had never sat. But right now it seemed so real, so alive! He saw shells tossed across a sandy shore, open mollusc shells like butterflies of different species. He also saw oyster shell halves with glistening pearls in their cores. He screwed up his eyes and shook his head. Once more he felt how tired he was, and he went to bed, leaving the stones on the table.

36

Despite all the tiredness in his body, Taras' sleep proved light and superficial, and just three hours later, at around ten in the morning, he opened his eyes, only to spend another twenty minutes lying on his back staring at the ceiling. His body came to its senses slower than his thoughts. And that same pearl, or more precisely, Wacław's mother-of-pearl kidney stone, still took pride of place in Taras' consciousness. He got up and went into the kitchen to look at the odd little stone through his magnifying glass again and was convinced, once and for all, that it had been neither a dream nor a vision.

He thought of Darka. She was probably fast asleep now after her night shift.

He imagined showing her this surprising stone, and telling her where he got it from. He imagined her surprise, her doubt. She probably wouldn't believe him!

At around midday, Taras dialled Darka's number and was delighted to hear her lively and sonorous voice answer after just two long rings.

"You're not still sleeping?"

"No," she replied. "I had to go to the dentist this morning."

"Why, did you break a tooth?"

"No, just a check-up. All in order!" She laughed. "They renewed my biting licence!"

"So when are we going to try that anti-allergic balm?"

"Why not this evening?"

"How about a little earlier? I've got something interesting to show you! You'll go crazy when you see it! In about an hour, perhaps?"

"But what is it you want to show me?"

"I'm not saying! Someone might be listening in on us! They could still take it away!"

"Well, if I like it, will you give it to me?"

"Wow, you're bold!" Taras laughed. "Alright, if you really do like it, it's yours!"

"Okay, then meet me at Kabinet in an hour!"

Taras was happy. He got in the shower, washed his hair.

As he went downstairs, he stopped suddenly, noticing that the fifth step was painted red. He squatted down and touched the step with his finger. The paint was fresh.

Taras stepped over it and went out to the courtyard, setting off down Pekarska towards the city centre with an easy gait. In the left pocket of his jacket was his magnifying glass with its comfortable metal handle. In the right was the kidney "pearl", wrapped up in a tissue.

Café Kabinet was humming like a beehive. Bright jackets brightened the mood, hanging on hangers and off the backs of chairs. At the tables, young female students sat and chatted, with just one bearded fellow sat alone by the window, sipping coffee and flicking through a photo album that he'd picked up from the bookshelf nearest him.

Darka arrived ten minutes later. Took off her green jacket, put it on the hanger and sat opposite Taras, her chin perched on her hands in their emerald-green satin gloves.

"Well, hi!" she said excitedly. "Have you ordered yet?"

"I was waiting for you." Taras lifted his hand as he said it, attracting the attention of the waitress passing behind Darka's back.

The girl stopped, listened to Taras' order and, after nodding, left for the bar.

"So, what have you got there?" Darka tilted her head to the side, giving Taras an arresting, playful look.

Taras took the folded tissue from his jacket pocket and unwrapped it. He took the pearly pea in his hand and lifted it to her eye level. The stone shone and different colours played over it.

"What's that?" Darka asked, leaning her whole body forward.

"You're not going to believe it!" Taras leaned towards her. "It's a client's kidney stone."

"I don't believe you!" Darka laughed. "You're kidding! Let me see!"

She took the mother-of-pearl pea and held it up for inspection. Taras enjoyed watching her face; its lively mimicry seemed to give away her every thought. The waitress brought the coffee, and Darka barely even noticed her! She inspected the stone with a child-like curiosity, holding it closer to her eyes, then holding her hand up to the window, as if checking the stone's opacity. Suddenly her face, without moving away from the pea, became surprised and troubled.

"It's getting warmer," she whispered, lifting the pea to her eyes again. "It's heating up, I can feel it . . ."

"It might just seem that way," Taras said condescendingly.

But Darka's face was now conquered by a joyful wonder. She took the mother-of-pearl pea in the fingertips of her left hand and seemed to listen in to it. Then she dropped it into her right palm.

Taras watched her, watched her distracted game with the stone, and thought about how easy it was to surprise her, just like a kid! But right now he just wanted to chat with her. Taras held out his palm, wanting to take back his "pearl" so that he, not the stone, had her full attention. Darka looked at the outstretched hand in surprise.

"I thought it was a gift," she said, looking down at the pea.

"Yes, of course!" Taras sighed.

"If there were more like that, I'd make myself a necklace!" she said dreamily.

Taras felt slightly annoyed, but then at that moment, something surprising happened. Darka moved her coffee cup from its saucer to the wooden table, and then placed the pea on the saucer, after which her left hand pulled off the long, satin glove from her right hand and she carefully picked up the mother-of-pearl pea with her bare fingertips.

Taras was struck dumb. It was the first time he'd seen Darka's bare hand. Refined, subtle, feminine – it paralysed his eyes. His mouth went dry.

"Strange," she whispered. "It really is warm! Maybe it's

alive? Look, there's no allergic reaction from my fingers! But I have such sensitive skin! It means it's perfectly clean . . . Oh, how nice!"

"Are you certain it's warm?" Taras asked doubtfully, slightly disturbed by the sight of the pads of Darka's slim, refined fingers squeezing the mother-of-pearl pea.

Darka shrugged, dropped the stone on the saucer and looked over her hand.

"Do you have any money on you?" she asked.

Taras took out one hryvnia.

Darka held out a fearful hand and touched her fingertip to the dirty, crumpled note. And immediately jerked her hand away again, her face filled with fright. She looked down at her finger. Taras watched as it started to go red. Darka's expression filled with self-pity and tears twinkled in her eyes. Taras wanted to hold her, calm her, console her.

Darka turned back to the stone lying in the saucer. She took it between the thumb and forefinger of her reddened, slightly puffy hand, which just a couple of minutes ago had been surprisingly beautiful and desirable, but now caused Taras sorrow and fright. He thought once again about how he needed to find a genius of an allergist, someone who would be able to cure Darka.

"Quiet!" Darka whispered suddenly, leaning over her bared, red hand. "Quiet!"

"I'm not talking!"

"Look!" she whispered.

Taras looked down. And he saw that the redness was slowly disappearing. And disappearing somewhat strangely.

The fingertips holding the stone were already clear of any unhealthy reddening, returning to their natural colour. After a couple of minutes there was no sign of the allergic reaction. Bewilderment slowly gave way to joy on Darka's face. Suddenly she turned to Taras, making him jolt like he'd just been given a small electric shock. Taras felt his lips go dry. He leaned across towards Darka. Their lips touched, and a new tender shock passed through to Taras' very heart.

Out of the corner of his eye Taras noticed the waitress was staring at them. He sat back in his seat.

Darka sat there with a conspiratorial look and switched between glancing playfully at Taras and returning her gaze to the mother-of-pearl pea in her hand.

"I've never had such a nice sensation," she said tenderly.

Taras smiled, at first thinking that she was referring to their first kiss. But her eyes, which had returned to the mother-of-pearl pea, made him doubt the veracity of his assumption. She was now holding the pea in the palm of her hand. Her forehead was scrunched up slightly in thought. Her eyes flashed with sudden resolution. She lowered the pea back to the saucer and removed the long satin glove from her left hand. Taras' breath caught. Now he could see both of her thin, graceful, musical hands. He didn't know if Darka played the piano, but he immediately imagined her fingers darting over the black and white keys. He could even hear the music they made: tender, quiet, mesmerising.

The stone appeared in her palm again, and this time she covered it with the other and froze again, staring at her own hands.

"It's a miracle," she whispered. "Thank you!"

Again, her eyes showered Taras in warm gratitude. He sat there, afraid of moving, afraid of distracting Darka from her miracle, to which he, Taras, was definitely connected, in some manner or other.

37

In overcast weather it's easy to imagine that it's evening already, even in the middle of the day. Especially if one is home alone, and the window is completely covered by curtains. That's why Oksana found no great difficulty in settling into a short daytime nap, so that later that evening, when she'd have to sing, dance and generally amuse a birthday banquet, she would be as fresh as a sparrow that's just learned to fly.

She changed into her pink flannel pyjamas and clambered up the steep stairs to the cupboard, to her comfortable little "nest", reminiscent of the nest of a stork. Oksana's body was compliant, and as soon as she had robed it in the soft pink flannel, it had wanted to go straight to sleep.

The alarm on her mobile phone was set for six p.m.; it was now half past two.

She shut her eyes. Even her feet, tired from the morning's walking round the city centre, stopped aching or complaining and went quiet.

And there, in that dark room, curtained off from the grey, rainy day, something made a knocking sound. It was nothing like the sound of the fridge, which sometimes began to grumble suddenly for no particular reason.

The noise persisted. It seemed to be coming from down below, from within the room itself.

Oksana sighed. She knew that it was the seagull in its cardboard box. The bird still had its beak wrapped in sellotape, and its wings bandaged up and strapped to the body so that it couldn't exacerbate its injuries with poorly-thought-through movement.

It must be uncomfortable for a seagull with a sealed beak, which only has its sellotape removed twice a day! Oksana pictured her own mouth being taped shut, but needing to speak, wanting to sing, or call out to someone she knew as they passed her in the street. No, doing that to a person would be a crime! But then a person doesn't bite without reason – it doesn't snap like a seagull! She remembered that the seagull had eaten the last two capelins from the fridge that morning, prompting a trip to the nearest grocery store for another kilo. On her way back, Oksana herself had eaten lunch – although that was putting it a little excessively – "eaten lunch". She'd pecked a little, like a bird. A cheese sandwich and a cup of tea! But she'd forgotten to feed the seagull. And now her thoughts were spiralling around the bird, which, she now began to understand, was just hungry and expressing its dissatisfaction through noise.

Oksana's guilty feelings towards the seagull forced her to get down from her nest. She got a few fish from the shopping bag, laid them out nicely on a small plate, as if the seagull would appreciate the beauty of its food deliveries, and returned to the room. She pulled the curtain back to reveal the cardboard box, and the room immediately lit up.

After dropping the plate into the box, Oksana held the

bandaged bird with her left hand, and used the fingers of her right to grip the end of the sellotape on its beak and remove it. The seagull, which only had its feet free, immediately opened its beak wide and froze for a moment in that position, keeping its beady little eyes trained on Oksana.

"What?" the hostess said to the bird. "Go on! Eat it! Fresh fish!"

The bird leaned over the capelins. It grabbed one, lifted it up in its beak and swallowed.

Oksana smiled. She prepared a new strip of sellotape to shut the bird's beak again after it had finished its lunch. But the gull suddenly thrashed its head around and gave a sharp and unpleasant cry-laugh, as though it had completely forgotten about the fish lying on the plate.

Oksana jumped back.

"You eat up now, and you can shout later, when you're free!" She nodded at the window.

But the seagull kept shouting, and its cries became louder and more repulsive. Oksana's head started aching.

"That's just what I need!" She sighed angrily. "Fine, if you won't eat, then I won't let your beak free until this evening!"

The seagull was clearly untroubled by the human's threats. It started to reel around the cardboard box, jumping and screaming. She could see it tensing its little body, which was shielded by its bandaged white wings as it tried to straighten them out.

The room suddenly seemed to smell of the sea. An unpleasant tang of seaweed rotting on the shore scratched her nose, and she sneezed.

Then, after pinning the seagull to the floor of the box with her left hand, she tried to close the bird's beak with her right and sellotape it shut. But it was like the seagull had lost its mind. It tried to bite Oksana's left hand, while she was trying to grab its beak with the thumb and middle finger of her right. But the beak was opening and shutting with the unbelievable speed of a barber's scissors, and suddenly Oksana felt a sharp pain and saw blood on her hand – the seagull had bitten the back of it. In shock, she lifted her hand to her face and felt hot blood pour down her wrist. A little further and the red would ruin her pyjama sleeve!

She jumped up and shot through the kitchen to the bathroom, turned on the cold water and put her hand under it. The water immediately turned pink. The unpleasant sea smell hit her nose again. Her mood was ruined, broken. The blood flowed as before, but now Oksana could see that the seagull had simply torn the skin. She looked round at the cupboard which held her first aid kit, and suddenly imagined herself that evening, in her stage costume with a bandaged hand. Just what I needed, she thought.

And once again, she was distracted by the smell of the sea. It now seemed that it was growing stronger and more saturated, and that it was coming from the cold water streaming over her splayed, wounded hand. She leaned towards the flow – the smell strengthened. She scooped some up in her left hand and brought it to her mouth. She froze, amazed.

The iodine sea salt burned her tongue and lips. And once more the seagull in the next room cried, an ugly, loud, sharp cry. And a strange clacking came from the tiled floor. She looked down and thought she saw small crabs, the size of five-kopeck coins, crawling under the bath, adroitly shifting their spindly legs.

Oksana frowned, trying to push air in and out of her full lungs, as an article she'd once read on reaching inner harmony had recommended. It didn't help. Then she got out the first aid kit. She dabbed the injury with cotton wool, then put a few drops of green antiseptic on it and pressed the cotton wool over it again. After that she bandaged up her hand and sat on a stool at her small kitchen table, which only had room for her.

Her head was hurting, the bird was screeching, her injury was throbbing. Absolutely nothing worse could happen to her today. She did her breathing exercises again, and it seemed to help a little. In any case, after she'd completed them, she had an entirely rational thought: call the housing authority and complain about the quality of the water.

She dialled the number and told the woman over the phone about the water and asked her to send a plumber and work out why on earth there was salty water in the tap. The lady proved a miracle of politeness. She assured Oksana several times in a soft voice that her complaint had been received, and that she would pass it on up the chain immediately. But Oksana wanted to vent, and she was in no way finished with her entirely meaningless phone conversation. Finally the lady herself said "thank you for your call!" in a calm tone and hung up.

Oksana did her breathing exercises again, but this time felt no improvement in her condition. She phoned Taras.

"Taras, dear! The seagull bit me!" she complained.

"Christ! You've still got it?! Let it go already! You're just making problems for yourself!"

"I need to call the vet first, to make sure its wings have healed!"

"So call her! You can let the vet sort your bite out while she's at it! Did it get you badly?"

"I was bleeding!"

"You want me to come over?"

"No, there's no need . . ."

And the seagull cried loudly again.

Oksana got up, walked into the room with her mobile still pressed to her ear and turned on the light. She looked at the unnerved bird. And a taste of salty water appeared in her mouth, and salty sea air in her nose. She turned to the window. Raindrops were racing down the outer surface of the glass . . . She looked down at the aquarium and, to her horror, saw that the fish were darting back and forth like madmen, pushing little ripples to the surface of the water.

"Hey!" she said. "I think I've worked it all out! Get everything valuable and run outside!"

"You what?" Taras asked, surprised. "Run where?"

"There's going to be an earthquake! Animals can feel them coming better than humans. That's probably why the seagull went crazy! And my fish are swimming around like mad! Look at yours!"

"I'm standing right next to them," Taras said calmly. "They're all in one spot, waving their fins lazily, no fuss . . ."

"Strange." Oksana sighed. "Then I don't know what to do . . ."

"First of all," Taras' voice became teacherly, "call the vet and get her to visit. Second, make yourself a herbal tea and calm down. Third, open the window and air out the apartment – fresh air also freshens the head! Got it?"

"Yes," Oksana said obediently.

"Then do what I've told you, and I'll call you back in an hour!"

The conversation with Taras calmed Oksana down and helped her gather her thoughts. First, she called the vet, and thankfully the woman from before was free and promised to come straight away. After that she opened the window. A moist, cool air tore into the room.

The doorbell rang. Oksana was surprised that the vet had come so quickly. But it was a different woman.

"I'm from the sanitary department," she said. "You complained about the water quality, and the housing authority called us."

Oksana nodded and let her into the hallway.

"I don't want to get your floors dirty." The woman, who was wearing a blue dress jacket and a long dark skirt, got a large test tube from her bag, pulled out its stopper and held it out to Oksana. "Collect some cold water in this!"

Oksana carried out the request. As she filled the tube, she once again picked up on the clear presence of a sea smell.

"Is this the first time it's been like this for you?" the woman asked, placing the test tube in her bag.

Oksana nodded.

"We've had dozens of cases like this in the last few weeks, but all the others have been on Hrushevskoho and Chornovol.

They had salty water start coming out of the taps for no reason over there, too. Some salty groundwater must have come up somewhere and seeped into a corroded water pipe. Your street hasn't had anything like that before! That's everything, thank you!"

"But what do I do now?" Oksana asked, seeing that the woman was getting ready to leave.

The woman turned around. "Don't do anything! On Hrushevskoho and Chornovol the salty water went away on its own, and their normal water came back. I think it'll be the same for you!"

Oksana, still troubled, sat in the armchair, feeling surprised by the sudden silence. The seagull had gone quiet!

The vet came an hour later. First she cleaned and re-bandaged Oksana's injury, then turned her attention to the seagull. She expertly shut the bird's beak with sellotape, and sellotaped its legs together expertly too; only after that did she cut open the bandages, freeing its wings. The seagull seemed to understand that it wasn't worth resisting and waited patiently for the vet to inspect its healed wounds.

"Everything's fine," the woman said at last. "You can let it go – unless, of course, you want to keep it."

Oksana shook her head.

"Yes." The vet nodded. "They aren't the nicest birds, and the smell . . ." She turned her head away.

"Does it smell like the sea to you in here?" Oksana asked cautiously.

"No, it smells of fish," replied the vet. "And it's cold!"

"I'm airing out the apartment."

The vet left, stashing her hundred-hryvnia call-out fee in her purse. Oksana stood over the box where the bird was lying, its wings free, but its feet and beak "bound".

"Well, that's it, time to say goodbye!" Oksana said decisively. She picked up the box and carried it into the hallway, where she grabbed the scissors from the windowsill.

In the courtyard, as rain fell on them, Oksana unwound the sellotape from the bird's beak and used the scissors to cut it away from its feet. The seagull seemed to be watching her suspiciously, maliciously.

Oksana was scared – would it attack her again?! After all, now it was a free bird.

But the gull craned its neck up to the square of sky between the courtyard's tall buildings. And then suddenly, with a loud flap of its wings, it jolted upwards.

Oksana watched it go.

38

The arms of the wipers threw water diligently from the windscreen. The road was glistening. Cheburashka cantered along with the energy of a faithful steed.

There were still four hours until the evening performance, which gave her ample time to go to Vynnyky for a chat with her friend Lesya – a woman whose care for unfortunate outsiders Oksana had always felt deserved praise. It was Lesya who had founded the homeless shelter, which she had named Oselya; these days it was not only full of life, but even in a certain sense *overfilled* with it, overfilled with the repeatedly broken human fortunes that someone unacquainted with the unluckly side of life would never be able to get their head around. A masterclass on restoring furniture, two small shops, another masterclass devoted to decorating plates. It was its own unique little world. But it was open to all who had fallen into a blind alley and were looking for a way out. On Thursdays they drove up to Gunpowder Tower to feed those who were hungry and unfortunate. Thursdays were also when any of Lviv's homeless population could come to the centre to take a shower or wash their clothes. Here, even in gloomy weather, there was always a sun shining. Shining and warming. And that sun was called Lesya.

Oksana drove down to the lake, turned right after five minutes, and began the descent down the winding road into the valley that cradled this large and heterogeneously designed Lviv suburb.

She left Cheburashka in the courtyard of the charity's premises and rushed into the building, only to stop immediately in surprise. In the usually empty, spacious corridor, from which you could walk straight through the door on the left into the shelter's office, a number of guests were sat on chairs lined up by the windows and by the wall on the other side. Washed, wearing clean clothes, but still carrying the imprint of life on the street on their faces. In the middle of the corridor stood Yezhi Astrovsky. To be more precise, he wasn't standing, rather moving in some kind of dance of his own design, clacking hairdresser's scissors around the head of a woman who was sat before him. Her face carried a blissful smile; her eyes were closed.

Taken aback, Oksana froze, unable to move an inch. Yezhi Astrovsky was thrilled to see her.

"Oh, hello!" he exclaimed, breaking off his dance. "I wasn't expecting you!"

"Same here!" Oksana snapped out of her trance and walked briskly into the office.

Shutting the door behind her, she nodded at the girl who did the bookkeeping and turned to the table where Lesya usually sat.

"She's gone out," said the bookkeeper.

Oksana sat on a chair next to the dresser, which held teacups, a sugar bowl and an electric kettle.

Lesya appeared five minutes later. Something about her had changed. Oksana was suddenly struck by how much younger her friend looked, and she had the seditious thought that Lesya was seeing a cosmetician.

"Well, how'd you like it?" Lesya asked.

"Like what?" Oksana didn't understand.

Lesya gestured at her hair, and suddenly everything became clear.

"Tea?" Lesya asked without waiting for her friend to evaluate her change in appearance.

Oksana nodded. Her thoughts were getting muddled and confused amid the array of the day's experiences.

"Woah, what have you got on your hand?" asked Lesya.

"A seagull bit me," Oksana answered, and her eyes went back to her friend's new haircut. Only now she was able to pay attention to how her facial features had changed. Before, when Lesya's hair went down to her shoulders and she just had it trimmed, without any other flourishes, her face expressed a softness and tenderness, and even when she got angry it was hard to credit it. Now her normally soft features were somehow intensified, and her nose seemed a touch sharper thanks to the scissors' effect on the geometry of her face.

"Did that chatterbox cut it for you?" asked Oksana.

Lesya smiled.

"You like it?"

"The haircut – yes. Him – no," Oksana declared openly.

And just then, as if his ears had been burning, Yezhi poked his head into the office.

"May I?" he asked, nodding a greeting to Lesya. "I thought I'd have a little break."

"Sit down, have a rest!" Lesya pointed him to the free chair. "Some tea, perhaps?"

"No thank you." Yezhi looked at the chair, but didn't sit in it. Instead, he walked over to the two friends.

His eyes stopped on Oksana's curls. She immediately felt uncomfortable.

"Remember, you promised to put yourself in good hands," Yezhi said with unexpected boldness.

Oksana's anger knew no limits.

"What do you think you're doing?!" She glanced at Lesya and immediately turned back to the hairdresser. "What kind of a dirty trick is this?! When and what did I promise you?!"

"Oh, sorry, you've misunderstood me!" Yezhi took a step back, as though afraid of having his ears boxed. "But you said that I could give you a haircut once I'd cut the hair of fifty homeless people."

"Well, have you?" Oksana asked distrustfully and a touch cruelly.

From the pocket of his chequered jacket Yezhi pulled out a sheet of paper folded in four. He unfolded it and showed it to Oksana.

"Forty-seven, here are their full names, you can check! Not a kopeck charged! And out there –" he nodded in the direction of the corridor – "another nine are sat waiting! That'll be fifty-six!"

Oksana suddenly felt awkward. He really was trying, after all – that much was clear.

"Okay," she muttered a little more softly. "You can cut it! But you have a queue out there!"

"Will you be here long?" Yezhi Astrovsky enquired.

"No, I've just dropped in, I'm heading straight back again," she replied. "I have work this evening."

Yezhi looked sorrowfully at Oksana's hair, stoking her irritation. He took his sharp chin in his right hand and shook his head.

"You're an actress, but you pay so little attention to your appearance . . ."

The statement didn't anger Oksana, but it clearly upset her, and Yezhi could sense he'd touched a nerve.

"Why don't I go and ask them? They'd probably let you skip the queue! They're in no hurry, after all, and you have work this evening! And I'll come back tomorrow for the people I don't get around to today. I promise!"

Oksana sighed heavily.

"Okay," she said, waving him away.

She went out into the corridor and sat down. Yezhi threw the sheet over her shoulders.

The scissors snipped, the comb's teeth ran through Oksana's curly hair. The first locks drifted down to the floor.

The insistent smell of cologne hung around Yezhi. The shelter's inhabitants, waiting for their turn, watched the skinny, graceful man with interest as he concentrated entirely on the curls of his female acquaintance.

Oksana herself now relaxed, zoned out. It suddenly seemed as if the whole business with the aggressive seagull had occurred several days ago, rather than today. Time seemed to drift away from her and hide around the corner. She was content to live in the sensation of the moment, allowing the spiced, alcoholic aroma of eau de cologne to knock the smell of the sea and rotting seaweed from her mind. And Yezhi's hands were exuding warmth like a cast-iron radiator. The warmth seemed to make her ears go red. She felt the urge to touch them, to check they weren't burning, but she was unable to easily extricate her arms from under the sheet pulled over her clothes. Suddenly embarrassed, she realised that her ears were burning from a sudden onrush of teenage shame. Something about this hairdressing performance seemed wrong to her, immodest. Like she shouldn't be letting a man make her beautiful! And indeed, Yezhi's persistence, which she was already thoroughly sick of, was proof that he wanted to make her a beauty entirely for his own satisfaction! Due to purely selfish motives. But she still wouldn't go for a coffee with him! She didn't like him as a person. Although the lengths he'd gone to just to appeal to or appease her had already taken him this far, to Vynnyky, to Oselya, knowing how much she cared both for Lesya and for her faithful team of helpers, and for the lost men and women who found it so hard to turn a new leaf in life, like trying to build a house alone.

39

That same evening, by a strange concurrence of circumstances, Alik Olisevych also appeared in Vynnyky. He appeared there after a phone call from Yurko Vynnychuk, who wanted to tell Alik something important, but said at the same time that he was not intending to visit Lviv in the coming week. Vynnychuk was not the kind of person to call about something trivial just to intrigue his comrades with riddles, so Alik decided to go and visit him. And now they were drinking wine at the table in the writer's new, recently finished home, discussing the last book fair, which, admittedly, Alik had not attended. Yurko was telling a very lively story, however, about a writers' booze-up in the courtyard at Kopernik 6, where the littérateur Mikhailo Vatulyak had laid out a crazy feast on the covered terrace by the entrance to his apartment. Alik listened interestedly at first, then drank homemade red wine with interest, listening with half an ear, and waiting for Vynnychuk to finally tell him the "something important". After all, some aspect of that "something important" would surely relate to him, Alik, directly. Why else would Vynnychuk have called him?

Alik finally ran out of patience and interrupted Yurko. "You wanted to tell me . . .?"

"Ah, yes!" Vynnychuk rubbed a hand over his forehead, as if he were trying to flatten out the wrinkles. "I saw that friend of yours, KGB. I wanted to tell you to keep him a little more at arm's length! I think he's lost it. He tailed me all night with a shotgun on his back! Can you imagine? I think you should tell the police about him, or else who the hell knows what he's gonna cook up next?!"

"Eh, he's fine." The old hippie came to his acquaintance's defence. "He's just searching for the Carpathian sea, like before."

"To shoot it with a shotgun?" Yurko gave Alik an inquisitive stare.

The hippie was unable to respond to this probing question.

"You surprise me!" Yurko's face grew serious, expressing something akin to disappointment. "I understand, of course, that we're all sadomasochists here, but you really take the biscuit! Making friends with a KGB who wouldn't let you live in peace and pray to your gods – sex, drugs and rock n' roll!"

Alik pursed his lips.

"First of all, he didn't stop me doing anything, if anything he sometimes helped. Secondly, I never prayed to sex or drugs! And thirdly, he's completely on his own now, and loneliness can make anyone go mad!"

"I value your humanism," Vynnychuk sighed. "After all, it's only a humanistic impulse that brought me to tell you this. He will not end well! A person who spends his nights driving around Lviv on a yellow scooter with a shotgun over his shoulder, following strangers, can't possibly end well. If there's a shotgun on the shoulder, sooner or later it'll go off."

"On the wall," Alik corrected his comrade. "If there's a shotgun on the wall! I know the expression – I'm the one that works in the theatre."

"I'm not talking about the theatre, I'm talking about life!" Vynnychuk waved him away. "But mark my words, if I see him again out at night in the city with a shotgun, I'll be calling the police and the psychiatrists myself!"

Alik tensed up. Something in the conversation was surprising him, putting him on edge, and that something was nothing to do with Ryabtsev. His thoughts bounced around, grabbing one another by the tail, piling up into a heap. And all of that on top of the homemade wine he'd drunk. A sudden funny thought came to him: "Wine with Wynnychuk in Wynnyky!". He sat there contentedly, savouring his newly invented tongue twister.

But Vynnychuk looked at his unfinished glass and stayed emphatically silent – for long enough for Alik to realise that he was embarrassed. And the realisation brought with it a question.

"Yurko, what was it you were doing out there? At night? In the city?"

Vynnychuk jumped, and switched from looking at the wine to looking at his friend.

"Well, going . . . walking," he said, but his voice lost its hard edge.

"Walking?!" Alik repeated, perplexed. "Well then, Ryabtsev was also probably walking, or scootering to be more precise, around the city. At night there are almost no cars around, and he loves driving around on that scooter . . ."

"And the gun on his back?"

"Nighttime is a dark time. Who knows who you'll bump into on your way." Alik lowered his voice, and stared intensely into the writer's eyes as he did so. "You said he was following you, right?"

Vynnychuk nodded.

"Must mean you were doing something." Alik realised he was analysing the situation aloud in almost exactly the same tone as Ryabtsev had recently used to analyse the goings-on in the city. "If you had been standing there, not doing anything, he would probably have just driven by . . . So what were you up to?"

The unexpected question stopped Vynnychuk dead. He grunted, got up sharply from the table and left. Alik, still perplexed, watched him go.

Yes, he thought. Strange people, these writers! Lord knows what's going on in their heads.

But it turned out that there was nothing strange going on in Vynnychuk's head. He appeared in the room again a minute later, carrying a sweating bottle of vodka in one hand and a teacup in the other, from which poked the heads of little salt-pickled cucumbers. His face was really far too serious for the goods he was carrying. It expressed something between doubt and thoughts that the thinker was not entirely happy to be having.

He placed the bottle on the table, moved the wine glasses to the side, got two spirit glasses from the cupboard and filled them.

"I'm going to tell you," he started a little haltingly, as if he were trying to work through his own thoughts on something at the same time. "But for you to understand me a little better, we need to drink."

Alik took a glass and looked at his comrade in mild confusion, unsure what was coming next.

"To mutual understanding." Vynnychuk lifted his glass, moved it to his lips, and paused for a moment or so before not-too-assuredly holding it out to Alik. The glasses clinked and returned to the table empty.

Alik picked up a pickle, bit it and gave it a juicy crunch. The host grabbed one too.

A silence beset them. It was clear that neither of the two men wished to be the first to break it. Yurko filled the glasses again.

After the fourth drink, Alik felt an uncontrollable relaxation in his body, and he got scared. How many times had he told himself: you can't drink vodka after wine! All the same, that moment always came, not too often, once every six months, when the wine ran out and there was only vodka left, or, as on this occasion, the vodka replaced the wine for some esoteric and not entirely clear reason.

"Well," the guest said slowly, giving his host a look that had been softened by vodka.

Vynnychuk wiped his lips.

"I'm writing a novel at the moment," he started.

Fear filled Alik's eyes. He thought his comrade was about to tell him the entire contents of his new novel, and that he'd deliberately filled him with booze to do so. So that Alik lacked the strength to get up and leave.

"I won't say what about," continued Vynnychuk, and Alik's heart relaxed; he went limp and hunched forwards, leaning his elbows against the tabletop and, like someone placing flowers in a vase, rested his chin in splayed-out palms that touched at the wrists. "But I have a character in there . . . this sailor from Odesa, who's randomly ended up in Lviv. Well, I thought, perhaps in the novel he could start up a romance with this married Galician girl . . ."

Alik closed his eyes.

"He-e-ey, don't fall asleep! Listen! Or else why did we drink the vodka?" Vynnychuk's voice, which sounded unexpectedly loud and harsh, forced Alik not only to open his eyes, but to lift his head from the "plinth" of his hands.

"Long story short, this Odesan started messing with the novel. And he wasn't the main character, so I took him out . . ."

"Took him out?" Alik wasn't understanding. "You mean you killed him off?"

Vynnychuk smiled.

"I guess you could say I killed him, but a better fit would probably be the word the English use for computers – I 'deleted' him, crossed him out entirely, that is. But when I was writing about him before, I had imagined him so fully in my head . . . His face, hands, manner of speaking, his gait . . . I mean I really saw him in front of me, like a living thing. And after I'd crossed him out, he came to me in a dream, swore at me, showed me a rude hand gesture . . . this one . . ." Vynnychuk lifted his right arm, bent at the elbow, while smacking his left fist against its inner curve. "And he promised to get me back for it, so that I'd remember him for the rest of my life. And then, one night, a few days after that dream, I was walking home down Pekarska after leaving a friend's place, when I saw him – in a sailor's jacket with a striped vest poking out at the bottom, and black trousers!" Vynnychuk's eyes were burning. "And he saw me and came at me like a tank, with his fists clenched. There was such aggression coming off him that I was scared for the first time in my life! I turned around and quickly left, almost ran! I think he wants to get revenge on me for kicking him out of the book . . ."

Alik shrugged, giving a wide yawn. "Okay, and why have you told me all this? To see if I believe in fairy tales?"

Yurko also yawned, wiping his temples with his fingers, and stealing a glance at the clock on the wall – midnight.

"I was explaining to you what I was doing at night in the city, when that idiot friend of yours started following me," Vynnychuk said, exasperated. "I was searching for this sailor, to talk to him. So he would leave me in peace . . ."

"Ahh." Alik nodded, regarding his host cautiously, like one might regard a dangerous madman.

"There, in that district, there's a lot of homeless people. Homeless people will have seen him, and they'll know what he looks like. After all, he also has 'No Fixed Abode'. I was just walking up to them one at a time, asking when and where they'd last seen him . . ."

"I'm spending the night at yours, alright?" Alik looked around and fixed his eyes on the sofa's blue-green tapestry throw.

"Of course, where else would you go at this time?"

The guest walked over to the sofa and, without undressing

first, lay down with his face to the ceiling. And fell asleep immediately. The host covered his comrade in a light blanket and, turning off the light, carefully shut the door behind him as he left.

40

Ryabtsev's worry for his doves and the fate of his city had once again given him insomnia. Just past one a.m., he took his hunting shotgun and went out into the street. It was a dry, cold night. The cold immediately stung his palms and brushed his cheeks.

The former captain walked over to the dovecote. He stood under it, listening.

If the city had a heart, he would probably at that moment have been able to hear it – that's how quiet it was. But the heart of the city was really hundreds of thousands of human hearts, and during sleep human hearts beat quietly, so as not to prevent rest.

Ryabtsev walked over to the fresh dove graves. He thought of the other, non-dove feather he'd picked up from the ground when he'd dug them. He got it out of his pocket.

And suddenly Ryabtsev was distracted by a distant bird's cry-laugh, sharp and unpleasant, forcing him to look up into the dark night sky. A moment later all was quiet again, but the silence that came to replace the bird's cry filled him with anxiety.

Ryabtsev wheeled his yellow Piaggio out of the dovecote,

locked the door, sat on the seat of the scooter then froze in indecision. He understood that as soon as he turned on the engine, the silence would scarper, disappear.

But his hands gripped the handlebars tightly, and the engine started muttering its dulled melody.

Sykhiv was quietly left behind. Late-night walkers trudged past here and there. A few were swaying, their gait giving away what they'd been doing before setting off back home.

Fifteen minutes later, the Piaggio was jolting across the cobblestones of the regular city roads. And then the former captain stopped and turned off the engine. On both sides of the street, all of the windows in the old buildings were dark. Quiet ruled here, and Ryabtsev found this quiet suspicious. He took the gun from its sheath, and then hung it back over his shoulder again. The scooter was left leaning against the wall of a house, the kickstand unused. He stood still and listened closely.

He could hear a sound coming from somewhere nearby, similar to the ticking of an old clock. Ryabtsev strained his ears. Then the "ticking" grew stronger and stopped being a "ticking". Ryabtsev could now distinctly hear someone's hurried footsteps. Something about the sound suggested that it was a woman.

A minute later she appeared and, clearly after noticing him, crossed to the other side of the road. She quickened her step. Ryabtsev, holding his breath, watched her go until she turned a corner.

Ryabtsev was suddenly lost. Something, the fatigue of either body or mind, made itself known to him, and he now cast about with dulled eyes, no longer alert but seeking help from any quarter. He suddenly felt entirely other in this place. Other and unwanted. The city stood firmly on the foundations of its homes old and new, the city clung vicelike to the earth beneath it with the roots of the thousands of trees that grew in the parks and squares, and along the roads within little stone borders. Such a city had no need for Ryabtsev's help. Such a city had no need for help whatsoever, indeed it could itself provide help to others. From the first to the last. Without a doubt, Ryabtsev was in more need of the city's help at that moment than vice versa. If there'd been a bench nearby, Ryabtsev would have collapsed onto it without a thought as to whether it was wet or not. The captain suddenly felt ashamed of his weakness, of his unmanly spirit. He pulled himself together, clenching his fists and gritting his teeth, strictly, militarily surveying his surroundings for enemies. And for a few seconds, the city seemed to stop being "at ease", responding to a call of "halt!". But at that moment the silence was broken by strange, oddly relaxed sounds of some sort. A drunken voice was approaching, accompanied by other, more distinct noises, and the intonations of this voice suggested to Ryabtsev that the man was chatting with himself while walking, giving out questions to the emptiness, that is, to the world at large. A passing drunkard was of no interest to Ryabtsev; he leaned against the wall of the house beside his scooter, waiting for the walker to amble on by. Waiting for the return of silence, so he could collect his thoughts, focus, and try to work out if this city really needed him, his shotgun, his trusty Piaggio, or even his strange desire to protect it from an invisible enemy, from a Carpathian sea hiding under the basements of these houses, and all the dangers that came with it. Or perhaps that writer with a high, sheening forehead and a spiteful countenance was correct? Perhaps it really was all nonsense, the fantasies of a lonely, unwanted old man?!

The drunk's voice sounded closer to him. "But the barges? The barges full of mullet?" Ryabtsev turned around. He saw in the darkness, about fifteen metres from him, a man on the shorter side, wearing a dark waist-length jacket that was reminiscent of Soviet military issue. He was swaying side to side, making little progress, and the bottle in his hand had a matte gleam to it. "I can't see the shore," the drunk opined to himself and the world around him. "I can't see it! Oh!" He stopped, his attention turning to Ryabtsev.

And then Ryabtsev began to feel awful. His heart began to ache, the air seemed salty, sea-like, his throat closed up and, most scarily of all, he could hear the sharp, repulsive cry-laugh of seagulls above him. Jerking his head up, he saw an unintelligible movement above the house and heard the sound of wings beating. And, sensing his strength leaving him, Ryabtsev managed to drag the shotgun from his shoulder, point the barrel upwards, and pull the trigger.

Out thundered a shot, not distinct, but "loose", dull, like on a hunt. The shot tore out of the iron barrel, penetrating the air and wrenching upwards, expanding its territory by conquest. Below, at the feet of the drunkard and the shooter, landed three bloodied seagulls, not dead, but wounded. And they began to writhe hideously on the pavement. One fell from the kerb to the road.

The drunk looked horrified. He fled wildly and awkwardly,

waving the bottle that was still gripped in his hand. The seagulls remained. And so too did Ryabtsev, his hand clutching at his heart, frightened to death and sharply feeling the finite nature of his own life for the very first time.

But his heart gradually calmed down. The air filled with moisture, the salt left it. Only the seagulls lying at his feet, two of which were no longer showing any signs of life, remained as evidence that what had just happened had not been the product of his, Ryabtsev's, own fevered imagination.

He would have stood there in that troubled state for a while longer. But a dim light fell down from somewhere above him. And the captain, lifting his gaze, saw that several of the building's windows had lit up. There was a screech as one of them opened. A woman's voice asked fearfully, "What's going on down there?", and a man responded, "Quiet, someone's probably been killed!"

And Ryabtsev realised that he had to go. He realised that he had woken people up with his gunshot. Woken them, but not awoken anything in them. That is, he had disturbed strangers who knew nothing of his existence, nor of the dangers that were threatening them all. And after a second, another thought appeared in Ryabtsev's head: the danger in this city was coming from himself, from Ryabtsev. It was he who had lost his mind and was now seeing, hearing, and even defending people from hallucinations that he himself had conjured up. He kicked the nearest seagull. Its body flew into the road. Flabbergasted, he caught himself thinking how these hallucinations of his were far stronger and scarier than all of those American horror films they advertised on the TV.

Somewhere in the distance a siren began to wail: one of the inhabitants had called the police, and now a car with flashing lights was racing this way.

He had never driven so fast down the cobblestone streets as he did that night. And he had never been so mentally lost before either, thinking of the dead seagulls on the pavement, the mumbling, stumbling drunk, and the smell of the sea, which still lingered in him. Had that really just happened? The siren sounded once more, somewhere behind him, but it neither got louder nor faded away.

41

At the hotel, Taras, out of breath and so not expressing his question very clearly, was not immediately understood. But once he had made himself clear, the girl, one of the two sat behind the little desk, shook her head.

"They already left. Half an hour ago."

"Where to?" Taras asked despondently.

"The station. Their train is in an hour and twenty minutes."

Taras rushed outside. It was a shame he'd left his car in the courtyard, but here at the Opera House he wouldn't have any trouble finding a taxi!

He noticed them straight away. The Poles were sat on high stools at the bar of the train station buffet, drinking coffee and chatting animatedly with the buffet's mature waitress, a woman of "Balzac age".

"Good day! How good that I've found you! I wanted . . ." Taras said falteringly, looking at Wacław. "I feel a little awkward. I didn't finish your treatment . . . There are still two stones left . . . And I, out of respect for your title . . ." Taras bowed a little, not taking his eyes from Wacław's face. Wacław nodded almost imperceptibly. ". . . I wanted to suggest that you stay. I'm sure that we can get it all done in one more night, and then you can return home at ease, so to speak . . . In working order. And for free, entirely for free!"

Taras gave Wacław a look so imploring that it made the Pole feel uncomfortable.

"I don't know," Wacław said quietly. "We've already made preparations . . . But if you think it'll be easy?! . . . I'd be willing . . . No, I'll pay, of course . . ."

Taras sighed with such relief that the Poles exchanged glances.

They treated Taras to a coffee and sat there for another twenty minutes, discussing when Ukraine would finally catch up with Poland, repeatedly coming to the intermediate conclusion of "never". Then two of the Poles left for their train, and Taras, with Wacław's little leather Louis Vuitton suitcase in his hand, led his princely client out to the station square to hail a taxi.

He took him back to the Leopolis, where the prince booked in for another night. A night which, as it happened, he wasn't planning to spend in his hotel room.

The second stone left Wacław's body at just past three in the morning on Krymska Street, by the unfinished villas. The last one came unexpectedly, exactly forty minutes later as they passed Lychakiv Cemetery. Here, unfortunately, the poor Polish prince had to stand holding the glass jar in an uncomfortable position for quite a while, around twenty minutes. And he would probably have stood there a little longer if suddenly, somewhere nearby, a gunshot hadn't rang out, making Wacław jump in fright. He screamed, and Taras could hear a pebble clink against the glass jar.

When Taras delivered Wacław to the hotel he looked awful, but Taras could discern a simultaneous joyous relief on his face. The same expression some women have after giving birth.

Back home again, in the kitchen, Taras looked over his winnings with curiosity. He was so happy it took his breath away. The stones were exactly the same! They had nothing in common with the usual grey concrete kidney stones. In front of Taras, on a clean white sheet of paper, lay two large pearls! Think of how happy Darka would be when he gave her these little pebbles!

His car stopped at the bureau de change on the "boomerang" turn of Franko Street at just gone six. Darka was overjoyed to see Taras, immediately slipping their ashtrays through the money hatch. And Taras decided not to rush the surprise. They drank their coffee and chatted away. She started telling him about the first pearl herself, telling him that she'd checked its efficacy a couple of times at home, and that her father, a man not easily surprised, had been truly shocked.

And just after Darka had said those words, Taras got out the little plastic tub for homeopathic balls and slid it through the slit of the bureau de change window.

"I've got another little gift for you!" he said mysteriously.

Darka poured the two pearls, awash with different colours, out onto her hand, which was covered in a burgundy satin glove.

Her mouth fell open and she looked from the mother-of-pearl peas to Taras' face. He could see amazement and gratitude in her eyes.

"God loves a trinity," Taras whispered, smiling.

"Where did you get them?"

"A gift, from an individual of royal blood."

"Yes." Darka nodded. "No ordinary person could make a gift like that!"

"And me?" Taras leaned forward, his forehead touching the cold window. "I'm the one giving you the present, you know!"

"Well, did I ever say you were an ordinary person?"

"Perhaps I'll wait for you to be freed, and we can go somewhere for breakfast?" Taras suggested, sensing that he was within his rights to ask for a little more of Darka's attention.

Her face darkened.

"I can't. Orest is coming for me at six. I need to go home. Papa always worries until I get back from work. I do his injections for him in the morning. Call me at around two, and we'll meet up! Okay?"

Going upstairs to his apartment on the second floor, Taras stepped over the fifth step, newly painted red. He went into his apartment and turned on the radio. It was still silent for now, but the clock suggested that in three minutes' time the radio would sing him his favourite lullaby – the Ukrainian national anthem.

42

That evening, Taras returned home in a romantic mood.

It felt like his date with Darka had not yet finished. That it was still ongoing. Only Darka was now with him in his heart – his heart and his thoughts. He thought back over the surprising events that had just unfolded, particularly when collecting her from her home. He had picked her up and they'd taken a walk together, holding hands like teenagers. But this time there had been no satin fabric between their palms. When Darka had removed the long burgundy glove from her left hand, he had immediately noticed some kind of bracelet bouncing around on her wrist. Staring at it a little closer, he had recognised one of the pearls he'd given her, now threaded on a leather cord.

"Papa punched the hole for me." The wrist with the bracelet was waved in front of Taras' face. "Now this hand is protected!" And she had smiled as lightly and earnestly as a child.

And the fingertips of the "protected" hand had reached out and touched his own fingers. And then they had held each other's hands for real, and they had walked, in the already approaching dark of the descending evening, along a street full of indifferent passers-by.

The doorbell made Taras jump.

"Oh! Excellent! I've finally caught you!" Yezhi Astrovsky trilled triumphantly.

Taras invited him in. His neighbour wasn't dressed for a day at home – bright trousers and a white and brown chequered jacket, under which his slim but well-built figure was accentuated by a fitted white turtleneck.

They sat in the kitchen, and while the kettle boiled, Yezhi drilled a piercing, wily gaze into the apartment owner.

"I have a request for you," he said eventually. "I want to have coffee with Oksana . . . Well, you understand! . . . You're not *blind* . . . I fear she won't come to mine again, but she'll come to yours! You invite her here, and I'll just drop by, as if by accident! I'll buy the coffee, don't you worry!"

"Yezhi." Taras sighed heavily. "You know what she thinks of you . . . well, not in a bad way, but just that she's her own . . . She doesn't need suitors . . . And she wouldn't be happy with you!"

"That's your opinion!" Yezhi interrupted him. "After I gave her a haircut, maybe her opinion of me changed too. And don't get the wrong idea! I don't want anything like that from her! I just like being near her. She radiates such energy! She's like Chernobyl! She warms me right through!"

"You? Gave her a haircut?" Taras gave his neighbour an uncertain and troubled stare.

Yezhi nodded.

"Not just her! First, I did almost fifty homeless people by Gunpowder Tower and at that shelter they've got out in Vynnyky . . ."

Taras rubbed his temples with his fingers, trying to concentrate. He was finding it hard to even think simultaneously about his neighbour and Oksana; it was unnatural how different they were, inhabitants of two parallel worlds that never intersected.

And yet, as it turned out, their worlds were intersecting all the same; and now that Yezhi had danced his ritual hairdresser dance around Oksana, he thought he could count on her warmer opinion of him!

"Have you been searching for negative vibrations, by the way?" Yezhi unexpectedly changed the topic of conversation.

"Vibrations?!" Taras repeated, looking gobsmacked at the hairdresser. "I'd completely forgotten about them! Damn! I've still got that machine!"

"Well, give it back then," his neighbour threw out calmly. "So you'll invite Oksana round for coffee?"

Taras nodded, now thinking about Simon Fyodorovich from the Laboratory for Paranormal Occurrences.

"When?" Yezhi asked.

"When what?"

"When will you invite Oksana round for coffee? Tomorrow, maybe?"

"No, first I need to take back this vibration measurer . . ."

"Let's do it together!" Yezhi suggested.

Taras absolutely did not want to go outside again that evening, he didn't want to leave the warm shelter of his little apartment. But thoughts of the instrument, lying unused on the floor in the corridor, started to annoy him.

"Well, okay then!" Taras waved his hand.

On the way to the laboratory, Yezhi recommended turning on the machine, in case they suddenly found themselves in range of any anomalous zones. From time to time, Taras checked both indicators, but the arrows didn't so much as tremble the whole way there.

Simon Fyodorovich himself opened the door to the laboratory. It was obvious from the look on his face that he was expecting someone else entirely.

"Here, I wanted to return it to you, so I wasn't keeping it for no reason," said Taras.

He hefted the machine and looked around, trying to figure out where to put it.

The vibration specialist sighed heavily. "Let's go upstairs."

They sat at the table again, just as they had a few nights ago. Only then the atmosphere of the conversation had been secretively alluring, whereas neither Simon Fyodorovich nor Taras regarded the instrument stood between them with any enthusiasm.

"So what happened?" Simon Fyodorovich broke the brief silence. "You were so enthusiastic! Taking the initiative, so to speak!"

"You know, I lost interest somehow," Taras confessed. "And for the last few nights I've not felt a single anomaly. Perhaps they've stopped?"

The vibration specialist looked at Taras with undisguised disappointment.

"They can't stop," he said firmly. "They can weaken, or the opposite, strengthen . . . But you've fallen in love, I take it? Suddenly become a happier man? . . . Hm? Happy people, while they're happy, don't notice anomalies, but that's only temporary. The anomalies are always there!"

Taras glanced at Yezhi, struck by Simon Fyodorovich's insight.

"Yes, I am truly happy," Taras admitted. "In any case, thank you ever so much!"

"Then perhaps *you* would be able to help science?" Simon Fyodorovich roused Yezhi from his thoughts and directed his gaze at the apparatus.

"No, thank you," said Yezhi. "I'm also happy, it seems!"

"That's an anomaly in itself," Simon Fyodorovich said bitterly. "Hundreds of thousands of unhappy people in this city, a whole heap of problems, and tonight I've had two exceptions turn up at once!"

Taras, catching the note of annoyance in Simon Fyodorovich's dissatisfied voice, got up from the table and laid a hand on Yezhi's shoulder. Yezhi jumped up in a hurry.

"Forgive us." Taras looked the vibration specialist in the eyes, at once sheepish and sympathetic.

Simon Fyodorovich saw them out. At the door they bumped into a sturdily built man in a brown sheepskin coat, his collar raised.

"Ah, come in, come in!" The vibration specialist was pleased to see him. "I've been waiting for you!"

Taras and Yezhi crossed to the other side of Arkhyvna.

"Did you see who'd come to see him?" asked Yezhi.

"Who? The guy in the sheepskin?"

"Yeah, it's that writer! Vynnychuk! Clearly he's got something similar going on . . ."

"Vynnychuk?" Taras asked doubtfully. "But is he really bald? He had such long hair before."

"You're getting mixed up! He never had long hair! Never! I'd put money on it, as a hairdresser! I used to cut his hair in the Soviet years!"

43

Alik Olisevych operated the lighting for *Swan Lake* entirely mechanically, without even having to think. He spent all three of its acts and all four of its scenes thinking about himself and the past. Whenever the Lviv Opera House put dancing swans on stage, Alik first pictured Leonid Brezhnev, and then himself, only much younger than he was now. The nation's misconception regarding Leonid Brezhnev's love for Tchaikovsky, and particularly for *Swan Lake*, was of course linked to the fact that the ballet had been played on repeat on all Soviet television channels the day that Brezhnev died. Sometimes Alik was reminded of the general secretary's funeral being broadcast on TV, how his coffin got caught as they lowered it into the grave, how someone had hunched over it and shoved it down, be it by hand or with some kind of instrument. Alik thought of these scenes at moments when his soul was quiet, after a few glasses of vodka, and then they seemed to repeat, only instead of Brezhnev, General Secretary of the Communist Party of the USSR, for some reason it was Jimi Hendrix lying there in the coffin, clasping his electric guitar to his chest. Everything else was unchanged: the guard of honour, the Kremlin wall, and the doddering colleagues of the deceased, their faces frozen in fear of death.

Yes, thought Alik, looking down on the dancing swan-ballerinas in their white flocks. Without Brezhnev, it seemed there was no way of making a logical chain from Tchaikovsky's ballet to the death of Hendrix! It was an altogether surprising train of thought.

This time, after waiting for the finale, and not being particularly surprised when nobody shouted "Bravo!", Alik switched off his lighting rig, paying no attention to the actions of his colleagues on the other side of the hall.

But outside a colleague caught up with him and reminded him that it was his birthday today and they simply had to drink a glass together. The fact that he hadn't invited him over to his house revealed yet another deterioration in his relationship with his wife.

Out of a feeling of workplace solidarity, Alik agreed. The birthday boy ordered two glasses of vodka and some simple *zakuski* in a nearby bar. Alik drank to his health, and then politely indicated he was ready to leave, but the birthday boy begged him to sit with him, even if for just half an hour. Alik could see the pain and longing in his colleague's soul. He thought about how the two of them were the only ones celebrating the man's forty-ninth birthday. They weren't even particularly close, despite nattering back and forth somewhat regularly, and Alik realised that his colleague wasn't just suffering in his marriage, but in his life more generally. After all, if a person has nobody to celebrate their birthday with, that means nobody around them knows when their birthday is; nobody takes any interest in them.

The birthday boy actually began complaining about his life after two glasses, but upon catching the momentary change in Alik's face, he went quiet and ordered more vodka. After that they confined the conversation to matters theatrical. Talking about the theatre always calmed Alik and put him in the mood for sleep.

After the third glass, his colleague began to talk more slowly, while Alik felt his tiredness more distinctly. He politely bid him farewell, after noticing the birthday boy was barely listening to him, and went outside.

The moist cold livened Alik up a little. He looked around, welcoming the dark, starless night to come, and set off with not too firm a gait back to the theatre, so that from there, like a plane, he could fly along the route to his house that he had long since programmed into his internal GPS, down Prospect Svobody and Chornovol Prospect to the very end of Zamarstynivska Street.

After around twenty minutes of leisurely walking, Alik noticed the tiredness shift downwards from his head and shoulders to his feet, making them heavy. He wanted to sit. He stopped, and suddenly staggered, like a thin birch in a strong wind. He looked back. The St Paraskeva clinic towered over the other side of the road. He surveyed his side of the prospect, focusing on the little courtyard of the nearby building. There, behind a low wooden fence, tree-stump stools were flanking a square table, which seemed just as suitable for both children's play and an adult picnic. Alik stepped awkwardly over the little picket fence, which was decorated in the colours of a children's playground – yellow and green. He lowered himself onto a stump and looked around him again. He noticed swings and a little wooden playhouse nearby. The playhouse was no more than a metre and a half in height, but Alik wanted desperately to get inside it and, finding a bed there only a touch too short for his height, lie down on it with his knees bent. But he already lacked the strength to get up from the stump.

An uncontrollable and unpleasant chemical reaction was taking place inside him. His body had started the night as a "stable" flask of liquid solution, into which he had poured vodka, a strong chemical reagent. Now everything inside him was fizzing, stormy, drumming against the inner walls of this living flask and a poisonous gas was floating straight up to his brain. It filled his head, making it feel somehow both heavy and empty at once, pushing at his eardrums from within – he felt pressure on his temples and forehead. And if his head had suddenly turned into a blown-up balloon, not tethered to his neck region in any way, it would have floated straight up, and drifted over the city like a crazed bird that has lost its way. His deep regret about the short but intense drinking session was the only healthy and whole thought left in there.

Pursing his lips self-critically, Alik blinked heavily. The night before him was as dark as it had been, poorly lit by two windows of a nearby building. The smell of the sea suddenly tickled his nose unpleasantly, making him sneeze. But he didn't have the strength to sneeze, so he just shook his head, chasing away the unpleasant sensations.

Then he heard an indistinct rumbling coming from somewhere off to the side, followed by approaching footsteps.

He could now smell the sea even more strongly. It was a salty, iodine smell, like rotting seaweed, thrown to the shore by a wave.

"I'll sit here, is that alright?" came a tired, drunken voice next to him.

On the next stump sat a bearded, hairy guy in a short, dark jacket. Large buttons stretched the jacket across his chest, and even his raised collar was buttoned up, thrusting the stranger's disorderly beard forwards as well as holding his head up, like some kind of post-operative "neck-corset".

"You feeling bad here?" the man asked, staring at Alik with a gloomy, dazed look.

"I am," sighed Alik.

"That's good." The man nodded and threw his back onto the non-existent back-rest of his tree-stump seat. He fell, swore an oath, got up and sat in his seat again.

"Why good?" Alik asked.

"A normal person should be feeling bad," the bearded man said more quietly, and somehow more indifferently. "I'm a normal person, see . . . I feel bad. So if you're feeling bad, it means you're normal too . . . Means you're also a fish out of water."

Alik thought about food, about how, if eaten properly while drinking, he would be able to peacefully walk home now, and after just an hour he'd be lying on his sofa, in comfort and warmth.

From above the birds began their sharp cry-laughs.

Alik lifted his head. He tried to look at the sky, but the wide brim of his hat was getting in the way.

"Seagulls," sighed the man, looking up himself. "Normally everything here avoids me like the plague," he continued after a short pause. "I'm out of place here! Trapped, like an old dog in a swamp! And I can't say anything good in your language . . . And none of you lot understand me!"

"What do you mean? I can understand you." Alik shrugged.

"You understand me?" The man livened up and leaned forward again to peer closely at Alik. This time Alik also managed to get a look at the face of his interlocutor, and his drunken, errant eyes. "You understand what's going on when a sailor turns up so far from the sea?! You understand?"

"A sailor," Alik repeated. "So, is that what you are, sir, a sailor?"

"Please, no need for 'sir's!" the man insisted. "It's stupid to use formalities at night! Night is no time for politeness! I've already been beaten and robbed several times at night!"

"Uh-huh." Alik nodded. "So what are you, a sailor?"

"I am." The man sighed sickly. "Sailed on a dry-cargo vessel. Odesa to Konstanz, Odesa to Istanbul, Odesa to Novorossiysk . . . You ever been to Odesa?"

"I have," Alik answered.

"That means you know what the sea is!"

Alik shrugged.

"A sailor should always be either on the sea or next to it." The man lifted his hands up in front of his face and studied them. Then he clasped them tight, as if he were grasping an oar, and started to make imaginary paddles through the air. "If a sailor finds himself far from the sea, he loses his mind. But the sea can save him!"

Alik realised that the man next to him was insane. And he began to feel scared. He kept watching as the man made another few invisible paddles with his oar, his eyes trained on some point ahead of him.

Then he lowered his oar, opened his hands and looked at them as if to check for blisters.

"The sea saved me!" He turned to Alik. "I nearly died when I came here for Halya! There's nothing to breathe in this place!"

Alik breathed in the air, trying to figure out its taste and smell.

"And then, when I was almost dead, the sea came to me, and it saved me," the man continued after a short delay. "Now I believe that the old sailors were talking to me, from when I first started! They said that when a sailor finds himself far from the sea, the sea will find him itself and . . . It's as if the sea is lodged inside him, he carries it with him, like a shot of vodka, until he returns to the sea . . ."

Here the man's head jerked forwards. A nauseous gurgling spilled from his mouth and he pressed a hand to his lips, frozen, his head leaning towards the earth.

Alik also felt pretty bad. His head was spinning, the smell of iodine returned to his nostrils and sat on the tip of his tongue. He could feel a tremor in his hands, so he put them on his knees.

"God, I feel bad," the man complained, lifting up his head.

"Maybe we should call an ambulance?" Alik suggested warily.

"An ambulance can't cure you of longing. Longing for the

sea ... Plus the doctors couldn't care less about an out of town vagrant!"

Alik thought he could feel the watery intoxication gradually letting him go. But he didn't have time to celebrate that at all before his heart started aching, his whole body encompassed by a cold, nasty shiver.

"Oh! It's hitting you too!" The sailor looked at his hairy interlocutor. "Go on, have a gulp, it'll let go of you! I know!"

He held out an open bottle of vodka to Alik.

Alik shook his head.

"As you wish!" The sailor smirked and took a few greedy gulps straight from the bottle.

The air around filled with even more salt. The seagulls laughed from above, repulsive and harsh. Alik threw a terrified glance upwards, knowing that he was no longer as drunk as he had been when he'd first sat down. An acute physical discomfort pierced right through him, beat him; he was cold, his chest was pounding, and on the tree stump next to him, with half a half-litre bottle of vodka, a drunken, bearded vagrant sat watching him calmly.

The vagrant suddenly sneezed, and Alik received a salty spray to the face, like a wave breaking on a quay.

"You've too much sea inside you!" Alik said, getting up.

The sailor's face became unkind. He lifted a weighty look at Alik, but the hippie was already looking straight up. He could hear flapping wings approaching. He thought he could see a seagull falling towards them. Alik sprang into action. The sound of his footsteps galloped across Chornovol Prospect, both back in the direction of the Opera House, and forwards towards the McDonalds. The echo became more and more sonorous as it bounced off windows and rang in the ears of the runner, drowning out the steps themselves and making him run even harder, the soles of his heavy boots slapping the tarmac, oblivious to the fact that he was running in the middle of the road, not on the pavement.

He soon tired himself out and stopped. Looked around. Realised that he had made it to Detka Street. Another couple of steps and he'd be on his familiar Zamarstynivska. The intoxication had almost left him and his body felt unusually light.

44

Alik woke up at around midday. There was a draught coming from the direction of the corridor somewhere, and after his heavy sleep he couldn't work out what was happening. He lay under his quilt, which he'd thrown a blanket over, but the quilt itself was quite short and, as often happened, his feet were poking out the bottom. Very much accustomed by now to this regular occurrence, Alik would use his feet to gauge the morning temperature in the room, and once he'd determined it, he'd get up and take two steps to stand at the "garden" sink attached to the wall.

This time, however, Alik was struggling to get up. His feet couldn't feel the temperature. Or more accurately, he couldn't feel his feet. His head was buzzing. It refused to help him remember his route home last night. The vodka, the bar, his co-worker; he could remember all of that. He even remembered leaving the birthday boy just in time, as he was slipping into a rage. After that he had floating images of tree stumps and a square table behind a low multi-coloured fence, and a bearded, dishevelled, homeless sailor. And none of it would have meant anything, but sitting next to that sailor, as he had started to sober up, Alik had felt that same shiver that had hit him several times before on Lviv's nighttime streets. Felt that same fear that always followed the shiver, stopping him from continuing his journey, and his heart, which had always pleased Alik with an unobtrusive and harmless presence in his chest, beating like never before. And then there were the seagulls, crying above him, and that smell of the sea, rotten and salty . . .

As he rubbed his wet hands over his face, trying his best to wash it while avoiding reviving those same feelings, Alik thought and thought about this homeless sailor. He was thinking because it seemed like he had forgotten something important.

Only when sitting at his table, looking through the window at the fence, and the lonely wooden toilet stall standing out there, did Alik remember another recent drink he'd had – in Vynnyky, at Vynnychuk's house. If only the vodka hadn't appeared after the wine back then, he could've remembered his writer friend's story before now. But, had the vodka not followed the wine, Alik would not have listened sober to that story, pulled together, as it had then seemed, from rags of raving insanity and an unhealthy writerly imagination. Vynnychuk had said that he went out at night to search for his hero, who'd run away from his novel . . . Or more precisely, he'd crossed out his sailor character himself, thrown him out of the novel, but then started fretting, thinking that the hero had in some way materialised in the city and posed some kind of threat to him . . . This was already material enough for a psychiatrist, in truth . . . Except that the bearded, dishevelled nighttime vagrant was somehow very reminiscent of this character that had been written out of the book.

Alik made up his mind. I need to phone Captain Ryabtsev. Tell him about this sailor!

And he looked around in search of his denim jacket, the pocket of which held his mobile phone. The jacket was lying by the sofa on the floor. His jeans and boots were also on the floor, a little closer to the door. Something was missing. Alik got up and looked around. He couldn't see his favourite wide-brimmed hat, which had protected him from rain, wind and even aggressive seagulls falling from the sky. He looked under the armchair, under the sofa, pulled back the curtain covering the alcove with the fridge and the TV on top of it. He checked every corner, of which there weren't many. But he still couldn't find the hat.

His mood worsened.

He called Ryabtsev. Told him about the sailor, about the smell of the sea around him and the seagulls overhead. And then about how when the sailor was clearly feeling nauseous, even more of the sea must have come out of his mouth, because the air became even salter and more iodine.

"And where was this?"

"Chornovol Prospect, somewhere at the start of it. I'd recognise it!"

"Well, have a rest," the former KGB captain said, lost in thought. "I'll come for you in an hour, and we'll go find out where the Lviv sailors live!"

45

Alik and Ryabtsev drove to the city centre through drizzling Lviv rain. The Piaggio stopped behind the Opera House, but they themselves – Ryabtsev under an umbrella, Alik in a hooded windbreaker – set off on foot down Chornoval Prospect.

They walked slowly. Now and then, Alik would stop to look to either side. In theory, he knew every corner here. After all, he had walked this precise route to and from work hundreds of times. Alik had easily come to learn the corner shops, cafés, kiosks, but were anyone to ask him to point out where he was on a map of the city, he wouldn't have been able to. On this too-familiar street, all need for orientation vanishes. The houses blend into the pavement, the pavement into the road.

"But what was it near?" asked Ryabtsev.

"Near?! There was something there ... A hospital ... That's it, St Paraskeva Hospital!"

Five minutes later they stopped before a three-storey building. In the courtyard, behind a green and yellow wooden picket fence, tree-stump stools protruded from the ground around a table.

Alik stepped over the fence.

"Here," he said firmly. He bent down, picked up a bottle from the floor and sniffed it.

His face changed. He lifted the neck of the bottle to his ear, listened, then gave it to Ryabtsev.

Ryabtsev also lifted it to his ear and froze. He looked bewildered.

"Sounds like the sea," he said, looking around him like he was searching for the sea in question. "We won't find him here by day. Maybe we should check the basement of this building . . . No, better to come tonight. No point wasting our time now."

"Tonight?" Alik repeated, his voiced drained of all enthusiasm.

"When normal people are walking around the city, the homeless hide in the basements. When people return to their houses, the homeless come out into the city. It's very much understandable," said Ryabtsev. "But nobody except the homeless people will tell us anything about this sailor. By the way, you said on the phone that you began feeling bad when you sat next to him?"

"Not straight away. While I was drunk, and he was too, I felt bad, but in a different sense . . . I mean, it was almost fine. Then when I started sobering up, it got to me."

"Badly?"

"Yeah, badly. At first, I was completely drunk! That's probably why it wasn't getting to me. Then afterwards even my heart started aching."

Ryabtsev considered this for a moment.

"Let's analyse this formally!" he proposed, turning to face Alik. "All of this devilry took place at night, or late in the evening. That means it happens when the homeless are drunk, if they've saved up all day for a bottle . . . And we know that you, when you came across an anomaly, were sober. Yes?"

"Yes."

"But yesterday you were drunk, and felt nothing until you sobered up. And you said to him, for some reason, that he had a lot of the sea inside him . . ."

"He said it himself. He said that a sailor suffers when he's far from the sea, and then the sea finds him and sort of . . . protects him. That is, he carries the sea inside him until he returns to the sea!"

"Yes-s-s . . ." Ryabtsev said slowly, thinking. "I know of a similar case! Back in the Soviet times, here in Lviv . . ."

"What, another sailor?"

"No, one guy from the army came over, he'd served in Afghanistan. And he was so used to war that he was suffering from withdrawal, and he'd roam around the city at night, scaring everyone. Not deliberately, it was just that something was coming off him. Some kind of suffering. His psyche was completely screwed! It was like he carried the war with him, just like this sailor carries the sea with him. And the war would sometimes push its way to the surface, to the outside world. At first, they thought he was a maniac of some kind, after all a few people got so scared of him at night that they nearly had a stroke. Psychologists were trying to figure him out, the police followed him everywhere. Finally, they took him in. He completely bared his soul to the psychologists, like they were his own mother. Explained how hard it was without the war . . ."

"And what did they do with him? Take him to the psych ward?"

"No, sent him back to Afghanistan. He died quickly, thank God."

"Why 'thank God'?"

"If a guy can't go without war, you need to send him to war . . . And, well, you won't stay alive at war forever. I meant that he found peace in death. All told, that's what he was looking for: death. Probably why he wandered around the city at night. But you'll find death quicker at war than at night in Lviv!"

"So maybe we need to send this homeless guy back to the sea?" Alik proposed.

Ryabtsev's eyes lit up.

"Well done! I had almost made it there myself, but you're quicker! Yes, that's the right idea! We need to rid the city of him . . . Maybe he's the real cause of all these anomalies!"

"Vynnychuk told me, by the way, that he had been searching for the sailor that night. Like he had written the sailor out of his novel, but he'd materialised . . ."

Ryabtsev turned and looked Alik in the eyes, a heavy look.

"Your Vynnychuk is the real anomaly!" the former captain blurted angrily. "You'd be better off keeping your distance from him! And in general, if this country had fewer writers, perhaps we'd be better off."

Alik, who at first had seemed ready to protest, kept quiet. The mutual antipathy between Vynnychuk and Ryabtsev was so obvious and strong that the most rational choice for Alik was just not to mention one in the other's presence. He understood that perfectly well.

"So then, shall I come for you at about midnight?" asked Ryabtsev.

Alik nodded.

46

After checking his email, Taras turned off the computer and relaxed. His next clients – once again from Poland – were coming the day after tomorrow. Two of them. And that meant both today and tomorrow, he could just enjoy life. And yet, Taras had a couple of doubts regarding the enjoyment of life this evening. After all, this morning Yezhi Astrovsky had politely reminded him of his promise to invite Oksana over for coffee. Whether Taras hadn't quite woken up yet at that moment, or he'd been in too light and relaxed a state of mind, for some reason he had called Oksana there and then in the presence of his neighbour and invited her over.

Yezhi Astrovsky, satisfied witness to the telephone conversation, had broken out into a smile, and after nodding goodbye, he'd left.

Taras sighed heavily. Yezhi Astrovsky's participation in their coffee drinking would not be amongst the most pleasant surprises Oksana could experience.

But the time had passed and the evening was getting close. In order to ease any possible tensions at the table, Taras bought an expensive cake at a nearby patisserie.

On the way home, carrying his sugary purchase, packed

in crinkling cellophane like a bouquet of flowers and topped with a decorative cone of bright red ribbon, Taras thought about Darka.

After all, tomorrow he was free, which meant he absolutely had to see her!

And here his thoughts turned to his Polish clients arriving the day after tomorrow. Would a prince or count be among them, and would he, Taras, get another pearl, maybe even two?! Then he'd gradually collect these precious pearls in a nice beaded necklace for Darka. He imagined it around her neck, glittering in all the colours of the rainbow.

The sky loomed lower, promising rain.

Leaving the cake in the kitchen, Taras threw off his jacket and took off his boots. The clock showed half past five. Oksana would be there at around seven. Yezhi would probably sit by the window and keep a close eye on everyone coming in the front door, and only once he saw her would he get himself ready to go the next floor up, avoiding the fifth step, painted red.

At half past six Taras' mobile rang. One look at the screen was enough to set his heart fluttering – it was Darka.

"Hi! How are you doing there?" he asked in a giddy voice.

"Better than ever!" she replied. "And you? You're not busy today, are you?"

"Well," he faltered. "I have guests today . . . but what is it?"

"Papa suddenly decided to invite you over for dinner. I was surprised myself! It's so unlike him . . ."

"For dinner? Today?" Taras was at a loss. "I don't know . . . I'll think of something . . ."

"Please!" begged Darka. "I'm scared he'll change his mind if it's not tonight . . . I'm surprised he's considered it at all . . . Plus he suddenly brought you up himself!"

"Got it," Taras said more decisively. "What time do I need to be there?"

"About seven."

"I'll be there, without a doubt!" he promised.

Taras hung up. He needed to think of something, and a plan began to come to him of its own accord, but it was a plan like a ticking bomb, the disarming of which would be very difficult indeed.

He went down to his neighbour.

"Yezhi," he said. "I need to go – right now. Can you meet Oksana at my place? I've already put everything out there."

Taras' neighbour looked at him guardedly.

"It'd be better if you waited for her and then left, if you wanted to leave us alone together."

"I don't want to leave you alone together," Taras said, slightly irritated. "It's just that something's come up . . . I'll try and get back as soon as possible . . ."

"Don't get angry," Yezhi Astrovsky back-pedalled. "I'm so greatly indebted to you! I'll meet her, you don't have to worry! And we'll wait for you together!"

47

Darka was waiting for Taras outside her house in a twilight slightly watered down by the dull light of a streetlamp.

The cold, unusually harsh leather of her glove brushed against his cheek. Taras was surprised. He was already so used to the soft, satin touch of her fingers, but here was leather! But winter was coming soon, after all, and every evening was colder than the last.

"I came out to meet you," whispered Darka, hugging Taras, pulling him closer to her. "And to warn you . . ."

"What is it?"

"You really don't know my father . . . He's a good man, but he might seem strange to you . . . So, just listen to what he says, and pay no attention to how he says it . . . Understood?"

Taras shook his head.

"But I'll listen," he promised.

She gave a terse smile and gestured for him to follow her.

The steps of the entrance hall seemed like marble to Taras. The staircases were lit up by wall lamps, and everything was shining clean.

"Is your father an oligarch, or a politician or something?" Taras asked carefully.

"No, we got lucky!" Darka turned while walking. "The apartment next to us was bought by a Kyiv deputy. He's here once a month and always brings a new blonde with him, to show her Lviv. But they refurbished the entrance hall!"

Darka's apartment was up on the third floor. The corridor was wide, almost two metres. Taras was surprised by how quiet it was.

Darka led her guest into a large living room. The oval dining table, like the soft furnishings, was too modern for the antique chandelier hanging from the ceiling, or the restored oak parquet, which creaked pleasantly underfoot. But this eclecticism of styles didn't irritate the eye. Nobody was seeking to brag about anything, as if everything in this apartment had happened of its own accord.

On the oval table, plates and bottles sat atop a beige linen cloth. On the right of each of the three plates was a yellowing ceramic cup, from which the operative parts of a knife, fork and spoon poked out like the tops of pencils. Taras was tickled by the creativity of whoever had thought to lay the table this way. He looked around to ask Darka, but she had already disappeared behind a door. From the direction of the door, which had already shut again behind her, drifted the smell of freshly fried carp.

The parquet behind Taras creaked. He turned around. Before him stood a man of average height, wearing a dark blue jacket over a slim black sweater and jeans. He was barefoot, his hands hidden in his jacket pockets, and looked at his guest with a furrowed brow. His lips shuffled, as if he were saying something silently.

"Good evening." Taras walked over to meet him.

The man's handshake was firm. He nodded.

"I'm Taras," the guest introduced himself, aware that the owner of the apartment was well aware of this fact. But he had to start the conversation somewhere.

The man nodded again. He pulled his right hand from the pocket of his jacket. Taras noticed something in it that looked like a torch. Darka's father lowered his gaze to the object, pressed a button on it that Taras couldn't quite see, and into the silence of the room came a soft humming. After that he pressed the apparatus to his throat, under his right cheek.

"Good evening," came his strange, seemingly mechanical voice, trembling and vibrating. "My name's Boris . . . Sorry for the sound . . . This is the only way I can talk . . . I had throat cancer, and the doctors removed my vocal cords. Let's sit!" Boris pointed at a comfy nook near the coffee table.

Taras lowered himself into the sofa, Darka's father into the armchair opposite.

"I'm very indebted to you," he continued. "I'll be honest with you: I didn't like you at first. Darka is my only daughter. I have my own medical problems, and since she was born Darka's had hers. We aren't a very healthy family . . . She has her allergies . . . They used to be triggered by nearly any-thing – house dust, poplar down, rainwater. But recently it's only been her allergy to money that's troubled her. I'm so happy you were able to help her!"

"Well, I . . ." Taras shrugged, shying away from the sudden praise.

"I really am very grateful," Boris went on. "When situations like this happen in fairy tales the king usually gives the young adventurer who's saved the princess from a deadly affliction half the kingdom and the princess' hand in marriage. I don't have half a kingdom, but I'm happy to give you my daughter's hand. Believe me, it's the most valuable thing I have . . ."

Darka's father sighed heavily and put the hand holding the device on his knee. Then he gave Taras a questioning look. But Taras was lost. His hands suddenly felt cold, and then he himself became somewhat chilly. He wanted to cover himself in a blanket. Head included. He thought Darka had invited him over just to meet her father, and that would have been entirely normal and natural. As it was natural for any father to want to get to know his daughter's suitor. He wondered if she knew what he was going to talk about?

This thought suddenly threw Taras from cold to hot.

"Yes, thank you," Taras mumbled. "I wasn't expecting . . . Forgive me! Darka is very dear to me, believe me!"

Boris smiled upon hearing this. He lifted the apparatus to his neck.

"I know she's dear to you. Or else I wouldn't have invited you! What you've done is a miracle, and I know that there are no miracles without true love."

Taras nodded and turned around to search for help, glancing towards the door Darka had disappeared through five minutes earlier.

"You understand . . ." Through sheer willpower, Taras was able to level his voice, ironing the shakiness and uncertainty out of it. "I haven't even proposed to her! I assume she doesn't know what we're talking about in here?"

Boris laughed, and live sparks appeared in his eyes.

"You've given her more than a proposal," he said. "I don't drink, but I can offer you a glass! Whiskey? Wine? Vodka?"

"Wine," Taras requested.

Once Darka returned, they sat at the dining table for a meal of fried carp and mashed potato, and a pickled cabbage salad to remind them that it was autumn outside. Taras drank red wine, Darka white and her father mineral water.

The atmosphere was quiet and peaceful, but Taras' face expressed a frightened happiness, and his eyes lit up in a peculiar way whenever they came to rest – as they often did, even against his will – on her bare hands, her slim fingers. On both of her graceful wrists shone a familiar pearl, worn on a thin leather bracelet. On a slightly thicker leather band around her neck hung a silver pendant in the shape of a heart, the size of a two-kopeck coin, in the centre of which was ably installed the third pearl.

48

Taras returned home in a strange condition, feeling neither his legs underneath him nor the night around him. The voice of Darka's father was still vibrating mechanically, like a wind-up talking toy, in his head. But what he'd said had been a much greater surprise than how he'd sounded.

He didn't even notice himself entering his courtyard on Pekarska, climbing up to the second floor, opening the door and turning on the light. He would have undressed just like that and gone to sleep without paying it any attention. But in the main room something crunched underfoot and he looked down to find a broken mug on the floor. There were dirty dishes on the table.

He remembered that while he had been having dinner with Darka, Yezhi Astrovsky and Oksana should have been on a date of sorts. Right now he could only guess how that had turned out. Perhaps the broken mug said more than enough. Taras could very easily imagine Oksana being beside herself. He didn't have the slightest doubt that his hairdresser neighbour could easily have forced her out beside her own self. Taras imagined in horror what Oksana must have thought when she realised she was going to have to have coffee alone with Yezhi, without her actual host!

He nervously got his phone out and saw the time on its screen – zero hours and forty-eight minutes. A little late to call.

Taras dropped limply into a chair at the table, chewing his lips in unease and catching the taste of Darka's farewell kiss. He sighed deeply. Decided that in the morning he would have to call Oksana and explain.

But in the morning, he was awoken by a racket. From somewhere nearby came the bang and whistle of a construction tool.

After pulling on his tracksuit bottoms and a sweater, Taras poked his head out of the door. And on the stairs below him he saw a fat man dressed in blue workers' overalls. He was kneeling with his backside towards Taras, planing away at something.

Taras went down a few steps and spotted Yezhi Astrovsky standing in his doorway, keeping an attentive eye on the work in progress. The red-painted step had been taken out and was now leaning against the wall, while the worker was installing a new one in its place.

"Needs some shaved off on the right!" Yezhi offered in a wheezy voice.

"I can see that," the fat man in the overalls grumbled. "I've already taken some off!"

Taras lodged his complaint. "You've started all this noise a little early!"

"How's this 'a little early'?" Yezhi asked, surprised. "It's two o'clock! When exactly did you get home, by the way? We waited ages for you!"

"You waited for me?!"

"Well, not 'we'. I waited ages for you. Oksana left earlier."

The worker in the overalls lifted his head to listen in on their conversation.

"See, there'll finally be a new step, completely silent," Yezhi said after a pause. "Oksana got really angry with me about it yesterday! Turns out I promised her I'd get it replaced a month ago! How am I supposed to keep track of all the promises I make?"

"Come by later!" Taras told his downstairs neighbour before returning to his apartment.

He was craving coffee. As soon as he'd made some, he remembered yesterday's chocolate cake. That's exactly what he needed right now: strong, bitter coffee and chocolate cake!

The cake was not in the fridge. Surely Yezhi and Oksana couldn't have eaten it all? Perhaps it was on a windowsill somewhere?

Taras returned to the main room, but couldn't find it there either. Troubled, and resigned to the industrial noise still coming in from the stairwell, he drank his coffee and waited for silence to set in again, at which point his neighbour would ring the doorbell, come in and explain everything. Only then would Taras understand what exactly he had to apologise to Oksana for.

Twenty minutes later it actually did go silent outside. And the doorbell rang almost immediately. Yezhi called Taras out to the stairs and guided him down to show him the newly installed wooden step. He asked him to step on it. Taras duly obliged, and it didn't give out the slightest sound.

"Try jumping!" suggested Yezhi.

Gloomily, unwillingly, Taras gave a couple of hops and nodded.

"You see?" Yezhi cried jubilantly. "Or hear, more like? After all, you can't hear anything! We put a thick rubber sole under it, I took it from a guy I know's boot!"

"Perhaps you should come over," Taras said insistently, looking up at his open door.

"Alright," Yezhi agreed. "But not for long. I'm not doing so good today."

49

Taras, sat at the table covered in the evening's dishes, looked inquisitively at Yezhi.

"Well, what happened here then?" he asked, looking at the fragments of mug on the floor.

"Eh, nothing much." Yezhi shrugged, also glancing at the floor briefly. "Oksana broke a mug – it was already empty . . . But we were chatting so sweetly. She kept asking when you were coming . . ."

"Uh-huh." Taras sighed, unconvinced. "And how was the cake? Tasty?"

Yezhi paled and shivered. His hand jerked up to his mouth, as if he were going to be sick.

"You feel bad?"

His neighbour nodded, got up and ran from the room. Taras went to the window and pulled back the curtains. Watched the fish swimming slowly in their aquarium. Gave them some food. And listened to the steps behind his back as Yezhi returned to the room.

"So what," he asked his neighbour. "You ate the whole thing?"

Yezhi sighed.

"Essentially, yes," he said with difficulty. "All of it. Only not 'you' as in 'us', generally speaking, more 'you' as in 'me' . . . But I didn't want to . . . Oksana made me."

"How did she 'make' you?" Taras asked, taken aback.

Yezhi's face assumed a pained expression.

"Well, all told . . . I'm the one to blame. I came on too strong. It's that I . . . I wanted to kiss her . . . But she said she'd only do it if I ate the whole cake. Well, I ate it . . . I felt terrible straight away. Couldn't sleep all night – my liver was hurting. I thought I'd have to call an ambulance . . . And I'm not feeling good now either! I'd best go back to mine."

"Should I call you a doctor?" Taras asked considerately.

"No, thank you. I'll manage, I'll manage." Yezhi got up and took small steps into the corridor.

There was slanting rain outside, and little regular drops were drumming against the window. Taras watched the water blur the image of the courtyard, taking away the lines and corners, smoothing everything.

The evening's conversation with Boris, Darka's father, drifted back into his mind to the accompaniment of the rain. And Taras, as if entranced by the droplets of rain racing each other down the glass, realised something that was both important and frightening in its simplicity: he had to – and he wanted to – propose to Darka. Before her father did so on his behalf!

His phone rang.

"You don't have anything to say to me?" Oksana asked without even saying "hello".

"I've been meaning to call for a while," Taras confessed. "But things just kept coming up."

"What's going on with you?" she asked, but her voice lacked its usual care and warmth.

"Why don't I come over, I'll tell you everything," Taras suggested.

"Alright, I'm at home. Come over!"

A walk in the rain calmed Taras a little and brought some order to his erratic thoughts. Twenty minutes proved long enough for him to rehearse the apologies he owed his oldest friend, and to devise a strategy for fluidly moving the conversation on to a topic that would distract Oksana from the date with Yezhi that he had "arranged".

Oksana looked surprised as she let Taras into the apartment. "Why are you looking so pleased with yourself?"

Taras hurriedly removed his smile. He became serious and a little unhappy again.

"If I hadn't known you so long, I would never have spoken to you again!" declared Oksana, sat on a pouffe on the other side of the table-on-wheels.

"Oksanochka!" Taras gathered his courage. "I'm sorry! It's not my fault! I didn't intend to leave the two of you alone! It's just that my fiancée called me and said that her father wanted to meet me urgently . . ."

The hostess's eyes bulged in surprise.

"You're getting married?"

Taras nodded helplessly.

"And you didn't even think to ask my advice?"

"I'm doing precisely that. As we speak . . ."

"Is it not a little late?" Oksana's face took on its usual caring and thoughtful expression.

Taras shrugged.

"But you're getting married for love? Not for anything stupid?"

Taras shook his head.

"She and I haven't even had any . . . close contact."

Oksana shook her head in shock.

"No, don't even think of it! I love her. That much I know! She's bizarre and charming and . . ."

"So what's her name?"

"Darka. She works in the bureau de change on Franko, you know, by the tram stop, right at the start . . ."

"Is that important?" Oksana asked, perplexed.

"What?"

"That she works in a bureau de change?"

"No," Taras replied. "Although, maybe, yes. Or else I wouldn't have met her . . . She had an allergy to money. I accidentally cured her of it . . . And . . ."

Taras suddenly went quiet. It seemed that even with a friend as old as Oksana, it wasn't worth telling her everything! She was still a woman, all the same. And when women hear about other women, they have completely unexpected thoughts and conclusions.

"You cured her?" Oksana asked.

"Well yes, only it's a complicated story . . . We'll come back to that . . . In short, I wanted you to be a witness at our wedding."

"Me?" Oksana was overjoyed. "Of course! But you need

to introduce me to her first! Sorry, I'm still annoyed about last night . . ."

"Oksana." Taras lowered his voice. "What happened between you and Yezhi?"

Oksana pursed her lips and wiped her forehead with her right hand.

"That idiot of yours said I was 'sweet' . . ."

"He's not my idiot!"

"Well, your neighbour then! He said I was sweet, and that he really wanted to kiss me."

"And you told him that if he ate the entire cake, you would let him?" Taras recalled Yezhi Astrovsky's story.

"No." Oksana shook her head. "I said that if he loved sweet things, he should eat the whole cake first, and then we'd see! He really did eat it, and his face went blue straight away. He got sick and waved his hand, telling me to leave! So I left!"

A weight lifted from Taras' heart.

"So you didn't break the mug?" asked Taras.

"No, once I'd left the apartment I heard something smash. It was probably that."

"Well, you should forgive him," sighed Taras. "He's lonely, nobody wants him . . . He's psychologically unstable . . ."

"He's extremely emotionally stable, and not at all lonely!" Oksana said maliciously. "He's already introduced himself to half of Oselya! He's made a myth of himself amongst the homeless, like he's some kind of saint who agonises over the fates of the unfortunate . . ."

"Why a myth?" Taras disagreed. "Seems to me like he has

353

that in him. Of course, he got to know you first, and then took an interest in the fates of the unfortunate after that . . ."

"So I was his first 'unfortunate' then?" Oksana retorted. And suddenly all of the malicious intent on her face transformed into something else, into sorrow. Except Taras couldn't tell if this sorrow concerned Yezhi Astrovsky or Oksana herself.

"Would you consider yourself a happy person?" Taras queried unexpectedly, after a short break in the conversation.

Oksana didn't answer right away.

"Normally I'm happy." Her voice dropped to a whisper. "Sometimes I get lonely, that's understandable. But I'm used to it, and it's easier for me like that. If I meet someone sometime that I can be happier with, I'll be thrilled. But I won't go searching for them . . . Loving someone is like helping them out, you know. Two people loving one another mutually is more like mutual aid than anything else . . ."

"Look at you, you're like Mother Teresa," Taras sighed, half-joking.

"And what have you got against Mother Teresa?" Oksana looked her guest in the eyes, softly but critically.

"Nothing – I like her. But are you not scared that one day they'll call you 'Mother Oksana'?"

"Not at all," laughed Oksana. "They won't call me that. "First they'd have to call Lesya from Oselya 'Mother Olesya'! You sure you don't want anything to drink?"

Taras thought for a moment. And he realised that he absolutely did not want to drink. He had never spoken so truthfully and openly with Oksana before. Then a thought crept up on him: Maybe she wants to drink? In that case, it would be no sin to join her!

And he nodded.

They drank a glass of cognac each.

"When's the wedding?" Oksana asked.

"Don't know yet. I still haven't proposed!"

"What do you mean you haven't proposed?" Oksana, bewildered, stared at Taras as though he were an idiot.

"No, I'll do it today. Absolutely. But I wanted to talk to you first."

Oksana liked what she heard.

"Let me know when and where you're having your next date! I'll come over and watch you together!"

50

As it neared midnight the rain paused to catch its breath. Alik went out into the courtyard and listened. Ryabtsev should already be there by now! Occasional cars passed the building in the direction of Bryukhovychi, their tyres squeaking on the wet tarmac. Nobody seemed to be heading towards the city centre.

Alik returned to his annex. He stood by the stove, whose iron rings were pouring a homely, kind warmth across the room. He sat in the armchair and yawned. If he wanted, he could turn on the record player and wake his body up, give it a shake with some good rock vibrations; but then his stepmother would wake up and bang angrily on the wall between their living territories, both under the same roof of Alik's parents' old home. He didn't want to disturb the old woman. Let her sleep! At her age, a peaceful night's sleep was a healthy thing.

Alik recalled the words of an old friend. After burying his father, the guy had said that when both of his parents were alive, they had really *lived*, and then when it was just his mother left, her life quickly transformed into "living out". And she only managed to live out another ten years: boringly, joylessly, but patiently.

And now Alik's stepmother was patiently living out hers. He gave a heavy sigh.

At twenty to one the familiar rumble of a scooter engine flew in through the open window. And Alik went once more out into the courtyard. He saw the former captain guiding his yellow Piaggio in through the open gate, the engine already turned off.

"Perhaps we should leave straight away," suggested Alik.

"We're going, we're going!" Ryabtsev nodded. "I'll leave the scooter with you. So I don't have to worry about it!"

Alik was confused. "But how will we get there?"

"I've called a taxi. Be here in five. We need to drink, don't we? And I never drive drunk. Well, almost never."

Alik helped Ryabtsev push the scooter into a small shed.

"Grab this!" Ryabtsev handed Alik a sports bag, in which something was clinking.

"What's in that?" asked the old hippie.

"Anaesthetics. A litre of vodka and some snacks," explained Ryabtsev.

A car stopped at the roadside on the other side of the building.

"Oh! That's for us!" The former captain smiled. "Opera House!" he instructed the taxi driver once they'd got in the back seat.

"Aren't you running a bit late?" the driver joked.

Ryabtsev ignored him. The car turned, almost grazing the enormous concrete tank defence that had been left on the Zamarstynivska kerb back during the Second World War.

"Or perhaps we should get out a bit earlier?" whispered

Alik to the former KGB captain. "We could go straight to the right courtyard!"

Ryabtsev shook his head.

"We'll walk from the Opera, just as you did that night! What if he's sat somewhere else?!"

It was deserted around the Opera House. The traffic lights on the prospect were working as usual, but they gave out their signals idly, because there were neither pedestrians nor cars present. The wet tarmac shone under their feet.

"Something's telling me that he won't be here tonight," Ryabtsev said sadly. "Do you always walk this way home?"

Alik nodded.

The windows of the surrounding buildings weren't lit, but the streetlamps were. A police car passed by. It slowed a little, as though the policemen wanted to take a closer look at the nighttime pedestrians. But after a moment the driver pressed the accelerator again and the car sped off.

The next traffic light switched from green to red. And suddenly Alik felt bad, and his heart started pounding. He staggered, losing his balance. He was frightened. He looked over at Ryabtsev to ask for help. And he saw that the captain had gone pale.

After wrenching himself around and shattering through his sudden pain and weakness with sheer willpower, Alik fled the junction at pace. Ryabtsev figured out what was going on and followed him.

They stopped about twenty metres from the ill-fated junction, both feeling a sense of release.

"He's there, he's there again," Alik whispered, looking over at the now-visible roof of the three-storey building sunken into the courtyard.

Ryabtsev nodded. "Looks that way." The former captain squatted down and waved at his long-haired acquaintance to do the same. "Time for a picnic. Apologies for the lack of amenities . . ."

The former captain waggled the zip as he opened his sports bag. He pulled out a newspaper, unfolded it, and laid it on the pavement. Then he placed a bottle of vodka and two disposable plastic cups, which were immediately filled, on top of the paper.

The sight of the full cups of vodka made Alik nauseous. Meanwhile, Ryabtsev pulled out sliced lard, two charred spring onions, a salt cellar, two slices of black bread and two boiled eggs. He looked up at the hippie.

"*Hiba hochesh? Musish!*"[19] he said with compassion and picked up a cup.

Alik picked up the other and put it to his mouth. It was good vodka, no smell.

"Right, come on then, to victory!" Ryabtsev downed his in a gulp. He immediately grabbed a spring onion and crunched his teeth into it.

They sat in silence for around three minutes.

"Let's have another," Ryabtsev said after the pause. "Just in case!"

They drank another glass of vodka each. Alik immediately felt his legs growing heavy. He got to his feet with difficulty and watched from above as Ryabtsev tidied the food, the vodka and the cups back into the sports bag.

The two cups of vodka had changed Alik's gait. He walked with a light sway. Ryabtsev's was more firm.

They stopped as soon as the edge of the three-storey house came into view.

"How robust are you feeling?" asked the former captain.

"About normal," sighed Alik.

"You see," whispered Ryabtsev. "It works!"

And suddenly above them came the sharp cry-laugh of a seagull. Both Alik and Ryabtsev craned their necks and saw several large white birds circling agitatedly around the roof of the building.

"Forward!" Ryabtsev commanded.

They turned into the courtyard. A large seagull was standing on the pathway that led to the low yellow and green fence, behind which, on one of the tree stumps by the square table, someone was sitting.

"There's two of them there!" whispered Ryabtsev.

"And one of them's in my hat," Alik added unhappily.

Ryabtsev and Alik approached the table. Above their heads flapped the wings of the disturbed seagulls. They cackled again, a repulsive, ear-splitting sound.

"Mind if we join you?" asked the former KGB captain.

The two people, sat opposite one another, turned to look. Alik was shocked to realise that he recognised both of them. Both the hairy sailor in the dark mariner's jacket over a dirty striped vest, with his, Alik's, brown leather wide-brimmed hat now sat quite snugly on his head, and his friend Yurko Vynnychuk, whose facial expression suggested that it was not wine he'd been drinking this evening. Yurko took his glasses from his nose, wiped them with a handkerchief, and put them back on again, staring at their uninvited and unexpected guests.

"If you've brought your own, take a seat!" said the hairy sailor.

Ryabtsev nodded, lifting up the sports bag to show them. "We have indeed."

Alik wanted first of all to take his hat from the sailor's head. But he held off, remembering the old adage: "Problems are solved through love, not force."

"So anyway, whenever we were approaching Marseilles –" the sailor started talking again, looking back at Vynnychuk – "we always kept the castle of the Count of Monte Cristo to our right. It was just there, right next to the port . . ."

"Huh?" Startled, Yurko Vynnychuk averted his eyes from Alik and Ryabtsev and stared at the storyteller. "And so, what, he was literally just sitting there?"

"Literally!" The sailor nodded with a heavy head. "And he wasn't alone! Our guys were there too . . ."

"Your guys?" queried Vynnychuk. He squinted again out of the corner of his eye at the uninvited guests who had sat down with them. "No, tell me how you ended up in Lviv!"

"Got to pour me something, or else my soul will be hurting!" the sailor requested.

Vynnychuk picked up a bottle of vodka from the ground and filled the empty glasses. He squinted in the direction of the newcomers again, but now somehow more fully. He managed a nod for Alik, but just looked at Ryabtsev disparagingly.

Ryabtsev put the sports bag on his knees, then took out

the food and laid it on the table; he put the bottle of vodka between himself and Alik before taking out the same disposable cups.

"Here?" the sailor said after a short pause. "Because of Halya, of course, because of the barmaid on our ship! She made such good macaroni *po-flotski*![20] I'd never eaten anything like it! It was like a narcotic! So I fell in love, like a mere whippersnapper! But she took that macaroni with her, and on the shore she signed off earlier than planned. She went home, back to Galicia. She told me her address, somewhere here, in Lviv. Only I forgot it. I've saved up three months of leave, and now I've come looking for her . . . After all, a man should keep hold of a cook like that! But when I asked people about her, they all sent me away with a flea in my ear!"

"But how were you searching for her?" asked Vynnychuk.

"Well, I asked if anybody knew a woman called Halya who cooked macaroni *po-flotski* better than anyone else . . ."

Vynnychuk shook his head mournfully.

"If anyone in Lviv is even able to make macaroni *po-flotski*, they'd never admit to it!" said the writer.

The eyes of the homeless sailor bulged at him. "What?"

"That stuff is like wartime rations!" explained Vynnychuk. "Only traitors to the Galician culinary tradition can cook like that!"

"See, if you'd taken her photo . . ." Alik jumped into the conversation, leaning his head to one side to peer under the hat, into the sailor's eyes. "It's easier to find a person with their photograph!"

The homeless man began to squirm. He wiped his fingers over his forehead and gave Alik a guarded look.

"I've seen you somewhere before!" he said after a moment.

"You and I sat right at this table and drank vodka, very recently!"

"Perhaps, perhaps," the sailor said distantly.

"And you've got my hat on your head!" Alik added.

"Yes." The homeless man nodded, and the brim of the hat repeated his nod elegantly and airily. "Perhaps it is yours . . . But you won't wear it after it's been on my grimy head!"

"Why wouldn't I?" Alik disagreed. "You wore it after it'd been on my own grimy head, didn't you?"

The troubled homeless man took off the hat and dropped it on the table, after which he stared even more fixedly at his long-haired interlocutor.

Alik carefully reached out his hand and took the hat, but he didn't put it on his head straight away. It went in his lap instead.

Yurko Vynnychuk stared at the former captain. "And how did you end up here?"

"We were looking for him." Ryabtsev looked at the homeless man.

"I found him first!" the writer declared with pride, and suddenly he grimaced in pain. He scrunched up his face, reached out for his glass, drank two mouthfuls of vodka and put it back on the table with an obvious, immediate relief.

"So when did you find him?" Alik enquired.

"Two hours ago."

"But I found him last night, ask him!" Alik nodded at the vagrant.

Ryabtsev coughed and started looking around with a searching eye. "Smells of the sea again," he said through another cough.

The vagrant sailor jumped, as if at the words he'd just heard. He shook his head and made a loud swallowing motion, then lifted his right palm to his mouth. His body shuddered as if he were about to vomit.

Above their heads, the seagulls' wings began beating again and the cry-laughs resumed.

Alik looked up in fear, into the invisible black sky. The sailor's nauseous moment clearly passed. He went quiet, falling into a daydream.

"It doesn't matter who found him first," Alik said amicably. "The main thing is that we get rid of him!"

"And how do we do that?" Yurko Vynnychuk shrugged. "Kill him, you mean?"

"No, he's your character, isn't he?" Alik laughed. "You've 'killed' him once already!"

Yurko stayed silent for a moment, then shook his head.

"Not mine," he said. "I would never have dreamed up Halya and her macaroni po-flotski . . ."

Alik's chest began thumping again. A growing unease crept up on him and he filled his glass with vodka. Knocked it back. The unease and pain went off somewhere into the darkness. His body became pleasantly heavy, while his head did the opposite, turning light and pliable, and his thoughts arranged themselves in a neat line like tin soldiers.

"We need to get him out of the city," Alik said to Vynnychuk in an entirely serious and convincing tone. "He only causes trouble! If you don't believe me, check how many people from this building –" Alik pointed at the sleeping three-storey block whose courtyard they were sitting in – "go to a doctor tomorrow with complaints about their heart!"

"But we don't have any complaints about our hearts, do we?" Yurko Vynnychuk laughed mischievously.

"That'll be the vodka," Alik said.

"Vodka creates an internal barrier that blocks his negative vibrations!" suggested the former KGB captain. "If we weren't drinking, we might as well call an ambulance immediately. And more likely than not, it would already be too late!"

"Yes, I've understood that," Vynnychuk muttered unhappily. "But still: where do we take him?"

"Send him home," suggested Alik. "To the sea! He's carrying the sea in him right now, and he might drown half of Lviv in it if we're not careful! You understand?"

Yurko Vynnychuk reached out a hand across the table and began to jostle the daydreaming vagrant by the shoulder.

"What is it, who?" the sailor grumbled before opening his eyes.

"So, do you have an apartment in Odesa?" asked Vynnychuk, leaning across to the former sailor.

"Yes, on Kotovsky, by the sea . . ."

"So what are you doing walking around here?" Vynnychuk said sternly.

"Well, my wife's there . . ."

"And what, she isn't going to let you in?"

"She probably would . . . But not in that way . . . Plus I've got no money for the trip . . ."

"We can get you the money," came the voice of Captain Ryabtsev again. "We just need to know where to find you a train that'll take you to the sea. Perhaps some kind of cargo train?!"

"Why a cargo train?" Vynnychuk looked at Ryabtsev in surprise, if not to say in anger.

"Firstly –" Ryabtsev gave a tight smile – "your friend reeks. And his clothes reek too. Besides that, his vibrations will wreak havoc on the other passengers. They'll start thinking there's some kind of infection on the train, they'll take it down a siding and put it in quarantine . . ."

Yurko Vynnychuk considered this. Alik looked at his writer friend, also trying to think of a way out of this situation. And he found one before the others did.

"I know where we can wash him and get him changed!" he said gleefully. "I washed there myself! In Vynnyky!"

Yurko Vynnychuk looked fearfully at his long-haired comrade.

"I sincerely hope you don't mean my house?" he asked.

"No, there's a homeless shelter there. Oselya. They've got a rack of clothes, a launderette and a hot shower. He can get a quick wash and pick out some new clothes."

"I will not change into civilian clothes!" the homeless man stated firmly. "I'll remain exactly as I am!" He wiped his black sailor's jacket down with his hand.

"And what vehicle are we going to take him to Vynnyky in?" asked Ryabtsev. "A sober driver can't get him there, and a drunk one is a danger behind the wheel!"

"I know a taxi driver who's always drunk at the wheel," Yurko Vynnychuk said calmly. "I'll call him!"

51

In the dead of night a silver Volga, either decoratively or defensively equipped with curved chrome tubing on all sides, picked up the four passengers from the courtyard of thirty-nine, Chornovol Prospect. The driver, Vanya, greeted only his acquaintance Vynnychuk on arrival, looking indifferently at the rest of them.

Alik sat up front, while Yurko, Ryabtsev and the homeless sailor arranged themselves on the back seats, putting the sailor in the middle, as though he might try to jump out en route.

Five minutes into the journey Vanya, a bulky and robust man of about fifty, threw back a slightly disturbed look.

"Something about you lot is making my head hurt!" he said irritably.

"We haven't said a word!" Vynnychuk retorted.

"Maybe that's why," the driver said, eyes back on the road. "Best start talking about something. Just quietly!"

"Or, perhaps, we could pour you a little glass of vodka instead?" Vynnychuk suggested.

Vanya was shocked. "What are you talking about?! I'm driving!"

"But did you not have a drink before you went out tonight?" Yurko Vynnychuk argued back placidly.

"Sure, I did. But that was before I started driving. I don't drink *and* drive!"

"Alright," sighed Vynnychuk. "Then we'll have to have a chat."

He looked at the gloomy, half-daydreaming sailor, then at Ryabtsev. He had no particular urge to speak to the former KGB captain, but there was no chance of getting any conversation out of the sailor.

"So, pan Captain, how did you come to realise that the ancient Carpathian sea had nothing to do with the anomalies?"

"It wasn't me," Ryabtsev replied calmly. "It was Alik! I always said he'd go far . . . He didn't actually go anywhere, to be fair . . . But he remained true to himself, and just as imaginative as ever."

"And the two of you never accidentally drank vodka together in the Soviet period?" Vynnychuk asked, not without a hint of malice.

"In the old Soviet era he drank port and I cognac, so we only crossed paths when I was working . . ."

"You can't drink cognac – beastly stuff," the sailor muttered suddenly.

Alik turned to Vynnychuk. "Yurko, stop picking on him. What's he ever done to you?"

Vynnychuk sighed, took his glasses from his nose, wiped them with a handkerchief he'd whipped from his jacket pocket, and put them back on again.

"My heart's beating pretty fast, for some reason," complained Vanya the driver.

"That's already pretty serious." Alik turned back, only this time he looked straight at Ryabtsev. "Pour everyone a glass, or else lord knows how this trip's going to end!"

Vanya the driver drank the first cup. He didn't even have to stop the car to do so. He applied the brakes, then emptied the plastic cup in one gulp and gave it back to Alik, before returning his right hand to the wheel. The second dose of the antidote went to Alik, and the sailor got some last of all.

They left the Vynnyky lake behind them to the right, and five minutes later the driver lowered his speed again for the winding descent into the suburb. Once they reached the Sviatoslav hotel, he came to a stop and turned to Yurko.

"Where now? Yours?"

Yurko's face betrayed a rash of swiftly moving thoughts. He shook his head.

"Where then?" Vanya the driver insisted on a concrete response.

"What's the time?" Ryabtsev asked sleepily.

"Half three," the driver replied.

Yurko Vynnychuk sighed loudly.

"I have a wife and a small child ... And a dog in the courtyard. It'll start barking and wake everyone up ... No. We really can't go to mine."

"Well, we'd be down in the basement or sitting in the kitchen," Alik said pleadingly. A new force had started pushing him towards a drunken slumber, and drunken slumbers differ from their sober counterparts in that they do not choose a resting place for the sleeper, who could lie down in any pigsty, flowerbed or roadside going.

"No," said Yurko, now more harshly.

"You could sit out by the veterans' hospital! There's a little table there, and a bench. And it's not even cold out today!" suggested the driver.

"Yes, that'll do nicely." Vynnychuk livened up. "And the people there mind their own business, they won't go calling the police on us!"

The driver took these words as a signal to action, and the car set off again.

Very soon it stopped on a wooded hill, where the road gave way to a dirt track. To the left and right stood a few two-storey buildings, each with two entrances. Behind the houses, unmoving, stood a pine forest. On the left a few little garage blocks were visible.

"The bench is just there, in the courtyard," the driver told them.

Alik sighed, then watched the fog that formed as a result of his sigh.

"Bit cold," he said. "Probably somewhere around zero degrees . . ."

"Not at all, four over," Vynnychuk insisted. "Will you be alright here until morning?"

"What about you?" asked Alik. "You're a local, we'll be safer with you . . ."

"Well, I was hoping to go home," Yurko muttered.

"Real friends don't abandon you in your hour of need," Ryabtsev announced to nobody in particular.

"You're not my friend," Yurko shot back.

"What about Alik?" Ryabtsev asked, staring directly at the writer.

"Alright." Yurko lowered his head.

Then, slightly swaying, he approached the open driver's door to settle up with Vanya. The car drove off.

All four of them went over to the wooden table and sat at the bench in the same positions as an hour prior, in an entirely different place.

Once again Ryabtsev opened his bag and took to serving everyone. Yurko Vynnychuk took two glasses made of real glass from his jacket pockets, and a fresh half-litre bottle from his inside pocket.

Alik looked around him. The air here was cleaner and fresher, and the sky seemed to stand out in brighter tones. It seemed to hang higher than it usually hung over Lviv. Just then, something unexpected diverted his attention from the sky. His eyes stopped on a lit corner window belonging to the building whose courtyard was hosting this enforced continuation of their nighttime picnic. The light in this window shone with an unusual, slightly orange yellowness. It suited the current night so perfectly! Like a traffic light frozen on yellow, screaming "Attention!". Alik looked around again. And he heard vodka gurgling as it migrated from bottle to glass.

He looked at Ryabtsev. He was amazed at how easily visible the former captain's face was to him. Even as they sat in total darkness, if you didn't count that window, casting down an improper triangle of light onto the courtyard.

"What time does this homeless shower of yours open?"
Vynnychuk asked Alik tiredly.

"Nine."

From above, over their heads, came the beating of wings, and two or three seagulls gave a simultaneous, penetrating laugh.

52

A sleepless night had put Taras in a bad mood. He wasn't expecting to fare any better tonight either, of course – he had a job arranged. But the job never materialised. Just before the appointed time, the client had phoned and told him that the train he was travelling on had hit a car on a level crossing outside Lviv, and thanks to the impact his stone had come out on its own. The Pole apologised politely and offered to treat Taras to a hotel breakfast as compensation. But Taras refused the offer. The news of the crash had embittered him, as though it had deprived him of not just one night's work, but his entire future. He lay on the sofa and closed his eyes, but sleep didn't come to him until six o'clock the next morning, when the anthem of his native land started up on the kitchen radio.

At ten a.m. he opened his eyes and immediately screwed them shut again, thanks to the sunbeam coursing through the uncurtained window. The sun, as it happened, was just what Taras needed, and like a green leaf on a tree, he soaked up its energy, feeling better and more lively for it.

And then he thought of Darka.

He got up and walked over to the window. Sprinkled some food for the fish, carefully watered the cacti, and experienced even more strongly the sun's warmth on his cheeks and bare shoulders. And, frowning, he pictured Darka walking up behind him to embrace him, her breasts pressing into his back. Her hands gave him warmth, too. To him, they felt hotter than the sun's rays.

He dialled her number.

"Hi!" he sighed happily after hearing her sonorous 'Hello!'. "Let's get lunch!"

"Let's! But where?"

"The Old Piano. One o'clock."

"Great, see you soon!" she said.

The sleepless night was forgotten. Taras walked to the nearest newspaper kiosk to buy a fresh issue of *Vysoky Zamok*.[21] On his return, he habitually stepped over the fifth step. It was only once he reached the door to his apartment that he realised what he'd done. Then he went back downstairs again and walked up one more time, this time without skipping it. Quite the opposite, in fact, he stepped on it with all his might. The fifth step didn't produce so much as a peep.

Life's changing for the better, he thought.

Ten minutes later the doorbell rang.

Yezhi was dressed in a black Adidas tracksuit, with trainers on his feet.

Taras was surprised. "Went for a run, did you?"

"No," answered Yezhi. "They brought a new shipment in at the 'Everything for a Hryvnia' shop. From Europe. Look at this stuff! Looks brand new! You making coffee?"

"Come on in!" Taras stepped aside to let his neighbour through to the main room.

"Well, how are things?" Yezhi enquired as Taras came over to the table holding a coffee pot.

"Fine. Only I don't have much time. I have something very important to do."

"Important?" Yezhi Astrovsky was intrigued. "What would that be then?"

"I'm going to ask a girl for her hand and heart . . ."

"Wow!" Yezhi's face became serious. "Do I know her?"

"No, the only one of my friends you know is Oksana! By the way, she's going to be my witness!"

"What, is the wedding that soon?" Yezhi's voice dropped to a respectful whisper.

"Very soon," answered Taras. "The sooner, the better!"

"Is she expecting?"

Taras waved away his neighbour's suggestion.

"No, but she will be soon. If everything goes to plan!"

"And who will be her witness?" Yezhi asked cautiously.

Taras froze. He hadn't given it any thought.

"I don't know," he said after a moment.

"Taras," Yezhi Astrovsky began, so sweetly it was as if he'd just put two full spoons of sugar in his mouth. "Choose me! We've known each other for quite a few years now!"

"What are you saying?!" Taras was truly puzzled. "What kind of wedding witness would you make?"

His guest took offence. "Why not?! I've been sober for a few months now, I look after myself, I help the homeless and I earn an honest living!"

"No, I don't mean that." Taras sighed. "A witness should be young and unmarried . . ."

"I am unmarried," Yezhi whispered. His face went pale, his jaw quivered.

"No," Taras said, more gently this time. "You aren't suitable. Sorry!"

Yezhi got up from the table and jerkily, as if all of his muscles had suddenly given way, fell to his knees before the seated Taras.

"Pick me!" he begged. "You don't understand how important it is for me!"

"Oksana won't like it!" Taras said, wavering.

"Only on the outside! She has such a tough exterior! But inside, in her heart, she'd be happy! You'll see! Women, they're all like that! They say 'no' loudly, just to then say 'yes' quietly. I'm experienced, I know what I'm talking about!"

"Well . . . I'm going to ask her first . . ."

"Don't! How are you not understanding me?" Tears filled Yezhi's eyes. "This is a matter of my life and death, you realise! If you don't pick me as a witness, then the day of your marriage will be the day of my funeral!"

"Yezhi, that's a poor attempt at blackmail." Taras pursed his lips.

"It's not blackmail, it's life! You couldn't care less about me! But I changed the step in the hallway for you!"

"For me?" Taras was angry now. "Perhaps you ate an entire cake for me as well?"

Yezhi Astrovsky, as if to defend himself, pushed forward his right palm.

"Let's say no more about that," he requested. "I, by the

way, don't walk on that step. I live below it! But you live up here, on the first floor!"

"Do you not come up to visit me via that step?! Get off your knees and sit back down!"

"Only if you promise you'll have me as a witness."

Taras suddenly felt tired. This is just what I needed on such an important day! he thought.

And he lowered his eyes to his neighbour, still kneeling before him in his black Adidas tracksuit and his white trainers.

"We'll see," he said.

Yezhi shook his head.

"I'm not leaving until you say yes!" he said unexpectedly firmly.

"Is this how you talk to ladies?" Taras shook his head in annoyance. "Fine. Yes . . . probably . . ."

"Yes or probably?"

"Probably yes."

"You said yes, you said it yourself," Yezhi insisted, getting jauntily to his feet. "Just don't forget to let me know when and where! I'll need to go to the secondhand shop to pick out a suit! Oh, but what day is it today?"

"Wednesday."

"Wednesday." Yezhi smiled. "I've got to go! I'm giving cuts to bums in Vynnyky today! Maybe I'll see Oksana too! Shall I pass on your best?"

"No, please don't!" sighed Taras.

Shutting the door behind his neighbour, Taras imagined in horror what Oksana would say when she found out that the other witness to the wedding would be Yezhi Astrovsky. No, he wouldn't mention it just yet.

And then the telephone rang. Oksana seemed to have sensed that he was thinking about her at precisely that moment.

"Well?" she asked. "Where can I get a look at your betrothed?"

"The Old Piano, one o'clock," he informed her.

"Excellent! Did you pick a restaurant right next to my place on purpose?! Thanks!"

53

Taras was only twenty or thirty metres from the restaurant when a biting hail started pattering from the sky, and the wind grew sharply colder. He stopped, quite surprised, and looked up to find hundreds of falling grains of ice. They hit his cheeks, smacked against the pavement and scattered underfoot like white sparks.

"Winter's here," he sighed.

All tables in the restaurant's main hall were full. The diners were chatting energetically. The words that tore themselves away from the general hubbub of conversation suggested that there were businessmen and lawyers amongst the patrons. The second hall, usually used for banquets, turned out to be almost empty.

Taras took a corner table. There was still twelve minutes until Darka arrived. But what if she got confused when she couldn't see him in the main hall?

He sent her a text message with his precise coordinates.

A waitress came over and handed him a menu. He ordered a bottle of Borjomi to start.

After running his eye down a long-since familiar list of dishes, he suddenly started thinking not of food, but of winter.

It really was just about to start, after all, and as always, the temperature of his daily life wouldn't be the only thing to change: so, too, would its rhythm. There was a seasonal break on the horizon in terms of work and earnings. Driving over cobblestones is a dangerous matter when they're covered in ice or snow. There was one comfort, however: his needs had never been great. He was capable of putting money aside for a snowy day. True, the coming winter might prove costlier. After all, there'd be two of them living in his apartment, so they'd need a little more money.

This thought returned his mind to Darka. He'd never heard a single good word from her about money. But that was down to her allergies, surely. And now? Now that he had accidentally cured her of this strange ailment? Perhaps now her attitude towards money would soften?!

His mobile rang in his jacket pocket.

"Hey!" came Oksana's whisper down the phone. "I'm behind you. Don't turn around! Everything's fine. Bon appetit!"

Taras was still cramming the phone back in his pocket when Darka appeared at the table. "Wow, you've hidden yourself away here!"

She had ruddy cheeks, a joyful smile on her face, and green satin gloves on her hands.

Taras jumped up and gave her a kiss on the cheek. He helped her take off her extravagant green goose-down coat. His eyes were glued to the gloves, but Darka took them off quickly as she sat down.

"How are things?" she asked.

"Good."

"Are you ready to order yet?" the waitress enquired politely.

"Just another minute!" Taras opened a menu and laid it on the table between himself and Darka.

"I want fish!" Darka declared.

"We have fresh carp, I warmly recommend it!" the waitress informed them in a business-like, trust-inducing tone.

If she had been young and good-looking, Taras wouldn't have believed her, but this waitress was over forty, and her pleasant, serious face seemed to suggest that she took responsibility for her words.

"Two of the carp, and another bottle of mineral water," he announced.

The waitress retreated. Taras watched her leave and decided that the moment had come for his important conversation.

"Darochka!" He looked her in the eyes. "I love you!"

"I know you do," the girl replied happily.

"No, you don't!" Taras shook his head. "I love you so much, I want you to become my wife!"

Darka froze.

"Have you properly thought this through?" she asked after a moment.

"Yes," Taras nodded. "Very properly!"

"I don't know," Darka sighed. "I have work, you know . . . We wouldn't be able to spend the nights together . . . You won't like it . . ."

Taras noticed tears glistening in Darka's eyes.

"What are you talking about?" he whispered, leaning over to her and taking her by the shoulders. "What are you talking about?! We just need to believe that it'll all be alright! And what do you need work like that for, anyway? Sitting all night in a late-night bureau de change?"

"Well what else can I do?" Darka asked uncertainly. "Sit all day in a daytime one?!"

"No, I have a completely new idea for you!"

"What is it?" Darka looked at Taras plaintively. "Oh, do say!"

"I will," Taras promised. "But first, say that you'll be my wife!"

Darka stayed silent. Her face dropped and she looked lost and disorientated.

"Well, do you want me to get down on my knees and beg?"

"Don't! What are you talking about?" She looked frightened. "It's full of people in here!"

Taras looked around and saw that there was no longer a single free table in their hall. His survey didn't make it as far as Oksana, presumably still sitting behind his back.

"Marry me!" Taras repeated in a whisper, only now his whisper sounded firmer and more insistent.

A few seconds of stillness and sighs later, Darka nodded.

Taras got up, embraced her, and kissed her again on the cheek. He tried to kiss her on the lips, but she diverted his face with a light touch of her palm.

"There's people here," she whispered.

"So Darochka, when can we formalise our declaration?"

"In the registry?" she asked. "Let's do it in spring, in April!"

"What?" Taras shuddered at what he was hearing. "Let's do it tomorrow! Or on Friday! But Thursday would be better! Let's do it tomorrow!"

"What's the rush?" Darka was surprised. "Usually it's only pregnant couples who get married in such a hurry." She smiled again.

"I am pregnant." Taras smiled too. "Pregnant with you."

Darka gave a resounding laugh. The people at the next table looked over.

"I'll need to tell Papa," she said. "But what if he's against it?"

"He's not, I already told him," Taras lied. "I even have witnesses for the nuptials! Well, one of them at least!"

"And who would that be?" Darka asked playfully. "One of your exes?"

"No, how could you! It's Oksana, a very old friend of mine."

"Will you introduce me to her beforehand?"

"Absolutely!" Taras gushed. "I can introduce you right now!"

"Now?"

Taras looked behind him and saw Oksana, sitting at her table in proud solitude. She suddenly looked a little afraid.

"Let's go and sit with her," Taras whispered.

And they both went to join the frightened Oksana.

"Oksana! This is my fiancée," Taras announced, indicating Darka, who also looked scared as she sat at the table.

Oksana and Darka stared at one another in not entirely amicable silence.

"What's up with you two?" Taras asked, sitting next to Darka. "Oksanochka, this is Darka, Darochka, Oksana!" He accompanied his introductions with elegant hand gestures.

"A pleasure," Darka sighed eventually. "So does that mean you knew you'd be a witness before he'd proposed to me?"

"But he has proposed to you?" Oksana asked guardedly.

"Only just now."

"And you . . . you agreed?"

"I did."

"Oh, thank God." A blinding smile appeared on Oksana's round face. "I was thinking, why are they coming over to sit with me? Have they had an argument or something?! You're so lucky, Darochka . . . More precisely, it's him that's lucked out." She threw Taras a dirty look. "He's such an oaf! He eats terribly and skips meals! Someone needs to keep an eye on him . . ."

"In what sense?" Darka seemed on edge.

"In a good sense." Oksana quickly corrected herself, realising she'd said something ambiguous. "He just doesn't look after himself, and if you're taking a man as a husband, you want him to live a long and healthy life! Or else what's the use in him!"

"I don't need any 'use' from him," said Darka.

"Oh, sorry! I'm so nervous, I'd better stay quiet!" Oksana announced, before hurriedly adding: "Plus I've got things to do! It was lovely to meet you." She gave Darka a genuine smile. "Forgive the motor mouth, but I really would be happy if you'd take me as a witness!"

Oksana got up, took her jacket from the coat rack and almost ran from the room.

"Strange friend you've got," sighed Darka.

"She's an actress, you see! She's always scared of coming

across as insincere. But she's a good person, all told! She helps the poor!"

Darka laughed. "Does that make you poor?"

"No, I'm lucky! But she also helped me!"

"Ah, you promised me something!" Darka suddenly livened up. "Remember?"

"When?"

"Today! You promised to tell me something, if I agreed to become your wife!"

Taras tried to remember.

"Regarding other work," Darka hinted.

"Ah! Precisely! I wanted to propose something to you. Well, it's that you do the same as I do, but with women! It's straight-forward. I'll buy you an old foreign import, and you can apply for your licence! I only work with men, after all . . ."

"But I haven't studied medicine," Darka said doubtfully.

"Neither did I. Gave up in my third year! But you don't need much of an education to get my know-how! If you want, you can get a licence as a 'folk doctor', or something like that. But you could also just do it as you are. The main thing is to be a good driver!"

"I'll think about it," Darka said seriously. "I am interested!"

54

Just before sunrise, every one of the two-storey building's windows suddenly lit up at the same time. Out into the courtyard came an elderly man in pyjamas, slippers and a grey *shapka-ushanka*, walking a small dog on a lead. The hat's ear flaps weren't buttoned up, so they shook around haphazardly as he bent over and unclipped the lead from the collar.

"Go on then, Filya, off you run! Do your business!" he said tenderly.

Filya sprinted over to the four dozing men slumped over the table. The dog first ran a lap of the sleepers, observing the quiet, and sniffing their feet and the buried table legs in great detail. Then it stopped and howled.

One of the men stirred and lifted his head. And the dog ran back to its owner.

"Vagrants barging in again!" the man grumbled, clicking his tongue in disapproval. "Filya, let's go to the sheds. We can have some peace and quiet there!"

And he went around the corner of the building. The dog raced after him.

"Hey, comrades!" Ryabtsev rubbed his eyes and got his phone out to check the time. "Wake-up call! Seven a.m.!"

Alik shivered. He lifted his head. His hand felt out his hat on the bench and he sighed with relief.

"Nearly froze," he said. "And my head hurts . . ."

Ryabtsev turned to the still-dozing Vynnychuk.

"Pan Writer, time to wake up!"

Yurko Vynnychuk muttered something incomprehensible in response.

"Well, yes." The former captain nodded. "Bohemians are never up this early!"

The word "Bohemian" clearly made it through to the writer's ears, and he wearily tore his head from his arms.

"It's still dark yet," he said sleepily, and yawned.

"All the lights are on in the building!" said Ryabtsev.

"But they won't be yet in mine," the writer said haltingly.

"Yurko," said Alik, his voice coming across surprisingly fresh and sober. "Do you feel alright?"

"What? Of course . . . I'm fine!" replied Vynnychuk.

"And you?" the hippie asked the former captain.

"Fine, my head's buzzing a bit is all. What is it?"

Alik Olisevych shared his observation. "Well, we've clearly all sobered up, and we're sat here with this sailor next to us!" He nodded at the sleeping homeless man.

"Okay, so what?" said Yurko Vynnychuk, not understanding the thrust of Alik's suddenly energised words.

"Well, the fact that none of us are suffering, even though we're sat right next to him!"

Vynnychuk considered this.

"Yes," he said. "Strange!"

"Nothing strange about it!" Ryabtsev waved away the

thought. "He sobered up as we did! You see, when he's sober, he's not dangerous! If he didn't drink, it wouldn't be a problem!"

"Precisely," agreed Vynnychuk. "Sober and asleep, he doesn't suffer at all, so he has no need to share his suffering with the world. He's entirely harmless for the moment! The main thing is not to give him anything to drink when he wakes up!"

"Do we even have anything to drink?" Alik asked. Feeling the top of his head getting colder, he took his hat from the bench and jammed it over his ears.

"I've got another bottle," said Ryabtsev, looking under his legs at the sports bag.

"Me too," admitted Vynnychuk.

"Perhaps we can pretend there's no more?" Alik proposed.

But they didn't manage to pretend. Ten minutes later the sailor woke up with a raging thirst, and with such a mean fire in his eyes that at his first mention of needing a further drink, Vynnychuk pulled the half-litre from his inside jacket pocket and put it on the table. The sailor's hand quickly and violently grabbed the bottle by the neck and pulled it towards him. He took off the lid and filled a cup.

"Wait a second." Vynnychuk stopped him. "I'm just about to run home to see the family, but you'll be heading down to the showers! Will you be able to find them?"

"How will we find them if we don't know where we are?" asked Alik.

"Just stick to that road the whole time, keep going down and down until you hit a wide street, then turn right. You'll work it out from there!" With that, Yurko hurried off down the route he'd just described.

"But when are you coming?" Alik shouted after him.

"I'll be there sometime around ten."

Alik sighed heavily, and suddenly he felt scared, and nauseous, and his heart was pounding, something he'd experienced more than a few times by now. He looked fearfully at the sailor and realised that he had just drunk another cup of vodka. Alik quickly poured some for himself and Ryabtsev. They drank hurriedly, paying no heed to the taste or strength, and the nausea and pain disappeared.

"Oh, how dreadful I feel," the sailor started muttering, looking around him. "Every morning the same! Just drying and drying!"

"Maybe you need something to eat?" Alik asked helpfully.

"Is there anything?"

Alik looked over at Ryabtsev. He picked the bag up from the floor. Pulled out a quarter-loaf of black bread, more charred spring onions and a small knife. He cut the onions and bread.

The homeless man poured the remains of Yurko's vodka into his glass and jettisoned the empty bottle under the table. Ryabtsev took his vodka unwillingly from his bag.

"Don't get too drunk," he said to the sailor. "We're going to get washed now. Time for a shower."

"One doesn't rule out the other," said the vagrant.

Ryabtsev poured for himself and Alik from his bottle.

"To your departure!" he said, looking into the murky eyes of the sailor.

"Where else can I go?" the homeless man asked back in a displeased tone.

"Home, to the sea."

"The sea is my home!"

"Exactly! Today we'll try and send you to Odesa!"

The vagrant, holding the glass at his mouth, stared at the former captain of the KGB.

"What, really?" he asked, his voice already slurred from the vodka.

"Really," Alik confirmed, looking very concentratedly at the sailor. "But only after we get you clean!"

"Right then, shall we go?" Ryabtsev looked over at Alik.

They got to the building that housed both the launderette and the shower room just before half past nine.

Alik banged on the door, then reached for the handle. It was unlocked. They went inside, and just to their left another door opened to reveal a red-headed woman in a white gown and slippers. She looked in surprise at Ryabtsev, or more precisely, at his sturdy boots.

"Good morning," Alik said. "I visited you not too long ago, if you remember!"

She nodded and smiled. "Yes, yes."

"We've brought a comrade to see you. He could do with a good wash," said Alik slightly searchingly.

"The shower's free," she said. "Go through! You know the way."

They led their guest into the room, the woman following. The sailor looked around fearfully, but sighed in relief at the sight of the shower cubicle.

"Thank God," he said in a trembling voice. "I really thought you were planning to harvest my organs . . ."

Ryabtsev and Alik looked at each other.

"On what grounds?" Ryabtsev shouted unhappily. From the corner of his eye he noticed that the woman was clutching at her chest behind them.

"Well, someone told me that they often trick bums here into going somewhere, pretending it's for a drink, then cut out their organs and sell them to oligarchs for operations."

"Why, you got any healthy organs in you?" Ryabtsev asked cruelly. "Your liver, perhaps?"

"Hardly the liver," the vagrant said thoughtfully.

"Well then get undressed and get yourself into that shower!" ordered the former captain.

"You wouldn't have any Validol?" the woman asked, wincing. "Feels like something's gripping my heart . . ."

Alik rushed over to her.

"Let's go out for some fresh air, quickly! Chop-chop now!" He took her by the hand and led her outside.

"The first aid kit is just there on the left, try that!" she asked.

Alik turned around. Attached to the wall was a plastic box with a red cross on the lid. He opened it and rummaged through the bandages, creams and medicines, fixing his eyes on a vial of calendula tincture.

"Here, you need to drink all of it! Quickly!" He turned agitatedly to the red-haired woman, twisting off the cap.

"It's mixed with alcohol . . . I'm not allowed, I've gone two years without a drop!"

"Take it! This is the only medicine that can help you right now, trust me!"

The woman lifted the open vial to her mouth and drank a little.

"All of it!" Alik repeated.

She drank the entire vial and froze, listening to her heart.

"It's going away," she whispered after a minute.

"Well thank God for that," sighed Alik.

He went back inside. The red-haired woman followed.

"You seem pretty clean today," she said to Alik, a smile appearing on her face, though she was clearly still unsettled by the sudden heart pain. "But you probably wouldn't say no to a shower either?"

"The main thing now is to get this thing washed!" Alik gestured at the vagrant, who was puffing away at the tangled, multi-coloured laces of his right boot.

The woman leaned a little closer to Alik and whispered: "Your friend smells bad."

"I know," Alik whispered back.

"Why don't I pick him out some new clothes?" she suggested. "I've got a good eye. He's a size 54, probably about 170 centimetres tall."

The woman left. And just in time, because Ryabtsev was finally getting the vagrant undressed. The homeless sailor's underwear was so tattered the holes looked like a deliberate pattern – it's possible it wasn't even his underwear.

"Alik," Ryabtsev called. "Pour me another half-glass, quick!"

"And me!" demanded the vagrant.

He finally swayed his way into the shower cubicle. Alik,

who had also drunk half a glass to guard against the sailor's vibrations, reached into the cubicle to turn on the water and check the temperature, then went over to the shelf where the shampoos were kept. He saw the familiar "nettle" variety, but opted for another plastic bottle, on which he could see a label with a handwritten note: "anti-dandruff and anti-flea". He opened the shower door, releasing a scorching plume of steam. Alik jumped back.

"You're cooking yourself!" he cried, plunging his hand back into the cubicle. He fumbled against the wall and fiddled with the temperature. Then he squirted some shampoo into his hand and slapped it onto the vagrant's wet hair.

"Give that a good scrub!" he shouted in his face.

After shutting the door to the shower cubicle, Alik went over to the table.

"You know," Ryabtsev said. "If we let him sober up, he shouldn't have any problems on the train. When he's sober, he doesn't affect the people around him!"

"That's unrealistic." Alik shook his head. "He'll find something to drink, and then . . ."

Ryabtsev gave a heavy sigh.

"Alright," he said. "I'm going out into the courtyard to phone a guy I know. His son works at the station. Maybe he can suggest something? It'd be best to put him in some post carriage or something, without any other passengers!"

Ryabtsev left.

The door of the shower cubicle suddenly opened. Alik turned around and saw a nude, washed homeless man, steam rising from his head.

"Any more of that shampoo?" asked the sailor.

Alik fetched the plastic bottle from the shelf. The homeless man took it into the shower and shut the door behind him.

The red-haired woman came back into the room, carrying some carefully folded clothes: trousers, sweater, shirts, socks. She put the pile down on the windowsill and looked over at Alik.

"There's some nice coats in there too. Even an old sheepskin one, but it's got no buttons at the moment."

Alik nodded his thanks, and the woman, satisfied with her good deed, gave him a quick smile, full of self-worth. Then she pulled on white cloth gloves, picked up the sailor's dirty clothes and took them away. Only his boots with their multi-coloured laces were left lying by the wall.

"They'll call me back," Ryabtsev informed Alik as he came back from the courtyard. "What's he up to, still washing?" He squinted at the shower cubicle.

"Let him be." Alik waved him away. "Water enriches sailors!"

The woman came in another couple of times while the vagrant was in the shower. But then she said she was going out to the shop, and asked them, should any other homeless people arrive, to hurry their comrade along.

Their "comrade", however, made his own way out of the shower soon after. His movements were evidence to the fact that he was starting to sober up again. He seemed on the verge of suggesting that it was time for another drink, but before he could his eyes hit the spot on the floor where he had left his clothes.

"What the devil is this?!" he said, troubled.

"They brought you clean clothes, just there, on the windowsill!" Alik said soothingly.

The vagrant looked doubtfully at the windowsill, frowned, and walked over. He picked up a crimson sweater, held it up to himself, then laid it back down and pulled the trousers from the pile.

"What is this shite they've given me, where are my clothes?" he asked. "This won't do! I had my vest and my sailor's jacket! I'm going nowhere without them!" he added harshly, but a moment later he dressed himself in the clean clothes and sat, resigned, at the table.

"I'll make sure they wash them," Alik promised. "The woman in charge will be back any minute!"

"It'll be two soon," Ryabtsev suddenly said. "But your writer friend appears to have forgotten about us!"

"He's probably messing around with his kid," Alik suggested. "Or the wife . . . Or the dog. I'll call him!"

But Alik only called him much later, four hours or so, once the vagrant's old clothes had been wash and tumble-dried, and once his appearance had been changed for the better thanks to a happy coincidence, or to be more precise, thanks to the timely appearance of a skinny, sharp-nosed, charitable and very chatty hairdresser. The hairdresser, whom Alik persuaded (not without difficulty) to drink two glasses of vodka to protect him from the dangerous bacilli flying through the air from the mouth of the sailor, trimmed his vagrant client very neatly, and even transformed his multidirectional beard into a neat, short display of facial hair – the kind you find on young university lecturers who don't want their students to mistake them for classmates.

Their plans for the evening also started to take form. The son of Ryabtsev's former co-worker informed him that the Lviv–Odesa train, departing this evening, would meet all of Ryabtsev's requirements: both conductors on board liked a drink, and nobody would call the train manager a model of sobriety either.

The red-haired woman began to look a little more sharply at the visitors once the sailor asked for vodka and the tall, long-haired man got out a bottle and poured a cup for all three of them. But they were calm and quiet about it, so the woman, despite a clear breach of the establishment's rules, didn't kick up a fuss, instead turning her thoughts to her past life, unpredictable and alcohol-fuelled. And the time flew by that way until six, when the moment came for the building to close and the guests to be politely seen to the door.

They went out into the courtyard, and that's precisely where Yurko Vynnychuk found them. The fresh face of the clearly well-rested writer filled Alik with envy.

Ryabtsev enlightened Vynnychuk at once regarding their plans for the evening. He asked him to call Vanya. And once again the silver Volga, gilded with welded chrome pipes, approached them and stopped. Vanya looked out of the car and nodded at Vynnychuk, ignoring the others.

Once they were aboard, the sailor requested more vodka. And Yurko Vynnychuk, having planned everything out beforehand, retrieved from his inside coat pocket another half-litre bottle, and from the outer pocket four metal cups, stacked one atop the other. Due to the cups' small size, the passengers and driver were forced to drink four times on the way to the train station to ensure that they arrived safe and sound.

From that point onwards everyone acted according to Ryabtsev's instructions. He knew the platform number, the number of the carriage, the forewarned conductor's name, and whose name they needed to drop to get him onside.

Thank God, the conductor met them with an already merry, drunken twinkle in his eye. He shook all of their hands, his palm proving somewhat moist, before leading them into a tight staff coupe. He determined which of them was travelling to Odesa with him and was particularly happy to see Vynnychuk take three further half-litre bottles and a litre canteen from who knew which pockets and place them all on the table by the window.

"It's the low season right now," the conductor said happily, surveying his potable gifts. "We've not got many passengers. No need to worry! We'll get there with no hiccups!"

"The main thing is that you don't bring him back!" Ryabtsev warned. "His wife's waiting at home for him!"

"It'll all be carried out in the finest fashion," promised the conductor, and his hand reached for the nearest bottle.

At twenty-two hours and fifty-nine minutes, train 228 pulled out of the platform, on which stood Alik Olisevych, Yurko Vynnychuk and the former Captain Ryabtsev, holding on to one another and swaying in unison. They stared attentively at the departing train's tail end, distinguished from the darkness by its reddish taillights.

Suddenly something changed in the air, and all three of

them sank their heads into their shoulders, as if they were expecting thunder or rain. But this fluctuation was nothing to do with the climate. From above they heard the multitudinous beating of wings, and against that sonic backdrop, large white birds pierced the air with their sharp cry-laughs.

Vynnychuk, Alik and Ryabtsev looked up and tried to work out what was going on. Above their heads in the sky swirled an avian whirlwind, consisting of thousands of seagulls, with new gulls flying up to meet it from all sides, joining the strange tornado with a cry. And suddenly the cries died away, only the wing-flapping continued up above them. And the stormy cloud of seagulls circling over the platform moulded suddenly into a wedge, a well-organised, sharp avian wedge of seagulls, which flew after the Lviv–Odesa train.

Alik, Vynnychuk and Ryabtsev were unable to tear their eyes from this wedge, from this endless white streak of birds, sweeping across the dark sky to follow the departing passenger train. And more and more seagulls kept flying up and arranging themselves at the tail of the wedge.

"Did you see that?" Ryabtsev asked in amazement. "All the evil spirits upped and flew away!"

Alik nodded and looked at Yurko Vynnychuk.

"So perhaps it really was your hero – the one from your novel?"

Vynnychuk shook his head.

"No; similar, but not him," the writer insisted. "But generally speaking, every character in every book has a prototype walking around somewhere out there, in the real world. That much I can tell you!"

398

"I'm not drinking for two weeks!" Alik Olisevych changed the topic of conversation. "Not a drop!"

"I'm doing a month!" Vynnychuk said decisively.

Ryabtsev looked at them sceptically and shrugged.

A week later, however, the three of them got together in Ryabtsev's dovecote. The late-autumn early evening was soundtracked by rain, quietening down and growing stronger again, its rhythm first slowing, then reviving. But inside the doves' little tower, warm air from the electric heater and the breath of the three men rose to the third floor, benefitting the birds, who stayed largely stationary due to the encroaching winter. One by one, they would suddenly stretch their wings and close them again, and their rustling added a strange, other-worldly comfort to the evening's atmosphere. Below, next to the yellow scooter, stood three open umbrellas, ready to shield their owners again in another couple of hours.

Ryabtsev had been waiting in the dovecote when Alik and Vynnychuk knocked on the wooden door. It turned out that he had been restoring order and making ready since lunchtime. The result of his preparations was a lavishly deco-rated (for a bachelor) table, on which sat sliced *Doktorskaya* sausage, sardines, herring fillets and other tasty goodies. In the centre of the table rose the glass obelisk of a bottle of Khortytsa.

"So then, we are now the liberators of Lviv!" said Ryabtsev

ceremonially, pouring out the vodka into glasses. "Only Lviv will never know!"

Yurko nodded. "The main thing is that the sailor doesn't come back!"

"He won't," Ryabtsev said assuredly. "It's been a whole week already! There's storms in Odesa, they showed them on the news last night!"

"Serves them right!" sighed Yurko Vynnychuk.

They drank to Lviv and its liberation, then had their *zak-uski*.

"I haven't just called you over for no reason," the former KGB captain said as he finished chewing a piece of herring.

Vynnychuk's lips were already preparing a sarcastic smile. But Ryabtsev looked at him so kindly and, at the same time, guiltily, that it wasn't quite brave enough to emerge on the writer's face.

"Today I'm going to surprise you," continued Ryabtsev. "But not now, later! Meanwhile . . ." He bent over to the floor, and after removing the paper from the stereo, pressed PLAY.

Vynnychuk and Alik froze.

The peaceful atmosphere was torn apart by the guitar of Jimi Hendrix. And suddenly smiles, entirely kind-hearted ones, without a note of malice or meanness, blossomed on the faces of Ryabtsev's guests. The doves flapped their wings up above, frightened by the rock.

"Yeah, that's the stuff," muttered a contented Alik Oli-sevych.

Hey Joe, where you goin' with that gun in your hand?

"Shame he never made it to Lviv in one piece," sighed Alik when the song came to an end and the owner of the dovecote pressed STOP. "We were waiting for him so bad! And guys all over the Union lived on standby, they'd be ready to hit the road at any moment! They'd all have hitchhiked it down as fast as they could, on the backs of trains and buses. If only he hadn't died so soon . . . in his 'Samarkand'!"

Yurko turned to Alik in surprise. "Did he really die in Samarkand?"

"That's what his last London hotel was called. He was there with his German girlfriend . . . But if he hadn't have died, we'd have all been at his concert, here in Lviv! The tour dates had already been announced . . . Well, not officially, obviously. But everyone knew . . ."

Alik dived into reminiscences. But Ryabtsev shook his head.

"He wasn't coming," the former captain said with a deep sorrow.

"But there were rumours going round!" Alik looked up at Ryabtsev. "Rumours like that don't come out of nowhere!"

"They didn't," Ryabtsev said with a sigh. "They were spread by the service . . ."

Alik was shocked. "But why?"

"There were two reasons. Firstly, we wanted to assess the speed that rumours travelled through a given environment; and then one general had the idea to gather all the hippies in

Lviv and put them through a 'tallying commission'. To see if we had them all under the microscope!"

"Yes, your 'microscope' left behind a cruel memory," said Yurko Vynnychuk, but his voice just sounded sad, without any of the usual haughtiness he usually showed towards Ryabtsev.

"Our old 'microscope' has just been passed to someone else," laughed Ryabtsev. "It didn't go away, and it wasn't given to a museum! But I've atoned for my sins! Alik, tell him about Jimi's hand."

"You mean the grave in Lychakiv?" asked Vynnychuk.

"Yes! Our Baltic comrades helped us out and, believe it or not, our colleagues in the CIA!" Ryabtsev looked Vynnychuk in the eyes with an open, earnest expression. "And then your Lithuanian friends took it from them and brought it over here . . ."

"The right hand or the left?" Vynnychuk wondered.

Ryabtsev thought for a moment.

"The right," he said uncertainly.

"But Jimi was a lefty, he played with his left," said Vynnychuk.

"He also played with his teeth," added Alik Olisevych.

"It doesn't matter." Ryabtsev waved them away. "And if you really want, we can get the whole truth established with DNA!"

"Why would we want the truth?" asked Yurko Vynnychuk. "Myths are always more important than the truth! Let's leave it all as it is! Here's to Jimi!"

Ryabtsev filled the glasses.

Alik proposed a toast: "Hendrix lived, Hendrix lives, Hendrix will live on!"

They clinked glasses and drank. And Ryabtsev reached once more for the stereo. The dovecote trembled pleasantly as it heard Jimi's voice:

> *Waitin' for the train, yeah*
> *Take me home, yeah . . .*

At around eleven, Yurko got ready to go.

"I've got to get to Vynnyky," he said, a little dazed because he was trying to work out how he would get home at this time. He didn't want to call Vanya and his Volga.

"What about the main event?" asked Ryabtsev.

"What's the main event?" Alik stared at the former captain.

Yurko was also distracted from his logistical concerns.

"Let's go downstairs! As soon as we're done, we can all head home!" Ryabtsev nodded at the hole in the floor, through which, after climbing up the stairs a couple of hours previously, they had emerged on the second floor.

Once they were downstairs, Ryabtsev pushed his yellow Piaggio to the left-hand wall, and kicked the straw aside from the square wooden hatch in the floor. He pulled it up and jammed a plug into the external socket connected to the accumulator.

The light turned on in the basement.

Alik took a peek downstairs.

"What's down there? A wine cellar?" he asked.

"It will be one day!" Ryabtsev nodded thoughtfully. "Here,

you can help me out. I'll hand you things, and you arrange them carefully!"

Ryabtsev went down. Vynnychuk squatted in front of the opening. His eyes "dropped" lower than he'd expected. The cellar was no less than three metres deep, and its walls didn't coincide with the walls of the dovecote, they were much further apart.

"Take this!" came Ryabtsev's voice from below, and in the hatchway appeared something wrapped in scratchy grey paper.

Yurko took from the hands of the dovecote owner a bulky, but not heavy object, about a metre long, and passed it on to Alik.

Alik put the package on the floor, and immediately received another one from Vynnychuk. Then another. After ten minutes Ryabtsev clambered out of the cellar and surveyed just over a dozen packages, arranged in two piles on the floor. Alik and Yurko stared questioningly at the former captain. But he just carefully picked up one of the packages and, looking up at Alik, handed it to him.

"That's yours!" Ryabtsev said. "You've probably heard that letters sometimes make it to their intended recipient twenty years later!" he sighed. "Think of it as lost post!"

Alik walked over to the scooter, lowered the package onto the seat and began to unwrap the paper. Beneath it he found a box with a drawing of an electric guitar.

"A Fender Stratocaster!" Alik blurted out. "Where's this from?!"

"This was sent to you from America in 1976. In the confiscation act it was described as 'Attempted import of an undesirable object in the guise of a musical instrument'. These ones –" he nodded at the other packages – "also failed to reach their addresses in time. Ideological confiscations. One of them was sent to Katsemona . . ."

"And what do you intend to do with them?" asked Vynnychuk.

"I don't intend to do anything with them. I've already done my part – confiscating the confiscations back in ninety-one. Now you'll take them and . . . you can give them to the guys who play rock! They're all new, all brand names!"

Yurko Vynnychuk took a handkerchief from his coat pocket, lifted off his glasses and wiped them laboriously, after which he hoisted them back onto his nose and looked down at his own branded box, inside of which sat another electric guitar.

"Does your son play the guitar?" Ryabtsev asked him.

"He's still small," replied Vynnychuk.

"Well, this is a guitar with growing room! They're beautiful. You could even hang it on the wall for aesthetic purposes, and then it'll be like Chekhov: if there's a guitar hanging on the wall, sooner or later it must make some noise!"

Yurko smiled. He liked the idea that a guitar could replace the rifle on the wall.

"Alright," he said, pulling his mobile out of his trouser pocket. "I'll take them home for now, and then me and Alik can decide what to do with them there!"

And he ended up calling Vanya the driver all the same, and gave him the address that he should pick them up from.

"We'll give you a lift," he said to Alik, stuffing his phone into the pocket of his coat. "Then in a week's time we can meet at mine. I don't think my wife will mind!"

Epilogue

Taras and Darka were married on the ninth of December in St George's Cathedral, and officially registered in the Galician registry office on Hrushevskoho. Yezhi Astrovsky was indeed a witness at their wedding, but it all went by peacefully. Oksana was a model of patience, as a result of which, through long and complicated discussions distantly reminiscent of discussions between Russia and Ukraine over the price of Russian gas, the hairdresser managed to negotiate the right to give Oksana a haircut no less than once a month. After the wedding, Darka left the bureau de change and moved in with Taras. The radio in the kitchen was unplugged until the coming of early spring, and the morning anthem no longer sounded in their comfy apartment. But in the evenings, they sometimes sat at the table and attentively read the secondhand cars section of the free ads in the papers.

Snow appeared outside. Fully-fledged winter finally came to Lviv. It fettered the city with its dampish cold, convincing its citizens to stay home more often and spend more time with one another.

One evening, Taras took Darka to the Opera House to see Franz Lehár's *The Merry Widow*. While there, he noticed in the left-hand lighting bay a tall, well-built, long-haired man who seemed very familiar. His attempts to remember where they might have met distracted Taras so much from the operetta that he only occasionally looked at the stage. Only once the audience stood to applaud the cast did Taras come to peace with his insufficient memory and devote all of his attention to his young wife, whom the performance had put in such a state of excitement that she couldn't help herself, giving her husband a kiss on the lips, directly in view of those around them, forgetting for a moment her usual shyness and modesty.

NOTES

1   "Good evening!" (Lithuanian)

2   Herba Devynia, or "Triple Nine", is a herbal liqueur most popular in Latvia.

3   Vladimir Volfovich Zhirinovsky (1946–2022)[1] was a Russian right-wing populist politician and the leader of the Liberal Democratic Party of Russia (LDPR) from its creation in 1992 until his death.

4   Small, bite-sized snacks or hors d'oeuvres, designed to follow each sip of spirits.

5   A rural single-home patch of land, often used for farming. Originated across Ukraine and in southern areas of Russia, in regions where Cossacks settled historically.

6   Oksana's car shares a nickname with a big-eared, fuzzy character from an old Soviet children's cartoon.

7   A central street in Odesa, Southern Ukraine.

8   A popular Ukrainian pop/rock band that formed in 2005.

9   The Pioneers was a state-run Soviet organisation similar to the Scouts in the West, providing extra-curricular activities for children aged 9–14. The Little Octobrists covered ages 4–9, and the Komsomol ages 14–28.

10   "Deficits" became a regular feature of late-Soviet life, particularly under Brezhnev in the 1970s. Common goods would go out of stock, leading to long queues outside shops when they eventually reappeared.

11 Gunpowder Tower (Ukr: *Porokhova Vezha*) was built between 1554–6, and is one of the last remnants of the old city fortifications.

12 A borrowed word from Polish, which in turn borrowed the form of shop from the German *Konditerei*. The shops sell sweets and desserts, with an emphasis on baked goods. The term is one of many linguistic examples of Lviv's entangled history with both Polish and Austro-Hungarian imperialism. "Szlachta" and "Szlachetna" mean "nobility" and "noble", respectively.

13 *Sukhoy*, the Russian adjective from which the surname "Sukhikh" is derived, means "dry", with connotations of unnecessary formality, frailty and withered-ness.

14 "Mykyta" is the Ukrainian equivalent of the Russian "Nikita", both sharing the same Greek origin. "Ryumach" is a similar de-Russification of the surname "Ryumachov", removing the typical Russian ending.

15 A *vatnik*, sometimes known as a *telogreika* (body-warmer), was a military-issue padded jacket, used as winter uniform from the Second World War to the 1960s.

16 Doctor Pi was a famous Ukrainian conman, who claimed to have memorised pi to thirty million decimal places and to be a practised brain surgeon, amongst many, many other things. In 2014, he was sentenced to eight years in prison for fraud.

17 A *marshrutka* is a privatised "public" transport system where minibuses travel pre-determined routes, closer to buses than taxis, but somewhere between the two. They originated in the USSR but were popularised across the former Soviet countries in the 1990s, as a substitute for crumbling public transport systems.

18 The title of an 1888 painting by Nikolai Yaroshenko, a member of the *Peredvizhniki* movement.

19 "You might not like it, but it needs doing!" (Ukrainian)

20 Literally "macaroni, navy style": pasta cooked with minced meat, onions and salt and pepper, a staple of old naval rations.

21 A daily newspaper available in cities across Western Ukraine. Produced in Lviv since 1946, when it went by the name *Lvovskaya Pravda*.

ACKNOWLEDGEMENTS

The author expresses heartfelt thanks to Andryi Ivanovych
Sadovyi, Mayor of Lviv, for the invitation to write a novel
about a city which was, is, and will always stay one of the
most interesting and beautiful city-enigmas on the map of
Europe. Thanks to the staff of the Leopolis hotel for their
kindness and the shelter and comfort they provided during my
visits – and for the exquisite food in particular. Thanks to the
protagonists of my story, Yurko Vynnychuk, Alik Olisevych
and Oksana Prokhorets, for agreeing to be my protagonists
and for allowing me into their lives and their biographies.
Thanks to Lviv friends old and new: Mikhail Vatulyak and
his family, Taras Voznyak, Galina Vdovichenko and many,
many others. Thanks to Yury Nikolishin and Apriori pub-
lishing house for gifting me a library of books about Lviv's
past and present; to Ruslan and the Old Piano Restaurant;
to the workers and regulars of the café on Virmenska, Café
Kabinet, the "round" cheburek shop in Bryukhovychi, the
grill-bar in Vynnyky, the unnamed bar on Starozensenska,
Café "Café" at 24 Povitryana, and the city's many other cosy
corners, which both consciously and unconsciously provided
me with spiritual warmth and a chance to relax. Thanks to

the organisers, visitors and volunteers at the Oselya-Emmaus centre for the homeless in Vynnyky, and the inhabitants of the city of Lviv for not noticing this visiting writer, and for aiding the writing of his novel by acting entirely naturally.

ANDREY KURKOV was born near Leningrad in 1961. After working as prison guard and a journalist, he found renown as a novelist with *Death and the Penguin*, now translated into thirty languages. Since the Russian invasion of Ukraine, Kurkov, whose novel *Grey Bees* was set during an earlier stage of the conflict, has become a crucial voice for the people of his country. He published his *Diary of an Invasion* in 2022 and also appeared on BBC Radio 4's *Letter from Ukraine*.

REUBEN WOOLLEY was the recipient of the National Centre for Writing's Emerging Translator Mentorship in Russian for 2020–21, mentored by Robert Chandler. Other translations include *The Gospel According To* by Sergey Khazov-Cassia.